The Forest of the Forsaken

By Joseph J Lee

Dedication

To my wonderful wife, Janel, thank you for being my rock and my biggest supporter. Your love and patience have inspired me and kept me going, even when the journey felt tough. You've always believed in me and my dreams, helping me turn my ideas into stories. This book is a reflection of our life together, a celebration of the love that has pushed me to write and the dreams we've shared along the way.

Readers: As you scroll these pages, be aware that there's a strange and haunting side to the stories within. They come from the reoccurring nightmares that have visited me at night and the long wait of twenty years to finally share them. Each tale carries a feeling of mystery and unease, reminding us that dreams can sometimes reveal truths we might not be ready to face. So, as you dive into this book, remember that the shadows of imagination can hold more than just stories; they can hold pieces of our deepest fears.

Copyright © 2025 by Joseph Lee
All rights reserved.
Published by: Limitless
ISBN: 979-8-218-88241-9

Prologue:

The Woodsman and the Witch

In the year of our Lord 1696, the town of Old Glory rose from the wilderness like a clenched fist of faith, planted stubbornly at the edge of a sprawling forest that brooded over the land like a watchful guardian. Folks around those parts treated the woods the way a child eyes the dark corner of a cellar—awed by its depth, yet certain something with too many teeth lurked just out of sight. The towering trunks, knotted roots, and snarled thickets seemed to breathe with ancient patience, and many swore the place sheltered forces that slipped beyond God's reach.

Wooden homes, built with plain pride and weary hands, lined the main carriageway like tired soldiers. Their timbers, softened by wind and years, wore the last traces of paint that time had nearly erased. Cypress shingles—chosen to resist rot—

still sagged under the memory of winters so heavy with snow they smothered the town into hushed stillness.

To the east, Big Mountain Lake stretched across the land like a sheet of polished glass, catching the dimming sky and throwing it back in somber reflection. A thin mist clung to its surface most mornings, whispering to anyone lonely or foolish enough to wander near. It was a strange kind of beauty—one that pulled you closer with shimmering light, only to tighten your stomach once you remembered how deep its waters ran.

Every Sunday, the people of Old Glory crowded into their simple wooden church, gripping hymnals with stiff-knuckled certainty. They believed the forest was the Devil's own cathedral, a shadowed kingdom where wicked spirits prowled for souls too slow to flee.

It was said the gloom seeping from those trees could stain a person's spirit. Anyone who wandered too close—anyone who lingered a moment too long among the tangled shadows—risked carrying back a mark: unseen, but unmistakable. Whispers in the tavern and murmurs in the marketplace told of women accused of slipping from righteousness into dark craft. Misfortune became evidence. Oddness became guilt. And in the minds of Old Glory's faithful, such women twisted into monsters deserving of the cleansing flame. Smoke still haunted memory here, drifting through streets like a ghost, reminding the townsfolk of pyres that once devoured the condemned.

In such a place, faith and fear wrapped around each other like serpents wrestling for a single throat. Old Glory breathed that tension and wore it like a second skin. Its people lived with one eye on Scripture and the other on the tree line, knowing the border between God's world and something far older lay only a few steps beyond their fences. The forest waited there, patient and watchful—a reminder that the past was never as dead as their prayers hoped and that some fears grow roots deeper than any oak.

As the first slivers of dawn crept over the horizon and spilled honey-gold light across quiet Old Glory, a familiar shape filled the doorway of the town's modest tavern. Hank, the woodsman everyone relied on whether they admitted it or not, stood there as if carved from the very mountains bracing the valley. The tavern, with its warm pastries, sour ale, and gossip thick enough to choke on, was where mornings truly began. And with Hank blocking the entrance, shoulders broad enough to shade half the room, his arrival settled over the place like a sudden change in weather.

His beard—a wild flare of red like a bonfire caught mid-roar —framed a face lined with deep, easy creases. Those eyes of his, bright as polished amber, held the glint of a man who'd seen hardship without letting it make him cruel. When Hank laughed, the sound rolled from his chest in booming waves, thunder rumbling across a summer field. Folks swore they felt it in their ribs; maybe they did. It was the kind of laughter that chased away morning gloom the way a hard wind scatters fog.

Old Glory loved Hank—honestly, not in the polite nod-over-the-fence way small towns often faked. His strength had become part of local lore, spoken with a pride reserved for miracles. He'd split logs thicker than a man's waist, hauled beams three men should've carried, and still had the breath and heart to patch a widow's roof or lift a farmer's fallen ox from a ditch. Yet it wasn't his muscle the town cherished most—it was the gentleness threaded through everything he did. He knew how to steady a man dragged down by bad luck or sit beside the grieving until silence stopped feeling like punishment.

When he stepped inside, the tavern welcomed him like an old friend. Warm bread filled the air, rich and yeasty, blending with the earthy scent of brewing ale. Voices buzzed—small jokes, early stories, the soft chatter people shared before the day hardened. Hank answered all of it with a wide grin, clapping friends on the back with such enthusiasm that more than one mug wobbled dangerously.

"Morning, friends! What wild tales do you bring me today?" he boomed, his voice filling the rafters and rattling the cups like a quick gust through the eaves. His presence threw heat into the room, a steady warmth like a hearth on the coldest dawn. People leaned toward him without thinking, drawn by the comfort he carried—solid, bright, dependable. In a town ruled by fear and superstition, Hank stood as stubborn proof that goodness still existed, and that maybe—just maybe—light could outshine whatever watched from the woods.

In the center of Old Glory—where whispers traveled faster than the morning wind and fear clung to the air like damp wool —Hank stood as the closest thing the town had to steady ground. Folks leaned on him the way they leaned on their faith: not always with understanding, but with desperate need. His big-hearted laugh and easy warmth reminded everyone that even with the forest brooding at the town's edge and old legends breathing down their necks, there was still room in this world for simple human goodness. As the sun climbed higher, spilling gold across the cobblestones and lighting up the worn faces of the people who called this place home, it was clear that Hank wasn't merely a woodsman. He was part of the weave that held the whole fragile tapestry of Old Glory together.

"Hank! Off to the woods again, are you?" Tobias the smith called, brushing soot from his arms. His voice rang with its usual clang, shaped by years of hammering iron. "You'll be dragging back enough wood to see us through the winter, I'll wager!"

"Aye!" Hank answered, his voice rich and warm, the kind that could chase the cold from a man's bones. "There's plenty in those woods this season. Leaves are down, and the timber's ready. I'll see to it every hearth is burning bright, Tobias."

People around them nodded, their faces carved with lines born of work, prayer, and quiet worry. Mary, the baker's wife—flour dusted on her sleeves like snow—added, "Mind yourself, Hank. Those woods can fool even the strongest men. Folks talk of witches hiding between the trees."

"Witches?" Hank barked out a laugh, tossing his mane of red hair back so it caught the morning light like sparks off an anvil. "I've roamed that forest more years than I can count. Not once have I crossed paths with a witch. Just keep clear of the darker corners, and you'll be well enough."

But as he cinched his belt and stepped toward the road, the chatter quieted like someone had smothered it beneath a heavy cloth. Old Man Fletcher—smelling as though he'd bathed in brandy instead of drinking it—shuffled forward. His eyes, sharp as chipped flint despite the tremor in his legs, locked on Hank.

"Mark me, lad," Fletcher rasped, breath sour enough to make a horse shy. "That forest ain't just a pile of timber. This time of year, the veil gets thin. Things creep through—things wrapped in beauty but born of wickedness. Women with strange gifts, if the tales hold true. Some say they whisper with spirits that never died."

Hank's brow lifted, a flicker of curiosity passing over him like a shadow from a drifting cloud—but fear had no place in his features. "Aye, I've heard those stories," he said, voice steady. "But I've walked those woods every day, and not a one's shown herself to me. I've crossed beasts with teeth like knives and tempers twice as sharp, but never a woman I'd fear. Nature's got room for all kinds, and I won't quake at the thought of one who seeks only to belong."

The townsfolk traded glances—quick, uneasy flickers, like birds startled into brief flight. Their faces formed a patchwork of admiration stitched with something colder and harder to name. They loved Hank; everyone did. He was a walking hearth fire. Yet admiration often leaves room for fear, especially in a place like Old Glory, where stories root themselves as deep as the pines at the forest's edge. And fear—true fear—was patient. It curled around the heart like the roots of an ancient tree, burrowing in, whispering warnings about the unknown and everything hiding just beyond daylight's reach.

The tavern thickened with that tension, the air heavy with thoughts no one dared voice. Then, from the direction of the church, a figure stepped into view—Reverend Samuel Goodwin. Even before he spoke, the crowd straightened, as if his presence alone brought them to order. His long black coat snapped in the breeze, giving him the look of a somber crow gliding down the main road. Behind him, the church rose into the pale morning sky, its steeple a pointed reminder to the heavens that Old Glory still sought protection. It was the town's anchor—some days more successfully than others.

"Hank," the reverend called, his voice carrying the weight of a man who had battled spirits no mortal had ever seen. There was an edge to his tone, sharp as a blade not yet drawn. The murmurs fell silent. "When you return, see me straightaway. The wood must be blessed before the town takes it. Evil clings to things it shouldn't."

Hank nodded, his expression tightening as the meaning settled in. Reverend Goodwin didn't speak like that unless something had truly rattled him. To the people of Old Glory, the forest was never just trees and shadows. It was a place where stories breathed, where old legends stretched their limbs when no one looked, where the line between reality and myth thinned to a spider's thread.

As Reverend Goodwin turned back toward the church, Hank felt something shift inside him—more than duty, deeper than obligation. Purpose. A whisper of dread he'd never confess. No one had given him the title of protector; he'd grown into it, the way bark grows around a scar. Now, standing in the morning light with the reverend's warning echoing through him, the weight of that role pressed harder than ever. In Old Glory, faith and fear walked side by side—and today, both seemed to have fixed their gaze on him.

Determination pushed Hank onward, each step a quiet vow to himself and to the town that leaned on his strength. Whatever waited in the woods, truth, darkness, or something writhing between the two, he meant to face it head-on. The townsfolk watched him go with a mix of pride and tight-throated worry, their eyes following long after he disappeared beyond the tree line. Admiration did little to smother the fear that he might return carrying answers no one wanted. Or worse, not return at all.

Crossing into the forest felt like passing through a veil. The air thickened at once, rich with pine sap and the faint sweetness of crushed wildflowers. Towering trunks rose on either side like silent spectators leaning in. Shadows stretched across the path as the canopy swallowed the morning light, narrowing the world into dim, green-lit corridors along the edge of Old Glory's wild borderland. Hank drew a slow breath, the scent of damp moss and rotting leaves settling deep in his chest— steadying him and unsettling him all at once. He'd known these woods since childhood, yet today they seemed to pulse with a restless hum, as if their secrets shuffled just out of sight.

His axe swung in a practiced rhythm, the sharp crack of metal on timber breaking the quiet. It should have soothed him —familiar motion, familiar sound. Instead, unease picked at him, first like a splinter, then like a finger tracing the length of his ribs. Something felt wrong. The air, perhaps. Or the silence. Or the sense that the trees were doing more than standing still.

Sunlight filtered through the boughs in thin, wavering shards, painting the forest floor with trembling patches of gold. Hank paused, wiping sweat from his brow, and studied the shapes around him. The trees loomed taller than they had moments before, their trunks warped, their limbs crooking upward like pleading hands. The canopy didn't just block the sky—it shifted in slow, deliberate breaths. The leaves whispered softly, not with wind, but with something older. Something patient.

"Come on, Hank," he muttered, tightening his grip on the axe. "Not scared of a couple shadows."

He swung again, the sound too sharp in the thickening gloom. But the prickling sensation along his spine remained, steady as a heartbeat. The stories of witches, demons, and wandering spirits crept through his mind like unwelcome guests. He'd laughed at those tales more times than he could count.

Yet here, alone in the hushed, watchful dark, even Hank could sense the forest listening.

Hank had no way of knowing that, not far from where he worked, a young woman was waking—someone the townsfolk spoke of with equal parts dread and fascination. Sarah. Her name alone could sour the tongues of Old Glory's elders; they treated it like a word better left unspoken. Yet here in the forest, she drew breath without fear.

She rose from her narrow cot in a cabin tucked so deeply into the woods that it seemed grown rather than built. Her hair, dark as raven feathers, spilled over her shoulders and shimmered where the morning light brushed it. The cabin was small and humble, crafted with care long before her birth. To the town, this place marked the edge of superstition—a den of spirits and wicked craft. But to Sarah, the forest was a sanctuary. Its trees stood like guardians. Its shadows watched without judgment. Whispering leaves, the sweet tang of earth, the birdsong carried on cool air—all of it wrapped around her with a tenderness the world beyond the trees had never shown.

Silence and solitude shaped her life. She had grown up with only the forest's creatures and the fading memories of her mother to keep her company. Her mother—gentle, wounded by the cruelty of others—had died several winters ago, leaving behind stories rooted in sorrow and resilience. She had spoken of Sarah's father in a voice tinged with both wonder and regret. The man had accused her of witchcraft to cleanse his own conscience, claiming she had bewitched him into sin. Fear and shame had driven her back to the cabin her father built, far from Old Glory's condemning eyes.

Sarah heard the tale many times, but it stirred no anger. Her father remained an idea, not a memory—a ghost without weight. She felt no longing for him, only loyalty to the woman who had raised her with unwavering tenderness.

She grew into the rhythm of the woods, letting it shape her heart and habits. She roamed the underbrush with easy grace, her steps soft on moss, her fingers brushing leaves as though greeting familiar companions. She learned which herbs clung to speckled sunlight, how the wind shifted when danger neared, and the difference between the crack of a warning branch and the sigh of a passing animal. The forest taught her its language—its dangers, its wonders, its secrets whispered only to those who listened with patience.

Sarah, with her quiet voice and gentle touch, answered in kind. She spoke to the trees as if confiding in old friends, sharing her hopes in murmurs as the breeze carried deeper into the woods. In return, the forest embraced her, its pulse syncing with hers in a bond older than memory.

But not everyone who heard its whispers understood them.

And not everyone who understood them were welcome.

And still, even with the forest's warmth wrapped around her, the town hovered over Sarah's life like a long, unbroken shadow—a forbidden world stitched deeply into her mother's warnings. Old Glory had been painted for her in stark, grim strokes: a village where suspicion grew thicker than ivy, where fear dressed itself as righteousness, and where anything unfamiliar was swiftly marked as sin. Her mother's voice drifted through her memory now, soft but firm. They will not understand you, Sarah. They will not forgive what they fear. A girl born of secrets, tucked away in a cabin, whispered about in sermons—what place could she possibly hold among them?

Sarah insisted she felt nothing for that distant world. How do you miss a place you've never walked? How do you long for people who wouldn't even speak your name? Yet somewhere beneath her ribs, something warm flickered—a stubborn ember of curiosity. It stirred in dreams, offering glimpses of cobblestone streets, lantern-lit windows, voices rising in laughter she had never heard. Beyond the trees lay another life, and a small, patient part of her yearned to see it.

She rubbed the last traces of sleep from her eyes and coaxed the hearth back into flame. Golden light spilled across the cabin walls, softening the edges of dawn. She reached for her notebook—a weathered volume stuffed with sketches of foxes, ferns, moonlit groves, and hidden corners of the woods she loved. Sliding it onto the shelf jostled a small stack of parchment. Several sheets slipped free and drifted to the floor. She crouched to gather them. The symbols drawn across the pages met her eyes at once—delicate, looping marks her mother had traced with reverent care. Enchantments, she had called them. Not mere drawings but pieces of an old craft woven through their bloodline. Each mark hummed with a quiet, lingering power, a faint echo of the woman who had loved her fiercely enough to shield her from a world eager to condemn.

Sarah ran her fingertip along one sigil, feeling that ancient connection spark to life. Then, with a steadiness rising in her chest, she collected her things and stepped out into the waking forest.

The morning air wrapped around her—crisp, cool, tinged with holly's sharp brightness and the musk of damp earth. She breathed deeply, letting the scent settle into her bones. A faint smile touched her lips. Out here, she belonged.

She moved between the trees with an easy, unthinking grace —part girl, part spirit of the wood. Leaves whispered beneath her feet in greeting, not warning. Birdsong laced itself through the air, guiding her along paths known only to her. The ancient trees seemed to lean closer as she passed, their branches murmuring secrets in a language she understood without ever having been taught.

Sarah's fingers drifted over the foliage with gentle precision, turning the gathering of roots and herbs into something close to a dance. Greens and browns shimmered under her touch— living colors pulsing with the earth's quiet heartbeat. Sunlight slipped through the canopy in trembling beams, sketching shifting patterns across the forest floor as if the woods were painting around her. Each step felt ceremonial, a thread tying her to the land that had raised her. She wasn't just collecting ingredients; she was honoring her mother, honoring the lineage that hummed beneath her skin. Every leaf she brushed, every stem she plucked carried that weight—reverence disguised as routine.

The forest offered its wonders with patient generosity: wildflowers blazing like spilled paint, a stream whispering secrets over smooth stones, the cautious tread of a deer moving through distant brush. Sarah paused often, breathing it in, her chest swelling with quiet gratitude. Here, she wasn't hidden. She wasn't feared. She belonged, woven into the forest's breath and heartbeat, its secrets and its magic. A single thread, yes, but vital to the pattern. The trees themselves seemed to know her name.

She knelt to gather a cluster of wild mushrooms, pale caps glowing against the dark soil. Before her fingers reached them, a sharp rustle cut through the stillness. Sarah froze. Her pulse hammered in her ears. She lifted her gaze, searching the shadows as a shiver crept up her spine. Something moved. No —something warned. Flickers of movement teased the edge of her vision, signs she had learned never to ignore. The forest spoke danger in a tongue only she could hear.

She rose slowly, breath caught in her throat, listening. Her sanctuary held its breath with her.

Deep in the same tangled expanse, Hank kept working, each swing of his axe ringing with steady purpose. Wood split cleanly under his strength, chips arcing through the air like slivers of gold. Winter demanded preparation, and he always met its challenge. Focused on the task, he never sensed the threat above him—not until the forest chose to reveal it.

The warning came as a groan—a heavy limb strained past its limit by cold and time. A second later, it snapped.

Hank's head jerked up, instincts flaring, but the falling log moved faster than fear. It crashed down with brutal force, slamming him flat. Air tore from his lungs in a broken gasp. Pain ripped through him like lightning, white-hot and merciless. The world tilted, blurred, then shrank into a tunnel of agony as he lay trapped beneath the crushing weight.

Above him, the forest stood silent.

Watching.

"Damn it!" Hank roared, but the forest swallowed the sound, smothering it beneath its ancient canopy. He clenched his teeth until his jaw throbbed, straining to lift the log, but the weight refused to budge. Pain surged through his leg—hot and blinding, like a blade twisting deep in the muscle. The shock left him dizzy, blinking against a world that wouldn't stay still. The forest, once familiar and steady, seemed to leer at him now, its silence heavy enough to feel like betrayal. He cursed the timber, the shadows, the trees that watched him without moving.

With a ragged grunt, he tried to roll aside, but the log held him fast. His vision wavered.

Sunlight speared through the branches in long, trembling beams as noon crept closer. Even the light felt distant, stretching away and leaving him in the thickening gloom beneath the trees. Leaves rustled overhead—not the comforting whisper he knew, but something colder, detached, as though the forest had already forgotten him. A terrible loneliness settled across his chest like frost.

But he wasn't alone.

Far away, Sarah froze mid-step, her breath catching. Hank's cry had torn through the woods like the howl of a wounded animal—raw and desperate. She felt the panic before she fully heard it, a ripple shuddering through the forest's pulse. The woods she trusted seemed to tremble, sending its warning straight into her bones. Something was wrong. Deeply wrong.

Her pulse quickened. She had spent her life avoiding people, slipping into the shadows whenever the townsfolk wandered too close. Their fear had teeth, and their suspicion burned hotter than their fires. But the forest urged her forward now, pushing at her with invisible hands.

She moved swiftly and silently as wind, following the muffled groans threading through the trees. The woods opened just enough to reveal a hulking figure pinned beneath a fallen log—Hank, though she did not yet know his name. Even broken, he looked carved from mountain stone, but pain had reduced him to a trembling heap. Her heart hammered, caught between fear and the instinct to help. If he saw her—truly saw her—would he look with gratitude?

Or would he see what Old Glory feared: a witch shaped by the forest's darkest corners?

"Hello?" she called, soft but steady, cutting through the thick silence.

Hank's head jerked up, eyes wide and wild with equal parts fear and agony. "Who's there?" he growled, though strain dragged at every word. "Show yourself!"

"I can help you!" she answered. Her voice carried gentle urgency, earnest and trembling, drifting toward him like a hand extended through shadows.

But to Hank—alone, hurt, and surrounded by whispers—it sounded too much like the start of a miracle.

Or a curse.

The shadows shifted, and Hank's pulse spiked as if the darkness itself had come alive. A sharp rustle tore through the trees, sending a jolt of raw fear up his spine. Driven by the terror of becoming another cautionary tale whispered in Old Glory, he gathered every ounce of strength left in him.

With a desperate heave, he shoved against the log. It rolled just enough for him to yank his leg free. Pain blazed through him, but he forced himself to roll aside, escaping the crushing weight that had pinned him.

His breath hitched as he scanned the clearing. Then he saw her.

A lone figure stood between the trees, caught in thin slivers of sunlight. Her hair shimmered like starlight poured over midnight, framing a face pale with uncertainty. For a heartbeat, Hank wondered if the old legends had come to life—if this was the witch the townsfolk feared.

Fear and fascination tangled inside him.

Sarah froze. Her gaze flicked from Hank to the restless shadows around them. "I—I am Hank," he managed, more curious than afraid. Her eyes widened when she realized he was free, and in that small, trembling moment, Hank understood: she wasn't a demon. She was terrified.

He stepped toward her, but she slipped away like smoke drawn into the trees. Sunlight caught her silhouette as she moved with uncanny grace, and the fear she carried clung to her like a veil.

"Wait! I mean no harm!" he shouted, his voice breaking with desperation. "Tell me who you are!"

A faint whisper drifted back to him as she vanished into the dark. "Sarah."

The rustling returned, louder now, as the forest seemed to swallow her trail. Hank's heart hammered as he searched the shadows for danger, but all he found was the lingering memory of her eyes—filled with sorrow and something he could not name.

He cast one last glance toward the place where she disappeared. "Sarah," he whispered, as if speaking her name might steady the unease twisting through him. Shaking his head, he gathered what wood he could and forced himself to continue deeper into the forest.

Yet the darkness followed him. The sense of fate tightening around them refused to fade. Something long buried was stirring, and he felt its pull with every step.

And somewhere in that same maze of trees, Sarah watched him go, her heart weighed down by the quiet truth neither of them dared to speak. "Hank," she whispered.

Chapter 1:
A New Beginning

Nestled between the rolling hills and the dense forest, Glory High School rose like an old stone castle, its tall spires stabbing at the sky. Weathered blocks of gray granite held decades of storms and whispers, and ivy curled up the walls as if trying to pull the whole place back into the earth. Students pushed through the heavy wooden doors each morning with the odd sensation that they were stepping into a place where the past still breathed alongside the present.

The schoolyard sat framed by towering pines and oaks that swayed in the breeze, their leaves murmuring as if exchanging secrets the wind refused to translate. Sunlight sliced through the branches in thin, shifting ribbons, scattering shadows across the ground that flickered like something alive. On still days, some students swore they heard faint whispers trailing through the air—too soft to understand, too persistent to ignore.

Just beyond the track, the forest leaned close, a dark guardian brooding over the edge of school property. The trees seemed to press inward, their gnarled roots creeping like fingers across the soil. In autumn, the leaves erupted into blood reds and molten golds, beautiful enough to lure anyone deeper—but there was always something unsettling beneath the beauty, a quiet reminder that the forest held more than color. It held stories—some sweet as sap, others bitter as rot.

On certain mornings, a thin fog hugged the ground, wrapping the school in a cold, damp shroud. The air smelled of pine and fresh earth, clean and sharp enough to sting the nose. Inside, laughter and chatter filled the halls, but beneath it all, there was always the rustling of leaves, the distant shriek of a bird—nature's reminder that it watched, waited, and never really slept.

As the school settled into its normal rhythm, a strange truth lingered: the forest had stories of its own, some eager to be found, others desperate to stay buried. Glory High was a place of friendship and learning, sure—but it was also an in-between space, where the ordinary brushed up against the extraordinary, and something just beyond the trees seemed to keep its eye on the students.

The classrooms buzzed with energy. Afternoon sunlight spilled through the windows, glittering in the dust like tiny sparks. In Literature 101, brightly colored posters lined the walls, each one a tribute to literary giants like Mark Twain, whose sharp humor brings laughter; Charles Dickens, whose vivid tales of struggle and resilience illuminate the human spirit; William Shakespeare, the master of words whose timeless plays evoke a range of emotions; and Jane Austen, whose keen observations of love and society still resonate today. They didn't feel like mere decorations; they felt like protectors of stories, watching over the room, daring the students to wander into their worlds. Each glance at these figures sparked curiosity and wonder, setting the perfect tone for a day.

In the back of the room sat Megan.

Her long, wavy black hair framed her thoughtful face as she slid into her usual seat—the one that let her see everything without being seen herself. Several months earlier, her mother's new hospital job had uprooted them, dumping Megan in a town she still wasn't sure she fit into. The move came right at the end of the school year, and she'd been dropped into Glory like a misplaced puzzle piece.

She tried to fit in, but failed miserably. Instead, she joined the art club and spent her lunch hours tucked away in the library, where the sweet smell of old paper felt like home. Some days, the shadow of her old life loomed behind her, whispering that she didn't belong here, but she pushed forward—quiet, observant, and far more aware of the world than most of her classmates realized. She didn't chase the chaotic currents of high-school social life. She preferred the worlds built from ink and imagination, the ones where she could get lost without feeling judged.

Amid that uncertainty, Megan was determined to make the best of her situation. She focused on her studies and tried to connect with her classmates, all while navigating the challenges of being a transfer student. Each day was a small step toward finding her place, and though she missed the familiar faces of her past, she held on to the hope that she could create fresh memories in this vibrant, bustling environment.

Though her unassuming nature often placed her on the outskirts of the social hierarchy, her intelligence shone through in the thoughtful comments she shares during class discussions. She has a unique perspective on life, and when she spoke up, her words were insightful and meaningful, but they sometimes went unnoticed amid the louder voices in the room. While her classmates exchanged stories about their weekends, Megan quietly observed, feeling a longing to connect and an appreciation for her individuality. She knew that her love for literature, while setting her apart, also gave her a depth of understanding that many of her peers did not yet grasp.

Megan found herself daydreaming about the stories and characters she loved so much as she settled into her familiar spot.

She often wondered if there were others like her, quietly hidden among the crowd, who also craved deeper conversations about the characters they adored, and the themes that spoke to their hearts. Next to her sat Aiden—her only real friend so far. Quirky, loyal, and bright enough to out-talk any science teacher, he flipped through his magazine with the excitement of a kid discovering a new galaxy.

"Hey, Megan!" he said, grinning. "Did you know a day on Venus is longer than a year? That's insane."

She laughed under her breath. "I can barely survive a day in high school. Venus sounds exhausting." Aiden chuckled and flipped another page—but before he could reply, the door swung open.

Ms. Emily Carter strode in, cheerful and glowing with that kind of enthusiasm teachers shouldn't logically have but somehow did. Megan sat up straighter.

"Welcome, everyone!" Ms. Carter announced, clasping her hands together. "Today, we're diving into the tragic love story of Romeo and Juliet." She paused, letting the curiosity settle. "And we're pairing it with a local legend—the tale of the woodsman and the witch. Two lovers, bound by fate, separated by fear."

A ripple of interest spread through the room.

Ms. Carter talked about Romeo and Juliet first—young love crushed under the weight of old grudges. Then she moved into the darker story, the one whispered around town like a warning. The woodsman who fell for a witch deep in the forest. A forbidden love, cursed by the town's fear of anyone who lived too close to the trees.

Megan felt something stir inside her at the mention of the witch. She wasn't sure why.

In the middle of the room, Thomas—the quarterback with the movie-poster smile—leaned back with a smug grin. Everything about him screamed confidence, from the tousled brown hair to the easy slouch of someone used to being admired.

Beside him sat his girlfriend, Lexi, the glittering cheerleader with a laugh like a bell whose bright blue eyes sparkled with mischief. She always seemed in high spirits, laughing and chatting with the other cheerleaders of Glory High. Although Lexi was clever and had her moments of insight, her focus on popularity and appearances often overshadowed her deeper thoughts. Together, they embodied the quintessential popular couple, thriving on the attention and admiration of their classmates.

As Ms. Carter continued to speak about the haunting tale of the Woodsman and the Witch, Thomas's smirk widened; he leaned over to Lexi, whispering something that made her giggle softly. "Care to share?" Ms. Carter asked, her tone light but edged with warning.

"Oh please," Thomas scoffed loudly. "That story is fake news. And soulmates?" He let out a snort. "Just a fairy tale to keep people entertained."

Lexi giggled, and the class cracked into laughter.

"Maybe it's not a fairy tale," Megan said softly but firmly. "Maybe love can be real, even if it's complicated. Romeo and Juliet believed it. And the woodsman and the witch—"

Lexi cut her off with a laugh sharp enough to sting. "You wouldn't know real love if it hit you in the face, Megan. You're not even from Glory. You don't know anything about our stories."

The laughter that followed felt like a slap.

Megan dropped her gaze, hiding behind her book, wishing she could disappear. Aiden leaned closer, trying to offer comfort, but she was already sinking into her anger and humiliation.

"Enough," Ms. Carter said sharply. "Debate is great—but not at Megan's expense." She shot Lexi a look that made the girl shrink in her seat. "Literature challenges us, yes, but it also teaches empathy."

Lexi huffed and muttered, "I'm just being honest."

Thomas smirked and spread his hands. "I'm just saying… witches? Magic? It's all make-believe. Stories to scare us away from the woods."

His words echoed in the sudden quiet.

And though he didn't know it, though most of them didn't feel it yet… something in the forest seemed to lean a little closer. As if listening.

As if waiting.

"Come on, babe. You don't need spooky stories to keep us out of the forest—it's creepy enough on its own," Lexi said with a teasing grin, nudging Thomas with her elbow. "But honestly? Some of these legends are actually interesting. Maybe there's more to them than you think." She flashed a bright smile, leaning in close so their foreheads nearly touched. "Besides, the world isn't totally lacking in love. I mean, look at us. We've survived three years of high school drama. That's practically supernatural."

Laughter bubbled through the classroom. Even Thomas cracked a smile.

"Alright, I'll give you that," he said, shaking his head. "But a woodsman and a witch? What are we supposed to get from that? Sounds like a bedtime story for little kids."

Ms. Carter, sensing the opening, stepped in. "That's exactly why we study these stories," she said, her tone warm but pointed. "They may sound like fairy tales, but they reveal things about who we are—our fears, our desires, the dangers of misunderstanding." She paused, scanning the faces in the room. "The Woodsman and the Witch isn't just about magic. It's about forbidden love. About how fear can twist people into making terrible choices."

Thomas lifted a brow, his skepticism softening. "So you're saying it's deeper than it sounds?"

"Much deeper," Ms. Carter replied with a spark of enthusiasm. "All stories—especially the strange ones—teach us something. Romeo and Juliet. The woodsman and the witch. They mirror our own lives more than we realize."

Lexi leaned back, nodding slowly. "Yeah… even the weird stories can hit close to home, I guess."

"You're absolutely right," Ms. Carter said. "Literature shows us parts of ourselves we don't always notice. Now—who wants to dig back into Romeo and Juliet and see how their world might echo ours?"

A ripple of energy moved across the room. Whispered excitement. Nervous laughs. The kind of spark teachers dream of igniting.

Ms. Carter wove the local legend into her lecture with surprising grace, tying themes of secrecy, fear, and longing directly into Shakespeare's world. "Love isn't always easy," she said softly. "It's misunderstood, challenged, and sometimes ridiculed. But it's still worth celebrating."

In the back of the room, Megan tried to focus on the lecture —but humiliation still burned warm along her neck. She could feel Thomas and Lexi's earlier snickering like needles pressing beneath her skin. Their easy confidence made her stomach curl.

She glanced at Aiden. Of course he was still buried in his magazine, flipping a page with total obliviousness.

Thanks for the backup, she thought bitterly.

She turned her attention to the tragedy of Romeo and Juliet, imagining herself not as the girl swept up in forbidden love, but as someone like Juliet—desperate to be seen, understood, and wanted. She didn't crave romance. She craved connection. Someone who looked at her and didn't see the "new girl," or the quiet girl, or the easy target. Just someone who saw her.

But in a room full of laughter and perfect timing and inside jokes she wasn't part of, Megan felt like an extra in someone else's story—present, but never important. The warmth other people seemed to float toward always stopped short of reaching her.

The bell rang sharply, its blare slicing through Ms. Carter's final words.

"Remember—your essays are due Monday! And finish act two!" she called over the rising chatter as backpacks zipped and chairs scraped the floor. The chatter of students increased as they continued packing up their belongings, excited for the weekend.

Megan packed her things slowly, each movement deliberate. Her fingers brushed over her notes as if she could absorb some kind of courage from the ink. At the front of the room, Thomas and Lexi were laughing again, their carefree voices echoing in her chest like an unwelcome reminder.

Aiden waited beside her desk, finally noticing her mood. He offered a small, knowing smile. "Don't let them get to you, Meg. They're probably just jealous of your brain."

"Oh, now you decide to chime in!" Megan said with a sarcastic tone. "Better late than never, Aiden," she added, forcing a smile while adjusting the strap of her backpack.

"Sorry, I just didn't know what to say, so it was easier to sit quietly," Aiden tried to explain.

Aiden shoved his hands into his pockets, his tone easy and calm. "Who cares what they think? Thomas and Lexi spend all their time chasing popularity. You're actually going to accomplish something. One day you'll be signing books for people like them."

Megan laughed softly. A real laugh. "You always know how to fix things."

"Hey, that's what best friends are for," he said with a playful nudge. "And seriously—your perspective matters. You see stories differently, and that's rare."

"Maybe," Megan murmured. "It just feels like a long way off. Sometimes I wish I could blend in. Just… be someone people don't pick apart."

As they stepped outside into the warm afternoon sun, the school behind them cast long shadows across the pavement. Aiden's voice softened.

"Fitting in is overrated. You have something they don't—something real. People lash out when they feel threatened. Jealousy's loudest when someone else shines."

Her chest warmed. She wasn't sure she believed him completely—but she wanted to. "Thanks, Aiden. Really."

"Anytime." He grinned. "Plus, you need at least one friend."

"Oh great," Megan joked. "So I'm the charity case."

"Absolutely. A full-time burden." He snorted. "On a brighter note, how about ice cream? That new place downtown has insane sundaes. We can work on our essays and pretend Thomas and Lexi don't exist."

Megan pictured a cold sundae, the swirl of whipped cream, the simple comfort of sweetness. "Yeah… I think I need that. Ice cream sounds perfect."

They walked through the neighborhood, sunlight stretching across the lawns and rooftops. The world looked calm, golden, soft—yet Megan felt weighted down by everything she didn't say aloud. She glanced at Aiden, warmth stirring in her chest. He had been steady since day one. Loyal. Kind. But no matter how close he stood beside her, she still felt the faint echo of loneliness trailing her steps, like a shadow that refused to let go.

Megan's attention drifted as she and Aiden followed the narrow path toward the town square. Her gaze snagged on an unusual willow tree standing apart from the others, its long, drooping branches swaying like tattered curtains in the breeze. The shadows it cast stretched across the ground in strange, twisted shapes that resembled ghostly silhouettes reaching for anyone who wandered too close. Its trunk coiled unnaturally, as if writhing in silent torment, and its dark roots clawed outward from the earth like skeletal fingers.

A chill crawled up her spine. The tree looked disturbingly familiar. It reminded her of the dreams that had been haunting her—dark, suffocating nightmares she couldn't shake.

In the most recent one, she was trapped in thick, mud-like sludge. It pulled at her legs with a terrifying patience, dragging her down inch by agonizing inch. The air had felt heavy, thick, impossible to breathe. Shadows with gleaming eyes lingered at the edges of her vision, their twisted silhouettes whispering, watching her sink. Their evil growls had rumbled through the darkness, cold and mocking.

The growl grew louder, becoming a frightening chorus that taunted her as she had tried to claw her way free, but the mud tightened around her. As her strength faded, the suffocating mud filled her lungs, crushing the last threads of hope. When she finally slipped beneath the surface, the shadows had laughed.

Now, staring at the gnarled willow, she couldn't shake the feeling that her dreams were more than stress or imagination—that something was lurking beneath the surface of her life, waiting.

With each step, she felt as if the tree was watching her, a silent guardian of secrets, and she shivered at the thought of what might lie hidden in the shadows beneath its twisted branches.

"Earth to Meg…" Aiden waved a hand in front of her face, snapping her back to reality. His playful tone softened the concern in his eyes.

"Oh—sorry. Just… spaced out." She forced a small smile, trying to banish the lingering dread.

Aiden tilted his head, the teasing slipping away. "You've been zoning out a lot lately. Everything okay?"

Megan hesitated. The dreams felt too strange, too heavy to explain. "It's nothing major. I've just been having these weird dreams. Hard to describe."

"Hey." He slowed his steps, his voice warm. "I'm here if you want to talk about it. Weird dreams, weird thoughts, weird whatever."

She laughed softly, grateful but unsure how to open up. "I don't want to dump all my weirdness on you."

"Meg," Aiden said gently, stopping her with a hand on her shoulder, "your feelings aren't a burden. If something's bothering you, it matters. Even if it feels silly."

Her chest tightened with a mix of embarrassment and relief. "I just... feel a little lost, I guess." She kicked at a loose pebble on the sidewalk. "Everyone else seems to know where they're going after high school. And I'm here obsessing over stories and legends like they're some secret map I'm supposed to decode."

Aiden's expression softened. "You're not lost. You're exploring. That's different." His smile tilted upward. "Besides, you have passion. That's more than most people can say. Your love for stories? It's going to lead you somewhere—maybe somewhere amazing."

A warmth spread through her chest, easing the pressure of all the things she didn't know. "Maybe."

"Definitely," he said, nudging her playfully. "Now—race you to the square."

Before he finished the sentence, Megan darted ahead with a laugh. "Too slow and way too predictable!"

Aiden's groan echoed behind her as she bolted through the intersection, the wind tugging at her hair. For the first time all day, the heaviness lifted.

When she reached the old-fashioned ice cream parlor, she paused to catch her breath. The striped awning fluttered overhead, and the bell above the door jingled with a cheerful ring as she pushed inside, welcoming them into a world of sweet delights. Cheerful pastel colors painted the shop's interior, and sweet scents of waffle cones, caramel, and rich chocolate wrapped around her like a warm hug.

Aiden jogged in after her, panting dramatically. "You cheated."

"Don't be a sore loser," she said, grinning.

They approached the counter. Megan's eyes sparkled at the sight of her favorite flavor. "Mint Chocolate Chip, please."

Aiden scanned the menu. "Banana split. Always."

Megan watched them pile the vibrant green mint ice cream high, dotted with rich chocolate chips, while Aiden's banana split was a decadent masterpiece, topped with whipped cream, nuts, and a cherry that beckoned for attention.

They found a small table by the window, sunlight spilling across the polished surface. As they ate, Megan savored the cool burst of mint and chocolate, letting the simple comfort settle her nerves.

"So," Aiden said between spoonfuls, "what do you want after high school? Really want?"

Megan traced a finger along the edge of her bowl. "I want to be an author. Write stories people can escape into. And maybe… travel. Find inspiration somewhere completely new."

Aiden's smile widened. "You'd be amazing. And it fits you."

"What about you?" she asked.

"Something in science, maybe environmental studies. I want to help—make a difference somehow."

"You will," she said, meaning it.

The rest of their conversation drifted easily, laughter replacing worries until the world felt soft again—safe, even.

By the time they walked home, the sun dipped lower in the sky, painting it in shades of orange and pink. Their steps slowed at her front porch.

"Thanks for today," Megan said, giving him a gentle smile. "I needed it."

"Anytime. Text me later." He gave a casual wave and headed off.

Later, curled up in her room surrounded by books, Megan let the events of the day wash over her. The sting of Thomas and Lexi's mocking still clung to her like dust. She opened her journal, letting ink spill across the page.

What if love isn't just about acceptance? What if it's about connection—even when the world thinks it's wrong?

Her words flowed effortlessly, unraveling her frustration, her longing, her dreams. She thought of the woodsman and the witch—misunderstood, whispered about and judged without truth. Their legend felt like a mirror held up to her life.

Why can't they see me for who I am? Why are people so quick to ridicule what they don't understand? Why does it hurt so much to be different?

Writing eased the tension in her chest. For a moment, she felt lighter—seen, even if only by herself.

As the night deepened, she curled into her favorite nook, lights dimmed to a soft amber glow. Thoughts of Romeo and Juliet drifted through her mind—not the tragedy, but the sincerity of their connection, the courage of loving despite the world's cruelty.

Maybe she could have something like that someday.

Maybe she wasn't as alone as she felt.

With that fragile hope warming her heart, Megan let her eyelids grow heavy, the weight of the day beginning to fade. The rhythmic sound of her breathing filled the quiet room, and her mind started to drift into a dreamscape, allowing her to easily surrender to sleep, embracing the possibility of a brighter tomorrow.

Chapter 2:
The Haunted Embrace

Megan stood at the far end of the track that circled Glory High's football field, but it didn't look like any field she remembered. The lines painted on the turf bled outward like open veins, white chalk smearing into the dark grass in long, pulpy streaks. Her heart slammed against her ribs, too loud, too heavy—each thud felt like a fist punching from inside her chest. The air hung thick and suffocating, a humid film that clung to her skin like something alive, something breathing with her.

A chill spidered through her bones.

The pine trees beyond the field towered in a warped line, their silhouettes stretched unnaturally toward the sky, as if every trunk had been pulled upward by invisible hooks. The moon overhead glowed a deep, unsettling red—more like a clot from a celestial wound—its light dripping across the field in sluggish, syrupy rays. It painted everything in shades of blood.

How did I get here? When did I walk outside? The questions slipped through her mind like whispers she couldn't grab hold of. Her voice didn't echo. It fell flat, swallowed instantly, as if the night itself were chewing it down.

A scream split the silence—high, shrill, shredding the still air like a blade tearing through wet fabric. It came from the direction of the school, but somehow also from everywhere at once, ricocheting through her skull. The sound was raw terror, vibrating with a throat-ripping desperation that made Megan's blood pulse cold.

She turned toward the school—but the trees were suddenly in front of her again.

Closer.

So close their cracked bark glistened with something thick and dark, sap or blood or both, oozing down their trunks in tar-like rivulets. She blinked hard. The branches writhed, curling like arthritic fingers eager to grab her. Panic constricted her chest.

This isn't real, this isn't real—

But the trees pulsed, as if breathing. The forest's darkness exhaled, warm and damp, brushing her face with the sour stench of rot. Every time she tried to step back toward the school, something tugged her forward—an unseen force tightening around her ankles like wire sinking into flesh.

Her breath broke into ragged gasps. The trees swayed without wind. Shadows pooled at their roots, slithering forward like spilled ink seeking her feet.

Something laughed in the darkness. A low, wet chuckle—like a throat full of mucus.

"Megan!" someone called behind her—far away, muffled, as if the voice had to break through thick layers of sludge to reach her. She whipped around, but school was gone, all that stood before her was pitch-thick absolute blackness. She stood in this emptiness confused.

Then something yanked her. A violent jerk, invisible hands closing like iron shackles around her wrists and ankles, wrenching her off her feet. She slammed onto the ground—mud splashed, thick and warm, the metallic reek of blood stinging her nose as the forest swallowed her whole in one choking motion.

The moment she crossed the tree line, the air pressed against her chest like a giant palm. Breathing became a struggle, like she had thick glue in her throat. The silence here wasn't silence at all —it was dense, pulsing, alive. A heartbeat she didn't recognize. A breath not her own.

Moonlight filtered through the canopy in thin, trembling shards, catching on crooked roots that writhed in the soil like pale worms. Each tree leaned inward, trunks bent at grotesque angles, bark splitting open in long gashes, revealing raw, wet wood beneath—fibers twitching like exposed muscle.

"Where… where am I?" Her voice cracked.

The shadows grew thicker, clinging to her like damp fabric. The darkness crawled up her legs, drank the color from her clothes, stole warmth from her skin. Every step sank deeper, the earth soft and spongy like decayed flesh.

Then a growl vibrated through the ground.

Deep. Resonant. Hungry.

It rolled underneath her feet, shaking loose dirt from the roots. She staggered backward, her breath turning to vapor that drifted upward unnaturally slow—as if time itself were hesitating around her.

The growl rose.

Multiplied.

Fractured into many.

From the shadows, shapes merged—fluid at first, like smoke learning how to walk—before snapping into freakish clarity.

Wolves.

But not wolves.

Their fur hung in ragged, matted clumps, slick with congealed blood. Patches of skin sloughed off as they moved, falling wetly to the ground. Bone jutted through their sides, ribs exposed in splintered crescents, some cracked open entirely as if something inside had clawed its way out.

Their eyes glowed a milky, corpse-white.

Their jaws hung too wide, the hinges cracked, tendons exposed and twitching as saliva thick as syrup dripped in long strings that sizzled when it hit the ground. When they bared their teeth, Megan saw more than just fangs, she saw pieces of their last meal still caught between them, long, torn scraps of flesh and knotted, matted hair.

They lunged forward, the forest floor quaking under their charge. Blood-streaked paws pounded the earth, splashing through puddles of dark ooze. A stench of rot and carnivore breath blasted toward her like a furnace of decay.

Run. The word wasn't her own—it slithered into her mind like a command. Her legs obeyed before her mind caught up. She sprinted through the twisted underbrush as branches whipped at her face, slicing thin lines across her cheeks. Shadows darted around her—wolf shapes weaving between trees, fluid and predatory, always just at the edges of her vision.

Broken branches clawed at her legs as she sprinted through the maze of darkness. Every leaf crunch sounded like a scream. The forest moved with her—twisting, rearranging, pulling her deeper. She could hear the wolves chasing her, their snarls echoing through the trees in a warped chorus.

She pushed herself harder, lungs burning, legs trembling. *Just a little farther*, she begged silently. But no matter which way she turned, the forest folded in on itself, trapping her in its endless, shifting maze. *Keep moving*, she gasped, but her voice sounded wrong—warped, echoing back at her with a distorted pitch, like something was repeating her words from inside her skull.

The wolves' breath hit her back—scalding hot, rank with rot. She could feel the heat of their bodies pressing in, could hear their tongues slapping against their teeth as they snapped inches from her heels.

Just when she thought they'd rip her down, a massive trunk loomed ahead. She dove behind it, slamming her body into the bark. The rough surface tore at her skin, tiny splinters embedding into her palms. She squeezed her eyes shut. Her heartbeat roared in her ears.

The pack thundered past. Paws pounded the earth like mallets, their growls echoed, shaking leaves loose from branches. She felt the vibration of their bodies—heavy and violent—rush by. Her chest rose and fell in shallow bursts, every breath scraping painfully against her throat. Fear throbbed through her muscles like an aftershock. Megan slowly turned, pressing her forehead to the cold bark, grounding herself, but her hands still trembled. The phantom memory of the wolves— their snarls, their hunger—clung to her like a residue that wouldn't wash off. The forest fell silent again.

Until—a raven shrieked.

A deep, vibrating caw that cracked through the quiet like a gunshot. Megan jerked her head upward. The bird perched above her, its feathers slicked back, eyes black as oil pits. Its beak gaped unnaturally wide, splitting at the corners, opening like a wound.

The world distorted. The trees warped into static, flickering shapes like a shattered TV signal. Colors bled together. Megan stumbled backward as a woman materialized through the haze. Long black hair flowed behind her as if underwater. Her face—a haunting blend of sorrow and serenity—she tilted toward Megan, eyes shimmering with glassy grief. She reached out, fingertips trembling, urging Megan closer. There was desperation in her expression, as though she had waited years for someone to finally see her.

Megan's breath caught. Something about the woman felt familiar or meant to feel familiar. Her eyes glistened with unshed tears as she reached out, her fingers trembling, skin pale as bleached bone. Megan took a step toward her just as the woman's arm twisted. Snapped. Lengthened.

Her bones stretched like heated taffy, bending at hideous angles as her jaw unhinged silently in a scream Megan couldn't hear—only feel, vibrating through her teeth like electricity.

Then she vanished—replaced by figures surging from between the trees—Pilgrim-clad men and women, their clothes torn, stained with decades-old gore. Their faces were twisted masks of fury, mouths stretched too wide, teeth jagged and broken.

Megan was surrounded as their clawed fingers latched onto her arms, tearing down her skin in ragged strips. Blood sprayed, warm and metallic, misting the air in a fine red cloud. She screamed as nails dug into muscle, scraping bone beneath. Their breath hit her face—sour, moldy, wet—as they shrieked in her ears, their voices merging into a throat-shredding agony.

As she closed her eyes, the world distorted again. Fire exploded upward as if the ground exhaled it. Flames twisted into a huge column of smoke, roiling with the towering figure of a red-bearded man.

His flesh rippled like something alive writhed beneath it. His beard was soaked in blood—fresh, wet, dripping down in thick ropes. His eyes burned with an ember-bright glow that flared every time he breathed. His shoulders bulged, tendons stretching, veins writhing like serpents beneath the skin. The air crackled with static once again. As he stepped forward, each thunderous step exploded through the forest. Shadows blasted outward like shrapnel. Screams erupted from everywhere.

His mouth opened wide—too wide—splitting from ear to ear, jaw dropping lower and lower until it nearly tore free. Rows of jagged, broken teeth jutted inward and outward, some fused together, some spiraling like drills, all slick with bloody drool. The smoke surged toward her with a guttural roar that seemed to tear itself out of the earth. Fire tore through the forest, debris raining down in clumps like burning flesh dropping from a butcher's hook. Smoke surged upward, churning, thickening, twisting into a massive, grotesque face—distorted, stretched, skin melting, eyes drooping down his cheeks like molten candle wax.

The smoke-face creature roared—a sound like metal scraping bone—and surged toward her with violent hunger.

Its maw opened, stretching so wide the world inside it turned black—and it lunged for her, teeth glistening, eager to swallow her whole.

"AAAAAAHH!"

Megan bolted upright in her bed, chest heaving, drenched in sweat. The morning light painted her room gold, almost too bright after the suffocating dark. She whipped her head around, expecting the bearded face to loom from the shadows. But her room was painfully ordinary. Her posters, her clothes on the floor, her desk—everything perfectly normal except for her racing heart and the feeling in the pit of her stomach that something still felt off. Like the nightmare hadn't fully let go.

The Next Morning…

The sun bathed the world in golden light the next day, a stark contrast to the darkness that had haunted her sleep. It was a beautiful Saturday, and Megan and Aiden escaped to the local park, seeking solace in the fresh air and gentle breeze. They settled at a picnic bench, the aroma of blooming flowers enveloping them, a reminder of life's small joys.

"I had the strangest dream last night, and they have been happening more and more over the last few weeks," Megan said, her brow furrowed as she tried to piece together the fragments of her nightmare. The memory of the dream lingered in her mind like a shadow, refusing to fade away. "Don't think I'm crazy or anything!" she pleaded, her voice rising slightly with urgency.

"Hah, we all have a bit of crazy in us," Aiden joked as he leaned closer, genuinely curious. "So what happened in the dream?"

Megan took a deep breath, gathering her thoughts as she prepared to share the unsettling details. "Well," she began, her voice steady yet laced with a hint of uncertainty, "I was chased by a pack of wolves through the dark forest. Their fur was matted and dirty, clinging to decaying flesh, and their bones stuck out beneath their skin. I could hear their growls echoing around me, a haunting symphony of hunger and rage."

She paused, the memory flooding her with adrenaline. "I barely escaped. Just when I thought they would catch me, I spotted a massive tree ahead. I hid behind its thick trunk, pushing myself against the bark as the wolves raced past me, their snarls fading into the distance. I could feel their hot breath on my skin, hear their claws scraping the earth just inches away. It was a close call." Aiden nodded, his expression focused as he listened intently.

Megan continued, her fingers nervously twisting a strand of hair. "There was this woman with long black hair. She looked so sad, like she was carrying a heavy burden. She kept reaching out to me, as if she wanted me to understand something important. And then there was a man with a red beard. He seemed powerful, but there was something terrifying about him too."

"What happened to them?" Aiden asked, his interest growing as he leaned forward.

Megan hesitated, searching for the right words. "The woman, I don't know, but the man, he… he turned into smoke. It was like he was being swallowed by darkness, and I could feel this overwhelming sense of fear. I don't know; it was all so vivid, but I can't make sense of it." She let out a frustrated sigh, feeling the weight of the dream pressing down on her. "It felt so real, like I was there, and now I can't shake the feeling that it means something."

Aiden listened attentively, his expression a mix of concern and curiosity. "That sounds intense. What do you think it means?" he asked, invested in her experience.

"Not sure. Dreams can be strange and confusing." Megan replied, "Especially this one!" Aiden said, trying to lighten the mood. "My mom always says they often reflect what's going on in our lives or what's on our minds. Maybe it's trying to tell you something about what you're feeling."

Megan nodded, considering his words. "I guess it could be. But it's just so eerie. I don't understand why I would dream about a forest, a pack of wolves, that unknown woman and man, it is so random. It feels like there's something deeper beneath the surface."

"You've always been someone who looks for meaning in things. Maybe this dream is pushing you to think about some of your own feelings or fears." Aiden encouraged, his voice calm and steady.

"Maybe," Megan said, her thoughts swirling. She appreciated Aiden's perspective. Talking about the dream somehow made it feel less heavy, as if sharing it allowed her to process it a little better.

Before Megan could gather her thoughts, a rowdy and obnoxious group approached, disrupting the moment and shattering the therapy session with Aiden. *Speaking of a pack of wolves*, Megan thought to herself as Thomas strode into the park with a swagger that commanded attention. Beside him was Lexi; her laughter ringing out like chimes in the wind. A cluster of football players and cheerleaders trailed behind them, their energy electric and overwhelming, descending upon the scene like a storm ready to unleash its fury.

The sound of their laughter bounced off the trees in the park, filling the air with an overwhelming noise that made it difficult for Megan to think clearly. It was a piercing sound, wild and carefree, but for her, it felt out of place. The bright colors of their clothes—red, yellow, and blue—stood out against the gentle greens and browns of the park, making her feel even more uneasy. As she watched them, a wave of anxiety washed over her, tightening in her stomach like a heavy stone.

"Hey, what are you two losers doing over there?" Thomas shouted, his voice thick with sarcasm as he pointed at Megan and Aiden. His smirk was big and confident, like he was enjoying the moment far too much. He loved being in control and making others feel small, and today was no different. "You guys sitting around like a couple of sad puppies? Come on, join the fun!"

Megan glanced at Aiden, who had a slight frown on his face, clearly not impressed by Thomas's antics. She could see the tension in his shoulders, just as she felt the same tightness in her own. "We were enjoying the day just fine until you guys arrived," Aiden replied, his voice steady but firm. "Not everyone needs to be loud and annoying to have a good time."

Thomas let out a loud, mocking laugh, as if Aiden's attempt to defend himself was the funniest joke he had ever heard. "Enjoying the day by just sitting here doing nothing??" he scoffed, shaking his head in disbelief at how clueless they seemed. "You guys need to lighten up! How can you just sit there while the rest of us are out here having a blast?" His tone dripped with condescension, and the disdain in his voice made Megan's stomach twist.

He turned back to his friends, who were giggling and whispering among themselves, entertained by Thomas's performance. They reveled in his ability to command attention, effortlessly shifting the mood with just a few words. Zack, leaning casually against a nearby bench, chimed in with a smirk, "Do you even know what fun is?" His voice held a mocking lilt, echoing Thomas's sentiment while adding his own twist. "You two are missing out on all the excitement of life. But I guess that's what happens when you're stuck in your little bubble, right?"

Anthony couldn't resist adding his own snarky remark. "Yeah, it's like watching two goldfish in a bowl—just swimming around in circles while the rest of us are out here splashing in the ocean!" His laughter rang out, and the group erupted in giggles, each one taking pleasure in the jabs at Megan and Aiden. With each snarky joke, the laughter felt like a heavy weight pressing down on Megan, amplifying her feelings of isolation and discomfort.

As the taunts continued, Megan's cheeks flushed with embarrassment, and she felt the heat of their mockery wash over her. It was as if the world around her had narrowed, leaving her and Aiden standing trapped in a web of ridicule while the others reveled in their amusement.

His tone was dripping with condescension, making it clear that he believed he was far above Megan and Aiden, as if they were beneath him. The way he laughed with his friends, their eyes sparkling with enjoyment, contrasted with the uncomfortable silence that had fallen over Megan and Aiden. Thomas reveled in his ability to manipulate the atmosphere, feeding off their discomfort while he basked in the spotlight, unaware of how shallow his version of fun was.

Megan felt a rush of frustration, realizing that they were worlds apart, not just in interests but in how they viewed life. While Thomas was living for the moment, seeking attention and validation, she and Aiden found joy in the simple things, even if they didn't fit the mold he had created. As Thomas continued to mock them, Megan felt her cheeks heat with embarrassment, wishing she could disappear into the grass beneath her. She took a deep breath, trying to shake off the negative energy surrounding Thomas and his friends. "We don't need to be like you to have fun," she said, trying to sound braver than she felt.

"Oh, look at that! The quiet girl has something to say!" Thomas shot back, his voice dripping with laughter as he turned back to his group. "What a surprise!" Lexi was laughing, her shiny blonde hair bouncing with each giggle. "Shouldn't you be hiding in a dark corner reading a boring book or something?" she called out, her voice sharp like a knife slicing through the air. "You two must enjoy being social outcasts?" Her words dripped with mockery, grabbing the attention of everyone nearby.

Megan could feel her heart race, and she glanced at Aiden, who looked equally uncomfortable. She wished Lexi would just back off. The laughter around them felt heavy, wrapping around her like a thick fog.

"Come on, Lexi. Leave them alone," said Amy, one of the cheerleaders. A mischievous glint danced in her eyes, contradicting her lighthearted words. "What if they're on a date? We wouldn't want to interrupt the lovebirds, would we?" Her comment elicited laughter from some onlookers, but for Megan, irritation bubbled just beneath the surface. The laughter felt like a sharp jab, a reminder of her isolation in a sea of friendship.

Jenna, the third cheerleader in the group, was striking with her shoulder-length black hair and athletic build. She rolled her eyes, unimpressed with Amy's attempt to diffuse the situation. "A date? Please! More like a pity party for two!" Jenna's voice dripped with sarcasm as she turned her attention back to Megan and Aiden, a wide, taunting smile stretching across her face. "Maybe you should just go back to your little corner where you belong. It's safer there." Her words were laced with disdain, an attempt to humiliate Megan further. The hostility in Jenna's tone was palpable, making Megan feel small and unwelcome, as if she were nothing more than an afterthought in this social hierarchy.

Megan clenched her fists, trying to keep her cool. "We're just trying to enjoy our time," she said, her voice steady but laced with frustration. "We don't need your approval to do what we want."

Lexi smirked, clearly enjoying the confrontation. "Oh, sweetie, it's not about approval. It's about knowing your place," she shot back, her laughter echoing around them like a cruel taunt.

Aiden spoke up, his voice stronger than before. "Worry about your own place, Lexi. No one wants to be around someone who gets off on others' embarrassment; it's petty."

There was a moment of silence as everyone processed Aiden's words, and Megan felt a flicker of hope. Maybe they wouldn't just sit back and take the bullying this time.

As the tension hung in the air, Megan realized that standing up for themselves was more important than ever. She took a deep breath, feeling the weight of the moment, and stood a little taller beside Aiden.

"Whatever," Thomas shrugged, dismissing them with a wave of his hand as he turned to his friends. "Let's go, guys. I don't want to waste my time here." Thomas turned to leave, tossing a ball at Anthony as they walked away.

Megan's cheeks were bright red with humiliation, the weight of their ridicule sinking in. She glanced toward the distant metal fence that bordered the forbidden forest, a stark reminder of the stories whispered about it. A sign that read, 'Do Not Enter' hung on the fence. Perched on the fence above the sign was a raven, its beady eyes watching them, cawing as if echoing her earlier dream.

Aiden, sensing her discomfort, leaned closer and whispered, "Just ignore them. They're looking for attention, and they'll get bored soon enough." His voice was low and steady, a comforting presence amidst the chaos.

"Yeah, you're right," Megan replied, though the laughter still echoed in her ears. She tried to focus on Aiden's words, finding solace in their friendship. "It just gets old, you know? I wish they could see beyond their own little world."

"Me too," Aiden said with a nod. "But we know better. Let's just enjoy our time here and not let them ruin it for us."

Megan smiled. As the laughter from Thomas and the three girls faded into the background, she felt a little annoyed but was ready to reclaim the moment for herself and Aiden.

"Okay, let's find a quieter place to chat," she suggested, trying to shift her mood. "I could really use a moment away from all this noise right now."

"Yeah, me too!" Aiden grinned, and together they turned away from the laughter, stepping into their own world where the opinions of others couldn't reach them.

As they walked away, Megan let out a breath she hadn't realized she'd been holding. "I don't know why they always have to be like that."

"They thrive on bullying others," Aiden replied.

Nodding in agreement, Megan stood up, her gaze lingering on the raven. It cawed again, a sound that resonated deep within her, sending a cold sensation coursing through her veins—a strange sense of unease washing over her. As they walked away from the chaos, she couldn't shake the feeling that the world around her was somehow connected to the dream, and that it was pulling her closer to mysteries yet to be uncovered.

Aiden walked beside her, concern etched on his face. "You okay, Meg? You seem a bit off today," he said, glancing sideways at her with a mix of curiosity and worry.

Megan shrugged, trying to brush off his concern. "It's just that weird dream. I know we talked about it, but I can't shake it."

Aiden frowned, his brow furrowing in thought. "Maybe the man and woman are your subconscious reacting to all the stuff Ms. Carter has been talking about. You know how fascinated she is with the urban legend of the woodsman and the witch of the forest. It's been brought up in class so often; your mind could just be processing it."

"Yeah, but this feels different," Megan replied, shaking her head. "It's like the dream is trying to tell me something. It felt so vivid, so real."

"Or maybe it's just your brain working overtime. You've been under a lot of stress with school and everything," Aiden suggested, though his eyes betrayed his concern. "It's normal to have strange dreams when you're anxious."

"But what if it's more than that?" Megan pressed, her voice tinged with concern. "What if it's connected to the stories we keep hearing? What if there's something out there, something we're meant to uncover?"

Aiden stopped walking, turning to face her. "Megan, I get that you're curious, but you have to be careful. Those stories regarding the witch and woods give rise to many superstitions. It's easy to lose yourself in them, especially with everything on your mind. Also, avoid entering that forest."

Despite his attempts at logic, a spark of resistance ignited within her. "Maybe," she said, "but what if there's truth hidden in those tales? What if the woodsman and the witch were more than just legends? I can't help but think there's something significant about them."

Aiden looked anxious as he ran a hand through his hair in frustration. "You will not drop this, will you?" he asked, his voice tinged with worry. Megan shot him an awkward smile and shook her head. "Fine. If it means that much to you, let's research the subject. But promise me two things." She met Aiden's gaze, tilting her chin up as she waited for him to lay down his conditions.

"First, we stay far away from the forest. Bad things always happen in that forest. I don't want you getting hurt or getting too caught up in something that could, and I hate to say this, end up being another Glory fairytale, like Thomas said." Megan shot him a disapproving look, raising an eyebrow. "Aiden? You and Thomas agree now?"

Aiden tried to defend his comment. "No… No… No… I'm not saying that! I'm just saying, what if that's all it is, Meg?"

Megan glanced away for a moment, the weight of his words hanging in the air. "And what's number two?" she asked, eager to get past the tension.

"Oh, for number two, you have to come to the movie in the park after the library," Aiden said, knowing he was playing with fire.

"Aiden!!! No way—come on," she protested, her eyes widening. "Everyone will be there, and I just… I don't want to deal with that right now!"

Aiden stood there, aware that he was treading on thin ice, realizing just how risky his words had been. "Aiden!!! No way—come on!" Megan exclaimed, her voice filled with disbelief. "Everyone will be there, and the last thing I need is more ridicule from those childish idiots! Ugh!" Her irritation surged to the surface like a pot about to boil over as she spun around, her hands clenched in frustration. With a heavy sigh, she walked away, her pace quickening as if she could escape not just the conversation but also the feelings that were swirling inside her. Aiden watched her go, a mix of regret and concern washing over him, unsure if he should follow her or let her have the space she needed.

"Meg! You love Edward Scissorhands! Remember when we first met you mentioned how it's a classic? Meg, please!" Aiden called after her, desperation creeping into his voice. He could see her shoulders tense, but then something shifted. Megan paused mid-stride, a spark of determination igniting within her. She turned back to face him, the thrill of possibility washing over her as the thought of uncovering the truth took root in her mind.

"Ugh, fine! Deal," she said, a resolute nod punctuating her words. Aiden felt a rush of relief and excitement. This was it! They were on the brink of something—an adventure that could lead to answers.

"Okay, it's getting late," Aiden said, glancing at the fading light of the day. "How about we meet at the library tomorrow morning? Let's say around nine?"

Megan's face lit up with a smile, the earlier irritation dissipating like mist in the morning sun. "See you then, buddy!" she replied, her voice cheerful again. As she turned back toward the path leading home, the sound of a raven's caw echoed in the background, a reminder of the mysteries that lay ahead. Aiden watched her go, feeling a mixture of excitement and apprehension about what they might discover together.

Once Megan arrived home, a familiar sense of solitude enveloped her. The house was quiet, a peaceful contrast to the noise of the park and the laughter that still echoed in her mind. She made her way to her cozy nook, that safe space in the corner of her room; she flopped onto her soft pillows and draped the warm blanket draped over her shoulders. This was her sanctuary, where she often escaped into the words of her favorite books or let her thoughts spill onto the pages of her journal.

Sinking into the corner, Megan pulled out her journal and a pen. The comforting weight in her hands grounded her at the moment. She opened to a fresh page and wrote, her heart racing as she poured out her emotions.

Today was rough, she started, the words flowing as she let her feelings spill onto the page. *I had the strangest dream last night—one that I can't seem to shake. There was darkness, a raven, and that woman with long black hair. It felt so real, like I was there, living it. The pack of wolves and the man with the red beard turning into smoke still haunts me.*

She paused, tapping the pen against her chin, trying to find clarity. *Maybe it was a warning? Or a reflection of my fears?* The questions lingered, swirling in her mind like the shadows in her dream.

Her thoughts shifted as she recalled the laughter of her classmates — Thomas, Lexi, and Jenna. *It's so frustrating how they always seem to belittle me,* she wrote, her grip tightening on the pen. *Lexi's comments cut deep, and their laughter feels like a weight I can't shake off. I wish they could see that there's more to life than fitting in and being popular. Why do they have to be so cruel?*

As she continued to write, she felt a sense of release. Each word was a step toward unraveling the tangled emotions inside her. *I want to be proud of my love for literature and the stories that speak to me. I want to find a place where I belong—somewhere I'm accepted for who I am, not judged for it.*

Megan felt the fatigue of the day creeping into her bones. Combining the emotional rollercoaster and the lingering remnants of her unsettling dream weighed on her. She leaned back in her corner, the soft pillows cradling her as she closed her eyes for just a moment, hoping to push the negativity away.

Just a few hours of rest, she thought, but as she drifted off, the line between wakefulness and sleep blurred, and she slipped back into the realm of dreams.

Chapter 3:
Echoes of the Past

The forest from her earlier visions rose again around her, swallowing the world whole. It wrapped her in darkness the way a cocoon smothers a dying moth. Megan stood at its threshold, the towering pines leaning in like eavesdroppers. Their long limbs swayed—not with any breeze she could feel, but with something older, something that noticed her. Nearby, a raven perched on a crooked stump, its beady eyes locked on her as though it had been waiting.

"Maybe this time I'll understand," she whispered. The words drifted out, soft as breath, and the trees almost seemed to lean closer to catch them.

She stepped forward. The dream thickened.

A heavier hush settled around her, smothering every sound. The forest rose like a cathedral built from bone—trunks twisted and warped, branches reaching down as if eager to brush her skin. When the raven cawed, its cry ricocheted off the silence like a warning shot.

Shadows rippled across the ground, pulling apart, reshaping. And then the woman appeared again—slipping free of the darkness like a memory Megan couldn't shake. Her hair, long and black as tar, drank in the faint light. Her face held a sorrow so sharp Megan felt it prick her skin. The air around her turned cold enough to sting.

The woman tried to speak, but clumps of dirt spilled from her mouth—wet, heavy globs splattering onto the ground. Megan recoiled, yet something about the woman's frantic motions tugged her forward. She was trying to warn her. Megan could feel it like a hand pressing against her spine.

She leaned in, straining to hear.

Pain snapped through her mind like a live wire. Sudden flashes streaked across her vision—faces screaming, flames writhing like serpents, silhouettes writhing in agony. Megan sucked in a breath, fighting the urge to look away, but the images kept coming, harder, faster.

The woman's voice clawed through the chaos, growing clearer.

"Stay away from the unholy!" she cried, and the desperation in her tone sliced right through Megan. "You must not let it consume you!"

"What unholy?" Megan shouted. "What are you talking about?" But her words scattered like dust, swallowed by the rising screams in the air.

The woman lifted a shaking hand and pointed.

Megan followed the gesture to the church standing in the distance.

Its silhouette looked wrong—wounded somehow—bathed in a sickly, unnatural light. Windows that should've glowed warm now oozed streams of thick black sludge, as if the building itself were crying tar. The goo dripped down the stone steps, pooling in the dirt like blood gone rotten.

Megan's pulse spiked.

"Are you doing this?" she yelled, but the woman didn't answer. She felt trapped between dread and curiosity, compelled by a force she couldn't name.

As her feet carried her closer, the church doors yawned open in a slow, conscious motion that felt less like wood moving and more like a mouth stretching wide.

Each step she took made the air colder. The wind whispered around her—voices snaking between the trees, old and full of warning. She was only a few feet from the porch when the doors slammed shut with a roar so violent the ground trembled.

"No!" Panic seized her. She shoved at the doors, palms slapping the cold wood. "Let me in! I need to understand!"

A scream exploded from inside.

Not human. Not animal. Something else. It wailed through her bones, rattling her teeth, shaking the air until even her heartbeat felt unstable. Megan clapped her hands over her ears, but the scream pushed through her fingers like needles.

The doors burst open.

The force threw her backward off the porch. She landed in a puddle of thick black ooze that sucked at her clothes and skin, cold and viscous as if alive. She clawed at the ground, but the sludge clung to her, pulling her down.

Footsteps creaked above her.

Her stomach dropped.

The reverend stepped into view—tall and lanky, his skin shining with a slick, serpentine sheen. His eyes were thin slits, gleaming with a predator's hunger. When he smiled, his lips peeled back to reveal fangs—long, sharp, too white.

"Ah, child," he hissed, his voice smooth and coiling, "I have been expecting you."

A forked tongue flicked from his mouth, tasting the air. Tasting her.

He moved with a rattlesnake's fluidity, each step deliberate, predatory. Dark drops of venom gathered at the tips of his fangs, falling into the ooze with soft, deadly clicks.

Megan's breath hitched. This was wrong. This was beyond nightmare wrong.

The reverend lunged.

Instinct took over. She curled into herself, arms wrapped tight around her head. She could feel the cold ooze climbing higher, gripping her like hands dragging her down.

Then—blackness. Heavy and sudden.

Her body jerked awake.

She shot upright in the soft corner of her room, drenched in sweat, breath coming in frantic bursts. Moonlight pooled through the curtains, pale and gentle, a stark contrast to what she'd just escaped. But the nightmare clung stubbornly, its claws still sunk deep.

Her heart refused to slow. She hugged her arms around herself, trying to hold the pieces together.

The reverend's fangs, that slick skin, his hissing voice—they lingered like smoke.

And the fear didn't fade.

It whispered in the back of her mind, persistent as a heartbeat.

"Just a dream," she murmured, though the shaky whisper felt like a lie even as it left her lips. Her heartbeat battered against her ribs. "What is wrong with me?" She tapped the side of her head—not gentle, more like she was trying to smack loose parts back into place—but the unease only deepened, that crawling sense that her nightmares weren't nightmares at all. They felt like warnings wearing the skin of dreams.

She drifted to her bed and sat down hard. Her mind spun, images from the night drifting through her thoughts like ash in a breeze—black ooze, screaming doors, the serpent-eyed reverend. She fought to keep her eyes open, but exhaustion wrapped around her like wool soaked in warm water, heavy and suffocating. No matter how she tried to resist, her eyelids sagged. The dark pulled at her. And she sank.

When Megan woke again, the sun was already filling her room, warm and golden, a sharp contradiction to the cold terror still clinging to her skin. Her heart thudded with leftover panic. The dream lingered in her bones like fever chills. She shoved her blankets aside and stumbled to her feet, her room momentarily unfamiliar, as if she'd crossed between two worlds and wasn't entirely sure which one she was in.

She showered quickly, dressed even quicker, and bolted downstairs. Her mother—still in her rumpled night-shift scrubs—watched her tear across the kitchen like a startled deer. Megan grabbed a single piece of toast.

"Bye!" she yelled on her way out, not slowing long enough to catch her mother's worried expression. She didn't want to answer questions she didn't have answers to.

Outside, the morning air slapped her awake. She sprinted toward the library, dew glittering on lawns like scattered glass. Houses along the street looked too normal—iced coffees in adult hands, neighbors waving lazy hellos, a golden retriever tugging its human down the sidewalk. Perfect little snapshots of peaceful life.

But Megan couldn't shake the creeping thought:

These dreams are messing with me. And they're trying to show me something.

She cut across the final corner and spotted the library—old brick, tall windows, a place that smelled like dust and forgotten stories. Aiden waited near the steps, bouncing on his heels.

Whatever he saw in her face made his own expression sharpen with focus.

Inside, the scent of old paper and worn leather hit them in a wave. The library felt quieter than usual—almost expectant. Megan and Aiden dropped into their usual table, its varnish worn smooth from decades of anxious fingertips and whispered secrets.

She took a breath and unloaded everything.

"The woman showed up again," she said, fingers tightening around each other. "And this time she pointed right at the church. It looked like Glory's, but… wrong. Sick. The windows were spewing this thick, black ooze—like it was bleeding something rotten. And the reverend—God, Aiden. He looked like Reverend Goodwin twisted into something… something a rattlesnake would kneel to." Her voice cracked. "He rushed me. I swear I felt his breath before I woke up."

Aiden leaned forward, eyes widening—not frightened, but fascinated in that way he got when puzzles handed themselves to him.

"The reverend? Hmm maybe we start with the town and churches history," he said. "If your dreams are connected to something real, Glory's past might tell us where to look."

Books piled fast. More than they needed. They combed through records—articles yellowed to near translucence, brittle pages that crackled under their fingertips, handwritten testimonies that looked like they'd been penned by trembling hands. The deeper they dug, the darker things became.

Women cast out.

Accused of witchcraft.

Banished into the woods, not killed—buried alive socially, stripped of name and home.

Every account struck Megan like a bell. Something resonated. Something familiar.

Could the woman in her dreams have been one of them?

She swallowed hard, the thought sticking to her throat like a lump of pitch. The stories felt personal. Too personal.

"What gets me," Megan murmured after a long stretch of reading, "is how it wasn't even always trials. Sometimes they didn't burn them or… torture them publicly. They just kicked them out. Banished them into the trees like the forest was a graveyard they didn't have to dig."

Aiden nodded slowly. "Isolation does more damage than fire. Think about it—cast someone out into the woods knowing they have no one, no way to survive. It's cruelty dressed up as righteousness."

"And it worked," Megan whispered. "They disappeared. No records, no graves, no names. Just—gone." She flipped another page. "And why does everything before 1730 stop? Like someone cut the timeline with scissors."

Aiden bit his lip. "Maybe no one wanted to remember. Trauma gets buried. People rewrite history because it's easier than facing the rot underneath it."

The silence between them grew heavy—thick with unspoken questions.

"What if we're looking too small?" Megan finally said. "What if Glory wasn't the only place doing this? If we compare witch trials from other towns… patterns might appear."

Aiden's eyes lit up. "Yes. Exactly. Regional records, old settlements, anything dealing with exile instead of execution. That could help us see the full story."

Megan felt hope flutter weakly in her chest. "Or we could talk to someone who actually studies this. Someone who knows how to read between the lines."

Aiden snapped his fingers. "Mrs. Archer. The historian from that guest lecture. She talked about gender persecution like it was archaeology—digging until the bones tell the truth. She said the trials we learn about are only the tip of the iceberg."

"Then she's exactly who we need."

They exchanged a determined look—two teenagers surrounded by dusty books and ghosts of the past, ready to pull at threads they didn't realize were tied to something still alive.

"Exactly," Megan said, the spark in her voice returning. "If anyone can help us make sense of Glory's history, it's her. She might point us toward regional cases or records we don't even know exist."

Aiden's enthusiasm dimmed just a little as he chewed the inside of his cheek. "How do we even get ahold of her? She's a university professor. Her schedule's probably packed. We should have backup plans."

"I can email her," Megan said quickly. "I'm pretty sure I still have her contact from that lecture last summer. I'll explain what we're researching, and ask if she'd be willing to meet or even just point us toward some resources." She tried to sound casual, but hope colored every word. "It's worth a shot."

"Do it," Aiden said, practically vibrating with energy. "If she gets on board, we might get access to things we don't even know to look for. Archives, databases… hell, maybe even stuff that never made it online."

They headed out of the library, pushing through the heavy wooden doors into the brightness outside. Sunlight poured over them, but all Megan felt was a tug of disappointment. No secret confessions in journals. No lost testimonies. No lightning bolt revelation tying her nightmares to Glory's past. The lack of answers somehow made the shadows feel heavier.

"I think we are done for now," feeling slightly frustrated. "Let's meet in a couple hours at the town square," she said, steadier than she felt. "I'll write the email and see if she responds. If she agrees to talk with us… it could change everything."

Even saying those words made her pulse jump—because it wasn't just history they were chasing anymore. Someone in Glory's past had screamed so loudly it was echoing into her dreams. Mrs. Archer might be holding the flashlight they needed.

"I hope she writes back," Megan added, the flicker of hope turning into a nervous knot.

"She will," Aiden said with a shrug so confident it was almost irritating. "She was obsessed with this kind of stuff. If we show we care about uncovering the truth, She'll see the passion." He nudged her playfully. "Besides, we're basically the poster kids for weird mysteries now."

Megan laughed, though insecurity tugged at her smile. "You really think so?"

"Absolutely," he said, grinning wide. "We're onto something big. I can feel it. No turning back now."

That warm, buzzing feeling of partnership lingered as they split paths—Aiden jogging off toward Main Street, Megan heading home with her mind still tangled in forests, witch trials, and the woman who haunted her nights.

Once inside her room, she shut the door and sat at her desk, her cozy reading nook glowing in the corner like a tiny lighthouse. She flipped open her laptop and began typing without hesitation.

Dear Mrs. Archer,

I hope this message finds you well. You might not remember me, but my name is Megan. I attended your lecture on women's history last summer…

The words poured from her fingers like water from a cracked dam. When she finally leaned back, she felt the weight of everything—dreams, warnings, shadowy forests—press against her lungs.

Then she glanced at the clock.

"Crap." The movie night. She'd promised Aiden.

"Why did I say yes?" she groaned, dragging her hands down her face. "This is so not my scene."

She grabbed a sweater, slung her bag over her shoulder, and stomped out the door. Every step felt like she was walking away from the mystery she wanted to drown in.

But by the time she arrived in the town square, the world had softened into a postcard. Twilight draped Glory in gold and purple. The scent of fresh popcorn drifted through the crowd. Leaves crunched under her boots. The screen towered above the families and couples settling onto blankets scattered like patchwork across the grass.

She spotted Aiden leaning against a lamppost—wearing a plaid flannel shirt, arms crossed, scanning the crowd like he was searching for trouble or trying to spot it before it spotted them. A twist of nerves tightened in her chest, uninvited.

"Hey! You made it!" Aiden called, face brightening as he waved her over.

"Wouldn't miss it for the world," she replied with the driest grin imaginable. She lifted a bag of caramel popcorn. "I brought snacks."

"Perfect. I need a sugar overload before the movie even starts." He pointed toward a blanket he'd spread out—blue and frayed at the edges, scratchy-looking but inviting in its own way.

The crew fiddling with the projector announced that Edward Scissorhands would start soon. Voices overlapped—laughs, greetings, whispered gossip. The air buzzed warm despite the cool.

Then, of course, chaos.

A group of high school kids bulldozed through the crowd, loud enough to drown out the speakers. Megan recognized them before she even fully turned: Thomas, Lexi, Jenna, and their entourage of cheerleaders and football players. A walking circus of perfume, cologne, and overinflated egos.

"Here we go," Aiden muttered. "Human fireworks."

"They live for attention," Megan said, rolling her eyes. "Typical high school royalty."

Right on cue, Randy barreled through the square—built like a refrigerator, attitude like a stubborn pit bull. In his rush to catch up with Thomas, he slammed straight into Aiden.

Aiden's drink exploded across his shirt like an abstract painting of sticky cherry soda.

"Watch where you're going!" Aiden shouted, stumbling back in shock.

And just like that, the night changed direction.

Randy turned, a sneer forming on his lips. "Maybe you should move out of the way next time, tiny!" he barked, his voice booming over the laughter of his friends. Behind him, two other football players—Jake and Tyler—exchanged amused glances, their snickers swelling the taunting atmosphere.

Jake, slightly taller than Randy, chimed in with a smirk. "Yeah, watch where you're going! We don't want you to get accidentally stepped on."

Tyler, known for his quick wit, added, "Or maybe you should just stick to the sidelines and out of our way!"

Their laughter erupted all at once, echoing through the square in a wave of mockery. Though the guys tried to play it off as harmless fun, there was a sharpness behind their words—an easy cruelty that came from power, ego, and an eager audience.

Megan felt heat rush through her. "That was uncalled for!" she snapped, stepping protectively in front of Aiden.

Before Aiden could respond, Reverend Goodwin stepped forward. His presence cut through the noise instantly. Tall, gray-haired, and always composed, he carried himself like a man used to settling disputes with nothing more than a steady look.

"Boys," he said, his voice calm but firm. "I think it's best you keep your negative comments to yourselves. We're here to enjoy an evening together, not create tension."

Randy shrugged, throwing his hands up. "I'm cool. It's just a little conversation. No problems here, Reverend. Just having fun." He sauntered backward, Jake patting him on the shoulder as he trailed behind, still laughing.

Randy tossed out one last jab. "See ya around, lil' homie, alright?"

Tyler followed with a cheesy finger gun and a wave. "Later, buddy!"

Reverend Goodwin cleared his throat as he turned back to Megan and Aiden, his expression softening. "My dear friends," he said warmly, "let not the unkind words of others weigh heavy on your hearts." His eyes gleamed with practiced wisdom. "Enjoy your night, and remember—kindness always triumphs over cruelty."

With that, he walked away, his footfalls almost too light for someone his size.

Megan turned to Aiden, worry etched across her face. "Are you okay? They didn't have to be such jerks."

Aiden brushed the incident off, more annoyed than upset. "I'm fine. Just surprised, that's all. It's not like I haven't dealt with these guys before. They're all bark—especially Randy."

But Megan noticed the tiny tremor in his hands as he tried wiping soda from his shirt. "Still," she muttered, "you don't deserve that."

Aiden's smile returned, soft but genuine. "Thanks for having my back. Really. It's good to know someone's looking out for me." He nudged her shoulder lightly. "Besides, we have bigger mysteries to uncover than high school drama."

"True," she said, though her jaw remained tight. "But still— you shouldn't have to put up with any of that."

Aiden shrugged and settled onto the blanket again. "Come on. Edward Scissorhands. Outsiders unite, right?"

Megan sat down beside him, but her eyes drifted to Reverend Goodwin.

Even as the projector crew finished setting up, he moved through the square like some strange, out-of-time figure— gliding more than walking, towering above the cheerful chaos around him. The families, the couples, the giggling kids… they all seemed so normal compared to him.

People approached him with an eagerness Megan found unsettling. Their greetings were overly polished, almost rehearsed.

"Good evening, Reverend! Blessings upon you!" a woman gushed, dipping into a small curtsy.

Goodwin returned each greeting with a velvet-smooth reply. "May your health be abundant, and your heart filled with peace."

The words seemed to wrap around people like a warm cloak, but Megan swore she felt something colder beneath the surface.

As he laid a hand on a little boy's shoulder and murmured, "May the light guide you," a shiver crawled up Megan's spine.

What light? she wondered. *And who decides who deserves it?*

She leaned toward Aiden. "Doesn't he seem… I don't know. Out of place? Like he's trying too hard to be some almighty figure."

Aiden squinted toward the reverend, who was now surrounded by a group of teenage girls, all of them smiling too brightly. "Yeah. It's like he's feeding off their energy. Not just respect—something else. Desperation?"

Megan nodded slowly. "He moves through crowds like he's royalty. They fawn over him, and he eats it up."

Aiden crossed his arms. "Creepy. Definitely creepy. I know people admire him, but this… this is different."

She forced her eyes back to the screen just as the film jerked awake. Shadows slid over one another—thin, twitchy silhouettes that didn't match the actors' movements. For a heartbeat they warped her vision, bending the world in a way that made her doubt her own footing. She told herself the prickle up her spine was nerves, just nerves, the same phantom unease you get when a storm scrapes its nails down a window.

But the sound changed. Not louder—closer. A low, breathy murmur spilled from the speakers, threading through the crowd like a draft slipping under a locked door. It rose, curled, and multiplied until it felt like the whispers weren't coming from the film at all, but from the dark folds beneath the benches.

Megan's breath caught as the screen shifted. The white border bled into a dull gray, and her stomach lurched. The projector rattled once, then steadied, casting a weak, uneven glow. The grotesque image she'd seen lingered in her mind like a stain—dark, heavy, impossible to scrub away.

Then the scent hit her. Metallic… wet… the the smell right after rain punches into soil, opening the earth. It gathered in her throat, heavy as copper. She imagined wings—thin, brittle ones —rustling just past the tree line. Waiting. Testing the air for her.

A hush rippled through the crowd. Someone at the back spoke—a woman's voice, almost too quiet to be real, too intimate to be meant for the group. Megan turned. A figure leaned forward in the shadows, head tilted like she was guarding a secret no one should ever hear.

"Do you ever feel out of place?" the woman asked. "Like you don't belong?"

Her eyes were locked on Reverend Goodwin, but Megan felt the question thread straight into her ribs.

Her own voice felt borrowed when she answered. "Sometimes. Sometimes I think I'm different, and everyone... sees it."

Aiden's voice sliced in from her right. "Meg, who are you talking to?" He looked toward the dark bench—empty. Completely empty.

"You are different," he said softer. "You're special. That's what they see."

Special. The word didn't calm her. If anything, the square seemed to pulse beneath her, like the ground itself was breathing too fast. Something pushed at the air—pressure without sound—tightening around her chest in an invisible grip.

Do you trust me?

The voice didn't come from the crowd. It rose from deep inside her, a whisper she hadn't heard since childhood nightmares she never told anyone about. Megan's throat cinched. She braced a hand on the blanket to steady herself.

Beware of him.

The warning coiled through her skull as she lifted her eyes toward the back wall, where the projector's beam died into a pool of crawling shadow. The film reached a sharp, unsettling note at the exact moment Reverend Goodwin turned his head and looked at her. His eyes weren't there; two voids stared back, black and bottomless. His mouth peeled into a grin so wrong, so jagged it looked carved with a blade. A grin that didn't belong to any preacher. A predator's smile worn on a holy man's face.

Megan's breath hitched. She blinked hard, once, twice—and the reverend's features snapped back into place. Normal. Human. As if nothing had happened.

The lights fluttered, dimmed, then spasmed violently. The projector spat out a thin, sickly glow as the screen washed in blinding white. The white color oozed, melting down into something brown and wet-looking. Rot crept across the picture, eating through the scene like mold devouring old bread.

From that rot, a face swelled into view.

A man—if the stretched, time-torn thing could still be called that. A rust-red beard crawled along his chin, flickering like embers about to die. The skin around it sagged and peeled in strips, exposing raw flesh beneath. His eyes were pits—empty, ancient pits that locked onto her with a weight that compressed her lungs.

His mouth gaped open in a soundless scream, teeth jagged like stone broken under a hammer. The face pulsed in the projector's light, beating slow and heavy, each throb pressing against her sternum like an unseen fist.

For a terrible second, she was certain the man would pull himself free of the screen and walk toward her—quiet, steady, unstoppable.

He didn't. He stayed suspended in the glow, a dead face pinned in place, staring straight into her.

A sour wave surged up her throat. She swallowed hard, but the taste clung like acid. The projector shuddered, flickered, steadied—its light going weak and washed-out.

She squeezed her eyes shut and in a silent plea, begged, *Go away. Please... just go away.*

When she opened them, the screen slowly bled back into normalcy, the colors smoothing back into place. The harmless scene returned as if the horror had never been there at all.

Megan exhaled in one shaky burst, her lungs finally remembering how to work. She shook her head, trying to dislodge the image; whatever evil she thought she'd seen—if it had been real at all—slowly slipped away like fog in morning light. But its memory remained. A dying ember waiting for a stray spark to roar back into flame. The air around her felt thick with things unsaid. Her heart thudded with a restless urgency, pulling her deeper into the mystery tightening around Glory... and around him. The crowd had fallen quiet, and the flickering film swept across the screen in warm, whimsical bursts of color.

Trying to ground herself, Megan reached for her popcorn and nudged the bag toward Aiden. He took a handful without tearing his eyes from the screen. Tim Burton's world unfolded like a dream—lovely, strange, tender. A place where difference was celebrated rather than feared.

The laughter and chatter of the crowd softened into a distant hum as she allowed the story to pull her in. But even as the film cast its spell, Megan couldn't fully shake the sensation simmering beneath her awareness—beneath Glory's painted charm were currents she didn't yet understand. Tension. Secrets. Something unresolved, coiled and waiting.

As Edward danced across the screen, she felt herself drift. The movie's magic wrapped around her like a blanket, but behind its glow lurked familiar shadows—echoes of the past she'd tried to forget. Those memories whispered to her now, reminding her that her journey was far from over. The film offered escape, but her fears pressed in, quiet and persistent, promising darker challenges still ahead.

By the time the credits rolled and the crowd dispersed, Megan felt wrung out and unsteady. She made her way home, the crisp night air clinging to her skin like cold fingers. Under a steaming shower, the chill finally loosened, melting from her bones. Wrapped in her oversized sweater, she sat before her laptop. The half-finished email to Mrs. Archer waited with its blinking cursor, patient and accusing.

What if she ignores me? Megan thought, biting her lip. *What if she thinks I'm just some foolish kid?*

The doubt pressed hard. She closed the laptop with a sigh and retreated to her cozy nook—a sanctuary of cushions, blankets, and warm lamplight. Curling into the softness, she reached for her journal, her most trusted refuge.

"Alright… let's sort through today's chaos," she whispered as she flipped to a blank page.

Her pen flowed across the paper. She wrote about the library —the disappointing dead ends, the cold facts about Glory's past, the exile and cruelty of the old witch trials that still sent a shiver through her. People were so cruel back then, she mused. Some days, it felt like the cruelty never disappeared—just changed faces.

She smiled softly, remembering the movie. "At least that was fun," she murmured. "I've always loved that film."

But her hand slowed.

Her thoughts drifted to Reverend Goodwin.

What's up with him? He helped Aiden… but something's off.

It's like he knows more than he lets on.

The thought sat heavy in her chest.

Wrapped in warmth, Megan's eyelids grew heavy. She tried to force them open. "I should finish that email," she mumbled through a yawn. But the words on the page blurred, the room dimming around her. Her pen slipped from her fingers, tapping the floor with a soft clatter.

The mysteries of Glory—the reverend's shadowed stare, the warped face flickering across the projector screen, that whisper curling like smoke at the back of her skull—followed her into sleep like unwelcome passengers. And when she finally surrendered to the dark, the house fell so still it felt as if the night itself were waiting for her to dream.

Chapter 4:
Unraveling Old Glory

Megan found herself in darkness, complete emptiness, something unexplainable dragging her back into its shadowy depths. She could still feel the soft brush of the wind against her skin, the coolness of the earth beneath her bare feet. The realization hit her like a fist to the ribs. Not here. Not again. Her lungs seized. "No—no, please —" The plea tore out of her, ragged and small, swallowed instantly by the trees. The air was thick enough to drink— damp, sour with rot, heavy with the musk of leaves long dead. Cold moisture clung to her skin like a fever breaking. The forest pressed in, ancient and watchful. Trees hunched above her, their twisted branches coiling like fingers ready to snatch her off the ground. Moonlight filtered through in thin, trembling strands, collecting on the dirt in pale puddles that pulsed when she stepped too close to them.

Her heart hammered so hard it made her vision tremble.

A gown hung from her shoulders—white once, now tired and sickly, streaked with old stains that looked too dark to be mud. The fabric clung to her thighs as if it knew this place intimately. Her bare feet sank into the cold earth, mud slipping between her toes, grounding her and trapping her in the same breath.

She glanced down at her skin. The paleness frightened her—dingy, smeared with grime, as if she'd been scraped raw by the forest itself. She looked less like a girl and more like something pulled from the ground. A wrongness curled in her gut, twisting tight, but she couldn't look away.

Her fingers brushed the bark of a massive tree. Rough. Too warm. Like it had a heartbeat. The trunk seemed to pulse beneath her touch, and a low sigh rattled its leaves. The sound crawled up her arm and settled at the base of her skull.

Something stirred in the shadows beside her. Something quick. Something close.

She froze.

A flicker of movement—dark shapes slipping between trees, watching her with intent that didn't feel playful. The forest felt alive with eyes. Every shift of shadow looked like it had teeth.

Megan forced herself to move. Branches creaked overhead like bones bending under weight. Her breath fogged in the cold, but her skin burned with nerves.

Then—rustling. A hard crack.

She spun, pulse skittering—

—just in time to see deer leap through the underbrush, too fast, too silent. Their eyes glimmered like polished stone, bright and wrong. A heavy shape lumbered after them: a bear, its silhouette hulking and predatory, but it barely registered her presence.

The forest wasn't ignoring her.

It was circling her.

She walked because stopping felt like dying. Her legs trembled with every step. When she reached a thin creek, its water caught the moonlight and threw it back at her like shards of glass. She crouched, driven by instinct or desperation—she didn't know which—and dipped her fingers in.

The cold stabbed her skin. Her breath shuddered out.

She looked down, expecting her face.

It wasn't her face that stared back.

A woman's reflection drifted up from the black water—hair flowing like dark ink ribboned through moonlight, eyes pale and bright enough to glow. Her face was carved from something ancient and soft at the same time. Her stare met Megan's with unsettling ease.

Megan jerked back, but the reflection stayed.

Watching.

Knowing.

A thrill—sharp, electric—ran up her spine.

Who are you? Why do you feel like you belong to me?

Her pulse stuttered. The woman's lips curved into a small, knowing smile that didn't reach her eyes.

The forest shifted.

The shadows deepened, weight gathering like an unseen crowd forming around her. The air vibrated with whispers, frantic and layered, brushing the back of her neck like cold breath. Figures—thin, wavering silhouettes—emerged at the edges of her vision, flickering like dying flames. They circled her, quiet and hungry, pulling her inward as though her heartbeat was a drum only they could hear.

Megan rose on shaking legs. Water dripped from her fingertips, cold as blood. The woman in the stream smiled wider as the whispers thickened, their rhythm ancient, primal, and far too familiar—like a song she used to know before she ever learned words.

The forest tightened around her. Every shadow leaned closer.

Then—A crack split the air.

Not a branch breaking.

Not an animal.

Something enormous.

The ground shuddered under her feet, vibrating through her bones. Megan staggered, heart leaping into her throat. Another crash—deeper, closer—rolled through the earth like distant thunder trapped underground.

The figures around her vanished. Swallowed whole.

Drawn by a force she didn't understand, Megan pushed forward through the choking darkness. Each step felt wrong, as if she were walking into a mouth that wanted to close around her. The trees opened into a small clearing—unnaturally empty, unnaturally still.

A massive fallen log crushed a shape beneath it.

A man.

Huge. Red-haired. Bearded. Wild.

He writhed beneath the weight, muscles bulging, veins standing out like black cords. His eyes burned through the shadows—sharp, feral. The sight froze the blood in her veins.

She should have run. Every instinct screamed it. But her fear tangled with something else—an awful, magnetic pull that held her in place.

Her vision warped. The world went soft around the edges, like she was sinking underwater.

Then she wasn't in her body anymore.

She was watching from the dark.

Hidden. Detached. Too still.

The man roared and heaved the log aside as if it weighed nothing. It crashed into the underbrush, shaking loose a shower of leaves. He rose—massive, snarling, scanning the forest like a beast hunting its lost prey.

Their eyes met.

Panic detonated inside her.

Cold. Violent. Immediate.

His face twisted—skin stretching, bones shifting, features wrenching into something monstrous. A roar erupted from his throat, inhuman and deafening, rattling the air until her ears rang and the trees shuddered.

Fire burst from his body. Real fire—thick, red-orange, licking up his limbs like hell had cracked open beneath him. Smoke poured off him in choking waves. The smell of scorched earth filled her nose, stabbing sharp enough to make her gag. Heat hammered against her even from her hidden place. The forest glowed with his flames. The shadows trembled.

And Megan knew—without understanding how—that this thing wasn't just hunting something.

It was hunting her.

The terror didn't just hit her—it swallowed her whole. It was raw, primal, the kind of fear that comes from a place older than thought. Every instinct shrieked at her to run, to tear herself out of the nightmare taking form in front of her. But Megan's legs turned soft and useless, barely holding her upright. She staggered backward, breath hitching in quick, panicked bursts.

The forest floor split open.

Vines shot upward like starving serpents, bristling with hooked thorns. They coiled around her ankles first, cold and slick, then wound up her calves, her waist, her wrists— everywhere at once. With a violent jerk, they yanked her into the air. The thorns tore into her skin, sharp as broken glass. Pain flared bright and hot, each puncture followed by the slow warmth of blood seeping down her arms and legs. Crimson streaked across her pale skin, glistening in the dim light like fresh paint on a corpse.

Suspended above the ground, she dangled helplessly, trembling as the forest shadows deepened into something watching. Something hungry.

Below her, the creature—something hell had coughed up—lifted its head.

It snarled, lips peeling back to reveal teeth like polished knives. Too many teeth. Too long. Its expression twisted into a grin that had nothing human left in it, a smile promising ruin.

Smoke boiled from the creature's body, thick and heavy. It clung to the trees, swallowed their shapes, then curled around her legs in lazy, searching ribbons. The nightmare felt alive, as if it fed on the darkness itself. She could feel it creeping toward her—cold fingers sliding along her spine, a whisper urging her to just give in and let the black swallow her.

Her heart thrashed against her ribs. Shallow breaths rasped through her throat. She was no spirit, no warrior, no creature born to take on monsters in the dark. She was just a girl suspended like prey while something ancient and furious stood below her.

The creature's jaw stretched wider, impossibly wide, and from deep inside its throat rose a sound that didn't belong in any living thing. A shriek—raw rage and torment fused into one blast—ripped through the air. It rattled the trees. It rattled her bones. Leaves shivered off branches like they were trying to escape the noise.

Then it charged.

A wall of fire rolled off its body, flames licking dangerously close to her dangling form. Smoke swirled and twisted around its monstrous silhouette as it sprang upward, claws reaching, teeth snapping.

Megan screamed. A sound ripped from somewhere deep—fear, pain, pure instinct. Her vision warped at the edges, darkness pressing in. The world spun, the forest tilting sideways, then slipping completely out of reach.

Everything went black. Megan jerked awake. A ragged gasp tore from her chest. Her lungs dragged in air like she'd been drowning. Sweat slicked her skin. Her heart hammered so violently she had to clutch her shirt just to steady herself.

Her bedroom materialized around her in familiar shapes—the bookshelf, the cluttered desk, the heap of blankets at the foot of her bed. But the comfort didn't sink in. The nightmare clung to her like damp fog, thick and heavy, its shadows still pooling behind her eyes.

She rubbed at her face, palms shaky. The monstrous man. The vines. That scream. They hovered in her mind like they hadn't come from a dream at all.

She squeezed her eyes shut, willing the images to fade—but they stayed, as stubborn as stains.

Some mysteries… are better left alone. The thought came unbidden, sinking into her chest. She wasn't sure if it was hers or left over from the dream.

She stood, legs unsteady, and stepped out of her reading nook. The morning sun filtered lazily through her window, warm and golden. It brushed across her desk, catching the edges of scattered notebooks and half-read library books. The light was soft, innocent—completely at odds with the nightmare she'd crawled out of.

She wrapped herself tight in the fuzzy blanket slumped over her chair, letting the familiar fabric cocoon her. It smelled faintly of lavender and the detergent her mom used—comforting, human, safe. She let its warmth sink into her skin, breathing slowly until the tremor in her hands faded.

When she shifted, something glinted on the floor. Her pen— knocked down during the night. It lay among rumpled pages like a charm she'd dropped mid-spell. She picked it up, running her fingers over the smooth plastic barrel, grounding herself one small sensation at a time.

Enough. Today would be normal. Had to be.

Still wrapped in her blanket, Megan padded down the stairs. The familiar groan of each step answered her like a sleepy greeting. As she reached the bottom, a warm, savory smell drifted through the air—eggs, toasted bread, something buttery. It curled around her senses, easing the knot in her stomach.

Her mom was home.

Keys jingled as Lily dropped them onto the counter. She still wore her hospital scrubs, the bright blue fabric crinkled and tired around the edges. Lily looked like a force of nature—petite but strong, her black hair falling in waves over her shoulders, her honey-brown eyes full of warmth despite the exhaustion shadowing them. She carried the faint sterile scent of the hospital mixed with her soft berry perfume—comforting in a strange, familiar way.

"Hey, sweetie!" Lily called, her voice bright despite the fatigue kneaded into it. "How was your weekend?"

Megan shuffled into the kitchen, blanket trailing behind her like a sleepy ghost. "It was okay," she said, mustering a small smile. "Just normal stuff. Reading. Shows. Nothing exciting."

Lily's smile held a flicker of relief. "Sounds relaxing. I'm sorry I missed most of it. It's been chaos at the hospital." She sighed, brushing her hair back with a weary hand. "I wish I could be here more."

"It's fine, Mom." Megan shrugged, though something tender tugged at her chest. "Your job's important. I get it."

"I still don't like missing so much." Lily's voice softened. "I miss our time together."

She turned toward the counter, pulling out ingredients for a breakfast sandwich. "Let me make you something. You need fuel."

At that, Megan's stomach growled loudly enough to answer for her. "Yes, please," she said, a little shy, a little relieved.

As Lily sliced the bagel, leaned against the counter, and let the morning loosen her shoulders, she asked, "So how's school? Any big projects?"

Megan hesitated, the nightmare's residue tugged at her mind. "Nothing major. History project due next week, but it's manageable."

"Good," Lily said, brightening. "You always do well. I'm proud of you."

Megan smiled, small but real. "Thanks. How was your shift? Anyone… interesting?"

Lily chuckled, eyes sparkling with that mix of disbelief and amusement only ER nurses carried. "Oh, you have no idea. We had a homeless man insisting he'd been chased through the woods by a giant with an axe."

Megan's breath stalled for half a second.

But Lily just laughed, shaking her head. "Quite the imagination. Honestly, though? I'm wiped."

Megan forced a smile. "Yeah… sounds like it." But inside, cold fingers traced down her spine.

The woods.

A giant with an axe.

A nightmare wearing the shape of truth.

And the day had barely begun.

Megan nodded, the weight of her mother's job settling heavily in her chest. "I know this probably isn't the best time to bring it up, but… are we moving again? I know you go where they need you, but…" She hesitated, her voice thinning. "I kinda like it here."

Lily froze. Her smile faltered, slipping away like a candle guttering in a draft. She looked off to the side, worry tightening the corners of her eyes. "I'm sorry, sweetheart. I know it's been hard on you. You've made friends. You've settled in." A tired breath left her. "I wish it were different."

Something knotted inside Megan, pulling tight. "I just… I like this place," she said quietly. "Some people are annoying—" she let out a small laugh, "—but it feels like home."

"I understand." Lily's voice softened to a tender murmur. "We're needed here right now, and we'll stay as long as we can. But sometimes my job means packing up and going where the hospital sends me. I don't always get a say."

Megan bit down on her lip, trying to swallow the bitterness creeping up her throat. "I just wish we could stay somewhere longer. It's hard to start over all the time." Her expression warmed, almost shy. "And… I finally made a friend."

Lily's features softened further. "I've heard you've been spending time with a boy named Aiden?" she asked, tilting her head with gentle curiosity.

Megan nodded.

"He sounds like a good friend," Lily said. "And I know how much this place has meant to you. But remember—no matter where we end up, you get to carry those memories with you. Friends can visit. Technology exists. And you…" She squeezed Megan's hand. "You can make a home anywhere. You've always had that strength."

Megan mustered a small smile. "I know, Mom." She didn't want to worry her. Didn't want her to see the exhaustion behind her eyes. "You should get some sleep. You look wiped."

"I think you're right," Lily admitted, sliding the finished breakfast sandwich across the counter. "But eat first. You need food."

The warmth of the bagel seeped into Megan's palms, grounding her. "Thanks, Mom."

They sat at the tiny kitchen table, the hum of the fridge and the soft morning light filling the silence between their small talk. Weather. The week's schedule. Ideas for a rare shared day off. For a moment—just a moment—normalcy wrapped itself around her like a blanket.

Lily glanced at the clock and sighed. "Alright. I'd better rest. I'll be here when you get home, okay?"

"Okay, Mom." Megan's smile held a touch of lingering warmth. "Sleep well. And… thanks for breakfast."

"Anytime, sweetheart." Lily brushed a kiss against her forehead, then disappeared down the hall, her bedroom door clicking softly shut behind her.

When the house settled again, Megan exhaled deeply. The sandwich smelled comforting, familiar—warm cheese, toasted bread—but the emptiness curled inside her anyway, as if fear had hollowed out a space sleep couldn't fill.

Still, she forced herself to eat. She needed the energy. Needed the anchor of something ordinary.

When she was done, Megan rose and headed upstairs to get ready for school. Halfway up the stairs, the memory of her unsent email flickered through her mind. She paused at her desk, opened her laptop, and—without giving herself time to overthink—hit send.

"Well. Let's see what happens," she muttered, a tiny thrill of hope fluttering beneath her ribs.

Snow blanketed the ground in thick, white silence....

Megan and Aiden dug through every scrap of Glory's past they could get their hands on. Old newspapers, brittle as autumn leaves. Library archives that smelled like dust and forgotten secrets. Dead ends. More dead ends. And Mrs. Archer —silent.

Their determination faded into frustration, then teetered on the edge of resignation.

By the time winter break finally arrived, the world outside had transformed. Strings of lights wrapped around porch rails and shop windows like bright veins, glowing in the early evening gloom. The cold air tasted metallic, sharp against the tongue. The landscape sparkled—but for Megan, the season felt strangely hollow.

She hadn't dreamed—not once—since the night the creature charged at her, flames licking its monstrous skin. The vivid imagery had dulled, losing its razor edge, but unease still lurked beneath her ribs like a bruise refusing to fade.

Aiden's voice cut through her thoughts. "Can you believe the first half of school's already over?" He sipped his hot chocolate, steam fogging the air between them. "Feels like we just started."

They sat bundled in separate blankets on her porch, their mugs warm in their hands. The scent of cocoa mingled with pine and cold winter air—cozy, familiar, grounding.

"Right?" Megan said, smiling softly. "Feels like yesterday I was the lost new girl trying to navigate the hallways. But… I'm proud of us. We survived midterms, dodged the popular idiots, and somehow didn't flunk anything."

Aiden let out a loud laugh. "Especially dodging Lexi and Thomas. Those two are like energy vampires. They live to annoy people."

"Seriously. But…" Megan's tone shifted, thoughtful. "I think we've grown this semester. Even if we didn't make a ton of new friends." She wrapped her blanket tighter around her shoulders. "I feel like I belong here now. And even though we haven't found much about the town…" She sighed, watching the snowflakes tumble through the gray air. "It feels like we're stuck. Maybe my imagination filled in the blanks."

Aiden shrugged, though his expression darkened with sincerity. "Maybe. Or maybe we just haven't found the right source yet. I'm surprised Mrs. Archer still hasn't replied."

"Me too." Megan frowned. "It's like we're chasing smoke. I keep wondering if there's even a connection between my dreams and Glory. Or if I'm just—God, I don't know—losing my mind." She chuckled weakly. "Those dreams were so real."

"Maybe," Aiden said. "But the mystery's still interesting. Even if we're going in circles."

Megan took a long sip of her cocoa, letting its warmth spread down her chest. "I guess you're right. And now that we're on break... we can relax. No research. No stress. Just..." She looked out at the snow-coated street. "Just breathing for a while."

But a shadow lingered behind the comfort—soft, quiet, and waiting.

"Exactly! We can actually enjoy the festivities without stressing over anything else," Aiden said, eyes bright with winter excitement. "Let's go ice skating at the park tomorrow. Come on—it'll be fun. We can forget about everything for a while."

"Ice skating?" Megan raised her brows, torn between nerves and budding excitement. "I don't know, Aiden!" The words came out as half-protest, half-laugh. The idea of stepping onto the ice made her stomach flutter—but in a good way. "But afterward, we are definitely getting that frozen hot chocolate. The one with the scoop of ice cream? It sounds ridiculous and magical at the same time."

Aiden grinned. "Exactly."

Snow drifted lazily around them, each flake catching the soft glow of the porch lights. Despite the unanswered questions about Glory's past—and the unsettling dreams that had once plagued her—Megan felt a warm, steady contentment settle over her. Friendship had a way of muting the shadows.

After nearly an hour of laughter, cocoa, and teasing each other about who would fall on the ice first, Megan watched Aiden head down the walkway toward his house. His footsteps left short, crisp impressions in the powder as he waved goodbye. The porch felt quieter without him, but the lingering warmth of the moment held her like a soft hand at her back.

Wrapped in her fluffy blanket, she stepped inside. The house greeted her with gentle warmth, and she made her way to her reading nook—a space tucked beneath her bedroom window. The blanket brushed her skin like the softest whisper. She curled into her corner, the lamp beside her casting a low amber glow across the shelves, the walls, the edges of her world. Familiar. Safe.

She opened her journal, its pages worn soft with use. Breathing steadily, she wrote:

Dear Journal,

Christmas is almost here! The lights around town are beautiful, and everything feels… different. Magical, I guess. I'm excited for the holidays with Mom. I really hope this year is even better than the last.

She closed the journal gently, placing it back on the shelf. A warm tide of peace washed over her as she crawled under her covers. The sheets were cool, the pillows soft, and the winter night hummed quietly beyond her window. No nightmares had touched her for weeks. Maybe—finally—she could rest.

She drifted into sleep with a faint smile.

Morning sunlight streamed across her bedspread, nudging her awake. Megan stretched, the good kind of soreness in her limbs, the kind that promised she'd slept deeply. As she blinked herself into consciousness, her phone lit up with a vibration on the nightstand.

A new email. The sender's name made her heart jolt.

Mrs. Archer.

She tapped it open, pulse quickening.

Dear Megan,

Thank you for reaching out—and I'm glad you enjoyed the lecture. Apologies for the late reply. I'd like to offer a last-minute meeting before I leave town for the holidays. I'll be grading midterms at the university for the next few days if you're available. My office number is below. Happy Holidays!

Megan bolted upright. This was it—the opening she'd been waiting for.

She texted Aiden immediately.

Guess what! I just got an email from Mrs. Archer! She wants to meet before the holidays!

Her phone buzzed almost instantly.

That's awesome, Meg! But my mom sprung this on me last night and won't let me go anywhere—family is in town. I wish I could be there.

I get it, she sent back, though disappointment tugged at her. *Family first. I'll update you after.*

She glanced at the time. Early afternoon. Before she could talk herself out of it, she dialed Mrs. Archer's number. Her heart fluttered like trapped wings. The phone rang twice.

"Hello, this is Mrs. Archer!"

"Hi, it's Megan," she said, keeping her voice steady. "I got your email and… I was hoping we could meet today."

There was a rustling of papers on the other end. "Certainly! I have an opening at three. Does that work?"

"Yes," Megan said, relief loosening something in her chest. "Thank you."

They exchanged details, and once the call ended, the reality hit her: today was the day.

She spent most of the early afternoon collecting her notes together and contemplating how she would present everything to Mrs. Archer. After she created a plan of action, which helped settle her nerves, she grabbed her backpack, and headed to the bus stop.

The bus rattled along icy roads, tires humming a low, steady vibration beneath her feet. Outside, snowbanks glistened under the weak winter sun, fields and houses blanketed in white. Wind whipped around the bus, producing a hollow, ghostlike moan that made the hair on Megan's arms lift. Anticipation and unease twisted together inside her. Would Mrs. Archer take her seriously? Or dismiss it all as teenage imagination?

The campus rose from the snowy haze like an aged sentinel, stone buildings towering and frosted at their edges. Megan stepped off the bus, her breath fogging in front of her. The cold pinched her cheeks, sharp and invigorating. The scent of coffee drifted from the student café, mingling with the metallic tang of winter air.

Following the map on her phone, she crossed the quiet campus until she reached a building with ivy-scarred brick walls. The vines were bare and brittle now, rattling faintly in the breeze.

She pushed open the heavy door.

The smell of old paper, cooled stone, and faint bergamot tea greeted her. Mrs. Archer's office was small but packed with towering bookshelves, old maps, yellowing documents, and artifacts that seemed to whisper history from their dust-soft surfaces.

Mrs. Archer looked up from behind her desk. Short dark-blonde hair framed her sharp but kind features, and curiosity gleamed in her eyes.

"There you are—Megan, right?" she said, smiling with warm sarcasm. "I'm glad you made it."

She leaned forward, elbows on her desk. "So. Tell me about your project."

Megan inhaled, gathering her notes with trembling fingers. "I… ran into a bit of a wall," she admitted. "Most of what I found was just routine town history—growth, development, local politics. Nothing meaningful."

She hesitated… then pulled out the articles she'd brought. "Except this."

She handed them over. "These reports mention women accused of witchcraft in Glory. They were exiled into the woods as punishment. But nothing goes back earlier than the mid-1700s. It all just… stops there. Like everything before it was erased."

The words hung in the air like frost, delicate and chilling all at once.

As Megan explained her findings, a cold ripple crept through her veins. Those women—banished, feared, punished—felt suddenly too close, like their shadows still clung to the bones of the town. She glanced at Mrs. Archer, hoping the historian might feel the same heaviness, the same wrongness whispering beneath the town's neatly polished surface.

Mrs. Archer arched a brow, a sly grin tugging at one corner of her mouth. "Exiled? Is that the story they went with?" Her tone dripped with dry amusement. "Those charming little folktales—and they always leave out the best parts. The truth is far more theatrical. Cities around here weren't exactly subtle in their approach. Glory included." She leaned back, eyes glinting with something dark and knowing. "Most of those 'witches' weren't just chased into the woods. They were strung up in trees. Drowned in creeks. And those the church found especially troublesome?" She gave a mirthless chuckle. "Purified by fire."

Megan's stomach tightened, a sick twist that made her throat feel too small. She'd hoped the rumors were exaggerations. They weren't.

Mrs. Archer's voice rolled on—light, almost playful, but tinged with something razor-edged. "Speaking of Glory—Old Glory, technically—did you know that in the early 1700s, a fire wiped the place clean? Torched it to the dirt. By the time they rebuilt, decades later, they gave it a shiny new name. Glory. Isn't that delightful? Like slapping gold paint over charred wood and calling it a blessing."

A slow chill seeped through the office, settling into the corners like fog. Megan could almost hear the crackle of that old fire, and feel the smoke thickening the air around them.

Without a word, Mrs. Archer reached into her desk drawer and pulled out several thick, battered books—spines cracked, pages yellowed at the edges—as well as a disk filled with digitized articles. She placed them in Megan's hands. "After that fire it doesn't surprise me you couldn't find anything, but these should keep you busy. And don't forget the archive in the library basement. It's practically a graveyard for forgotten stories. If you can get in, that is. But something tells me you'll manage." She gave a small, knowing nod.

Megan held the stack carefully, the weight of the books mirroring the weight settling across her shoulders. Excitement flickered inside her, cut with fear and sharpened by curiosity. She felt like she was standing at the mouth of a cave, its darkness beyond whispering secrets.

"Remember," Mrs. Archer said, returning to her shelf with a smirk, "history twists itself. Your job is to straighten it out—if you're brave enough to look."

She paused, glancing back. Her expression shifted, shadows passing through her tone. "And a warning—whoever crafted that little 'exiled into the woods' bedtime story must've had a reason. Truth tends to fight back when you dig too close to it."

A hush settled between them. Megan swallowed, nodding slowly. The mystery around Mrs. Archer seemed to thicken like smoke, leaving her with a final reminder that the past wasn't just old—it was buried. And things buried weren't always meant to be disturbed. But Megan's resolve only burned brighter.

She stepped out of the office, the door groaning shut behind her. The corridor's icy air slapped against her skin, stealing away the last of the warmth from inside. Mrs. Archer's words echoed in her mind, relentless. *Come back when you're done. We'll talk more.* The invitation lingered like a candle guttering in a draft.

On the bus ride home, time stretched thin and slow. Megan stared out the window as snow blurred past, a white smear against the gray sky. Her reflection stared back—wide-eyed, thoughtful, haunted—as visions from Mrs. Archer's revelations unfurled in her mind. Women shoved beneath freezing water, their screams bubbled away into silence. Bodies swinging from tree limbs, limp and swaying like grotesque ornaments. Flames climbing over skin, over bone, until nothing was left but ash and echoes.

The cruelty of it pressed into her chest like a fist. *How could people have done that? How could entire towns have watched and let it happen?*

The questions hollowed her.

Stepping into her house felt like entering another world entirely—warm, soft, and quiet. But the numbness clung to her like frost. She texted Aiden, hoping for comfort, conversation, anything to ease the heaviness. No answer. Probably family distractions, but still, she wished he was there.

After a short shower, steam washing some of the chill from her bones, she curled into her nook. Pillows hugged her sides, blankets draped over her like a cocoon. She opened her journal. The pages looked almost too clean, too innocent for what she needed to spill onto them.

She wrote everything—every disturbing detail, every image clawing at her mind, every emotion that refused to settle. Her handwriting wavered at times, the words blurring as she tried to process the brutality of it all. Hangings. Drownings. Burning. All done in the name of purity, fear, control.

A sadness—not quiet, but crushing—settled over her. It was hard to imagine those women as anything other than shadows now, but their agony felt vivid and real, pulsing through the lines of her journal.

When the last sentence curled across the page, exhaustion swept over her. She closed the journal gently, almost reverently, and slipped beneath her blankets.

Night crept into the room, heavy and still. Megan let her eyes close, her thoughts drifting like ash on the wind—dark, slow, inevitable—until sleep finally gathered her and drew her under.

Chapter 5:
Whispers of the Vanishing

Old Glory rose before her in a crooked sprawl of buildings and dirt lanes, its silhouette warped against the low, colorless sky. The town felt wrong in the way a body feels wrong just before it collapses—upright, breathing, pretending. Narrow houses leaned inward as if conspiring, their clapboard siding split and weather-gnawed, windows black and watchful. Smoke clung low to the air, sour and stale, carrying the mingled stink of damp wood, animal waste, and something coppery that tightened Megan's throat. The street lay silent, not abandoned but restrained, as though sound itself had learned better than to linger here.

She stood at the edge of the main thoroughfare, boots planted in rutted earth hardened by countless wagon wheels and forgotten footsteps. The ground should have been firm.

Instead, it yielded slightly beneath her weight, as if the town itself resented being touched. A pressure settled behind her ribs, slow and insistent, making each breath feel borrowed. Somewhere deeper within Old Glory, something shifted—wood creaked, a shutter tapped once, then stopped—small noises swallowed immediately, like secrets smothered before they could escape.

The buildings seemed to crowd closer as she moved forward, their roofs sagging, their porches bowing under invisible strain. Iron signs hung from rusted brackets, swinging without wind, groaning softly like tired throats clearing themselves. Doorways yawned open, dark and expectant, their thresholds worn smooth by generations of hands and feet that had passed through and never fully returned. The town watched her with the patience of something that knew it had time.

Her next step sank into a strip of churned earth slick with old rain and rot. Mud swallowed the heel of her boot with a thick, obscene sound, tugging as if reluctant to let go. The air grew heavier, pressing damply against her skin, clogging her lungs. Her pulse hammered, sharp and uneven, each beat echoing too loudly in the hollow street. Then—without warning —the world lurched.

Light fractured the air, sudden and brutal, tearing through the gray like a blade.

And the town vanished.

The force of it slammed into her skull and dragged her under, hurling her headlong into a vision that reeked of smoke, fear, and unfinished sins.

A woman screamed, a sound so sharp it pierced the woods like a blade. Megan saw her being dragged toward a towering tree, wrists bound by a coarse rope that chewed into her skin, leaving angry welts. She fought, legs kicking, but the rope only tightened. A crowd swarmed around her, faceless in the low light, their silhouettes flickering like they were lit by some unseen fire.

"Purify the witch!" someone roared.

A man stepped forward—the reverend—robes hanging from him like a funeral shroud. His face was mostly shadow, but his eyes burned bright, feverish.

"Rid our world of this demon!" His voice rose with a kind of sacred fury, the kind that could make sane people dangerous.

Megan's heart hammered so hard it felt like it would bruise her ribs. The flash snapped again—another scene, worse, colder.

Someone forced a woman into a churning stream. Her cries ricocheted off the banks as she clawed at the muddy edges. Water surged over her face. She kicked wildly, trying to keep her head above the surface.

"Drown her!" a voice hissed from the dark. "Let the waters cleanse us!"

Megan clutched her skull with both hands, nails digging into her scalp. *How could people do this? How could a whole town be so convinced of their righteousness they'd trade their humanity for it?*

With each vision, the dread clawing at her grew sharper, more insistent. The forest seemed to pulse with it. It felt alive— feeding on the terror of the dying.

Then another jolt of light—someone tied to a stake, screaming as flames licked up her legs. The fire painted the onlookers' faces in demonic reds and oranges. They stared, transfixed. Some even smiled.

"Burn the witch!" they roared, voices uniting into a monstrous chorus. "Free us from her curse!"

The smell hit Megan next—burning flesh, hair, cloth. It filled her nostrils, coated her tongue, settled heavy in the pit of her stomach.

"This isn't real," she whispered. But her voice trembled. She didn't sound convinced. "It can't be."

But the visions didn't stop.

Figures appeared at the edges of each scene—shadows with hollow eyes, their faces blurred but watching. They leaned just close enough for her to feel their breath on her neck.

"You shouldn't be here!" they whispered.

Her heart kicked. "I'm… I'm trying to understand." The words scraped out of her, barely audible. "I didn't know it was this terrible."

Her resolve buckled. Every new flash chipped away another piece of her certainty. The reverend stood in each scene, a dark anchor, his sermons twisting the crowd into a frenzy. *They think they're saving themselves*, she realized, ice trickling down her spine. *They think they're doing good. But all they were doing was feeding the darkness—giving it a shape, a purpose, a reason to grow.*

The women's screams bled together into a single, horrid hymn. With every death, something stirred in the forest. Shadows peeled off the suffering, forming warped specters. They sprinted between the trees, bodies contorted, eyes blazing with a fury that felt older than the woods themselves. Their innocence had been burned away, crushed under the boot of fear.

The forest quaked beneath them, leaves trembling as if the entire place recoiled. Trees whispered of the wrongs committed here. Nature itself held its breath.

Then came the reverend again, his voice booming over the carnage: "Look upon your sins! Let the flames purify you!"

His followers dropped to their knees, praying to a sky that had long since stopped listening.

The ground trembled under Megan as if rejecting the memory. The women's cries echoed inside her skull, a desperate chorus begging for acknowledgment. Her throat tightened.

"STOP!" she tried to shout, but the word scraped out weakly. "No more... please." Tears streaked down her cheeks.

One final flash—the brightest yet—a woman swallowed by fire, her mouth open in a soundless scream. Then the darkness lunged, devouring her soul, ripping her into shadow like she was nothing but smoke.

Megan collapsed to her knees. Useless. That was the word that echoed through her—raw, bitter.

And then, as suddenly as they'd begun, the visions snapped away.

The forest's oppressive weight eased, though not fully—never fully. Megan knelt at the border of the trees, her breath shuddering, the cold clinging to her like a second skin. Shadows slithered back into the treeline, but their shapes lingered just long enough to let her know they were watching.

She rose on shaky legs, turning back toward the woods. Dark figures hovered there, eyes glinting, carved from the same nightmares she'd just witnessed.

The forest would always remember what happened here. And now, so would she.

A hollow emptiness swallowed her, deep and aching, echoing with the screams of the vanished. Megan lay curled deep in her blankets, a makeshift cocoon against the winter chill that seeped through the thin windowpane. Outside, snow drifted down in heavy, muffled sheets, soft enough to seem peaceful—almost holy—yet the calm felt miles away from the storm twisting in her chest. As she shifted, the stiffness in her muscles announced itself, the aftermath of a night spent tensed against dreams that didn't feel like dreams at all.

Her eyes cracked open. The skin beneath them throbbed faintly, tight with dried tears. She swiped a hand across her cheek and felt the gritty residue her crying had left behind. The weight of last night's visions—every scream, every flame, every desperate face—pressed down on her like someone sitting on her sternum.

She pulled the fuzzy blanket closer, burying her chin in its softness. It helped a little. Not much.

Why does it hurt this much? The thought trembled across her mind like a whisper she didn't want to hear herself say aloud. *Why do these nightmares keep coming back? I thought I was done with them.*

She inhaled slowly, then exhaled through her nose, hoping to settle the dread clawing at her gut.

After a long moment, she reached for her phone. Her fingers wouldn't stop trembling. *Hey, just checking in. I had my meeting with Mrs. Archer yesterday. I need to talk to you about it.*

She hovered over the send button, chest tight with a strange mix of hope and dread. Aiden had always been the one who could talk her down from the ledge, but recently… he'd felt far away, like someone fading behind a fogged window.

The message finally sent.

Minutes crawled by—heavy, sluggish, torturous. She started to convince herself he wouldn't reply when her phone vibrated against the comforter.

Sorry, just woke up! How did it go?

Relief flushed through her so quickly she almost felt lightheaded. *It was overwhelming. Mrs. Archer shared dark history about Glory—hangings, drownings, women burned alive. It's… a lot.*

She paused before continuing, *There's a hidden archive in the library's basement. It might have more.*

Aiden responded almost instantly. *Wow… that's heavy. But I'm pretty sure the library doesn't open back up until after the holidays. So we'll have to wait.*

Frustration flickered across her chest, then simmered down into reluctant acceptance. *I didn't even think about that. I just… I feel like I have to know the truth. It's like the voices of those missing women are calling for someone to pay attention.*

Another buzz. *As soon as my cousins head home, we'll pick this up. My mom's just being impossible.*

A small, tired smile tugged at her lips. It wasn't much, but it was something. The heaviness in her chest loosened a fraction.

"Thanks, Aiden," she murmured into the empty room, pulling the blanket tighter around her shoulders. Outside, snow kept falling—quiet, relentless, like the world was trying to cover something it couldn't quite bury.

Winter break faded into a blur…

The holidays had finally passed, leaving only the quiet press of snow and the soft isolation of her house. Megan spent most of the days alone, poring over the materials Mrs. Archer had given her. Her mother worked double shifts at the hospital, slipping in and out of the house like a ghost. Megan barely saw her except for a coffee mug left in the sink or a coat draped over a chair.

The pages spread across her bedroom floor became her company—stories of Old Glory's hidden sins, the long-buried cruelties no one wanted to mention. The more she read, the more real everything in her dreams began to feel. Too real.

When school resumed, she felt something spark inside her—a strange, renewed sense of purpose. Noise filled the hallways again. Backpacks slammed shut. Kids laughed too loudly. And between all that, she met Aiden for quick conversations that always tilted toward the same subject.

"Did you go through the stuff I sent you?" Megan asked one afternoon as they navigated the chaotic hallway.

Aiden nodded, expression dark. "Yeah. It's… worse than I expected. Those drownings, the hangings—God, Meg, it's like the women are still begging for someone to see them."

A shiver slid through her ribs. "Exactly. That's why we have to get into the basement. There might be something down there. Records. Proof."

By Friday afternoon, they cornered themselves in a quiet spot in the cafeteria with a notebook between them.

"So, what's the plan?" Aiden asked, uncapping his pen.

Megan leaned in. "We need to know where the basement entrance is. How many rooms are down there? And whether it's locked. If it is, we can't draw attention. We only get one shot."

Aiden scribbled fast. "Weekend might be best. Or right after school. Less foot traffic."

"Right. And if it's locked," Megan said, lowering her voice, "you distract the librarian. I'll try to find a key."

He gave a short nod. "And we take pictures of everything. No lingering."

"Good." A faint thrill ran through her, brushing against her fear. "Today is Friday, we will go after school. Nobody's going to be in the library—they'll be rushing to escape for the weekend."

Every class crawled by in slow motion, like someone had hit pause periodically throughout the day. Megan's mind kept leaping ahead to the library's basement—the hidden archive, the truth buried in dust and darkness. What if they got caught? What if something was down there waiting for them? Something that had been waiting a long time.

When the final bell rang, she practically shot out of her chair.

She and Aiden walked in tense silence across the courtyard, their breath puffing out in small white clouds. Her heartbeat thudded hard, too loud in her ears. By the time the heavy library doors came into view, her palms were damp.

Inside, rows of towering shelves cast long shadows under the dim afternoon lights. The familiar scent hit her—old paper, floor polish, dust that tasted like secrets. At the back, a thick red rope blocked off a narrow set of stairs. A sign dangled from it: AUTHORIZED PERSONNEL ONLY.

Behind it, half-hidden at the bottom of the steps, she saw it: a metal door, old and dull, as though it had been waiting a century for someone to touch it.

Megan cast Aiden a quick look. His jaw was tight; his eyes were on the room around them.

"Keep watch," she whispered.

He nodded once, tense.

She ducked beneath the rope. Every creak of the wooden steps sounded like it echoed across the entire library. Her heartbeat filled her ears. She reached the door, her fingers trembling as she grasped the handle.

The cold metal bit into her skin.

She turned it slowly.

The soft click of the mechanism sounded unnaturally loud—like the building itself had just woken up.

"Great. The door's locked. Just our luck."

Megan sagged, shoulders collapsing inward as she drifted back to Aiden's side.

"Don't worry," Aiden murmured, a stubborn spark lighting behind his eyes. "I'll handle this."

He scanned the room until his gaze snagged on the librarian—a thin, brittle woman with her gray hair ratcheted into a bun so tight it could've snapped. Reading glasses dangled halfway down her nose, giving her the look of someone who spent nights knitting sweaters for ten cats while muttering to herself about overdue fees. Megan wasn't sure whether to be amused or alarmed.

"Alright—just keep her busy," Megan whispered, nerves and excitement blending into one jittery hum in her bloodstream.

Aiden nodded once, then strolled toward the librarian, launching into an enthusiastic monologue about new arrivals. Megan hovered behind a row of shelves, listening to his voice rise and fall—harmless, cheerful, the sort of tone that put people at ease. It was almost ridiculous how good he was at this.

She peeked over her shoulder. Perfect. Aiden had pulled the librarian far from her desk, the woman leaning toward him, hanging on his every word.

Megan slipped forward.

Her hand darted behind the desk, fingers brushing cold metal before closing around the ring of keys. Her pulse jumped. By the time she reached the locked basement door, her hands were shaking so badly she nearly dropped them. After fumbling through several wrong ones, the correct key slid home with a quiet, blessed click.

The door groaned open.

A wave of cooler, mustier air curled up the stairwell and brushed against her face—old, heavy, almost wet. Megan stepped inside. The single bulb hanging from the ceiling buzzed weakly, throwing jittery light over the basement. It didn't feel like a library. It felt like a place where evidence went to die.

Caged storage units lined the walls like jail cells. Boxes piled on boxes. Forgotten junk. Dust thick enough to taste. History clung to the place like a smell.

Her palms dampened as she moved deeper.

She dug into the boxes—town records, meeting minutes and brittle papers scarred by age. Inked notes crawled across the pages, chronicling the early days of Old Glory. Parish declarations. Property damage claims. Incorporation documents with faded signatures that looked more like ghosts than names.

Land deeds bearing the surnames of families she'd seen etched on headstones.

Then she found the labeled boxes—years scrawled on the sides in permanent marker.

One box snagged her attention like a hook: *Transcripts / Testimonies.*

The smell of old paper puffed out as she lifted the lid. Letters, dozens of them, written by trembling hands. Accounts of strange lights, strange figures, strange noises in the woods. The ink smeared in places, as if the writers' hands had been shaking.

She skimmed lines—panic-soaked statements about things stalking the edges of the town, things no one wanted to admit they'd seen. She shoved them into her bag before she could overthink it. Then—unlabeled boxes. Her breath hitched.

Inside were drawings—rough, black-ink sketches of buildings swallowed in flames. People fleeing. Shadows bending in unnatural shapes amid the firelight. The lines were so frantic they almost vibrated. She tossed pamphlets, articles, any scrap that felt important into her bag. Her fingers were numb with adrenaline by the time she returned the boxes.

She was about to leave when she saw it: a box hidden behind a stack, its edges wrapped in layers of old tape.

Something in her gut twisted.

She pulled it forward, peeled back the lid, and stopped breathing.

Binders.

Each was packed with missing-persons posters. Faces stared up at her—faces from decades apart, frozen in fear, or hope, or confusion. Some children. Some adults. Smiles that felt wrong in the sterile fluorescent light. The weight of them hit her chest like a stone. She flipped through page after page, snapping pictures as fast as her phone could manage. Names. Ages. Last known whereabouts. Lives that had simply evaporated.

One loose photograph slid free from the binder. Megan picked it up, her breath hitching as the image sharpened. The reverend stared back at her—same narrow jaw, same hollow eyes—but the clothes were wrong, the grain too old. He stood beside a cluster of stern-faced townsfolk she didn't recognize. It was Reverend Goodwin but... not him. An echo. A bloodline. An ancestor wearing his face like a hand-me-down mask.

She flipped the picture, fingers trembling, and read the faded ink bleeding across the back: *Reverend Marcus Goodwin and beloved congregants — 1904.* Her stomach dropped. Grandfather, maybe. Or something worse.

When she turned it over again, the reverend's figure had vanished.

The air left her lungs in a sharp gasp. The photo slipped from her hand and drifted to the floor in a lazy, soundless fall. Megan didn't move. Couldn't. A prickling sensation crawled up her arms as the room tightened around her.

That's when she heard it—a brittle crackling seeping from the farthest, darkest corner of the room, as if something old had just woken up.

She froze.

The sound shifted—crackle to scratch. A deliberate, crawling scratch. Megan angled the hanging bulb toward the noise, nudging it with shaking fingers. The light swayed, jerking shadows across the walls.

Then it landed on him.

The reverend clung to the ceiling like an oversized insect, his limbs splayed at impossible angles. Elbows and knees bent the wrong way, jutting out like broken branches jammed back into a dying tree. His spine arched in a sick curve, vertebrae clicking one by one as he shifted his weight.

And his face—it wasn't a face anymore. The flesh had folded inward and split outward, reshaping itself into something swollen and arachnid. Eight glossy eyes bulged from the warped skull, each reflecting the swinging light like tiny wet marbles. Below them, rows of needle-thin teeth pulled apart into a ragged, quivering grin that stretched too wide, as if eager to split further.

Megan's breath snapped shut in her throat.

The bulb slipped from her trembling fingers, swinging wildly on its frayed cord. The room fractured—light, dark, light, dark—each flicker revealing warped glimpses of the creature above her.

On the next flash, it was gone.

Silence lasted only a heartbeat.

Then—tap-tap-tap-tap-tap

A frantic skittering, fast and sharp, scraped across the ceiling. The sound jittered down her spine like a broken zipper. Something heavy shifted above her, its weight cracking the old plaster. Dust sifted into her hair.

She fumbled for her phone, fingers numb, breath stabbing in and out. When her thumb finally struck the flashlight, the beam exploded across the ceiling—just in time to see it sprint toward her, racing upside down with horrifying speed, its joints pistoning sideways, its mouth unhinged in a wet, bone-deep howl that vibrated through her ribs.

It dropped suddenly, dipping into the beam—its limbs slamming into a stack of old boxes, sending them scattering in a violent avalanche. Cardboard burst open, contents spilling like guts across the floor. The creature twisted through the wreckage, skittering in frantic darts, its legs punching tiny cracks into the cement with every frantic step as it tried to reach her.

Megan staggered back, heart clawing at her throat. One of its legs struck the ground, narrowly missing her—fear jerked through her muscles; her foot shot out and connected with its slick flesh. The creature flipped to the floor with a sickening, wet thud. It writhed on its back like a spider that had lost control of its body, legs flailing, abdomen pulsing as if swollen with something alive inside. It righted itself in a sudden, jerking snap of motion.

Those eight eyes locked onto her.

It jumped towards her—Megan squeezed her eyes shut, bracing for bone, for teeth, for fire tearing into her skin.

NO.

The voice came from inside her.

Not hers.

Not human.

And the creature exploded. A violent burst of black smoke tore outward, swallowing her whole. The world vanished in a choking cloud. The smell hit first—rot and burnt hair and something sickly sweet, like fruit left to liquefy in the sun. Her eyes stung instantly, tears burning hot trails down her cheeks.

The smoke curled around her, thick and alive, pressing against her mouth, her ears, her skull—and then it peeled away, thinning into tattered ribbons before dissolving completely.

Megan stood alone in the silence.

But her heart knew: the thing wasn't gone. Megan gasped, stumbling backward. Her knees nearly buckled. "Come on," she whispered to herself, shoving everything she could grab into her bag. "Come on—go, go, go—" Fear took her by the scruff of the neck and hurled her up the stairs.

The bright library lights hit her like a slap. She blinked until the shelves sharpened into view again. Aiden and the librarian were still tucked in the corner, deep in conversation— completely oblivious.

Her pulse hammered so loud she wondered if the whole room could hear it. She forced herself toward the exit, dropping the keys on the service desk with a sharp metallic clatter. Her bag dragged at her side.

With every hurried step, Megan felt the weight of her bag thudding against her back—heavy, overstuffed, alive with the secrets she'd stolen. The thrill of it spiked through her veins, a cocktail of adrenaline and budding terror. For a moment she glanced over her shoulder, expecting the librarian to burst through the doors, shrieking about stolen keys and restricted archives. But the library remained behind her, still and silent, a keeper of secrets she'd just ripped from its ribcage.

She rounded the corner and yanked out her phone, thumbs flying. *Meet at my house!* She hit send so fast she barely registered the words.

The familiar streets of her neighborhood wavered strangely —like she'd stepped into a dream wearing her own skin wrong. Snow-loaded trees leaned over the road like pale sentinels, their branches sagging under winter's weight as the sky smoldered a dull, storm-gray above them.

Getting home became everything. A single need. A tunnel vision pulse in her skull.

Her bag tugged at her shoulders like hands—cold, insistent, reminding her of what she carried: the missing-persons posters, testimonies scribbled in panic, brittle documents whispering the old bones of Old Glory. Every passing car made her flinch; a distant horn made her heart leap into her throat. The excitement roared up again—raw, electric—chasing off the fear for a heartbeat before it surged back twice as sharp.

By the time she reached her porch, her hands were trembling so badly she nearly dropped her keys. She shoved her way inside, slamming the door behind her as warmth curled around her body like a blanket she didn't feel she deserved.

"What the hell was that…" The words spilled from her in a thin, shaky whisper. She slid down the wall, bag clutched to her chest like a lifeline. Images of the spider-thing—the reverend's warped, impossible face—flashed behind her eyelids. Eight glossy eyes. Teeth like tiny razors. The way it moved, skittering, wrong. The scream that felt like it tore through her instead of the air.

Had she really seen it? Or had the darkness and her own imagination twisted together into something monstrous? She didn't let herself think too long.

She bolted upstairs.

Once inside her room, she dumped the contents of her bag onto the carpet in a papery explosion. Pages fluttered and drifted, landing like dead leaves across the floor.

She got to work, her hands steadied as she sorted—methodical, focused. Legal documents in one pile. Community pamphlets in another. Witness reports, parish declarations—each stack growing, the narrative of the town slowly knitting itself together in front of her. A strange reverence settled over her. She wasn't just a student anymore. She was a custodian of the buried, piecing together a truth that someone—or something—had gone to great lengths to hide.

By the time she finished, her room had transformed into a chaotic museum exhibit. Yellowed pages, curled pamphlets, brittle ink. Every surface drowned in Old Glory's shattered history. The air tasted like dust and cold paper, tinged with the faint winter draft slipping beneath her window.

Her phone buzzed. *Almost there. 5 minutes.*

She exhaled—half relief, half dread.

The knock came sooner than expected, slicing through the house's tense quiet. Megan's stomach lurched, memories of the basement creeping up her spine in cold fingers. She forced herself to the door.

Aiden stood there, breathless, snow clinging to his hoodie. His expression shifted from concern to alarm when he saw her face.

"Megan—Jesus. Are you okay?"

She swallowed hard. "Before we start… I know how this is going to sound." Her voice quivered. "But something was in the basement."

Aiden stepped inside, closing the door behind him like he expected the night itself to follow them. "What do you mean?"

Megan's pulse hammered as she searched for words. "I heard scratching. Then… I saw it. The reverend—but not him. Not really. It was like a spider wearing his skin. Eight eyes. Teeth. Hanging there in the corner." A shiver rattled through her. "It jumped at me. And then…" She stopped remembering a singular word inside her head. NO, it wasn't her; it was a woman, a voice she didn't recognize. "Umm, it exploded into smoke."

Aiden blinked at her. "Are you serious? The reverend was a spider creature?" His voice cracked between disbelief and dread. "What the hell, Meg!"

"I know how insane it sounds," she whispered. "But it felt real. I heard it after it disappeared. Scurrying. Watching. I thought I was losing it."

"What if it's still down there?" he muttered, voice barely a breath.

"I didn't look." She hugged her arms around herself. "But I don't think it was random. I think it was trying to scare us off."

Aiden moved closer, fear tightening his features. "This is way bigger than old records. Something doesn't want us finding whatever it's hiding."

He followed her upstairs, but froze in the doorway of her room. "Oh my god, Meg… it looks like a tornado had a panic attack in here."

Despite everything, she snorted. "It's organized chaos. Legal documents here, pamphlets there, witness reports over there." She pointed at each island of paper.

He crouched beside a pile, sifting carefully. Megan turned to her desk, printing every photo she'd snapped. One by one, they slid out—faces, dates, places where children and adults vanished without goodbyes.

She made a new pile.

Missing Persons.

"Think these can help us figure out what happened to them?" Aiden asked quietly, running a thumb over a faded deed.

"Absolutely." Megan didn't hesitate. "Every detail matters. If we can connect anything—names, dates, locations—maybe we'll understand what Glory's been hiding."

She added the printed photos to the growing mound. A sea of faces—mostly teens—stared up at them in silent accusation. Their eyes followed her, pleading for answers. The stack loomed larger than any of the other piles combined, pulsing with a cold, urgent weight.

For the first time, Megan realized the truth: They weren't just researching history anymore. They were digging up bodies.

"Look at this," Aiden murmured, brow knitting as he studied the growing pile. "There's… so many. Maybe we should be extra careful."

Megan nodded, throat tight. "Yeah. And most of them are teenagers." She slid him a sideways glance. "Do you recognize any of them?"

He shook his head slowly. "No. I don't remember hearing about anyone disappearing. But that doesn't mean it didn't happen. It's just…" His voice trailed into a grim whisper. "Unsettling."

They crouched at the center of their paper battlefield, sifting through the next handful of documents. "Here," Megan said, tapping a witness report. "Girl vanished last summer. Someone saw her near the old forest." She grabbed another sheet. "And look—this one mentions weird noises in the same area."

"You think it's connected?" Aiden asked, leaning closer.

"Maybe. If the forest is involved… it could explain why so many kids are gone."

Aiden's face tightened. "But how have we never heard about any of this? No school announcements. No social media posts. No search parties." His voice cracked with a rising unease. "Nothing."

The question hung between them—heavy, accusing.

Hours slipped by as they pored over timelines, sightings, minutes from old council meetings, and community responses that now read like half-truths or deliberate omissions. The deeper they dug, the more the town's history felt like a wound sealed too early—infected underneath.

Daylight eventually bled out, leaving the room awash in gray shadows. Aiden checked his watch, exhaling reluctantly. "I should head home. But… we're picking this up tomorrow, right?"

"Definitely." Megan tried to keep her disappointment from spilling into her voice.

After he left, she lingered by the door a moment, feeling the quiet close in around her like a thick blanket. She took a quick shower—trying to wash off the day's fear and dust—and threw on her oversized sweater. It swallowed her whole, a comfort she desperately needed.

She curled into her reading nook, hugging her pillow, journal balanced on her knees. The blank page felt like a confession booth.

Today was exhilarating and terrifying, she wrote. *We finally got into the basement. We found so much—too much—and yet not enough. But then… that creature and the voice that… protected me.*

Her pen hesitated.

She scanned her dim room, irrationally expecting something to be perched in the corners.

The memory slammed into her again—the reverend's warped, spider-like face, eight slick eyes glinting in the dark. Those teeth. The way its limbs bowed all wrong as it clung to the ceiling, watching her like a hungry thing that had waited centuries. A shiver prickled across her skin, leaving goosebumps in its wake.

She forced herself to keep writing. Fear clawed at her ribs, but beneath it was a spark—hot, determined. If something was trying to scare her away, she couldn't let it win. Not now. Not when the truth was finally starting to breathe.

She tapped her pen, gathering the threads of her thoughts. "That creature won't stop me," she said aloud, the sound thin but steady in the quiet room.

What is this parish declaration? she wrote. *Why does it keep showing up with legal documents and missing persons reports? How does it all fit?*

Frustration and curiosity tangled inside her, pulsing through her handwriting. The parish declaration felt like a hinge—a point on which everything else turned. She could feel it. The truth was close. Close enough to taste. She just had to dig deeper, read harder, stay awake longer… or let her dreams drag her further in.

Her excitement built again, swirling like heat. *What if the answers were buried in these stacks? What if the community had hidden something monstrous in plain sight?*

She yawned hard, the journal slipping closed. Navigating around the paper towers on her floor, she felt like she was moving through an archive of ghosts. Each pile whispered for her attention.

She crawled into bed, the soft mattress dipping under her tired body. But rest didn't come easy. Her mind churned with missing faces, legal terms, forest maps, and that lingering image of eight eyes glistening in the dark.

Why do I feel like I'm missing something?

The question echoed softly as her eyelids grew heavy. The room blurred. Her thoughts drifted. And finally, she slid under, into the murky realm where her questions waited to twist themselves into nightmares.

Chapter 6:
The Light of Truth

Sunlight spilled through Megan's curtains in bright, uninvited streaks, crawling across the carpet and lighting up the towers of old papers scattered everywhere. The room looked like a storm had blown through and left nothing behind but forgotten stories—yellowed pages, brittle legal slips, and handwritten notes that smelled faintly of dust and basement air. Megan rubbed the sleep from her eyes just as her bedroom door creaked open.

Her mother stepped inside, still in her wrinkled hospital scrubs. The sharp scent of antiseptic floated off her like a second skin, mixing oddly with the warm morning light. Lily blinked hard, as if she thought she might be hallucinating after a long shift.

"Megan! What—what is all this?" she gasped, eyebrows lifting so high they nearly touched her hairline. "It looks like a landfill exploded in here."

Megan pushed herself up, heartbeat ticking faster with guilt. "It's just research, Mom. I found some documents at the library."

Lily pinched the bridge of her nose but couldn't quite hide the concern shadowing her expression. "Research," she repeated, skeptical. "Or is this one of your… creative conspiracy theories?" The teasing tone softened the words, but her eyes told the truth—she was worried.

Megan forced a small, sheepish laugh. "Not a conspiracy. I'm researching weird occurrences from a few years ago. Including some missing high school students. There's something about it all that feels… important."

Lily's shoulders dipped, some of the tension easing but not disappearing. "Sweetheart, these are real families. Real grief. I don't want you wading into anything dangerous."

"I know," Megan said gently. "I just… I feel like I should help."

Lily studied her for a long moment before letting out a tired sigh. "So it is one of your conspiracies. Meg, I always give you your space to explore these beliefs, just promise me you'll be careful. I can't lose you, too." Her voice cracked ever so slightly.

"I promise." And she meant it.

Lily leaned in, brushing a kiss to her forehead—warm, grounding. "Good. I'm getting a shower before I pass out on my feet. Keep it down, please. And… Megan?"

"Yeah?"

"You can always tell me if something is wrong."

Megan smiled. "I know. Thanks, Mom."

Lily slipped out, closing the door softly behind her. Megan sat there a moment, blanket pulled tight around her shoulders, letting the quiet settle. Her mother had raised her alone since Dad died—never smothering, never hovering—but always solid in the background. A safety net woven from exhaustion, love, and too many night shifts.

Megan gathered the stack of legal documents and shuffled toward the stairs, blanket dragging behind her like a cape. The morning chill nipped at her ankles, but the fuzz of the blanket chased it away as she descended.

In the kitchen, she laid the papers on the table and fired up the coffee pot. The rich aroma filled the room, warm and comforting. She slid a strawberry toaster strudel into the toaster and listened to the low hum of the heating coils. The smell of sugary pastry soon joined the coffee, and her stomach gave an appreciative growl.

With breakfast ready, Megan settled at the table, blanket wrapped snugly around her shoulders again. She opened her laptop, the screen's glow flickering across her tired face. Her fingers danced across the keyboard.

Parish Declarations.

The definition popped up instantly.

Eighteenth-century legal documents used to report damage to properties," she read aloud. "Requests for aid or funding from the church during restoration…"

Her brows knit together. Each word seemed to latch onto the next, forming something heavy and unsettling in her chest.

"The church is always in the middle of the community," she muttered. "And now we've got legal records, sales slips, and parish declarations tied back to them. But where do the missing kids fit in?"

Her mind flashed—uninvited—back to the dream. The old church was blazing with an unnatural glow. Thick ooze bleeding from its windows, slithering down the stone steps. Doors slamming shut as if the building were alive. And the reverend—his face gone serpent, fangs bared, a forked tongue withering as he stared at her from the porch.

Her stomach twisted.

Was the dream-woman trying to steer her away from the church? Away from whatever was happening to the missing people? Or from the reverend himself? Megan remembered the serpent creature that had crawled out of her nightmare, and the spider thing that came for her when she was awake—as if the terror didn't care whether her eyes were open or closed. Both hunting her. The thought wrapped cold fingers around her spine and squeezed.

She hugged the blanket tighter and leaned back in her chair, staring at the morning light pouring in through the window. It felt wrong—too bright for the dark weight simmering in her mind.

But she pushed forward. She always pushed forward.

Megan clicked deeper into her search, chasing every thread she could find. Old church histories. Local scandals. Parish funds. Community disputes. Anything with even a whisper of relevance. With each new page, her pulse quickened.

She wasn't imagining it. Something connected all of this. She just didn't know what yet.

"I'm not turning back," she whispered, steadying her breathing. "Not now."

She tried another search.

Churches involved in missing persons. Nothing.

She tried again.

Christianity missing persons. Still nothing.

The blank search results stared back at her, cold and indifferent. Her heart sank, but only for a breath.

Because buried in the silence was something else—a pulse of determination, steady and stubborn. If there were answers, she would find them. Even if she had to dig through every shadow in Glory to get there.

Frustration simmered under Megan's skin, but she shoved it down and forced herself to keep typing. The laptop's bluish glow washed over her face, giving her reflection in the screen a ghost-like shimmer. She felt close—close enough that her chest buzzed with nerves. Something was hiding just past what she could see.

Then she typed it.

Christianity township sacrifice ritual.

"Bingo," she breathed—half laugh, half gasp—as the search exploded with results.

Her eyes skimmed the text, widening. *Christianity replaced physical sacrifices with its new covenant. In contrast, earlier cultures offered animal or human sacrifices to appease deities…*

The words crawled across her brain like cold fingertips.

Could the church have clung to anything older? Anything darker?

The idea rooted itself deep in her gut, twisting hard. The fear felt electric, but so did the excitement. She leaned closer to the screen, drawn in as if the glow itself were whispering secrets.

Her searches spiraled—pagan traditions, fertility sacrifices, harvest rites. Ancient stories lit her screen with eerie colors: torches burning in midnight fields, drums pounding like distant thunder, offerings buried under moonlit soil. She could almost hear the whispers of old prayers, almost feel cold earth packed beneath her nails. An icy wave rolled over her as she imagined those rituals not as myth, but as history. Maybe local history. Maybe Glory's history. And maybe—an idea not impossible, not completely insane—the disappearances in town weren't random at all. She grabbed the books Mrs. Archer offered and flipped feverishly through their brittle pages.

Megan stopped on a page with weird ink markings in the margins. *Early settlers in the Old Glory and surrounding regions had practiced a rough, fearful form of paganism, worshipping earth spirits and old forest gods long before the arrival of Christian missionaries. Over generations, those beliefs were supposedly "converted" into Christianity, the old rituals buried beneath hymns and Sunday sermons.*

Megan scanned back at those strange symbols and she felt a cold certainty crawl across her skin—maybe some pieces of that older faith hadn't died. They had simply learned to hide. Her stomach knotted, and she pressed a shaking hand against her ribs. The kitchen felt too quiet, too still.

Her phone buzzed suddenly, slicing through the tension, making Megan jump.

A text from Aiden lit the screen:

I know you're up already. Find anything yet?

Her fingers flew.

Hey! Deep in a rabbit hole. Found stuff about original religious practices and old rituals tied to both paganism and Christian churches. Nothing solid but interesting enough to freak me out. Come over? Want to go through the missing posters. Maybe you'll recognize someone.

She hit send and sat back, heart thumping hot and fast. The kitchen clock ticked like it was counting down to something. She kept checking the phone, waiting for—

Buzz.

I'm on my way.

Relief washed through her so quickly it left her dizzy. But beneath it lurked another feeling—something darker. A low, creeping dread whispering that maybe they were edging toward something real. Something dangerous.

She gathered her notes, hands trembling despite her determination. Shadows flickered in the corners of the kitchen, shifting just enough to make her breath hitch.

By the time Aiden's light knock met her door, her pulse was a hummingbird in her throat.

Megan opened the door. Morning sunlight splashed across the porch in soft gold, but the warmth didn't reach her bones. "Took forever," she exhaled, pulling him inside. "You won't believe what I found."

She led Aiden into the kitchen where the documents lay scattered like a crime scene—parish declarations curled at the edges, brittle legal slips yellowed with age.

"These documents are connected," Megan said, tapping one with a shaky finger. "I learned the church acted like an insurance provider in the eighteenth century. People filed parish declarations instead of claims."

Aiden frowned. "Why does that matter?"

"Because," she said, excitement flaring again, "the church didn't just offer help—they held collateral. Property deeds. Partial ownership until debts were paid. Look." She handed him a stack of thin, fragile pages. "See who the grantee is?"

Aiden scanned them, brow creasing. "The church... So they owned pieces of half the town?"

"Exactly."

He folded his arms, thinking. "It's logical, but... it's too neat. What would the church want with all that power? Is there any real link to the missing kids?"

Megan took a trembling breath. "Maybe. Look at this."

She dug through the mess and pulled out printed pages on pagan rites—harvest rituals, fertility sacrifices, and blood offerings to protect communities during harsh seasons. The text felt alive in her hands. Aiden leaned closer, skeptical but unable to tear his gaze away.

"These rituals," Megan whispered, "were meant to protect towns. Ensure good crops. Strong offspring. Survival. And a lot of those practices may not have disappeared—maybe they morphed into early Christian customs."

Aiden lifted an eyebrow. "You think the church in Glory adopted pagan sacrifices? Human sacrifices?"

"I know it sounds insane," she said. "But maybe some version of their old beliefs survived here. Maybe that's one reason Glory feels stuck in another century. And if I'm wrong—then what else explains the disappearances?"

Aiden set down the papers, finally serious. "Okay, that is a lot of maybes, but I get it."

Something in her—the same thing that woke her with bruises, the same thing that whispered at the edge of sleep—tightened like a warning.

Whatever they were about to uncover…it didn't want to stay hidden.

Megan's mind drifted—unwelcome, but relentless—back to Aiden's real reason for being here. The posters. The cold faces staring out from printed paper. The ones she couldn't unsee.

"That brings us back to the missing persons cases," she murmured, forcing her voice steady. "If my theory's off… then something else is behind all this. And honestly?" Her throat tightened. "The church's grip on this town feels too powerful to ignore."

Aiden nodded, pushing down whatever doubt still clung to him. "Exactly. That's why I came. We have to look at the recent cases again —really look—and see what jumps out now that we know more."

The memory of those photos flicked open inside her like a wound. Sunlit faces. Frozen smiles. Gone.

"We have to find a pattern," she whispered. Determination sparked under her trembling unease as they sifted through the stacks. Each page rasped like something alive, something restless, and Megan felt the pressure of their search tighten around her ribs.

She shoved aside a thin stack and froze. "Here—these are the last five years." She thrust the posters toward him, praying the paper might finally give up a truth.

Aiden leaned in, his expression sharpening with every line he read. "No… no…" His voice dropped into a low murmur. After several minutes flipping through the posters, he suddenly stopped. "Wait—Amber Langley." His breath hitched. "I knew her back in elementary school. I thought she moved away with her dad. But this…" He shook the poster once, lightly, like testing whether it was real. "This says she went missing three summers ago. That doesn't make sense."

A jolt shot straight into Megan's heart. The closeness of the connection—the way it snapped their investigation into something personal—made her hair stand on end.

"If Amber's disappearance ties into all this…" Her mouth had gone dry. "We have to follow it."

Aiden exhaled. "Her mom still works at the grocery store downtown." He hesitated, dread flickering in his eyes. "If she'll talk to us."

"Maybe," Megan said, brushing her thumb along the paper's edge. "But we need to be careful. People don't just forget their kids. If she's been silent this long, someone made her that way."

Aiden nodded slowly. "Still—we should try. She might open up, especially if she remembers me. And you…" His gaze softened. "People trust you."

Megan chewed at her lip, weighing every worry. "Only if you're sure. If she's hiding something dangerous—"

"It's a risk," he said, steady now. "But not going is worse. And we'll go together. Safer that way."

She inhaled deeply, forcing her heart into a calmer rhythm. "Tomorrow afternoon, then. We'll go together. And afterward…" A shiver rolled through her. "We come back here. Talking anywhere too public—especially about the church—feels like begging to be overheard."

The Next Day

The afternoon sun cast a too-bright glow over Glory, the kind of blue sky that felt like a lie. Megan and Aiden stepped into the grocery store, the bell chiming cheerfully above them as her pulse hammered in her ears. The aisles looked aggressively normal—bright colors, smiling logos—like the world was mocking the weight pressing down on her chest.

Mrs. Langley stood at the counter, her face worn thin by grief. Her eyes found theirs, and something in the quiet sorrow behind them made Megan's heart contract.

"Mrs. Langley?" Aiden asked, his voice softer than she'd ever heard from him. "I... I went to school with Amber."

Recognition flickered—and immediately drowned beneath grief so raw it almost felt like heat. "Amber," she whispered. "My sweet girl. Everyone moved on. I thought everyone forgot about her."

"We didn't," Aiden said gently. "It always felt... unfinished. Like she slipped away too fast. Everyone said she left with her father—"

Mrs. Langley's entire expression snapped. "Her father?" Her voice sliced through the air. "Is this a joke?"

Before Aiden could backtrack, Megan stepped in. "No joke. That's what people said. But we found posters... posters that say something very different."

The woman blinked hard, confusion twisting into dread. "Come with me," she said suddenly. "It's my break."

The back of the store was dim, the air thick with the sour scent of spoiled produce and old cardboard. Mrs. Langley led them into the loading area, then turned, face pale.

"What posters?" Her voice wavered with something dangerously close to hope.

"A dozen from the library," Megan lied smoothly. "We think Amber's disappearance might be tied to the others."

The words hit the air with a thud. Mrs. Langley's hands curled into fists on the edge of a metal table, her knuckles whitening. "Others? You shouldn't be involved. None of this is your burden." Her voice cracked. "I wasn't a perfect mother. I needed help. People—powerful people—told me she left with her father. They said it was best. But I know my daughter. She loved that church and her friends, she wouldn't go. Not with him. Not like that." Tears slid down her cheeks, glistening in the dim light. She wiped them away sharply. "Did you tell anyone else?"

Megan and Aiden exchanged a single, quiet glance. "Only people we trust," Aiden said.

"Good." Mrs. Langley's gaze swept the loading area as though expecting shadows to shift. "Keep it that way." She swallowed hard before continuing. "There are stories about the church. Old stories. The kind folks whisper only after dark. Prayers that don't feel Christian at all—more like something ancient." She shivered. "I'm not saying it's connected. I'm saying the timing is too strange."

A cold knot tightened in Megan's stomach.

Mrs. Langley stepped closer, her voice almost a rasp. "I looked for Amber myself. I followed every rumor. Every lie. And eventually… I found out she went into the forest." Her jaw trembled. "She never came out."

Megan felt the breath punch out of her.

Aiden leaned in. "Are you sure?"

Mrs. Langley's eyes filled with something dark and certain. "The Reverend Goodwin knew," she whispered. "They all did. When Amber vanished, they wrote her off. Called her unstable and said she needed a fresh start. They lied about everything."

Mrs. Langley let out a weary sigh, her shoulders sinking as if pressed down by years she hadn't asked to carry. "I sound like a crazy woman," she murmured, rubbing her trembling hands together. "But I demanded answers—help—and everyone treated it like nothing was wrong. Like it was all… normal." Her voice frayed, then thinned to a whisper. "So yes. I'm sure."

Her gaze lifted to Megan's face—and froze. Something fragile flickered there. "I'm sorry, Megan," she said, looking away quickly. "Those eyes… you remind me so much of my little girl. Curious. Always asking questions." She swallowed hard. "But sometimes curiosity takes us places we shouldn't go. Maybe you ought to let this go too."

A faint flicker in the overhead lights made the shadows around the aisles deepen, stretching long and strange across the linoleum. Megan felt her breath hitch. "I just want to help," she whispered, unsure if she meant it for Mrs. Langley or herself.

Megan and Aiden exchanged a glance—a silent "You say it", before Megan stepped forward.

"Mrs. Langley, we've found some… disturbing things. About the church. Its past. Its hold on the town." Her voice dipped, wary of the quiet pressing in around them. "Do you know anyone who worked there? Someone who might've seen things… or heard things?"

Mrs. Langley answered almost instantly, like she'd been waiting for the question to surface.

"Sister Abigail," she said. "Go to Sister Abigail. She lives in a little cottage near the forest line." A shiver ran through her voice. "She talks to shadows. Always has. Eccentric, yes—but when Amber went missing, she and I spoke." Mrs. Langley clasped her hands tightly. "Abigail said she saw Amber walk into the woods alone. But that's not the part that terrified me. She swore church officials were there… praying. Chanting."

Aiden's eyebrows shot up. "You think she'd talk to us?"

"I don't know." Mrs. Langley shook her head. "Just be gentle with her. She's been through a lot. And she's not as strong as she used to be."

Aiden glanced toward Megan, whose rigid posture betrayed the storm brewing inside her. He turned back. "What about Mayor Thompson? He loves bragging about Glory's history. Maybe he knows something."

Mrs. Langley let out a humorless laugh. "He loves talking about himself. And about how he 'rescued' this town." Her expression shifted—fear creeping in like a draft. "But if you're looking for real history… yes. He knows a lot. If you coax him, right he may talk." She paused, eyes shining with worry. "But don't go telling him your theories. He won't tolerate anything that chips away at his perfect little picture."

Her tone hardened. "You two have good hearts… but too much curiosity. Stirring up a beehive will only get you stung. So take my advice—let it go."

The knot in Megan's stomach drew tight, like someone twisting a rope inside her. "I'm sorry," Megan said softly. "But we can't. Not anymore."

Mrs. Langley met her eyes again—this time without looking away. "Then be careful, dear." Her words dropped like stones in the room. "Some things beneath that church must stay buried. And some people will make damn sure they do." Mrs. Langley looked at her watch. "I need to get back; please don't do anything reckless."

They agreed, leaving Mrs. Langley and returned to the square, the morning air felt colder than before, swallowing their breath as they walked in silence. By the time they made it back to Megan's room, the weight of the store's conversation sat on both of them like a bruise.

"What did she mean by buried?" Megan asked, shutting her bedroom door with a soft click. "Do you think she meant like… literally? Or was that a warning about the info regarding the church?"

Aiden paced, fingers digging through his hair. "I don't know. But none of it sounded good. If her warning was metaphorical, it was terrifying. If it was literal? Even worse."

The room seemed darker than it should've been. The corners looked deeper somehow, the edges of the bookshelves smudged with shifting shapes. Megan's breath stuttered. A faint whisper—like someone dragging their finger along wallpaper—seemed to move along the wall behind her. Her palms dampened. The air felt close. Watching. Still, the pull—toward answers, toward the truth—tugged hard.

"Do we keep going?" she asked, her voice steadier than her heart. "For Amber. For Mrs. Langley. We can't stop now… right?"

Aiden stopped pacing and met her eyes. His face was pale but determined. "Right. We can't turn back. If the truth is out there—even if it's dark—we need to find it." He hesitated, then added, "But Meg… what about your visions? Your nightmares? Why you?"

Megan swallowed, tracing the faded lines of a centuries-old map spread across her bed. "I don't know. But everything points back to the church. If they were involved before… they might still be hiding something now." Her fingers twitched. "There's probably, like… some evil council behind all this."

Aiden snorted. "A literal council of bad guys. Sure." But his smile faded quickly. "We still need to speak with Abigail. But I think we should start with the mayor."

He pulled a crumpled newspaper clipping from his pocket. "Oh! And look what I found on my way out." He handed it to her.

Megan leaned in, the headline shouting back: *Legacy of Influence: Exploring the Generational Bloodlines of Three Pivotal Figures in the Town of Glory.*

A photo sat beneath it—Mayor Thompson, Sheriff Jenkins Sr., and Reverend Goodwin—standing shoulder to shoulder, almost staged like a family portrait.

"They look like best friends," Megan muttered. "Can I keep this?"

"Of course. Evidence pile," Aiden said, gesturing to the chaos scattered across the floor.

Megan nudged him. "Shut up."

Then she grew serious again. "You're right. We start with Mayor Thompson. If anyone knows how far the church's influence reaches—or what's been buried—it's him."

Aiden nodded, excitement and dread tangling in his expression. "And we investigate the entire 'Legacy of Influence.' If Sheriff Jenkins Sr. helped cover up disappearances..." He exhaled shakily. "Who knows what else they've hidden."

"Sounds like a plan," Megan said, her eyes brightening with that reckless spark of excitement she always tried—and failed—to hide. "Let's start at the town square. The late Mass should be ending soon, so we might catch people on their way out. But remember—we keep everything we found to ourselves."

Aiden gave a sharp, decisive nod. Together, they stepped out of Megan's warm, lived-in house and into a slap of brisk afternoon air. It bit at their cheeks, waking them up, sharpening their senses. Aiden shoved his hands into his pockets, the cold needling his fingers, but the anticipation buzzing in his chest was warmer than any coat.

The town breathed around them—the distant clang of the church bell releasing the congregation, the muted ripple of voices drifting down the street.

They were almost at the square when a familiar pack materialized in front of them: Thomas, Lexi, Jenna, and Randy. Lexi's grin flashed first—sharp and delighted, the kind kids wore right before they pulled wings off a fly. She marched forward and yanked Megan's bag right off her shoulder.

"What's this?" she cackled. "Homework on a weekend, nerd?"

She flung the bag open. Papers burst out and scattered across the pavement like startled pigeons—missing posters fluttering into the street, the faces of lost kids staring up at the sky.

"Hey! What are you doing?" Megan dropped to her knees, scrambling to gather them.

That was when Jenna spotted Amber's poster.

Her whole face changed. It twisted into something raw and furious, as if an invisible match had been struck inside her.

"Amber?" she choked out—and then her voice roared. "Amber? What sick game are you playing? You don't even know her! Why do you have these?"

Megan froze, her hands full of paper, her breath caught halfway between her ribs and throat. "I'm just trying to help—"

"Help?" Jenna lunged toward her, shoving Megan so hard she stumbled backward, the posters slipping from her fingers. "You can help by minding your damn business, you psychotic, heartless wannabe detective! You don't get to throw around her name like a toy. You don't know what it's like to lose someone!"

Aiden moved instantly, anger tightening his jaw. "Jenna, stop! This isn't—"

"Stay out of it!" she screamed, turning her fury on him. "You knew Amber! You—of all people—should be furious she's doing this! But no—you're just as heartless as she is."

Randy grabbed Jenna's arm. "Enough! Not here." He dragged her back as she still shouted, her face blotchy with grief and rage.

Lexi snickered. "Seriously, Megan. Get checked out by a shrink."

Thomas leaned in close—too close—and said with a voice dripping false sympathy, "Hey, do you think your mom would cry if you ended up on one of these missing posters?" His smile was poison.

Aiden rushed to Megan, helping her to her feet. "Are you okay?" he asked, his voice tight.

Megan nodded, though her hands shook as she shoved the last posters into her bag. "I can't believe they just... how could Jenna think I'm heartless?"

Aiden watched the group disappear around a corner, his jaw clenched. "Amber was her best friend. That doesn't excuse it. But it explains the blind anger."

They continued toward the square, both weighed down—by guilt, by confusion, by the sharp aftertaste of confrontation.

The church rose over the town like something ancient and waiting, its tall windows darkened, the sky's gray reflection smeared across them like dead eyes. Megan's stomach tightened. She still felt Jenna's shove on her body, still heard the accusation echoing in her skull.

Residents poured from the church in small clusters, exchanging smiles and murmured goodbyes. But one figure sat apart from the warmth of the crowd.

Charlie. The town drunk.

His body sagged against the church's stone wall like he'd melted there years ago. His clothes were wrinkled and stained, hanging off him as though they belonged to someone bigger, someone healthier. His hair was a stringy, tangled mess, and his skin looked like old parchment—worn, tired, and creased by stories no one ever wanted to hear.

But it was his eyes that truly captured attention—the haunted look in them hinted at the burdens he carried. They displayed a shadowy blue hue that shimmered, like he could see the underbelly of Glory—every secret slab of rot—and was clinging to what little sanity hadn't been eaten by it.

Aiden and Megan exchanged glances, sensing that beneath Charlie's rough exterior might lie insights into the town's hidden truths. Aiden leaned closer. "Should we talk to him?"

Megan hesitated. Something in her chest thrummed uneasily. But she nodded. "Yeah. I think we should."

As they approached, Charlie's gaze lifted, glinting with suspicion and something sharper—a warning, maybe.

"What do you want?" he rasped, his voice rusted from disuse.

"Hi… Charlie, right?" Megan asked softly. "I'm Megan. This is Aiden. We were hoping to—"

"Talk?" He snorted, nearly coughing. "Why would you wanna talk to me?" He smelled of whiskey, cold nights, and hopelessness. "I don't want to talk. You best leave now. Now."

The sudden aggression made Megan step back. Aiden lifted his hands slowly, palms out. "We didn't mean any harm. Rumors about missing teenagers… we thought you might've seen something. That's all."

Charlie's eyes flicked over them—calculating, dismissive, troubled.

Megan swallowed. "We're sorry to bother you," she whispered.

They backed away, returning to the noise of the square. Megan stole one last glance over her shoulder—Charlie hadn't looked away. His stare clung to them like a warning stitched into his skin.

"Maybe… maybe we should stop for today," she muttered.

"Yeah," Aiden said softly. "It's been a lot. And Jenna…"

Megan winced. Her throat tightened. "I don't understand why she hates me for trying to help."

"She's grieving," Aiden said gently. "Everyone grieves ugly, but Jenna—she's drowning in it."

Megan nodded, though her eyes stung. "Let's just go home."

When she reached her house, she barely registered Aiden's quiet goodbye before sprinting upstairs, her heart racing with an array of emotions.

The moment her bedroom door shut, she collapsed onto her bed, face buried in her pillow. The tears came fast—violent, hot, uncontrollable. The words Jenna had hurled at her reverberated mercilessly in her mind: *psychotic, heartless!* Lexi's taunts echoed just as vividly: *You need to get checked out by a shrink.* And Thomas's haunting question lingered like a specter: *Think your mom would cry if you ended up on one of these missing posters?* The weight of their disdain pressed down on her, suffocating and relentless.

Each insult replayed with perfect clarity, slicing her from the inside out. Her chest shook with silent sobs that left her gasping for air. She curled into herself, a tight ball of grief and humiliation, as though she could hide from the voices still clawing at her mind.

The room around her blurred. The world outside vanished. All she could feel was the crushing weight of their words. It wasn't just their cruelty—it was the way it cracked something inside her. A small, steady part of her she'd relied on. Her confidence. Her purpose. Her belief that she could help without becoming the next name whispered in fear. Even as her sobs faded into raw sniffles, the heaviness stayed. A shadow curling under her ribs, settling in her bones.

Town secrets could wait—but the unease didn't. It followed her into sleep as she cried herself into exhausted darkness.

Chapter 7:
Confessions of the Damned

Megan stirred in her sleep, caught between the last tremors of a dream and the pale smear of dawn bleeding through her curtains. The soft, breathy rustle of fabric drew her back to herself. Warmth pressed at her side—the familiar weight of her mother. Lily sat on the edge of the bed, exhaustion carved into the small lines around her eyes, but there was love there too, glowing faint and steady like a candle that refused to die out.

"Megan, wake up, sweetheart." Lily whispered, brushing a few strands of hair from Megan's forehead. Her touch felt gentle, grounding, almost painfully normal. "It's time to wake up for school."

Megan shifted beneath the covers, clinging to the cocoon of warmth. A cold pulse throbbed under her ribs—the fading afterimage of a dream she couldn't remember but still felt in her bones. *Something followed me out...* a voice whispered in the back of her mind, *Let me in*. She cracked her eyes open and forced a small smile, pretending she hadn't heard it at all.

"I'm tired, Mom. I didn't sleep very well."

The words slid out slowly, thick and unpleasant. Her mouth tasted sharp afterward, like copper, like she'd bitten down on something that bled and never stopped. She pressed her tongue to the roof of her mouth, trying to ground herself.

Lily didn't answer right away. Her gaze drifted past her daughter's face, lingering somewhere over her shoulder, as if she were listening for something just out of reach. Then she frowned. "Is that why you've been so quiet lately? Is something..."

"Yeah. Just tired." She cut in before the question could finish forming.

It was another lie. Or maybe it wasn't. The truth had started to twist in on itself, knotting so tightly she couldn't tell where it ended and the lies began. "I'll get up and take a shower," she said. The words sounded distant, like they'd come from the end of a long hallway. "You should get some rest too, mom."

Behind her, the house creaked—not settling, not the familiar sounds of old wood—but Lily leaned in and kissed her cheek. Warm lips. Warm breath. Then she pulled away and left the room.

The door clicked shut.

Megan realized she'd been holding her breath. When she finally let it out, the air turned colder, thin against her skin, as if something else had been waiting in the room—waiting to breathe with her.

She showered, letting the warm water pound against her shoulders. For a moment she closed her eyes, soaking in the sensation—but the back of her neck prickled. That crawling, needling feeling again. Like someone watching her through frosted glass. When she opened her eyes, a shadow slipped against the shower curtain—just steam, she told herself, but her chest tightened anyway.

By the time she dressed and wandered into the kitchen, she felt hollowed out, scraped thin. She made a breakfast sandwich out of habit, not hunger. The toaster popped; warm bread filled the air, a smell that should have steadied her.

Instead, something else crept beneath it—damp earth, decomposing leaves ground into mud, and the kind of rot that clung to an old boot long after you'd scraped it clean. Her stomach tightened.

She blinked, and the scent was gone.

She grabbed her backpack, her half-written notebook of thoughts and nightmares, and stepped outside into the brisk East Coast morning. The wind bit at her cheeks. The town felt empty, stretched thin, as if Glory held its breath the same way she did.

Why do I feel so damn lost? she wondered as she walked towards school. She should have felt something—excitement, nerves, anything recognizable. Instead, everything pressed down on her, dense and unyielding, as if the air itself had gained weight.

She rounded the corner near the school and saw Charlie slumped on a bench, hood over his hair, posture sagging like he was trying to fold himself out of existence. A surprising warmth prickled inside her chest, soft and almost tender.

She placed her breakfast sandwich beside him a small, stupid kindness. But it grounded her somehow. *Maybe he needs it more than I do*, she thought.

She turned to leave. Something clawed at her attention—like she was being watched—but when she glanced back at Charlie, he didn't move. *Stop being paranoid*, she told herself. *Jesus, get a grip.*

Charlie's eyes, though she didn't see them, cracked open as she walked away.

At school, Glory High loomed ahead, its brick walls dark against the gray sky. Megan felt a twist in her gut. The building always felt old, but today it felt… aware. The crowd of students buzzed—laughing, complaining, living—but she felt like she was underwater, listening to everything through thick glass.

Then she saw them. Jenna, Lexi, and their glossy-faced entourage. Their expressions soured when they saw her, eyes sharp, judgmental, hungry in a petty, recognizable way. But beneath their stares, Megan felt another set of eyes—lower, colder, something slinking behind them in the shadow cast by the school entrance.

She swallowed hard, and forced her feet to keep moving.

She buried herself in her schoolwork through the day, ignoring the gossip that swirled around her. Whispers felt louder than usual, threading between the walls. Once, she would've sworn she heard her own name hissed right behind her ear, but when she turned, there was no one there. Just a drifting hint of pine.

Aiden slid into the desk beside her, his voice low. "Megan… Have you noticed anything weird around school lately?"

Her skin prickled. The pencil trembled in her hand.

Just the shadows shifting when they shouldn't. Just the dreams bleeding through daylight. Just the sense that reality was slipping, soft and unreliable, like wet paper tearing between her fingers.

Her thoughts skidded and collided, refusing to settle.

"Umm, weird—I'm not sure," she said, too quickly. "I've just… been in my own world."

Aiden looked wounded, but he let it go. The bell rang. She gathered her things, her limbs heavy as if she were moving through syrup.

"I'm not feeling well," she murmured to him before he had a chance to ask. "I'm going home."

"Let me walk you," he offered, concern softening his voice.

"No."

Her voice cracked. She forced a smile anyway. "I just need space. I'll be fine. Everything's fine."

The lie stuck in her throat this time.

Something behind her—too close, though she hadn't heard it move—answered anyway.

No... it isn't.

The words didn't reach her ears at all. They took root inside her head—cold, deliberate, yet she turned away from them anyway.

The walk home felt endless. Every step dragged heavier than the last, as if the street itself were trying to drag her down into its cracks. The sky dimmed to an iron-gray bruise, the sinking sun stretching long, crooked shadows that slithered across the pavement. She hugged her arms around herself.

That's when she saw him—Charlie. He wasn't slumped this time. He stood straighter, strangely alert, eyes clearer than she'd ever seen them. The change unsettled her more than his drunkenness ever had.

"Hey, Megan."

His voice was steady... softer, almost careful. "Thanks for the sandwich this morning."

His sincerity knocked something loose inside her. She blinked, startled.

"Oh—no problem," she said, fumbling over the words. "I'm glad you're okay."

Charlie's expression cracked open for a moment. Vulnerable. Raw. The kind of look people get when they're standing too close to the edge.

"I'm sorry for how I acted," he said. "I've seen so much... too much. And somehow the bottle and being alone became my way of coping."

Megan's chest tightened. Empathy flickered through her—sharp, sudden. "We all have our battles," she whispered. "Even I do."

She stepped back, the weight on her shoulders unbearable. "Have a nice day."

Charlie nodded, though the movement seemed half-hearted. "Thank you," he murmured.

He watched her walk away, something restless churning in his eyes. "I see your struggles," he called after her, voice trembling. "I'm not that different. I'm an outcast too. A walking disappointment."

She froze. Her breath scraped against her throat. *This has been my life for as long as I can remember*, she wanted to shout. Instead, she turned, frustration and vulnerability twisting together.

"This is how it's always been," she said, the words rushing out before she could stop them. "I chase mysteries—conspiracies—whatever my mom calls them. Usually, they're just voices in my head. But this time... this time feels different. Something's wrong. I can feel it."

Charlie's expression darkened, a sharp weight settling in his eyes.

"Do you hear them too?" he whispered. "The voices... telling you something isn't right?"

Megan stiffened. Shadows twisted behind him, shapes stretching and curling with the fading light, like hands clawing at the edges of the room. Her throat went dry.

Charlie's gaze remained steady, though a flicker of fear moved behind his eyes. "Those voices… they never stop. Always warning me, whispering that something's wrong—always leading back to the church." He swallowed. "Maybe it's all in my head. But the church owns my family's land. Has for generations. I don't know the whole story, but they've held it over us my entire life."

Megan's lips parted, cold and hesitant. "What do you mean something's wrong?"

He looked away, his jaw tightening. "Everyone thinks I'm just the town drunk," he said quietly. "I drink because it's the only way to quiet the voices, but I see things other people don't."

His voice cracked. "I see the church gatherings. The ceremonies. And afterward…" He swallowed hard. "People are just gone."

He rubbed the back of his neck, his hand shaking. "I notice people disappearing. Teenagers. Whole families. They leave without warning." His eyes flicked back to hers. "I don't know if it's connected, but I can't ignore it."

A shiver crawled up Megan's spine, settling coldly beneath her skin. The wind rustled the trees—sharp and brittle. She thought she smelled smoke. And pine. And something like burnt hair.

"You need to say something," she said, desperation clinging to her words.

"Megan, no."

Charlie's voice shook. "If I do, I risk everything. Myself. My family—my kids—" His breath snagged. "I've already ruined enough. The drinking. The guilt." He swallowed hard. "It cost me my marriage. Now I'm a stranger in my own house. A ghost my kids don't know how to look at."

He dragged a hand across his face, but it did nothing to hide the tears.

Megan stepped closer, heart aching. "When did you first notice these disappearances?"

He swallowed hard. "About a year ago. But truthfully? The pattern's been longer. Every summer, around the solstice, the reverend hosts some 'gathering.' Afterward… people vanish."

His voice dropped to a whisper. "That's all I know…"

Something inside him broke then. He buried his head in his hands, fingers digging into his scalp like he wanted to tear the thoughts out.

"The voices are too much," he choked. "I'm losing my mind."

Megan sat down on the bench next to him. His body flinched like he expected a blow.

"You're not alone," she said. "I do hear them too."

He lifted his head slowly. Gratitude flickered there—but so did something else. Fear. Paranoia. The sense of someone watching from behind the trees.

"I shouldn't have told you any of this," he muttered. His eyes darted around the street. "No. No, I've said too much. I need to go. I'm sorry—just—forget this."

He backed away before she could respond, then turned and walked quickly, shoulders hunched, as if expecting something dark to swoop down on him at any moment.

Megan watched until he disappeared into the growing dark. The air around her felt thick, humming with tension. The secrets of the town pressed in, suffocating. She hugged herself tightly, her feet finally forcing her forward.

Once home, she ate mechanically, the food turning to paste in her mouth. She washed the dishes without really seeing them. Her thoughts spun, tangled and frantic. The house creaked softly, each sound too sharp, like the walls were leaning in to listen.

When she finally retreated into her nook, she felt her body sag with relief. Her sanctuary. Her hiding place. Her last bit of normalcy.

She opened her journal beneath the warm lamp light, the smell of old paper comforting and familiar. The pen rested in her shaking fingers.

What is happening in this town? she wrote, hand trembling.

Why do I feel like something terrible is coming?

The thought of the approaching solstice gnawed at her. Time slipping away. Breath by breath.

Who will be next?

Her heart hammered. The shadows in the corner of the room seemed to shift—slowly, deliberately.

She pushed through the panic.

I can't quit now. There is something about the church. If I don't… I'll never forgive myself.

She closed the journal, pressing her palm against the cover as if sealing the words inside could somehow steady her. But even in the quiet of her nook, she couldn't shake the creeping dread.

Something was coming.

And it was getting closer.

Weeks had slipped by since that unsettling talk with Charlie, and the halls at school simmered with a kind of quiet electricity —whispers that cut off when Megan walked by, sideways glances that pretended not to be glances at all. She felt them, every last one. But instead of shrinking under it, something else had taken root inside her. Something steadier. Sharper. Like resolve crystallizing in her ribs.

Aiden had become her anchor through it all. They spent afternoons holed up in the library, buried under yellowed clippings and brittle pages that smelled like attic dust and time. "We can't let fear stop us," he said one evening, tapping a headline about another missing hiker. "Whoever's behind this isn't going to stop. Neither can we."

Megan felt a flicker of heat in her chest—courage or stubbornness, she wasn't sure. "I know. We'll figure it out. Whatever it takes."

The weight of their mission hung between them, heavier than the stacks of newspapers. But together, it felt... doable. Almost.

When school let out, Aiden lingered to talk to Mrs. Carter, leaving Megan to walk home alone. She'd barely made it past the town square when she heard her name.

"Megan!"

Charlie came stumbling toward her, his silhouette washed in late-afternoon sunlight. The sight of him made her stomach tighten. He looked worse than before—eyes darting, breath hitching like he'd sprinted the whole way.

"I feel like someone's watching me," he blurted, twisting his hands together. "I needed to warn you. Be careful—there's something out there." His voice dropped. "I don't want anyone else getting hurt because of me."

The tremor in his voice cracked something inside her. This wasn't the usual jitteriness she'd seen in him. This was deeper. Darker. As if something had been gnawing at him from the inside out.

Megan stepped closer, lowering her voice. "Charlie, hey—listen. You're okay. No one's following you. You're just being cautious." She tried to anchor him with a gentle smile, but his gaze skittered around her like he was searching for something hiding in the corners.

"No, you aren't listening to me." His voice pitched higher, raw and quivering. "I've been having these dreams. I can feel someone behind me. Watching. Waiting." He clutched his head, fingers digging into his scalp as if trying to stop something from getting in—or out.

Megan's pulse kicked up. "Charlie, breathe. Just slow down. You've been through a lot, but you're safe right now."

The words didn't calm him—they frayed him further. His eyes turned wild, pupils blown wide. Then, without warning, he jerked upright.

"Safe?" he barked. "You're just a kid, Megan. You don't get it. I'm not safe. I have to go."

Before she could react, he spun and bolted toward the edge of town, leaving her frozen on the sidewalk. She scanned the shadowed street, but there was no figure lurking, no movement she could see.

"I hope he's okay," she whispered, though the words felt thin.

Charlie didn't stop running until the town square blurred into a smear of color behind him. His breath tore in and out, cold and sharp, the sweat on his back chilling in the evening breeze. Every sound stabbed at his nerves—crunching gravel, a distant crow, the wind scraping through dry leaves.

"They're out there," he muttered. "I know it. I can feel them." He kept glancing behind him, expecting to catch a flicker of movement just beyond his sight. He never did. That somehow made it worse.

The path narrowed as it led him toward the forest at the edge of town, funneling him forward with quiet insistence. Ahead, the trees rose into an immense black wall against the bruised purple of dusk—trunks hunched and uneven, branches clawing skyward like crooked sentries trying to choke the last of the light from the sky.

Charlie slowed, a tight knot forming in his throat. The certainty pressing at the back of his mind told him this was the only place left where he could disappear. Where the watching would stop. Where no one would follow.

He swallowed and whispered, "Are you sure?" The words sounded weak, already unraveling the moment they left him.

He knew the stories. Everyone did. Campfire warnings muttered under breath, names spoken once and never again, as if repetition might draw attention. People went into those woods and didn't come back. Entire lives erased between one step and the next.

"You'll protect me," he said aloud, though his voice faltered on the words. At the edges of his vision, the dark stirred and withdrew, gathering and thinning like smoke drawn in and slowly released. Wind slid through the branches with a sound too intentional to be chance, winding through him, settling in his chest, coaxing him forward.

Safe, the thought surfaced unbidden. *Quiet.*

His gaze fixed on the dark between the trees. "They went in," he whispered, thinking of the missing, of all the unanswered questions, "and they never came out."

Still, his feet carried him forward.

The forest seemed to beckon him—with the eerie welcome of something that opened its arms only for the already half-lost. Maybe it's safer in there, he thought wildly. At least the open air won't swallow me whole. He stepped closer, watching the undergrowth shift, the branches writhe, the shadows breathe. "Where are you taking me?" he whispered, his voice cracking. "Is this… safe?"

The path narrowed ahead, funneling him forward like it had a purpose of its own. The trees leaned inward, black and massive against the bruised purple sky, branches twisting as if to block retreat.

"You're not leaving me behind, right?" he asked, half to himself, half to someone—or something—that wasn't there. His hands trembled, but he kept moving. "I'm… I'm listening. I'm doing what you said."

The darkness thickened around him, swallowing the last hints of town. The rusted fence came into view. "Should I… go through this?" he whispered. Metal groaned as he pushed past, jagged edges tearing his arm, drawing blood he barely felt. "I'm still okay, right?"

Cold pinched his skin, and the forest seemed to lean closer, taller, watching. "Am I going the right way?" he asked, swallowing hard. Leaves crunched underfoot, a soft answering rustle echoing from deeper in the shadows. He stumbled forward, looking around. "You said no one is following me… right?"

The darkness ahead rippled, almost alive. He froze, blinking. "Are we almost there?" His voice shook, betraying the fear he tried to smother. Branches shifted like bent limbs, shapes forming angles that made no earthly sense. "Just trees… just wind," he murmured, but his own words rang hollow.

Something paced just beyond sight, matching his steps, sliding along with him. "I'm… I'm listening. I'm doing it," he whispered. "I'm not turning back. Am I making you happy? I'm… I'm doing what you told me."

The forest seemed to breathe around him, dark forms flickering at the edges of his vision. Footsteps followed, slow, deliberate, patient. His instincts screamed: run.

He didn't. Not yet.

The murmurs drifted through the trees, threading close, coaxing, circling. "Where do I go now?" he asked, voice small, desperate, obedient. And still, he walked on.

"Charlie…"

"Charrrr–lieee…"

The whispers curled around him in a slow, sinister drawl, each repetition a needle sliding beneath his nerves. He stopped walking. His heart hammered against his ribs as he strained to locate the source—yet all that met him was thick, ancient darkness.

Ink-black forms bled in and out of the treeline, stretching like silhouettes made of spilled ink swirling in water. They flinched and twisted with each blink, whispering things too low to understand, pressing against the fragile edges of his sanity.

"Hello, where did you go?" he whispered. "I can't hear you. Are you still there?"

The forest listened.

And then—

it answered.

A face pushed out of a tree trunk ten feet away, the bark bulging before splitting open. Yellow eyes, threaded with red veins, glared from within. Bark peeled back in a grimace, stretching into a grin full of splintered, wooden teeth. Red moss draped from its jaw like a beard soaked in dried blood.

Charlie's breath hitched. He couldn't move.

The forest floor churned. Mud and vines boiled upward, knotting together into legs—spindly, trembling—then a torso hunched and dripping, vines writhing beneath its skin like worms trying to escape. The creature lifted its head and smiled the same awful wooden smile.

"No," Charlie gasped. "The voice said I was safe here!" His voice cracked, echoing uselessly between the trees. The creature didn't lunge or growl; it simply stood there, grinning, as if his terror amused it.

Panic detonated through him. He spun and ran.

The forest warped with him, the path twisting back on itself. Roots snatched at his ankles. Branches clawed his face. Something cold and impossibly long brushed the back of his neck. "Get away from me!" he screamed, stumbling forward as shadows pressed in tighter, dragging their whispers across his skin. The creature followed—not visible, but unmistakable, its presence swelling behind him like a rising tide.

"You lied to me!" he cried. "This was a mistake! I shouldn't have listened!"

The footsteps behind him quickened—heavy, hungry.

Run.

He sprinted blindly, lungs burning, vision shaking. The voices swelled into a vicious chorus, chanting behind his ears, weaving into the crunch of twigs and the thunder of his own heartbeat.

"Just—get—AWAY!" he roared, adrenaline cleaving through him.

The forest didn't listen.

His foot snagged on a half-buried strip of the fallen metal fence the forest had concealed like a trap. The jolt drove him forward helplessly, and before he could catch himself, he slammed full-force into an upright shard of the fence; the rusted iron tore into his side with a wet rip, and his scream shot out of him before the pain even hit. For a heartbeat he was weightless. Then agony crashed over him in a white-hot wave.

Still, he ran, clutching his bleeding side. He pushed himself onward until the trees finally spat him out into a clearing. Moonlight poured over him. Air filled his lungs again. For a stunned second, he believed he'd escaped.

Then the heat in the wound ignited—crawling under his skin like something alive. His fingers trembled with the realization.

Behind him, the treeline shivered, shapes rearranging themselves with quiet, patient malice.

Watching. Waiting.

Five days since escape from the darkness...

Charlie stumbled through the town square like a dying animal. His shirt clung to his side, soaked in dried blood and fresh seepage. Sweat plastered his hair to his forehead. His skin had taken on a grayish, sickly pallor.

The fever hit hard.

Reality melted.

People in the street became warped—eyes too wide, smiles too sharp. Their faces twisted into masks of suspicion, hate, disappointment. Their voices carried whispers that clawed at his ears.

"They're all against me," he rasped, stumbling past a bench. "They want to see me suffer."

Every laugh sounded like it came from the trees.

Every shadow stretched too long.

Every person seemed to watch him the way the forest had.

And somewhere beyond the edge of town, deep in the dark, something answered his fear with a low, eager creak—like a branch bending under fresh weight.

Driven by delusion, Charlie lashed out at anyone who came near him, convinced every moving shadow belonged to the conspiracy hunting him down. If a branch twitched or a figure shifted at the edge of his vision, he'd whirl toward it with a guttural scream, swinging with wild, panicked strength.

"Stay back!" he'd roar, voice raw and splintered, stumbling through brush and mud like a wounded animal. Each outburst left him more alone, more hunted by the phantoms that clung to the inside of his skull. The infection burned through him, chewing reason apart, feeding on every spike of fear until he barely resembled the man he'd been.

The forest had followed him home. And it wasn't letting go.

Charlie became a ghost in daylight—vacant eyes, twitching hands, whispering to things nobody else could see. The darkness he'd run from pressed in on him no matter where he staggered, merging fantasy with reality until everything blurred into one nightmare.

Megan sat curled on the couch, half-zoned out, flipping through channels just to fill the silence. Her mind drifted until the sharp tone of Breaking News sliced through the room. She blinked, straightened, and felt her stomach twist as the broadcast shifted to a shaky cell-phone video.

Charlie filled the screen… or what was left of him.

His hair stuck out in filthy clumps, plastered to a face so pale it looked bloodless. His eyes were hollow pits rimmed with cracked red vessels, darting everywhere as if the air itself threatened him. He lunged at people in the street—random, unsuspecting townsfolk—and chaos exploded around him. Screams pierced the background. Someone dropped their groceries. A child wailed. Shattered glass glittered under the frantic camera light like spilled stars.

Megan's pulse hammered.

The footage trembled as deputies rushed in. Charlie fought with animalistic strength, foam bubbling from the corners of his rotting teeth. When one deputy tried to grab him, Charlie shrieked—a high, broken sound—and his eyes streamed tears of blood, leaving thin, dark trails down his face.

"Charlie, please!" one deputy yelled, desperation cutting through the panic.

But reason couldn't touch him.

It took three men—then four—to pin him down. Even then, he thrashed so violently they nearly dropped him. Megan watched, hand trembling at her mouth, as he kicked and screamed, spitting blood-tinged saliva across the pavement.

By the time deputies hauled him into custody, Megan was already crying.

Megan couldn't sit around not knowing what happened. After repeated calls and quiet persistence, they finally relented, granting her a brief visit under strict conditions: Charlie would remain in his holding cell, no exceptions.

Megan hugged herself as she stepped beneath the cold fluorescent lights, the air sterile and unforgiving. Her legs felt like wet paper as she entered the holding area, every step heavy with the weight of what she might find on the other side.

Charlie turned.

The sight hollowed her out.

"Stay away!" he bellowed, stumbling toward the bars. Before she could react, his hand shot out, fingers closing around her wrist with a crushing, frantic strength. Megan sucked in a breath, fear punching through her chest.

"Charlie, it's me—it's Megan—stop, please—"

"They're coming for me!" he rasped. His pupils trembled, swimming with terror. "You have to go! You have to go!"

She tugged, trembling, but his grip only tightened.

And then—self-destruction.

With a sudden, feral lurch, Charlie hurled himself forward and smashed his skull against the bars. The impact wasn't just a sound—it was an explosion, a metallic clang fused with the dull, sick thud of bone meeting iron. The whole cell shuddered. Megan felt the vibration in her teeth.

"Charlie—STOP!" she screamed, voice cracking.

But he didn't hear her. Or couldn't. Or something else was driving him.

He reared back and slammed his head again, harder, the crash ringing out like a hammer striking a soaked slab of meat. Blood sprayed across the bars in a bright, violent arc, flecking her face with warm droplets. Megan staggered back, horror ripping through her.

"HELP! SOMEBODY—PLEASE!" she shrieked, but the deputies barely moved, frozen in disbelief as if their brains refused to process the carnage happening feet away.

Charlie didn't slow.

He rammed his skull into the metal a third time, the blow strong enough to rattle the hinges. His skin split wide, peeling back to reveal flashes of white bone beneath. Blood ran, then gushed, pouring down his face in sheets, dripping from his chin, pattering onto the floor in rapid, sticky beats.

He screamed as he did it—raw, guttural, an animal being torn apart from the inside out. His voice shredded into wet gasps, but he still threw himself forward again.

This time the sound was wrong. Deep. A nauseating crack that echoed like green wood snapping under an axe.

Megan's breath seized mid-scream.

Before anyone could reach him, he struck the bars one final time.

Something gave.

His skull split with a freakish, hollow pop—bone separating under force it was never meant to meet. Blood and gray matter splattered the bars in a thick, sickening burst. Deputies lunged for Megan, dragging her back as she fought to get away, her voice tearing out of her throat in pure, choking panic.

The cell door slammed shut behind her as the world narrowed into a ringing haze. She turned just in time to see him fall.

Charlie collapsed in a twitching heap on the concrete, his head no longer a recognizable shape but a ruined, pulped mass. Blood pooled rapidly beneath him, thick and syrupy, spreading in warm ripples across the floor. One of his eyes bulged grotesquely from the torn socket, dangling by a slick strand that swayed with the tiny, dying convulsions of his body.

His face—what remained of it—looked clawed from within, torn by fingers that had never touched his skin. The bruises already blossoming across his cheeks formed grotesque patterns, as if something had been carving its way out.

He twitched once, violently—bones clicking—then went terrifyingly still.

Megan's scream didn't even make it out of her mouth. Her body locked, stiff and cold, as if terror had reached down her throat and frozen her from the inside.

The deputies dragged her backward through the hallway, her shoes scraping across the floor. She couldn't blink. Couldn't breathe. Couldn't look away.

She stared at Charlie's ruined body until the cell door, the bars, and the pooling blood disappeared from sight.

Later, back home, darkness pressed tight around her like a living thing. Shadows clung to the corners of her room, pooling thickly under the bed and along the walls, as if waiting for her to close her eyes. She lay curled beneath the covers, trembling so hard the mattress shivered beneath her. No matter how tightly she wrapped the blankets around herself, she couldn't get warm; the chill from the cell still clung to her skin.

Her mind kept replaying everything—the cage-like bars, the spray of blood, the wet crack of bone splitting open. The echoes of it wouldn't stop. They rattled around her skull like loose stones. Every time she shut her eyes, she saw Charlie's face collapse, saw his eye swing free, saw the gore glistening in the fluorescent light.

Worse was his voice. That cracked, frantic pleading right before something inside him broke. It clung to her, curled around her like a whisper she couldn't outrun.

She pressed her hands against her ears, but the memory still bled through.

Just before sleep finally dragged her under—slow, heavy, suffocating—one question rose from the coldest corner of her mind, bubbling up like something breaking the surface of a frozen lake:

Who was coming for him?

And then—quieter, sharper, infinitely worse—

were they coming for her next?

Chapter 8:
The Gathering Storm

The soft glow of morning crept through the curtains, pale sunlight stretching across the room in thin ribbons that wavered like ghosts on the walls. Megan stirred beneath the covers, her sleep restless and broken, her dreams still ringing with blood and metal. Her eyes blinked open to the blurred silhouette of her mother standing at the edge of the bed.

"Megan," Lily whispered, gently shaking her shoulder. "Wake up, sweetheart. I need to talk to you."

A low groan escaped Megan as she dragged the blankets over her head. "Just a few more minutes, Mom," she mumbled, her voice thick and tired.

But Lily's tone darkened with urgency. "Honey, it's important. The sheriff came by the hospital today. He told me about Charlie."

The name hit like a stone dropped into cold water. Megan sat upright, heart thudding hard enough to bruise her ribs. "What did he say?"

Lily exhaled slowly, her expression a mix of sorrow and something like helplessness. "He said you witnessed Charlie's breakdown… and his death. He wants to come by later to speak with you."

A wave of nausea rolled through Megan, sharp and sudden. She had hoped the details of that night would stay buried somewhere deep and unreachable. "I'm fine, Mom. I can handle it." But the words wavered on her tongue, hollow even to her own ears.

Lily shook her head. "I think you need to stay home from school for a few days. What you saw—events like that can stay with people. Megan, this is trauma. Someone died."

"But I can't just stop everything," Megan protested, desperation slipping into her voice. "Aiden and I are—"

"Megan," Lily cut her off gently but firmly. "I know you and Aiden have been digging into things. You said it was harmless. But now someone is dead, and whatever you two are tangled in clearly isn't harmless. I need you to stop before this gets worse."

Megan clenched her jaw, frustration and guilt tightening together like a knot in her chest. "I get it. I'll… I'll step back." A lie, flimsy and fragile, but she couldn't bear to worry her mother any more than she already had.

Lily's features softened, and she leaned forward to press a kiss to Megan's forehead. "Thank you. I love you. I just want you both safe."

"I love you too," Megan whispered, though uncertainty gnawed at her insides as Lily slipped out of the room.

When the door clicked shut, silence wrapped itself around her like a second blanket. Megan sagged back against the pillows, her thoughts spinning in cold, frantic spirals. Her mother's love was a comfort, but it also pressed down on her—too heavy, too smothering. The investigation had become a lifeline, a way to reclaim control after months of nightmares, fear, and whispers reaching for her. But Charlie's violent death hovered over her like a storm cloud, threatening to split open.

She grabbed her journal from the nightstand, flipping to an empty page. Her hand trembled as she wrote, the words scratching across the paper:

I can't let this go. I need to understand what changed Charlie—and who... or what... got to him first.

The shadows in the corners of her room seemed to pulse, darker than they had any right to be. She tried to breathe evenly, but every inhale felt tight, shallow. The day ahead loomed uncertain, but one truth anchored her:

Fear would not stop her.

It never had.

The hours passed in a quiet, uneasy blur...

Megan emailed her teachers, pulled the blankets up to her chin, and spent most of the day drifting between half-sleep and intrusive memories she couldn't shake. The house felt too still, every creak of the floorboards making her flinch.

A soft knock at her door broke the silence.

"Honey, the sheriff is here," Lily called.

Megan's palms instantly slicked with sweat. Sheriff Jenkins. She had known the conversation was coming, but dread still curled coldly under her ribs.

"I'm right here with you," Lily said, appearing in the doorway. "If anything feels like too much, just look at me and I'll handle it."

Megan nodded, swallowing tightly. "Okay… thank you."

She pulled on her oversized sweater and sweatpants—the soft fabric a small shield—and wrapped herself in her fuzzy blanket before heading downstairs. The sharp, familiar scent of coffee drifted through the kitchen.

Sheriff Jenkins sat at the table, a solid man with a compact, athletic build. His clean-shaved scalp gleamed under the overhead light, and his trimmed beard framed a face that could have been intimidating if not for the warmth in his ice-blue eyes. He looked up as she entered and offered a gentle, steady smile.

"Hey there, Megan," he said, his voice low and calming. Though they'd met before, he greeted her like they were starting fresh. "Thanks for sitting down with me."

"Of course, Sheriff," she said softly. She poured herself a cup of coffee and drowned it in sugar, hoping the sweetness would cut the bitter dread coiled in her gut. She took her seat.

He wrapped his hands around his mug, watching her carefully. "Your mom said the last few days have been rough. I want you to know—there's no pressure. You can tell me whatever you feel ready to tell."

Megan nodded, gripping her cup as if it were an anchor. "It's just… a lot. The school, the town, and then Charlie…" Her voice trailed off, thin and trembling.

Sheriff Jenkins took a slow sip of coffee, the steam drifting between them like a thin veil. His expression softened but stayed serious, a balance he seemed practiced at. "I understand, Megan. It's a lot. Feeling overwhelmed doesn't make you weak —it makes you human. Just take your time."

The kitchen felt oddly sealed off from the world outside; the warm air, the smell of coffee, the soft hum of the refrigerator— all of it wrapped around them in a fragile cocoon. Megan drew in a deep breath, bracing herself to peel back the tangled layers of fear and confusion knotted inside her since that night.

The sheriff leaned forward, forearms on the table, his icy-blue eyes focused. "Let's start simple. How did you know Charlie?"

Megan hesitated, choosing her words carefully. "That's just it —I didn't. Not really." Her voice steadied, though uncertainty lingered beneath it like an undertow. "I only met him a week or two ago. He was sleeping on a bench near my school. I left him a breakfast sandwich because… he looked like he needed someone to care. Later he thanked me, and we talked. Just small stuff. He seemed… normal. Like someone who just needed a moment of kindness." She swallowed hard. "When he walked away, he wasn't upset. He was fine."

Jenkins nodded, prompting her gently. "And that was the only time?"

"No." The word scraped out of her. "There was another day. He looked different. Disoriented. He kept saying someone was following him." Her stomach clenched at the memory of the frantic darting of his eyes. "I didn't understand. Before I could ask more, he bolted." She pressed her fingers against her mug. "I saw the news report and thought maybe I could help. You know… be a familiar face at the station."

The sheriff raised a brow. "Did he seem intoxicated? Any noticeable injuries?"

She sifted through the memory, searching for details she might've missed. "No. No smell of alcohol, no injuries I could see. Just fear."

"Alright." Jenkins sat back. "Tell me what happened at the station."

A cold shiver ran down Megan's spine. Her throat tightened. "He looked awful. Like he hadn't slept in days. His eyes were wild." Her voice trembled. "He told me to leave. He said they were coming for him. That I had to go." The weight of those words pressed against her chest again, compressing the air in her lungs. She saw the concern deepen in the sheriff's eyes.

"Did he say who?" Jenkins asked gently.

"No." Her voice dropped to a whisper. "Just he seemed scared of someone. I backed away, and then he—he started hurting himself. I yelled for help, but the deputies were slow, and I watched him fall. I watched him die."

"Megan," the sheriff interrupted softly, "that's enough. Take a moment if you need it."

Beside her, Lily's expression softened with a mother's instinctive pain. "Sweetheart, take your time. We're right here."

Megan blinked hard, pushing back the sting of tears. "I'm okay. Really," she whispered.

Jenkins gave Lily a small nod before continuing. "Did you ever see anyone following him? Anything unusual?"

Megan's gaze flickered toward her mother, silently pleading for space. "No. I looked around when he mentioned it, but I didn't see anyone," she said, voice thinning at the edges.

Lily, sensing the unspoken boundary, kept her hands folded tightly together. "Sheriff... she told you she barely knew him. She was simply being compassionate toward someone in need. Nothing more."

The sheriff nodded. "I understand. And she did the right thing. We need more young people willing to help others, especially with everything this town's been through." He gave Megan a soft, earnest look. "Don't let this change who you are."

Relief and exhaustion washed over her in a single heavy tide. "Thank you," she murmured. "Can I... go back to my room now?"

"Of course." His voice warmed. "You've helped more than you realize."

Megan stood, her blanket slipping from her shoulders, but before she could step fully into the hallway, she caught the low murmur of her mother's voice behind her.

"You mentioned the community experiencing a lot," Lily said. "Is there anything we should be watching for?"

Megan froze just beyond the doorway, heart tightening as if bracing for an impact.

The sheriff's tone shifted, more guarded. "We're investigating several missing persons cases from last summer," he said. "Teenagers mostly. We warned people to stay out of certain areas—posted 'Do Not Enter' signs around the forest—but some still went. And some never came back."

A pulse of dread thumped in Megan's ribs. The forest. Always the forest.

Sheriff Jenkins continued, "Aside from that, this is the first violent incident we've had in decades." A sigh left him, heavy. "My father retired last year. This job felt like a birthright, but… big shoes to fill."

Lily's voice sharpened with concern. "Should we be worried about anything else?"

He hesitated. Megan felt the pause like a cold breath crawling up her spine.

"Just stay alert," the sheriff said finally. "Report anything strange. Look out for each other. We're a small town—we survive by sticking together."

Megan slipped into the hallway, her pulse racing as she made her way toward her bedroom. The dim light, the quiet of the house, the echo of the sheriff's warnings—they all pressed around her like a tightening sleeve. The forest. The disappearances. Charlie's last words. Everything aligned in a way that made her stomach twist.

Something dark was threading itself through their town, and the closer she came to the truth, the more certain she felt:

It wasn't done with her yet.

Once she slipped back into the cozy corner of her room, Megan wrapped herself in her worn, soft blanket and nestled against her favorite pillow—the one that still faintly smelled like lavender detergent. The dim room felt safer than the rest of the house, safer than the whole town, really. She pulled out her phone, the small glow cutting through the quiet like a lifeline. Her fingers trembled as she typed.

I don't think the sheriff is involved, she wrote.

She hit send before she could overthink it, then leaned back against the wall, chewing her lower lip, heart thudding in her throat.

A buzz.

Aiden: Why not? You okay?

His messages were blunt, but she could feel the worry pulsing between the words. She sucked in a breath, trying to steady the fog of tension that wrapped around her like an extra blanket she didn't want.

He seemed genuinely concerned about me, she typed. I know it sounds weird, but I think he cares about this town. And he said they're actually investigating the disappearances.

Another buzz.

Aiden: I don't trust him yet. Something's off. Might be an act. Just be careful, alright?

His protective edge lit a quiet heat in her chest—comforting, grounding—but she still felt the hollow ache of not having answers.

She typed, I want to attend the town hall meeting later this week.

Before she could second-guess it, a gust of wind moaned outside her window. Leaves scraped across the siding, branches rattled against one another, and the whole world seemed to pause—an uneasy breath held in anticipation of something unseen.

A knock startled her.

Lily peeked inside, worry shadowing her face. "You have a minute, kiddo?"

Megan nodded, though her pulse still raced from the jump scare.

Her mother stepped in, shutting the door behind her with a soft click. "Between us... is there anything you didn't tell the sheriff?"

The question hung between them like fog. Megan searched her mother's face, then forced her voice steady. "No, Mom. We just talked about life. Charlie mentioned his family, nothing else."

Lily's brow arched, unconvinced. "Then why didn't you mention the missing people you've been researching with the sheriff? You think it's important, don't you?"

A surge of frustration cracked through Megan's chest—hot, fast, tinged with guilt. "Because it didn't feel relevant. And he was focused on Charlie—on what happened. I didn't want to dive into random theories while he was worried about... all of that."

Lily exhaled slowly, massaging her temples. "This isn't some rumor mill, honey. These are real people. Missing people. You might know something without realizing it. Please... just be careful about what you tell people—and what you hide."

Megan nodded, the weight of her mother's concern settling over her. "I know. I'll be more careful. I just... want the truth before I say something stupid."

"Good." Lily pulled her into a quick hug. "You're not in this alone. I'm here. Always." She moved toward the door. "Dinner's in the microwave when you're ready."

When her mother left, Megan felt both lighter and more suffocated. Comfort and pressure tangled in her chest like two hands pulling in opposite directions. She stared out the window, into the dark that pressed tight against the glass.

"What are you hiding?" she whispered to the night, uneasy.

After several days away from school time she technically needed, though the memories still stalked her like shadows clinging to her ankles. Yet today felt different. Less crushing. More bearable.

Today was the town hall meeting.

With her mother's reluctant blessing, she met Aiden at the entrance of the old brick building in the town center. Anxiety hummed in the air like static electricity. Residents crowded together—neighbors, teachers, classmates—faces marked by confusion, fear, and curiosity.

Inside, Sheriff Jenkins stood directing people toward seats and open wall space. At the front of the room stood Reverend Goodwin, brows drawn in solemn concern; beside him, the retired Sheriff Jenkins Sr., arms folded; and Mayor Thompson, looking wrung-out but resolute. They looked like a trio set to brace against a storm steadily sweeping toward them.

"Thank you all for coming," Reverend Goodwin began, voice steady but shadowed with worry. "We're here to discuss the tragic events surrounding Charlie's breakdown and the… attack that followed. We must come together to understand, and to prevent anything like it in the future."

Megan exchanged a look with Aiden. His hand brushed hers —steady, grounding. She squeezed back.

A ripple of whispers cut through the room.

"Why did he do it?" Mrs. Henderson cried out, her voice cracking.

Tom—who grew up with Charlie—spoke next, his face pale. "We thought he was just struggling. No one thought he'd… snap. It was like he changed overnight."

Sheriff Jenkins stepped forward, raising his palms to calm the rising anxiety. "We're working to understand what led to this. Mental health matters—we can't ignore the signs."

He paused, glancing toward a sobbing woman in the front row.

"Charlie's family has allowed us to share a significant discovery from the autopsy."

Gasps and murmurs broke out.

"Calm down," he urged. "Listen, please."

He continued, "The medical examiner found a two-inch cut on Charlie's abdomen. Severely infected. Doctors believe the infection may have contributed to his delirium and violent behavior."

A cold shiver ran through Megan's chest. She could still picture Charlie's haunted eyes. It wasn't him, she thought. Not the real him.

"This makes sense," she whispered to Aiden. "He wasn't himself at all."

Mayor Thompson stepped toward the crowd. "This discovery reminds us we must take mental health seriously. Charlie struggled, yes, but in recent days he deteriorated— talking to himself, wandering near the forest, even slipping through a hole in the fence."

A wave of unease rippled across the room.

The forest—again.

"We may never fully understand what happened," the mayor pressed on. "But our community must talk openly about mental health and support each other."

For a moment, the room seemed unified—fear binding them, hope struggling to rise.

Then Mrs. Martinez, usually so composed, stood with trembling hands. "Isn't it too late for that? How can we believe things will be different now? What if… what if this happens again?"

Her voice broke on the last word, and the whole room went silent—hollow, brittle—waiting for an answer no one seemed prepared to give.

The moment the crowd's attention snapped toward Megan, a cold whisper curled through her mind—they will all turn against you. Their collective gaze felt like a noose tightening, and as the overhead lights flickered, the town hall seemed to darken in a single breath. "She knows what happened to Charlie, don't you, witch!" someone shouted, the accusation ripping through the air like a serrated blade. Reverend Goodwin's voice followed, slithering across the room. "Yesssss… she is infecting our town." His grin stretched unnaturally wide, the teeth—razor-lined and glistening—catching the dim light, while his eyes hollowed into black pits that reflected nothing but malice, thickening the air with a suffocating dread.

As his words poured over the crowd, their faces warped into a grotesque mask of fury, fear, and something feral—an ancient instinct demanding blood. They surged forward as if animated by a single monstrous will. "She did this to Charlie!" a man screamed, spit flying as his features twisted into something barely human. "She brought this evil upon us!" another shouted, fingers trembling as they pointed at her like they could burn her alive with blame alone. "Purify the witch!" the room roared, their voices bleeding together into a fevered chant that echoed like a death knell against the wooden rafters.

Panic clamped around Megan's throat. The mob blurred into a wall of snarling mouths and bulging veins; their hatred was thick enough to taste—metallic and suffocating. Sweat slicked their foreheads as their rage frothed into violence, the Reverend towering in front of them like a puppeteer reveling in the chaos. His grin widened further, impossibly wide, feeding off the frenzy until it felt like the floor itself trembled beneath Megan's feet.

A rope snaked around her neck before she registered the movement, tightening with every frantic jerk as she clawed at it. She gasped, each breath thinner than the last, her heartbeat thundering in her ears as she kicked and thrashed. Her screams tore through the hall while hands hoisted her toward the rafters, the Reverend's laughter pealing through the darkness—high, cold, and delighted. The room vanished into shadow, the hatred pressing against her like a physical weight, the rope biting deeper as she fought for air.

A hand squeezed hers—warm, human, real. Aiden's. The vision snapped apart like shattered glass. The crowd, the rope, the darkness—all gone. Megan blinked, trembling back into the soft hum of the town hall's fluorescent lights. Aiden leaned closer, whispering, "Hey… you're pale. You okay?"

She stood abruptly, throat tight. "I need air." The words stumbled out as she pushed outside into the cool night, the chill brushing her skin like ghost fingers. Instinctively, she reached for her neck, half-expecting bruises, half-expecting the rope to still be there. The phantom chants echoed in her mind—They will all turn on you—a malignant lullaby that refused to fade.

Inside, Reverend Goodwin's voice droned on, distant and hollow. "On Sunday following the seminar, I will be available for discussion. I will be working with the sheriff to help maintain peace and order." The crowd murmured, weighing the implications, their whispers stretching thin across the room.

As the meeting ended, neighbors filed out in uneasy clusters, their conversations buzzing with worry and thin hope. Aiden stepped outside and immediately spotted Megan by the entrance. She didn't wait for the question. "Sorry... all the talk about Charlie was too much. I needed air." Her gaze drifted across familiar faces that suddenly felt unfamiliar.

"I get it," Aiden said, concern edging his voice. "Honestly, the meeting felt useless. Too many conflicting explanations— alcohol, injury, stress? Feels like a giant cover-up."

Megan nodded, his frustration mirroring her own spiraling unease. Fear, sadness, and a tremor of determination churned within her. She caught sight of Mrs. Henderson speaking passionately to a cluster of parents. "If we don't talk about this, how will we help our kids?" she argued. Aiden nudged Megan lightly. "At least people are talking. Better than nothing."

"Maybe," Megan said, though the whisper still lingered— They will all turn on you—poisoning every sliver of hope. "But talking isn't enough. We need action, not just panic and meetings."

As the last of the townsfolk drifted toward their cars, Megan and Aiden spotted Mayor Thompson near the entrance, greeting families with the ease of a man who'd worn his smile for decades. Aiden leaned close, whispering, "This is our chance. Let's get something out of him." Together, they moved through the currents of fear rippling through the crowd, carrying with them the dark legacy of the town's witch-trial past.

"Just like back then," Aiden murmured, "fear ruined innocent lives. We can't let that happen again—not with Charlie, not now."

Megan nodded, her pulse quickening. "Exactly. If we don't learn from those witch hunts, we'll make the same mistakes. We need truth, not another mob chasing shadows."

With fear and determination tightening her chest, Megan stepped forward and greeted the mayor. "Mayor Thompson, it's an honor to meet you," she blurted, the words tumbling out before she could steady herself.

"Hello, Megan," he said warmly. "We heard what you witnessed. How are you holding up?"

She drew in a breath, grounding herself. "It's been a lot. My mom kept me home for a few days, and at first I was annoyed, but… it gave me time to think. I've been reading about the town's history—the witch trials, the fear that spiraled into tragedy. It feels important now, especially with the rumors about missing teens and everything that happened with Charlie. I'm starting to understand the weight this town is carrying."

A shadow flickered across the mayor's face before he smoothed it away. "Missing teenagers? I haven't heard any such rumors," he said, clearing his throat. "But yes, every town's past has faced some dark days. We've done our best to move past them. Just look—we're thriving, wouldn't you say?" He gestured toward the dispersing crowd as if they were evidence of success.

Aiden stepped in smoothly, his tone respectful yet probing. "Yes, it appears that we are thriving, sir, and I admire what you've accomplished. I'm aiming for a career in politics myself one day, and I'd love to know what lessons you believe we must carry forward. What issues still need addressing to keep Glory moving in the right direction? What can we do to help?"

The mayor's smile sharpened, self-satisfied. "Ah, youthful ambition. It's refreshing." He paused, folding his hands. "The greatest lesson is simple: division and misinformation nearly destroyed this town once. Those days taught us the value of unity—and of trusting strong leadership to guide us through fear."

Mayor Thompson straightened, his chest lifting with the pride of a man who believed he'd earned every inch of his authority. "As for current issues," he continued, "while we've made significant strides, there are still challenges we must address—economic revitalization, improving public safety, and fostering deeper community engagement. These areas are where the next generation, like you, can make a true impact." His eyes fixed on Aiden, gleaming with something between encouragement and ambition. "If you want to accomplish what I have, immerse yourself. Attend meetings like this. Volunteer. Build your network. It's how you position yourself as a leader in Glory."

He paused, letting the weight of his own story hang in the air. "Remember, desire isn't enough. Change requires dedication, perseverance, sacrifice, and a clear vision. If you're willing to put in the work, the rewards will come."

Megan leaned in slightly, her gaze attentive, her tone softened with a practiced sincerity that invited honesty. "It seems you—and generations before you—have had a lot of success tackling those challenges," she said. "I'm sure not everything in our past was negative. What do you think are the most important historical actions we still follow today? And how have they evolved to keep the town successful?"

The question pleased him. His smile stretched, slow and deliberate, as if he were choosing which truths to reveal and which to leave buried.

"Ah. A strong inquiry," he said. "The most important lessons we carry are born from endurance and cohesion. There were times in our history when survival wasn't guaranteed—when standing alone meant vanishing. We learned, painfully, that we endure only when we stand together. We listen to every voice, we close ranks when necessary, and we confront threats directly, without hesitation. That understanding is the spine of Glory. It always has been."

He paused, allowing the weight of that statement to settle before continuing, his voice lowering just enough to suggest confession rather than pride.

"And as a community shaped by faith," he went on, "we've never forgotten the old ways of seeking guidance—prayer, ritual, shared sacrifice. Compassion and forgiveness guide us publicly, yes, but beneath that lies something older. A recognition that belief binds people more tightly than law ever could. Our past taught us that unity must sometimes be... enforced, for the greater good." His eyes flicked briefly toward the Reverend. "We are fortunate to be led by a man who understands that responsibility—and who would do anything necessary to protect this town."

The smile returned, measured now, practiced.

"The practices we uphold today aren't relics," he said. "They're the framework that keeps us growing, keeps us safe. They remind us that while we cannot undo what was done before us, we can ensure it was not done in vain. When something threatens the health, the progress, or the future of Glory, we do not hesitate. We come together, as we always have, and we stop it—quietly, efficiently, and as one."

He folded his hands. "That's why I've pushed for greater mental health awareness. It helps us recognize instability early. It allows us to guide people back into alignment before they hurt themselves—or the town. Protection doesn't always look kind in the moment, but it ensures that Glory continues to grow, untouched by forces that would see it rot from the inside."

Megan felt a flicker of accomplishment spark inside her. Beneath his polished phrasing were truths she and Aiden needed—insights confirming the deep entanglement of faith, town history, and collective responsibility. "Thank you, Mayor. Your guidance means a lot," she said. "It's inspiring to see how far Glory has come. We want to help it keep moving forward."

They exchanged parting nods before walking away, an unspoken understanding simmering between them. What they had gathered was valuable—but there were currents beneath the mayor's words, deeper and darker truths woven into his emphasis on unity, sacrifice, and the reverend's unwavering influence. It created a sense of urgency that crawled under Megan's skin.

As they stepped out into the fading daylight, the sky erupted in fiery reds and deep oranges, casting an eerie glow over the lake. The water mirrored the sky, reflecting it in shimmering streaks that looked too intense, almost violent. Shadows stretched wide across the landscape, long fingers creeping over the ground as if reaching toward them.

"That was… a lot," Aiden said finally, breaking the silence. "I don't even know what to think."

Megan brushed a strand of windblown hair from her face. "I know. But did you notice how uncomfortable he got when I brought up the missing teens?" Her voice dropped. "And the Reverend doing 'anything' for the community? Does that include sacrifice? Human sacrifice?" She held Aiden's gaze, her words heavy with implication. "And when he talked about unity and faith and sacrifice—didn't it feel like he was admitting something? Like the town's guilt is collective? But who exactly is part of that 'everyone'?"

The question lingered between them, charged and unsettling.

By the time Megan made it home, relief and unease braided themselves tightly in her chest. Aiden gave her a reassuring smile before heading off. "We'll figure this out," he said gently. "We always do." His confidence steadied her—but only for a moment.

Back in her room, Megan slid beneath her blankets, though the warmth did little to quiet her thoughts. The twisted image of the reverend from her vision clawed it's way back into her mind—the needle teeth, the hollow eyes, the way the crowd had turned on her without hesitation. Their faces had warped with the same rage and fear that had once fueled the witch trials. *Is this what the victims felt back then?* she wondered, a chill crawling over her as she imagined the terror of being wrongly condemned.

She stared at the ceiling as questions piled in her mind like stones. Beneath the town's celebrated unity and its carefully maintained image lay deeper fractures—secrets festering, truths buried. She could feel them now, lurking beneath every friendly smile, every prayer, every perfectly rehearsed speech.

Her eyelids grew heavy. Her breaths slowed. As she drifted toward sleep, one final thought tightened around her like a thread pulled taut:

The next meeting might not just reveal what was wrong with the town—it might reveal what was waiting for her.

Chapter 9:

Threads of Fate

The night split open with a roar of thunder, violent and relentless, each rumble rolling across the sky like a warning meant for her alone. Lightning ripped through the clouds in jagged veins, illuminating a sky that looked charred and burning from the inside out. The world flickered between darkness and a hellish glow, as if the heavens themselves were on fire.

Megan stood frozen, breath snagging in her throat, as the impossible unfolded above her.

From the swirling, storm-torn sky, thousands of missing person posters and torn pamphlets came pouring down—spiraling, tumbling, screaming silently through the air like lost souls finally breaking through the veil.

They smacked into muddy puddles with soft, sickening slaps. Ink bled and ran, staining the water black, turning the reflections into grotesque smears of faces she almost recognized. The posters writhed in the puddles as if something beneath the surface pulsed. The once-human features twisted: eyes collapsing into black pits, mouths stretching wide in soundless agony.

Then the whispers started.

Soft at first—then growing, multiplying, overlapping until the storm itself seemed to breathe them.

Help me.

Please… help me.

The chorus clawed at the inside of her skull, worming through her thoughts until she could barely hear her own heartbeat.

Megan squeezed her eyes shut, but the screams followed her inward. When she opened them again, the world around her had shifted.

She was standing in the ruins of Glory.

The remains of the town spread before her in a skeletal sprawl—burned-out buildings hunched against the storm like broken tombstones. Shattered windows gaped like empty eye sockets. Doors hung crookedly, swaying in the wind, groaning in protest. Dark figures drifted across the cracked stone streets— shadows that seemed to breathe, to watch, to wait.

A chill crept across her shoulders, raising the hair along her arms. It felt like the past itself was muttering at the edges of her vision, desperate to be remembered.

A low murmur tugged her attention toward the back of the decaying church.

A group of townsfolk stood clustered together, their movements slow and wrong—jerking and shuffling, as though their limbs were guided by strings. Their faces were sickly pale, stretched tight over their bones, eyes dull and hungry. They looked half-dead.

Half-returned.

Fear squeezed Megan's heart, but curiosity—dark and uncontrollable—pulled her forward.

As she stepped closer, she saw the small figure at the center of the crowd.

A little girl. Ten, maybe younger. Her eyes were wide with terror, lips trembling in a silent plea. The townsfolk closed in around her like predators.

The reverend emerged from behind them, towering, his face swallowed in shadow. His skin looked carved from stone, his movements deliberate and cruel. When he reached for the girl, Megan's stomach lurched. His hand was rough, massive, swallowing her delicate wrist. With a dull, rusted blade, he sliced into her skin.

"Come now, child," he growled, his voice a guttural vibration that scraped against her nerves. "The forest awaits your sacrifice."

"No!" Megan's scream tore out of her, raw and shaking. "Let her go!"

The reverend turned his head toward her slowly—not normally. Not naturally. His head swung toward her in a snapping arc, his neck bending like wet paper.

His eyes caught the lightning, flashing like sharp, fractured glass. Madness blazed within them, a madness so cold it froze the breath in her lungs.

Then his mouth began to open—and open—and open—far beyond anything human. Bones cracked. Flesh stretched then peeled away as a wet popping sound echoed in the air.

The shriek that erupted from him was inhuman—high, piercing, a banshee wail that sliced through the storm and straight into her skull. Megan dropped, palms clamped over her ears, tears springing to her eyes as the sound gouged at her mind.

She tried to move. She couldn't.

The scream pinned her to the earth.

The girl stumbled forward, reaching toward Megan with a trembling hand.

"Please!" she cried, her voice breaking through the storm like a shard of glass.

But before Megan could rise, the townsfolk shoved the child into the waiting darkness of the forest. The trees swallowed her whole. A deafening roar rose from the woods—furious, ancient, hungry.

The townsfolk froze.

Even the reverend's bravado cracked; his face twisted into horror as he staggered backward, retreating from whatever stirred within the treeline.

The world spun.

The ground tilted sideways.

Colors bled and melted as the scene dissolved into a swirl of motion—time jerking forward like a broken film reel.

Suddenly, another child appeared—an eight-year-old boy this time—dragged forward by a trembling adult. The knife flashed. The forest swallowed him, too, and his scream lodged itself in Megan's bones, vibrating through her like a live wire. Another child was dragged forward—screaming—then hurled into the waiting dark, and another after that, and another, a sickening procession of small bodies offered up without mercy. Dozens of them—dragged, shoved, offered, consumed—their cries folding into the trees until the forest itself seemed to breathe in their terror.

The townsfolk grew healthier with each offering—skin filling out, eyes brightening, their bodies straightening as if drinking vitality straight from the sacrifices. Glory rebuilt itself in fast-forward—the ruins stitching back together, burned beams regrowing fresh wood, flowers blooming where ashes had fallen.

It was too much.

Far too much.

Static clouded her vision, buzzing violently behind her eyes. She squeezed them shut, desperate to shut out the nightmare. When she opened them, the scene had paused mid-motion.

A figure broke from the stillness.

Amber.

Not the bright, smiling girl from the missing posters—but a blood-soaked version of her. Her hands dripped crimson, the blade in her grip slick and gleaming. Her eyes were wide, frantic, holding the weight of something indescribably terrible.

She stepped toward the forest, trembling. Each movement looked agonizing, as though invisible hands tugged at her bones. The darkness beyond the trees pulsed in slow, hungry breaths, a living thing waiting for her to cross its threshold. Amber reached the tree line, the tips of the branches arching toward her like skeletal fingers eager to claim their offering.

For a moment, she stood perfectly still—caught between the dying light and the suffocating black.

Then she turned. Her gaze snapped to Megan with a precision that felt deliberate, unnatural.

Megan froze, breath stalling in her throat as the world around them fell into a suffocating silence. Even the storm seemed to retreat, the thunder stuttering into a distant echo as if afraid to interrupt the exchange.

Amber's eyes—once bright and full of life—were hollowed out, ringed in shadow, yet burning with a desperate awareness. They shimmered with the kind of terror that had no words, the kind that burrows under the skin and lives there.

Her lips parted, trembling.

Her chest heaved with thin, shaky breaths.

Blood dripped steadily from her fingertips, trailing down the blade she clutched as though it were the only thing keeping her tethered to the world.

Megan felt the ground tilt beneath her, nausea twisting in her gut.

Amber lifted her chin just enough that the weak, flickering light caught her face. It revealed a girl caught in two places at once—one part sacrificed, one part fighting to crawl back into the world of the living.

Her mouth moved slowly, shaping silent words.

Megan... help me.

The plea wasn't spoken, yet Megan felt it inside her—like a cold hand closing around her heart. The air thickened, pressing against her skin until her knees threatened to buckle. The forest behind Amber seemed to lean forward, swallowing the space around her, eager to drag her in.

Amber's expression contorted—fear, pain, resignation, and fury—then settled into something darker... a warning.

As if she wasn't just begging Megan to save her—she was begging her to run.

Static roared in her ears, a harsh, electric shriek that scraped along her skull and smothered every coherent thought. The world wavered at the edges, colors bleeding into one another like melting paint.

"Megan!" a voice cried behind her—urgent, familiar, the voice of the woman who had haunted her earlier dreams, sharp enough to crack through the storm rattling inside her mind.

Megan couldn't turn; she couldn't even breathe. Her legs felt fused to the earth, swallowed by the nightmare itself as cold pulses of fear surged through her, hollowing her chest and numbing her limbs. What happened to Amber? What were those people? What kind of monster is the reverend? The questions spun in a frantic, tightening loop until her lungs seized, and all around her the darkness seemed to lean closer—pressing in, tasting the air, watching her with a patience that felt predatory and impossibly aware.

"Please, we have to help her!" Megan cried, whipping her gaze back to the woman frozen in place. Terror stretched the woman's eyes wide, her face drained to a corpse-gray pallor. Her lips trembled, as if she were trying to hold back a scream—or something else was forcing its way out. Her fear didn't just show; it radiated, a cold pressure that sank straight into Megan's ribs and tightened like a fist around her heart.

"We can't save her. You don't—" The woman's voice cracked into a desperate whisper as she seized Megan's arm. Her fingers were icy, brittle as bone, clutching her with a dead woman's strength. "Whatever is out there… it wants you too. Save the girl, or save yourself!"

Megan tried to wrench free, panic igniting like sparks beneath her skin. "Let go!" she shouted, but the woman's grip only constricted, compressing her arm until a numb, sick ache pulsed through her. Then the air warped around them—an audible crack, like snapping joints—and the woman's form rippled, spine twisting in a way no living body could endure.

She didn't let go.

She transformed.

Her face collapsed inward, features melting like wax dragged over embers. Rotted-black fabric bled across her skin until the shape standing before Megan was tall, crooked, and unmistakably wrong. The reverend—what remained of him—stood where the woman had been, his body stretched into a grotesque parody of a man. Shadows clung to him like wet tar.

Without notice something sharp and heavy slammed into her abdomen, knocking the air from her lungs. Megan flew backward, smacking the ground hard enough to rattle her teeth. Cold mud splashed against her face, thick and icy, sliding into her ears.

Before she could gather breath enough to scream, the creature dropped onto her, pinning her to the earth. Its weight was suffocating, crushing her ribs, draining the strength from her limbs. The ground beneath her softened—then gave way— mud swallowing her inch by inch like a hungry mouth.

The creature's face hovered inches from hers, its breath hot and rancid, curling down her throat as it hissed, "We got you now."

Lightning tore open the sky, flashing white through the storm. And then everything collapsed into darkness—thick, final, absolute. Megan's scream vanished inside it.

She jolted awake with a strangled gasp, sitting bolt upright in her bed. Her heart hammered painfully against her ribs, each beat a frantic reminder she was still alive. The familiar outlines of her bedroom swam into view, but the nightmare clung to her skin like damp soil. She gagged and lurched for her trash can, retching until her stomach cramped. The taste of mud lingered —grainy, earthy, wrong—coating the back of her tongue.

Just a dream, she told herself, trembling. But dreams didn't usually leave a taste.

Morning light seeped faintly through the curtains, but it did nothing to ease the dread curling tight in her chest. Images lingered like after-burn: the screaming children, Amber's terrified eyes, the town twisted beyond recognition, and that thing—that version of the reverend—bearing down on her.

Hands still shaking, she grabbed her laptop. If these nightmares were trying to tell her something, she needed to put every detail down before they slipped away. She began typing, fingers trembling with adrenaline, each keystroke punctuated by the echo of that last warning: Save the girl or save yourself.

She wrote about the reverend's warped shape, the children and teenagers sacrificed like lambs, their faces locked in terror. She wrote about the sensation of dying—the mud swallowing her, the weight crushing her breaths flat. Every detail felt like a shard of something bigger, something she was finally starting to uncover.

When she finished, Megan leaned back, chest tight, fingers hovering above the keys. The nightmare replayed in her mind, sharper than any previous dream. That warning—*Save the girl or save yourself*—lodged beneath her rib cage like a splinter.

What was she supposed to choose? The questions pressed against her skull like fingers, cold and insistent. *What kind of girl needed saving—a victim, a witness, or someone already marked by the darkness? And what would it cost her?* The thought slithered through her mind, leaving a chill in its wake, because some prices weren't paid in blood or fear—they were paid in pieces of yourself you could never get back.

She got up, pacing the small room. The girl's face—pale, terrified—flashed in her mind. The reverend's distorted scream followed. Megan wrapped her arms around herself, trying to steady her breath. The memory of those cold, crushing hands burrowed under her skin.

"I can't just sit here," she whispered, voice cracking under the weight of everything clawing at her. "I can't do nothing." The fear twisting in her stomach slowly hardened into something sharper, a trembling but undeniable resolve.

She snatched up her phone with shaking hands and typed a message to Aiden: *Another nightmare. Worse than before. I need to see Sister Abigail tonight.*

Her pulse thudded in her throat as she waited, the silence stretching thin—until his reply blinked onto the screen: *Will you be in school?*

Megan exhaled shakily, her fingers barely steady enough to respond: *No. Mom says I can go back Monday. She says I need another day.* She hit send and wiped her palms on her blanket, nerves sparking beneath her skin.

His answer came quickly: *Okay. I'll meet you after school and chores.* Relief flickered through her—small, fragile, gone almost as soon as it appeared.

She hesitated, watching the cursor blink like a pulse, then typed: *Can we meet at my house? I need privacy.*

Another beat, then: *Sounds good.* The words offered comfort, but it was thin—like trying to shelter behind paper in a storm.

For a moment, hope and dread tangled in her chest. Maybe together, they could figure out what these dreams were— warnings, memories, something worse. But time felt slippery, thinning like the last seconds before a storm breaks.

She stared out the window. The wind stirred the leaves, whispering against the glass. Something dark hummed at the edge of her awareness—something patient. Watching.

Hours blurred. A sudden knock yanked her from her thoughts. Heart pounding, she rushed to the door. Aiden stood there, worry etched across his face.

"Hey... how bad was it?" he asked.

Megan led him to the kitchen table, turning her laptop toward him. "Just read."

As he scanned the screen, the color drained from his face. His brows knotted, his mouth tightening with every line. "Megan..." His voice cracked. "I—I don't know what to say. Something's seriously wrong. These aren't normal nightmares."

"Are they memories?" she asked, barely breathing. "Could they be connected to the disappearances?" Saying it out loud made her feel unhinged.

Aiden opened his mouth… then closed it. Fear flickered across his face—raw and unguarded.

Megan threw her hands up, pacing. "These dreams are making me crazy! I feel trapped inside something I can't wake up from."

"What if you're not supposed to do anything?" Aiden said softly. "The woman said, 'Save the girl or save yourself.'"

"So you think I should do nothing?" Megan snapped, anxiety twisting tight. "I could never live with myself."

"You might not have to worry about living with yourself." He tried to joke, but his voice shook. "Stubborn as you are… what's our next move?"

Megan steadied herself, pushing through the fog clouding her mind. "Abigail. She's the only one who might understand."

Aiden nodded slowly. "Mrs. Langley said she lives in a cottage near the forest. Behind the church, I think."

Megan didn't wait. She grabbed her coat and headed for the door. "We need to go before dark. Are you coming?"

Aiden managed a weak grin. "And let you walk into danger alone? Not a chance."

By the time they reached the valley behind the church, dusk had slipped over everything like a heavy shroud. The last streaks of sunlight bled out behind the hills, turning the sky a bruised violet. Shadows stretched long and skeletal across the sloping grass, which was only now waking from winter's chokehold—patches of green poking through the frost-bitten earth like timid survivors.

A narrow dirt road wound through the valley like a forgotten ribbon, curling past gnarled trees that leaned inward, their branches twisted like arthritic fingers. In the distance, a cottage materialized through the thickening gloom—small, crooked, and half-swallowed by shadow. Smoke drifted lazily from its chimney, rising into the twilight with a ghostly expansion that made the entire valley seem to hold its breath. A damp chill clung to the air, carrying the scent of thawing earth and something older beneath it, something that felt... watched.

Wind tore through the trees as Megan and Aiden trudged down the dirt path, their footsteps muted in the softening ground. Every rustle seemed to come from just beyond the edge of the clearing. Every shape in the forest seemed to lean closer, as if listening.

"Just... don't pay attention to the trees," Aiden muttered, though his voice trembled. "Mrs. Langley said Sister Abigail knows more about the church than anyone."

Megan rubbed her arms, fighting the creeping sensation that something was threading its way between the trees, pacing them. "What if she refuses to talk? What if she knows something that puts us in even more danger?"

Aiden stepped closer, determination flashing through his unease. "We need answers. Abigail is our best chance. Turning back isn't an option."

Megan swallowed hard, nodding. "Almost there. But Mrs. Langley said she's… unstable." She hesitated. "I don't think this is going to end well."

The last of the day's light died as they approached the cottage. Darkness rolled in quickly, swallowing the landscape whole. A faint flicker glowed inside the window—candlelight dancing in jittery spasms. Smoke curled from the chimney, warm and rich with firewood and something faintly herbal, drifting into the cold night air.

Megan stepped onto the creaking porch and knocked on the weathered door. "Miss Abigail?" she called, though tension squeezed her voice tight.

A voice rasped from inside, sharp as tearing fabric: "WHO'S THERE?"

Aiden inhaled shakily. "It's Aiden and Megan," he said. "We need to speak with you."

"GO AWAY!" Sister Abigail snapped, her voice cracking like a whip.

Megan's pulse spiked. "Please," she insisted, forcing the words out. "Something feels wrong in town. We think the church is involved. Five minutes. Then we'll go."

A long silence followed—thick and pulsing—before the door creaked open on its own, revealing only a sliver of blackness. Candles flickered inside, casting warped shadows across an elderly woman's face.

"The church," Sister Abigail murmured, her tone shifting. Her lined features softened slightly in the candle glow. "A delicate subject in this place. Too many prefer to forget." She peered out into the dark, scanning the trees as if expecting something to be right behind them. "Come in. Quickly now."

She pulled them inside and shut the door fast, her hands trembling.

Inside, the cottage was cramped and dim, lit only by candles and the glow of a low fire. Sister Abigail hurried to gather dusty pillows—filthy things that looked dragged from a basement or worse—and tossed them around a small table.

"Explain," she said, settling into her creaking chair. "Tell me what you think is abnormal."

Aiden motioned for Megan to speak.

"We looked into Glory's history," Megan began. "We found… concerning documents at the library."

Abigail stared at her unblinking, as if peeling every layer off the girl with her gaze. "Go on."

"We found parish declarations, legal records, even old pamphlets," Megan continued. "Some of them hinted that Glory took part in witch trials. Everything public says exile was the punishment—but a university professor hinted it was much worse." Her voice dropped. "Have you seen anything strange?"

"Strange?" Abigail leaned forward, her eyes narrowing with a knowing glint. "You mean the phantoms in the trees? The screams that wander the forest at night?" The air seemed to tighten around them as she spoke. "This land is old. The things that live in the woods are older. Spirits, demons, witches…

whatever they are, they protect what's theirs. Leave them be, and perhaps"—she paused—"they'll leave you be."

She reached for a fire poker and stirred the flames. Sparks spat upward, casting frantic shadows across her lined face.

"You're right that something isn't right with the church," Abigail continued. "But you know only the surface. Glory was built on suffering—on accusations, fear, and blood. The church hunted anyone who didn't conform. They say the wronged souls never left." Her gaze drifted far away, as if hearing echoes only she could perceive. "Many believe justice still calls from these woods."

Megan's heart thudded painfully. "What do you mean? What's happening in Glory?"

Abigail sighed—a long, exhausted exhale that felt like it carried decades of pain. "This land remembers. Pain lingers here like rot under the soil."

Aiden shifted uneasily. "And the disappearances? Are they connected?"

Abigail nodded once, sharply. "Of course. Some in town think offering their innocents keeps the darkness calm." She looked toward the fire again, her voice dropping. "I've seen children led into the forest for church rituals. I want no part of it."

Megan tensed. "I can't ignore that. If I do, these dreams—"

She stopped herself, heart thudding.

Sister Abigail's head snapped toward her. "Dreams?"

Megan froze.

"Let me see your hands," Abigail said.

Reluctantly, Megan extended them. Abigail traced the lines with a cold, gentle finger, studying every crease.

"You're sensitive," the old woman said softly. "You feel the emotions of the living… and the unrest of the dead. Pain clings to you. It leaks into your dreams." Her voice narrowed into something solemn. "You haven't been sleeping well, have you?"

Megan's heart plummeted as she glanced at Aiden. A cold wave of anxiety surged over her, flooding every corner of her chest. How did she know? The question spiraled through her mind, tightening like a steel band around her ribs.

"No," she admitted, her voice thin and trembling. "I've been having… dreams. Except they're not dreams. They're nightmares and visions—horrible ones—and they won't stop even when I'm awake. It feels like they're trying to tell me something, but I can't make sense of it."

A shadow of concern passed over Abigail's lined face, but her calm never wavered. "I saw it immediately," she said, tone soft but unsettlingly certain. "You are special, my dear." Her eyes glimmered with knowing warmth, the kind that made Megan's skin crawl. "Your dreams are so vivid because they're reflecting this town's buried horrors."

A sick twist rolled through Megan's stomach. "So my nightmares are visions of… things that have happened?" Her voice cracked. "But why now? Why me?" She searched Abigail's expression, desperate for an answer that didn't terrify her.

Abigail leaned forward, palms pressing into her knees, giving her words the weight of something ancient. "Technically, yes. But you must tread carefully. Visions are never neutral—they're shaped by the storyteller. And storytellers, living or otherwise, are unreliable."

The fire crackled sharply behind her, casting strained shadows against the walls. Abigail's eyes drifted toward the flames, as though drawing warmth—or courage—from them. "There are forces protecting this land. Powerful ones. But if you let them, they will warp your judgment. Manipulate your choices. The truth you're seeking hides deep in the shadows. If you stumble blindly into it, you may provoke a wrath you are not prepared to face."

Aiden stiffened beside Megan, the tension in the room coiling around all three of them. Abigail continued, her tone strangely tender:

"A gifted young woman like you, feels everything amplified. When there is unrest—fear, anger, or grief—you absorb it. And this valley has plenty of those unsettling feelings. More than you realize." Her gaze sharpened. "It's likely tied to the disappearances you mentioned."

Aiden swallowed hard. "So what does that mean for her? Can she stop it?"

Abigail turned to him slowly, her gaze shimmering with hard-earned wisdom. "She can protect herself, yes. But only if she learns to anchor her mind. Without clarity, the nightmares will keep bleeding into her waking world."

A spark of hope flickered through Megan's chest, faint but stubborn. "Is there a way to do that? To actually stop them?"

"Yes, my dear," Abigail said gently. "With practice, you can shut out the noise."

Megan leaned forward. "What do I do?"

Abigail rubbed her chin, thinking. "Are there places where you feel safe? Energized?"

Megan hesitated—then nodded. "My nook. In my room. It's by the window… pillows everywhere. That's where I write."

A small, almost relieved smile touched Abigail's lips. "Good. Claim that space. Make it sacred. Shut out any energy that isn't yours. Once you build that boundary, you'll start hearing your own emotions instead of everyone else's."

The warmth in her tone quickly cooled.

"But remember—when you peel back the layers, the shadows thicken. To move forward, you must face the nightmares. All of them. And trust each other, because the path ahead won't be walked alone."

Megan nodded slowly. Determination simmered beneath her dread. Outside the window, night had settled over the valley like a suffocating veil.

She and Aiden walked home along the dirt path, swallowed by the pitch-black stretch of trees crowding the trail. The forest loomed on either side—massive trunks rising like pillars, branches twisting overhead in a tangled, skeletal canopy. Shadows crawled across the underbrush, reaching long, fingerlike shapes that seemed to stir as they passed.

Every sound felt amplified: the crunch of gravel underfoot, the rustle of unseen movement in the leaves, the faint snap of a distant twig. The woods felt awake. Aware. Watching.

"Do you hear that?" Aiden whispered.

Megan couldn't even nod—her breath caught halfway up her throat. Something in the forest was shifting, pacing them. She felt it, deep under her skin, like a pressure building behind her eyes. The whisper of leaves. The hush of something large keeping rhythm with their steps.

"Just keep moving," she managed. "We're almost home."

She tried to anchor herself in the thought of her nook—the soft pillows, the blanket that smelled faintly of fabric softener, the small lamp that cast everything in a warm, honeyed glow. She clung to that image like a life raft, forcing herself to picture sinking into it, wrapped in comfort, safe.

But the woods didn't release them easily. Shadows flickered at the edges of her vision, dancing shapes that retreated the moment she turned her head. The air thrummed with an unnatural tension, as though something hidden held its breath, waiting.

By the time the faint outlines of their homes emerged, Megan felt wrung out. When they finally stepped into the thin safety of the porch lights, it felt like breaching the surface after being held underwater for too long.

Inside, she rushed straight to her nook. She wrapped herself in her favorite blanket, breathing in the familiar softness. The safe warmth steadied her shaking hands as she reached for her journal. She began writing everything—Sister Abigail's warnings, the forest's whispers, the feeling of eyes tracking her through the dark.

Words blurred across the page as exhaustion crept in—heavy, irresistible, a slow, warm tide pulling her down by the ankles. Her pen slipped from her fingers, tapping the notebook with a hollow little click as her lids fluttered, then sagged, too weighted to fight.

The room around her softened, edges dissolving into a muted haze, her sanctuary folding around her like a cocoon. And finally, she surrendered to the hush and warmth of her blankets, slipping helplessly into sleep, carrying the darkness of the night with her as if it had been waiting in her hands all along.

Chapter 10:
Revelations in Ruin

Megan woke to a pale wash of morning light slipping through the narrow gap in her curtains, casting soft, shifting shapes across the walls of her bedroom. Birds chattered outside—cheerful, insistent—while the distant hum of passing cars drifted in from the road. The sounds felt muted, as if filtered through water, present but far away. She pushed herself upright, rubbing the grit from her eyes, and the memory of the previous night surfaced all at once, tight and breath-stealing. Unease settled into her chest, familiar and heavy, the kind that never quite faded no matter how much sleep she got.

She moved slowly down the hall toward the kitchen, guided by the warm, sweet smell of pancakes. The scent should have been comforting, something that grounded her in the ordinary rhythm of mornings. Instead, it tightened something low in her stomach. Lily stood at the stove, flipping pancakes with practiced ease, her hair loosely pulled back, her posture relaxed in a way Megan both admired and resented. When Lily noticed her, she smiled—bright, reassuring, effortless—as if the world had not shifted overnight.

"Mornin', sweetie," Lily said lightly. "I made your favorite—blueberry pancakes."

"Thanks, Mom," Megan replied, forcing the words out past the knot in her throat. She hovered in the doorway for a moment, watching her mother's movements, sensing the weight in the room that neither of them acknowledged. The silence between them felt rehearsed. Her instincts prickled. This moment—the setup, the tone—felt like something she had already lived through once before.

"Why don't you sit down?" Lily said, turning from the stove. The brightness in her expression dimmed, replaced by something careful, measured. "We need to talk."

Megan's heart sank. She took a seat at the table, her gaze fixed on the plate Lily set in front of her. The pancakes looked impossibly fluffy, steam curling upward in soft tendrils, but her appetite vanished completely. She knew this conversation. She had sat in this same chair before, listening to the same pauses, the same gentle delivery that tried to soften a blow that never really softened.

Lily took a slow breath and folded her hands together, bracing herself. "Megan, honey… my contract at the hospital is over at the end of the summer. We'll be moving back to Chicago."

The words hung in the air, heavy and suffocating. Megan felt heat rush to her face, her stomach twisting painfully. "What?" she blurted. "But I have one more year of school. One year." Her voice trembled despite her effort to steady it, disbelief sharpening quickly into anger.

"I know," Lily said gently, reaching across the table to squeeze her hand. "But this time is different. Chicago will be permanent. No more bouncing around. We can finally settle."

Megan pulled her hand away and pushed the plate aside, the sight of it suddenly making her feel sick. "What about my friends?" she demanded. Her voice cracked despite herself. "What about my life here? You know I hated Chicago. You know I was finally happy."

Guilt flickered across Lily's face, her eyes shining. "I wish I could change it," she said softly. "I do. But you won't lose everyone. You can visit, and they can visit us—"

Megan stood abruptly, the chair scraping loudly against the floor. "I need to be excused," she muttered, already backing away, already retreating before her tears betrayed her.

She slammed her bedroom door behind her and collapsed onto her bed, burying her face into her pillow as the sobs tore free. Grief came in choking waves—grief for her friends, for the fragile sense of belonging she had fought so hard to build in Glory, and for the life that already felt like it was slipping through her fingers. Her thoughts spiraled, tumbling over one another. The forest. The church. The unanswered questions threaded through the town like veins beneath the surface. If she were leaving, she couldn't leave without understanding what she had walked into.

The shower water scalded her skin, steam curling around her like a temporary cocoon, but it did little to quiet her mind. When she stepped out, wrapped in a towel and breathing hard, something inside her had shifted. The pull of the forest returned—not as fear, but as resolve.

She dropped to her knees and dragged the boxes from beneath her bed, dust rising in the sunlight as she rummaged through old belongings. Her fingers closed around a small, weathered pocketknife—her father's. The metal felt cool and solid in her hand, grounding. Memories surfaced, sharp and bittersweet, and she clenched it once before slipping it into her pocket. The weight of it steadied her, a quiet reassurance she didn't fully understand.

She emptied her backpack onto the bed, books and loose papers scattering across the floor. Slowly, deliberately, she packed what she needed—bandages, a flashlight, a thick sweater, snacks—each item placed with care. Not panic. Preparation.

Outside, the air had cooled, evening shadows stretching long across the road as she stepped off the porch. Purpose hardened her stride. She pulled out her phone and typed quickly.

Going into the forest to find answers.

The reply came almost instantly.

You promised!

Guilt flared, sharp but brief. *Mom says we're moving back to Chicago, she typed. I can't wait.*

There was a pause. Then, *meet me at the valley. Don't go without me.*

She hesitated only a moment before replying. Her heart hammered as she pocketed her phone and continued on, adrenaline humming beneath her skin. The forest loomed ahead, dark and watchful, branches whispering softly as if recognizing her return. For once, fear didn't slow her. Something steadier took its place.

She stopped at the edge of the valley and drew in a deep, steadying breath. The forest waited—patient, silent, full of answers she was no longer willing to ignore.

"Megan!"

She turned as Aiden emerged from the path, breathless and flushed, chest heaving as he skidded to a stop in front of her. Sweat glistened along his hairline, his expression caught somewhere between worry and disbelief. "You're moving?" he demanded, words tumbling out too fast. "Tell me you're joking."

Concern etched every line of his face, raw and unguarded. Aiden had always been protective, but now the urgency was unmistakable, as if the thought of losing her had pushed him to run harder than he ever had before. The forest loomed behind them, silent and unreadable, and Megan knew that whatever happened next would set something in motion she couldn't undo.

She pushed the conversation aside before it could slow her down, forcing it into a corner of her mind where it couldn't interfere. Emotion would only cloud things now. Focus mattered more. "We'll talk about that later," she said, keeping her voice firm even as her chest tightened. "Something in this forest made Charlie sick. Whatever's out there isn't random. We need to pay attention and be ready."

As she spoke, Sister Abigail's words surfaced unbidden, looping insistently in her thoughts—ease your mind, go to a place of comfort, set boundaries, let nothing invade your space. Megan clung to the advice, repeating it silently as she pictured an invisible line drawn around herself, a quiet perimeter she refused to let anything cross. It wasn't courage exactly, but it steadied her.

Without waiting for Aiden to respond, she turned and headed toward the dark opening between the trees. Each step was deliberate, measured. Her heart beat hard against her ribs, but she didn't slow. Behind her, Aiden hesitated, doubt flickering across his face as he stood rooted at the forest's edge.

"Megan, wait," he called.

She glanced back over her shoulder, her hair lifting slightly in the breeze. "You don't have to come," she said quietly. "You can stay here if you want. I'll be fine. I promise I'll come back."

The promise lingered between them, fragile and uncertain. Aiden clenched his jaw, visibly wrestling with himself, then shook off his hesitation. Without another word, he hurried forward and fell into step beside her. The closer they came to the forest's edge, the heavier the air grew, thick with damp earth and decay. The trees rose high above them, their branches knitting together overhead and dimming what little light filtered through.

"Are you sure about this?" Aiden asked, his voice lowered as the shadows deepened.

Megan nodded. There was no hesitation left to hide behind. "I need the truth," she said. "About Charlie. About everything. And I'm done letting fear—or moving—decide things for me."

Aiden studied her for a moment, then said nothing. The understanding passed between them quietly, weighted but mutual. Together, they crossed into the trees.

The forest closed around them almost immediately. The ground softened beneath their shoes, uneven and slick with fallen leaves. The familiar sounds of the valley faded until they were gone entirely—no birds, no breeze, no distant traffic. The silence felt deliberate, pressing in from all sides. Megan's skin prickled with the uncomfortable sense of being observed, though she couldn't pinpoint from where. The trees leaned inward, their trunks scarred and twisted, as if shaped by time rather than growth.

Something moved between the trees.

Megan stopped short. "Did you see that?" she whispered.

They continued forward cautiously, breaths shallow, every snapped twig sounding far too loud. Light filtered weakly through the canopy, casting warped shadows that shifted subtly when she wasn't looking. Then the trees thinned, opening into a small clearing. At its center lay the remains of an old campsite—collapsed tent poles tangled in weeds, rusted cookware scattered across the ground, and a knife half-buried in the soil beside a strip of frayed cloth bleached nearly white.

Aiden crouched and lifted the knife carefully, examining the corrosion along its blade. "This has been here a long time," he said.

Megan's stomach tightened as her dreams surfaced unbidden—Amber standing in shadow, her hand clenched around something sharp. "My dream," she murmured. "Amber was holding something like this. What if she came here?"

Aiden's gaze swept the clearing, his shoulders tensing. "Or ran."

The air seemed to thicken, heavy and close, and then they heard it.

Children's laughter drifted through the trees—high and light, threaded with the sound of a people crying. The noises overlapped unnaturally, echoing and bending as if the forest itself were replaying them. Megan's breath caught. "Aiden," she whispered, "tell me you hear that."

His face had gone pale. "Yeah," he said. "We need to leave."

A sudden gust of cold air swept through the clearing, sharp enough to cut through Megan's clothes. The laughter lingered as they moved quickly toward the far edge of the clearing, fading only when the trees closed around them once more.

"Stay close," Megan said under her breath.

They pressed deeper into the forest. Time behaved strangely there—minutes stretched, steps repeated, and the cold seemed to deepen with every turn. Shadows shifted at the edges of Megan's vision, disappearing whenever she tried to focus on them. The trees crowded closer, branches brushing their arms, roots rising unexpectedly beneath their feet.

Then, after what felt far longer than it should have, they stepped into another clearing.

A cabin stood at its center, sagging and half-consumed by vines and brambles. Its windows were shattered, its door hanging crooked on rusted hinges. Megan's pulse quickened as old rumors surfaced—the witch, the hermit, the stories whispered around town but never spoken aloud. Standing there, faced with something undeniably real, she understood why no one ever questioned them.

Inside, the cabin was not what Megan expected.

There was no altar. No cauldron. No overt signs of ritual or worship. Instead, the space felt like a home left behind too quickly, as if whoever had lived there had meant to return but never did. Peeling wallpaper curled away from the walls. A chair lay tipped on its side near the table, one leg snapped clean through. Dust coated every surface, but beneath it lingered the faint impression of warmth—of ordinary life interrupted.

Books were scattered across the floor, their spines cracked, pages warped with age. Megan knelt and flipped through one carefully. The margins were filled with symbols she didn't recognize, interspersed with rough sketches of plants, animals, and unfamiliar constellations. Melted candle stubs dotted the corners of the room, their wax pooled around small crystals embedded into the floorboards. When Megan brushed her fingers over one, it vibrated faintly, like something humming just below hearing.

Her attention caught on a journal resting beneath the table.

It was thicker than the others, its cover darkened with ash and charcoal smudges. She opened it slowly. The first pages were filled with drawings of forests and streams, animals curled in sleep, hands cupped around firelight. The images were gentle, almost tender, and for a moment her shoulders eased.

Then she turned the page.

The drawing stared back at her with unsettling clarity. A man, broad and heavy-set, his beard wild and unkempt, his eyes rendered with an intensity that made her breath hitch. There was something wrong in the way they were drawn—too alert, too knowing. Not imagined. Remembered.

"Megan?" Aiden said quietly. "What is it?"

Her throat felt tight. "It's him," she said, the words barely audible. "The one from my dreams."

Aiden stepped closer, peering over her shoulder. "Are you sure?"

She nodded, her hands trembling as she traced the edge of the page. "I've seen him before. Not like this—but I know him."

The cabin shifted.

It wasn't violent or sudden, just a subtle change in pressure, like the air thickening. The temperature dipped. Wood creaked somewhere deep in the walls, and the door behind them swung shut with a dull, final thud. The sound echoed longer than it should have.

The light dimmed.

Shadows gathered in the corners of the room, stretching slightly out of place, as if the angles no longer matched the walls. A low murmur drifted through the space—not voices exactly, but the suggestion of them, overlapping and indistinct. Megan felt it brush against her awareness, intimate and unwelcome, like someone standing too close.

She slid the journal into her bag, her movements careful now, deliberate. Her pulse thudded hard against her ribs. "Aiden," she said, keeping her voice low, "we need to go."

She reached for the door and pushed.

It resisted.

The murmuring deepened, pressing in from all sides. The air felt damp against her skin, heavy with the smell of earth and old smoke. The walls seemed closer than they had a moment ago, the space subtly wrong.

"Window," Megan said sharply.

Aiden didn't argue. He grabbed her hand and pulled her toward the far side of the cabin. They stumbled through overturned furniture, their steps clumsy in the dim light. Dead vines were pressed tight against the windowpane, their shapes webbed across the glass.

Aiden grabbed a stool and brought it down hard.

The glass shattered outward, scattering into the brush below. Cold air rushed in, clean and sharp. Megan climbed through first, scraping her palms as she dropped to the ground outside. Aiden followed immediately after.

For a moment, neither of them moved.

The cabin stood behind them, silent and still, its dark windows empty. No sound followed them out. No movement. Just wood and shadow, as lifeless as it had looked before.

Then the forest shifted.

Leaves rustled without wind. Branches creaked and adjusted, settling. Megan's unease returned in a slow, creeping wave. She pushed herself to her feet, tugging Aiden upright with her.

"We can't stay here," she said.

They ran.

Not in panic, not yet—just fast enough to feel the forest closing in around them. Branches brushed their arms. Roots snagged at their shoes. The path twisted subtly, refusing to straighten. The farther they went, the darker it became, the air thick with damp bark and decay.

They didn't stop until the trees thinned.

Light spilled through ahead, soft and pale. The valley opened before them, familiar and wide. Relief hit Megan so suddenly her knees nearly buckled. They were almost clear.

She took one more step forward—

—and something tugged sharply at her ankle.

She cried out as her foot was yanked backward, her balance snapping. She hit the ground hard, the breath knocked from her lungs. Panic flared as she twisted, trying to pull free.

A thick vine had wrapped itself around her ankle, dark red and rough with thorns. It tightened slowly, deliberately, pressing into her skin as if testing her weight.

"Aiden," she gasped, her voice shaking. "Something's got me."

The forest around them remained quiet, watching.

Cold followed—unnatural and wrong. It crept up Megan's leg in slow pulses, leaving a sticky slime on her skin. Her stomach rolled violently as she dug her fingers into the earth, nails bending and snapping against packed soil. The vine tightened with steady determination, dragging her backward inch by inch toward the shadowed trees.

"Megan!" Aiden shouted. He skidded to a halt and turned back, panic flaring across his face. "Get up—now!"

"I can't," she cried, terror breaking her voice. "It won't let go."

The ground beneath her shifted.

Not violently—just enough to notice. The soil ahead of her sagged inward, collapsing into a shallow depression that hadn't been there moments before. From it rose a wet, sucking sound, slow and rhythmic, as if something beneath the surface were breathing. The vine jerked sharply, pulling her closer, and Megan felt a sudden, nauseating pressure beneath her—as if the earth itself were aware of her weight.

She screamed and clawed harder at the ground.

"What the hell is happening?" Aiden yelled, stumbling back a step, his face drained of color.

"Please—get it off me!" Megan sobbed.

Aiden dropped to his knees and grabbed the vine with both hands. It was slick and cold beneath his grip, resisting with surprising strength, tightening instead of loosening. The soil trembled faintly. The hollow in the ground deepened just a fraction, enough to make Megan's heart slam painfully against her ribs.

"Hold on," Aiden said through clenched teeth, straining.

The vine pulsed beneath his hands, releasing a sour, rotten stench that made Megan gag. The cold crept higher along her calf, numbing and invasive, like something probing for weakness.

"Hurry," she whispered, tears streaking down her face. "Please."

Her fingers brushed her pocket.

The knife.

Her father's knife slid into her palm, its familiar weight anchoring her just enough to think. She swung downward, slashing at the vine. The blade bit into dense, rubbery flesh. It resisted, shuddering beneath the impact. She struck again, breath coming in sharp gasps.

The knife slipped free and vanished into the mud.

"No—no—no," she whimpered, plunging her hands into the muck, panic detonating as her fingers searched blindly. She found the handle and wrenched it free, screaming as she drove the blade down with everything she had left.

The vine recoiled abruptly, loosening its grip before snapping back toward the ground. It retreated into the soil with a wet, agitated sound, disappearing as if it had never been there.

Megan scrambled upright, barely steady on her feet.

The ground shifted again.

Not rising. Not forming anything solid. Just moving—swelling slightly beneath the surface, as though something large had turned over below. The soil rippled outward in a slow wave, then stilled.

A deep sound followed—not a voice, not quite—but something close enough to make Megan's blood run cold.

Aiden grabbed her hand. "Now," he said urgently. "We're leaving."

They didn't wait to see what else might surface.

They ran.

The forest resisted them, branches tugging at their clothes, roots catching their feet, but the valley's light broke through ahead, pale and undeniable. Megan's ankle screamed with every step, but she didn't slow. She couldn't.

When they finally burst into the open, sunlight washed over them, warm and blinding. They collapsed into the grass, lungs burning, bodies shaking.

Behind them, the forest stood silent.

Megan lay there staring at the sky, the blue too bright, the clouds too peaceful. Her ankle throbbed fiercely, already swelling beneath torn fabric, dark marks blooming along her skin.

After a long moment, she turned her head toward Aiden. "Did… did that really happen?"

He nodded, chest still heaving. "I don't know what it was. But it wasn't nothing."

She squeezed her eyes shut. The memory of the vine tightening, the ground shifting beneath her, replayed with sickening clarity. "It felt like the forest wanted me," she said quietly. "Like I wasn't supposed to leave."

Aiden followed her gaze back to the tree line. "Yeah," he said. "That's the feeling I got too."

They lay there a while longer, neither of them eager to stand. The valley looked the same as it always had—open, harmless, familiar—but Megan knew better now.

Whatever lived in that forest hadn't chased them.

It had simply let them go.

They pushed themselves up from the grass, both moving stiffly, but Megan sucked in a sharp breath the instant she put weight on her ankle. Pain flared hot and immediate, radiating upward in a dull pulse that made her vision blur. The skin was already swelling, stretched tight and tender, a dark bruise beginning to bloom beneath the surface like something trying to surface.

"Easy," Aiden said, stepping closer without thinking. His voice softened, concern slipping back into place as naturally as breathing. "Let's get you home and ice that before it gets worse."

The walk back felt longer than it should have, the familiar paths suddenly distorted by exhaustion and shock. Every step sent a steady throb up Megan's leg, a reminder of how close she had come to not making it out at all. The adrenaline that had carried her through the forest drained away, leaving behind a hollow vulnerability that made the world feel too quiet. "I still can't believe what happened," she murmured, shaking her head. "It doesn't feel real. Like it belongs to someone else."

Her house came into view, blessedly ordinary—white siding, familiar windows, the porch light flickering on as dusk crept in. Inside, the air smelled faintly of laundry detergent and warmth, grounding her in a way the forest never had. Megan limped to the couch and eased herself down with a quiet groan, lifting her ankle onto a pillow. Aiden disappeared into the kitchen and returned moments later with a bag of ice already slick with condensation.

"Here," he said gently, handing it to her.

She pressed the cold pack against her ankle and hissed, then slowly exhaled as the sting dulled into numbness. The silence that followed felt heavy but not uncomfortable, like the stillness after a storm has passed but before the air fully clears. Almost without thinking, they both reached for their phones.

"Let's figure out those symbols," Aiden said, leaning closer so their shoulders nearly touched. "If they meant something, we should know what."

A chill crept over Megan as she unlocked her phone. The symbols no longer felt abstract or academic—they felt intentional and deliberate, like a language she had stumbled into without permission. "If we understand them," she said quietly, "maybe we'll know how to avoid whatever that was next time."

The living room filled with the cool glow of their screens as Megan typed witchcraft symbols into the search bar. Images flooded in—sigils, runes, circles layered with meanings that shifted depending on culture, intent, and era. Her brow furrowed as she scrolled. The sheer volume was overwhelming.

"Where do you even start?" Aiden muttered. "There are hundreds of variations."

"I know," Megan said. "Every symbol means five different things depending on who used it."

Aiden paused, then straightened slightly. "Wait. I think I've got something." He angled his phone toward her. "These are pagan elemental symbols. Air, water, earth, fire."

Megan leaned closer, recognition flickering. "Those were in the cabin," she said. "On the walls. On the pages."

"They're often arranged around a pentagram," he continued. "And the orientation matters. A lot."

That word lodged uncomfortably in her chest. "I'll check Wiccan symbols," she said. "There might be overlap."

She switched searches, scrolling through flowing designs meant for protection, balance, harmony. The artwork was beautiful—but wrong. None of it matched what she remembered. "These don't fit," she said finally. "Most of these are meant to protect. To heal."

"Unless someone used them wrong," Aiden said quietly.

He scrolled again, expression tightening. "If the pentagram is inverted—or the elements are placed improperly—it can be used to channel negative energy. Curses. Binding rituals."

Megan hugged the ice closer to her ankle. "Binding," she repeated. "Like trapping something."

Aiden looked up. "You said your dream showed children. Being offered to the forest."

Her stomach twisted. She nodded slowly.

"What if those weren't offerings," he said. "What if they were sacrifices?"

The thought settled heavily between them. Megan swallowed. "That would explain the anger," she said. "But not why it's still there."

Aiden's gaze drifted toward the darkened window. "Maybe whatever was done was never undone."

Megan followed his stare, the weight in her chest tightening. The house felt safe—but thinner now, like a barrier that could be crossed if something wanted to badly enough.

"Then we need to be careful," she said quietly. "Because whatever's in that forest doesn't feel finished."

Aiden nodded once. Neither of them said it out loud, but the truth was already there.

They hadn't escaped the forest.

They'd only left it behind—for now.

The clock ticked loudly on the wall, each second stretching longer than the last. Megan stared at her phone, scrolling through pages that all blurred together, the answers slipping farther away the more she searched. Nothing fit neatly. Nothing offered clarity. The symbols felt just out of reach, like a language she almost understood but couldn't quite translate.

Aiden finally locked his screen and leaned back against the couch, his gaze drifting toward the darkened window as night settled in outside. He exhaled slowly. "We're not getting anywhere," he said. After a beat, his tone shifted, more careful. "And there's something else we need to talk about."

Megan's shoulders tensed.

"You said you're moving," he continued, turning to face her fully. "You're my best friend. I deserve to know what's going on."

She looked down at her ankle, at the bruising already spreading beneath her skin, deepening as the minutes passed. "My mom's contract is ending," she said quietly. "The hospital in Chicago offered her a permanent position."

Aiden nodded, absorbing that. "Chicago doesn't sound all bad," he said after a moment. "How do you feel about going back?"

Megan shook her head immediately. "I hate it." The word slipped out sharper than she meant, and she winced before taking a breath. "I didn't have friends there. Not really. It's huge and cold, and I always felt invisible. Like I didn't belong anywhere."

Her voice wavered as the truth settled in. "Here… I finally feel comfortable. And now it feels like everything's being ripped away again."

"No need to stress, Meg," Aiden said gently. "The move isn't soon. We've still got time."

He sounded hopeful, casual even, as if time alone could soften the edges. Megan knew he meant well, but the words landed hollow. He hadn't spent his childhood packing boxes, learning new hallways, starting over again and again. To him, leaving was an event. To her, it was a pattern.

She sighed, shoulders slumping. "It's not just the move," she admitted. "I won't even finish high school here. In a few months, it's like this part of my life just… ends. I want to enjoy the time I have left, but it already feels like I'm saying goodbye."

Aiden dragged a hand through his messy hair, his familiar crooked smile appearing as he searched for something reassuring. "We'll figure it out," he said. "Together. Your mom said I could visit Chicago, right?"

Megan nodded, though the faint spark of hope flickered uncertainly. "Yeah. I guess. It just won't be the same. Everything's changing all at once, and it's… a lot."

"Well then," Aiden said, lifting his hands dramatically, "I guess I'll just have to visit constantly. Weekly FaceTime—nonnegotiable. I'll come out whenever I can. We'll plan trips. I'll even pretend Chicago is my favorite place on earth."

She let out a small laugh despite herself, though tension still lingered in her brow. "You and your optimism."

"It's a survival skill," he said lightly. "Besides, distance doesn't erase people. And hey—Chicago pizza alone makes the move defensible."

That earned a softer laugh. "You're impossible."

"And loyal," he added, meeting her eyes. "No matter where you go, this doesn't disappear."

Warmth settled in her chest at that, easing something she hadn't realized was clenched. "Thank you," she said quietly. "I needed to hear that."

Aiden glanced at the clock and groaned. "I should head out. My mom's probably already checking the driveway." He paused at the door, concern slipping back into his expression. "You okay?"

Megan nodded. "Yeah. Just… thinking."

He gave her one last look before leaving, the door clicking shut behind him. Alone again, Megan leaned back against the couch, listening to the steady rhythm of the clock. The house felt calm and unchanged—but she knew better now.

Some things were already shifting.

And there was no stopping that.

"Take it easy on that ankle," Aiden said, his tone turning serious as he stepped toward the door. "And promise me you'll write tonight."

"I will," Megan replied. "Thank you, for everything. For being here."

After he left, the house settled into an unnerving stillness. The quiet pressed in on her, heavier somehow than the chaos of the forest had been. She climbed the stairs slowly, favoring her ankle as a dull ache pulsed in steady rhythm with her thoughts. In the bathroom, she scrubbed dirt from beneath her nails, watching muddy water spiral down the drain. When she looked up, her reflection startled her—tired eyes, flushed skin, someone who looked older than she had that morning.

Why does everything have to change?

She pulled on her oversized sweater, the fabric soft and worn in all the right places. It grounded her, familiar and comforting. At least I still have this, she thought, clinging to the small certainty.

Curled into her favorite corner of the bed, pillow tucked tight against her chest, Megan opened her journal to a blank page. The pen hovered for a moment before the words finally came.

I was reckless today. I went into the forest knowing it was dangerous—and I brought Aiden with me.

Her handwriting wavered slightly as she wrote about the vines, the dark pit, the way the ground itself had seemed to turn against her. She paused, eyes drifting to the bruised ring around her ankle, already deepening in color.

Dad's knife saved me. But when I stood up… the earth had a face. Watching me. Smiling.

Her chest tightened at the memory, but she kept writing, refusing to look away from it.

And then Mom told me we're moving back to Chicago. I'm scared—not just of leaving, but of losing the only place where I finally felt like I belonged.

The pen slowed as her thoughts softened, settling into something quieter.

Maybe this move is another beginning. Maybe Chicago isn't the end. But something in Glory isn't finished with me yet. I can feel it.

She closed the journal and slid it beneath her mattress, relief and unease settling side by side. As she lay back, moonlight crept across the walls, pale and watchful. Somewhere in the distance, an owl called, the sound hollow and lingering.

Megan closed her eyes. Sleep came slowly—gentle and fragile—while beyond the edge of town, unseen and patient, the forest waited.

Chapter 11:
The Burning Truth

Megan woke to sunlight and silk. For a few dazed seconds, that alone felt wrong, the sensation lodging in her chest like a splinter she couldn't quite reach. The light spilling through the curtains was warm, honey-colored, the kind that belonged to late spring mornings and open windows—not the flat, anemic winter glow that usually bruised her bedroom walls. The sheets beneath her were smooth and cool, gliding against her skin when she shifted, untouched by sweat or panic, not knotted and damp from another night of clawing herself awake. When she pushed upright, her hair slid over her shoulders in loose, glossy waves, heavy with product and care, brushing against skin that felt unfamiliar beneath her polished fingernails—smooth, sun-warmed, taut in places that should have been soft. Her body felt… finished, like something that had already been decided for her.

A thin unease crept up her spine. This wasn't how waking ever felt.

She swung her legs over the side of the bed and froze, breath catching halfway out. The injury from her and Aiden's reckless adventure into the forest was gone; her ankle smooth and unmarked, as if it had never known pain.

When she turned her head, she noticed an outfit laid out neatly on the chair—clothes she would never wear, folded with deliberate precision, as if someone had rehearsed this moment down to the smallest detail. A tight white crop top, fabric crisp and unwrinkled, paired with high-waisted jeans shaped for hips she didn't own, the denim dark and new. A leather belt lay coiled on top, its silver buckle catching the sunlight like an eye that knew it was being watched. Everything about it screamed intention. Presentation. Approval.

Popular.

The word slid into her thoughts uninvited, and her stomach clenched hard enough to make her dizzy. This wasn't her room —she knew that with a certainty that made her throat tighten— but it was close enough to mock her. The same bed. The same dresser. But scrubbed clean, edges softened, and stripped of the mess that proved she existed. No notebooks piled like barricades. No half-filled coffee cups. No journal bleeding ink onto the carpet like an open wound. Even the smell was wrong. Instead of paper and dust and cold air, the room breathed out sweetness—perfume, hairspray, something floral and artificial that coated the back of her tongue.

She stood slowly, bare feet sinking into plush carpet that felt too thick, too forgiving, as if it might swallow her if she stayed still long enough. When she lifted her eyes, the mirror caught her before she could look away.

The girl staring back at her smiled automatically.

It wasn't wide or manic—just easy, practiced. Lips glossy. Teeth straight and white. Tan skin glowing as if lit from within. Long lashes framing eyes that looked confident, alert, unafraid. Her posture was effortless, spine straight without tension, shoulders relaxed, like she had never learned how to brace for impact.

Megan raised a hand, heart thudding. The reflection mirrored her with lazy perfection, fingertips brushing the glass at the same time, warmth meeting cold.

For a flicker of a second, she thought the girl might hesitate. That she might blink wrong. But she didn't. "Is this me," she whispered.

A car horn cut through the moment—sharp, impatient, invasive. Megan flinched like she'd been struck. Her pulse spiked as she crossed the room and pulled the curtain aside.

A convertible Mercedes idled at the curb, its silver paint gleaming obscenely bright against the street. Jenna lounged behind the wheel, sunglasses pushed into her hair, elbow draped over the door as if she owned the road. Lexi leaned across the passenger side, laughing at something on her phone, already recording. Amy sat in the back, legs crossed, boots hooked casually over the edge, chewing gum with bored authority.

They looked inevitable.

Jenna leaned on the horn again. "Megan! School starts soon, let's go!"

The sound carried weight—expectation pressing down on her ribs, the unspoken rule that she belonged with them, that this was where she was supposed to be. That if she didn't move, she would be late not just to school, but to herself.

Megan opened her mouth to call back, to protest—but nothing came out. Her throat locked, her voice swallowed by the certainty that no answer existed. Her hands trembled as she backed away from the window, pulse racing far too fast for a dream that felt this solid, this insistent.

She dressed without thinking. The clothes slid on easily, fitting her like a second skin, clinging in places that made her hyperaware of her body, molding her into someone she didn't recognize but apparently knew how to inhabit. Each movement felt rehearsed, muscle memory borrowed from a stranger. When she came downstairs, her feet carried her through a spotless kitchen, past gleaming counters and untouched surfaces, past a mirror that reflected a girl who didn't look scared enough—and that terrified her more than anything else.

The front door flew open.

Lexi grabbed her wrist, nails digging in just enough to remind Megan she was real, laughing as she dragged her outside. "There she is. Took you long enough."

Megan stumbled into the car, knees scraping leather that smelled expensive and new. Jenna twisted around, eyes scanning her face with performative concern. "You didn't even do your makeup?"

Before Megan could answer, Lexi was already rummaging through a cosmetic bag, shoving brushes and tubes into her lap. "Hold still. We can't have you looking like you just rolled out of a grave."

The words hit wrong. *Rolled out of a grave*, Megan thought.

The car lurched forward.

Lexi leaned in close—too close—her perfume sharp and chemical, burning Megan's nose. As she swept a brush beneath Megan's eye, something in her face slipped, subtle at first, like a mask losing its grip. Her pupils bled outward, swallowing the whites until her eyes became wet, bottomless pits that reflected nothing. The skin around them sagged, softened, then began to slide, melting like wax left too close to heat. Her cheek sagged downward, splitting to reveal slick pink muscle beneath, fibers twitching as if still alive.

Megan gasped, jerking back as Lexi's face continued to collapse in slow, intimate ruin, flesh sloughing off in ribbons that clung briefly before letting go. Beneath it, there was no skull. No structure. Just hollow darkness, vast and empty, staring back at her.

Megan squeezed her eyes shut and blinked hard.

"Stop moving, silly. You're gonna mess it up." Lexi rolled her eyes, her perfectly intact, mascara pristine.

Laughter filled the car, bright and normal, spilling over the leather seats and bouncing off the windows in a way that should have been comforting—but wasn't. The road rushed beneath them, tires skidding slightly to a fault in the school parking lot, leaving faint black streaks on the asphalt, the smell of burning rubber mingling with the sharp chemical tang of Lexi's perfume. Megan gripped the edge of her seat, stomach twisting as the ordinary scene—laughter, sunlight, the hum of an engine—felt just slightly off, like the world was tilting beneath her feet without her permission.

The school rose ahead, impossibly large, its wooden doors towering like something ancient and judgmental, more church than classroom. When they stepped through the gates, the noise of the courtyard softened, bending around them. Students parted without being asked, eyes tracking their every movement. Whispers threaded through the air, prickling Megan's skin like insects skittering just beneath it. "Look—it's them," someone hissed. "The Fearsome Four of Glory."

The words snagged in her head, repeating until her vision stuttered. The scene stretched, warped—the wooden doors lengthening, darkening—until the smell of incense and cold stone flooded her lungs.

She stood inside the church with Aiden at her side.

The Reverend's voice boomed from the pulpit, bright and energetic, layered with something eager beneath it. His eyes shone as he spoke of devotion, of sacrifice, of giving oneself fully to God and community. The congregation leaned forward as one body, breathing in sync, every face tilted toward him. Megan's skin prickled. The air felt compressed, as though the walls were slowly breathing inward, testing how much space she needed to survive.

In the far corner, half-swallowed by shadow, a woman rocked back and forth.

Her lips moved in a broken chant, syllables tripping over one another, wrong and arrhythmic. Her head jerked sharply, snapping side to side with sharp, unnatural angles. Her arms began to twitch, then jerk violently, elbows bending the wrong way, joints popping softly. Fingers clawed at empty air. Her legs kicked against the pew, wood thudding as her body convulsed.

"Do you see her?" She asked Aiden, but Aiden ignored her; no one looked at her.

The chanting grew louder, faster, drilling into Megan's skull until her teeth vibrated. The woman's outline blurred, edges trembling as if she were being erased. Megan tried to stand, to scream, but her body refused, limbs heavy and distant. The woman smeared like wet paint dragged by a careless hand and then vanished entirely, leaving only empty space and the lingering echo of her voice scraping along Megan's thoughts.

The sermon ended, the Reverend's voice fading into silence, leaving only the faint echo of hymns and the sharp, lingering scent of incense. The massive wooden doors creaked open, swinging wide as if inviting something in, and cold air rushed into the church, slicing across Megan's skin and curling around her like a living thing. The sudden chill carried with it the faint, metallic tang of blood, or maybe it was just her own pulse hammering in her ears, leaving her shivering despite herself.

Outside, Megan saw Charlie standing near the steps, hands in his pockets, posture loose, face normal. Relief slammed into her so hard it nearly dropped her to her knees.

"Charlie," she said, moving toward him with excitement.

He looked up—and his face cracked.

Bone split with a wet pop, skull peeling back like broken doors. One eye bulged free, dangling by a slick cord, swinging as he moved. The other rolled aimlessly, blind. His exposed brain pulsed inside the open cavity, gray and veined, throbbing in obscene rhythm with her heartbeat, each pulse forcing blood to slosh over shattered bone. The smell followed—rot and copper and something sweetly wrong that clogged her throat and made her gag.

Megan looked away, forcing her gaze to the ground as a bitter lump formed in her throat. "I'm sorry I couldn't save you," she muttered, the words tasting hollow as disappointment washed over her.

Charlie stepped closer, completely normal now, hands casually tucked into his jacket pockets, the easy slouch in his shoulders making him seem grounded, real, almost impossibly ordinary after the brief glimpse of what he could become. "Hey,

I am saved, Megan," he said, voice warm, unbroken. "It's good to see you." He glanced over his shoulder and motioned toward the steps, where a woman and two girls stood waiting. "I don't think you've met my family yet." The woman smiled first—soft, tired, kind in a way that felt earned. She held one girl's hand while the other leaned against her hip, both daughters bundled in coats too big for them, cheeks flushed pink from the cold. "This is my wife, Anna," Charlie continued, pride threading his voice. "And these are my monsters." The girls laughed on cue, one waving shyly, the other giving Megan a solemn, curious stare like she was being sized up for something important. "They won't bite," Anna said gently. "Much." They all laughed, and the sound settled around Megan like something practiced and safe.

Megan smile. "Very nice to finally meet you!" Something inside her kept snagging, her eyes drifting to Charlie's temples, his eyes, his mouth, waiting for the split that didn't come. The moment stretched, normal and almost sweet, yet the air around him felt wrong—too still, too careful—like reality was holding its breath, daring her to relax.

Suddenly a hand closed on Megan's shoulder.

She spun at the sudden weight on her shoulder and jumped, the breath tearing out of her chest.

"Reverend!" The word slipped from her before she could stop it, sharp with surprise, her pulse leaping as his fingers tightened just a fraction too much. He stood close—closer than necessary—his hand resting with practiced familiarity, possessive in a way that made her skin crawl even as his smile remained gentle, rehearsed, perfectly calm. "I'm so proud of you," he said warmly, eyes bright with something that felt a shade too intent. "You've come so far."

As he spoke, his face betrayed him in fleeting, horrifying glimpses. His skin seemed to darken in irregular patches, stretching tight over ridges and angles that shouldn't exist beneath human flesh. The planes of his cheeks sharpened unnaturally, jutting like broken stone, while his smile stretched wider than any kindness could hold, curving into something predatory. His teeth lengthened, pointed and uneven, catching the dim light as if eager for blood. His eyes sank back into shadowed hollows, the sockets glowing faintly red, a slow, smoldering ember that made his gaze feel like it could burn straight through her. Every subtle shift of his features pulsed with menace, and for a fleeting second, she saw not a man, but something hungry, patient, and utterly inhuman, waiting just beneath the surface.

Megan squeezed her eyes shut, forcing herself to will the image away, and when she opened them again, the Reverend's face had returned to its familiar, human shape, calm and unthreatening.

"Megan, will you join us for solstice prayer?" he whispered.

Before she could answer, the world snapped. The oppressive darkness lifted like a drawn curtain, and familiar contours rushed back into view.

Megan stood in the church again, dressed in white. The gown clung to her damp skin, heavy with incense and sweat. She chanted with the others, words spilling from her mouth without permission, vibrating through her bones. When she turned, the congregation knelt, heads bowed. The reverend stood above them, knife glinting in his hand.

"Your turn, my child," he said softly. "Give yourself to Glory."

"No," Megan choked, backing away, panic clawing up her throat.

He moved faster than thought. The blade flashed in front of her eyes, slicing deep as it tore across her neck. Heat burst outward. Blood surged immediately, thick and unstoppable, spilling down her chest as her hands flew up too late, fingers slipping in the wet ruin while her breath shattered into a choking, broken gasp. She clawed at the wound, fingers slick and useless, blood bubbling between them. Her lungs seized, dragging liquid instead of air. She gagged, iron flooding her mouth as the world dimmed and narrowed.

Megan bolted upright, screaming.

Her room swam into focus, dark and achingly familiar. She gasped, hands flying to her throat—unbroken, whole. Air ripped into her lungs in harsh, uneven pulls, each breath burning as if she'd been drowned and dragged back too fast. The clock on her nightstand glowed red—3:00 a.m., the witching hour, Megan thought—its numbers glaring like a warning rather than a simple mark of time, searing into her vision and making her skin crawl, each flicker of the display echoing the rapid, uneven thrum of her pulse. Silence pressed in around her, dense and attentive, the kind that felt aware.

Of course another nightmare. Should have known from the beginning, she thought, the words sharp with bitter certainty.

Megan scanned her shelf for her journal, voice low and uncertain. "Weird… I left it right here," she muttered as she found herself reaching for empty air. Her gaze dropped—and there it was. Her journal lay on the floor, edges curled and worn, a small, tangible anchor to reality in the midst of the disorienting dark. She reached for it, fingers trembling, needing the weight of something solid in her hands. As she leaned down, a sudden skittering made her freeze. Something—fast, jointed, impossibly wrong—scrabbled across the carpet, its movements too deliberate, too alien. It vanished under her bed before she could see it clearly, leaving only the echo of wrongness and a creeping, crawling sense that the shadows themselves had teeth.

Her heart hammered, each beat a frantic drum in her chest. She snatched her phone from the nightstand and flicked on the light, the glow harsh against the dark corners of the room. Leaning over, she peered beneath the bed, eyes straining for even a hint of movement.

Nothing.

Her shoulders sagged as she eased back upright, setting her phone carefully on the nightstand. "What is wrong with me?"

she whispered, breath shaking, the warmth of panic pooling and coiling in her stomach like molten lead.

The mattress groaned beneath her, then dipped—slowly, impossibly—like something unseen had settled just out of sight. A cold, crawling awareness slithered up her spine: she wasn't alone.

A smell crawled into her nose—rot, heat, old blood. Charlie's mutilated form hauled itself onto the bed, skull split open, brain pulsing wetly. His loose eye swung wildly, tracking her. Hot, rancid breath washed over her face as his hands clamped around her legs, fingers digging in, mouth working as slurred, gurgling sounds spilled out. "You did this!"

Megan screamed, waking again, sunlight slicing through her window, the scream still tearing out of her throat.

It didn't feel like morning so much as an obligation—daylight arriving out of habit rather than intent. The sun hung low and thin beyond the glass, its glow pale and sickly, as if even it hesitated to look too closely at Glory. Megan hugged her knees to her chest, eyes squeezed shut, voice tight with lingering dread. "If that's what being popular is… I don't want it," she muttered, shivering despite the weak light, the memory of the dream crawling along her spine like a warning she couldn't shake.

Her room surfaced piece by piece as her eyes adjusted. Plush pillows crowded the corner where she read at night, still bearing the faint crease of her shoulder. Books lay stacked unevenly on her desk, some open, others splayed facedown as if abandoned mid-thought. The air freshener her mother insisted on using hummed softly from the outlet, releasing its synthetic calm into the air. The scent turned Megan's stomach. It felt invasive, like something attempting to overwrite the truth.

Today was her first day back at school.

The realization settled into her chest with conflicted weight. A small, treacherous spark of anticipation flared there—an idea of routine, of bells and hallways and familiar misery she understood. Normalcy, or at least the performance of it. But the spark didn't last. Beneath it, dread stirred, thicker and slower, coiling with patient intent. That feeling had become familiar over the past few days, always present, never loud—waiting.

Her ankle throbbed beneath the blankets, a deep, pulsing ache that felt older than the injury itself. It wasn't just pain; it was memory. The forest. The vines. The moment the ground had given way beneath her like a mouth opening to swallow. She and Aiden hadn't just almost gotten hurt—they'd almost disappeared. That truth clung to her, impossible to shake.

Megan pushed herself upright, refusing to linger. She wasn't going to let the ache dictate her day. The moment her feet touched the floor, a sharp burst of pain shot up her leg, bright and immediate. She hissed through her teeth, gripping the mattress until it passed. When she stood, her ankle protested again, stiff and uncooperative.

In the bathroom mirror, she lifted the hem of her pants and froze.

The bruise had spread.

What had once been an angry ring was now a wide bloom of darkened flesh, mottled purple and bruised blue, its center nearly black. It looked wrong—not like a healing injury, but something settling in. For a fleeting, irrational moment, Megan thought it was growing, creeping outward while she slept. The thought made her pulse stutter.

Stop it, she told herself, turning away from the mirror.

The shower did little to help. The water scalded, then chilled, never settling, steam gathering thickly around her like a presence that refused to leave her alone. She dressed quickly, tugging on her oversized sweater—soft, familiar, grounding—before slipping into the hallway.

The house was too quiet.

Each step down the stairs felt amplified, her ankle sending dull reminders up her leg. The stillness pressed in until the sound of movement from the kitchen finally broke it—drawers opening, a pan set down too carefully. Her mother's presence brought a brittle kind of comfort, fragile and easily shattered.

The kitchen smelled of strawberries and toasted pastry, overly sweet. Megan's stomach growled out of reflex, but the tight knot beneath her ribs killed any real hunger. Staying meant conversation. Staying meant questions she wasn't ready to answer.

"Megan!" Lily called, turning from the counter. Relief crossed her face, quickly chased by concern. "There you are. Did you sleep any better?"

"Yeah. I slept okay," Megan said, the words coming out clipped and sharp, defensive before she meant them to be. She busied herself near the counter, avoiding her mother's gaze, though she could feel it on her—measuring and worried.

Lily stepped closer anyway. Her eyes dropped to Megan's leg, narrowing when she spotted the bruise peeking out. "That doesn't look okay," she said quietly. "What happened?"

"It's nothing. I tripped," Megan replied too quickly, waving it off like a nuisance. "I wasn't paying attention."

Lily's concern hardened. "A bruise like that isn't nothing. Are you sure you don't need to see a doctor? I can call—"

"No."

The word cracked through the kitchen louder than Megan intended. Her pulse spiked instantly. "I—I have to go to school," she added, forcing steadiness into her voice. "It's just a sprain. I'll be fine."

She turned away before her mother could argue, grabbing a toaster strudel and slinging her backpack over her shoulder like armor.

Lily sighed behind her, heavy with things she wasn't saying. "I know you're upset," she said gently. "But I love you."

"Yeah. You too," Megan muttered, already reaching for the door.

Outside, the air felt damp and oppressive, thick in her lungs. She moved quickly, the ache in her ankle flaring with every step, though it faded beneath the louder hum of unease buzzing beneath her skin. The bus arrived with a hydraulic hiss, and she climbed aboard, dropping into a seat near the front.

As it pulled away, the vibration traveled up through the floor and into her bones. Houses slid past the windows, warped slightly by the glass, and every jolt in the road echoed through her leg—and through her thoughts. Her mother's face. The move they hadn't discussed. The forest. The thing beneath the ground.

The bus lurched to a stop.

Glory High loomed ahead, its brick exterior catching the morning light in a way that made it look rigid and unwelcoming. Megan stepped down, adjusting her grip on her backpack, forcing her shoulders straight.

That was when she saw them.

Jenna. Lexi. Amy.

They stood near the entrance, not welcoming like her dream. Their posture was tense, but their attention locked onto Megan instantly. Arms crossed. Smiles sharpened.

"Look who it is," Jenna drawled, her voice slicing cleanly through the morning chatter. "The ghost of Glory."

Heat rushed up Megan's neck. She shifted her weight instinctively, trying to hide the limp, but her ankle pulsed in protest.

"Back to haunt us," Jenna continued, eyes flicking over her sweater with practiced disdain. "Still wearing that thing? Bold choice."

Amy giggled, stepping closer. "Did somebody hurt her wittle ankle?" Her voice dripped mock concern. "Poor baby."

Lexi snorted. "What was it this time? Trip over your own imagination?"

"At least she has some color now," Lexi added, satisfaction bright in her eyes. "Didn't think ghosts could tan."

Megan's hands curled into fists, nails biting into her palms. Her throat tightened, words swelling uselessly behind her teeth. She kept her gaze forward and walked faster, forcing herself past them toward the doors, every step burning—but she didn't stop.

She wouldn't give them that.

"Don't think I forgot about Amber, you heartless psycho!"

Jenna's voice followed Megan like a thrown object, sharp and intentional. The name struck with physical force, knocking the breath from her lungs mid-step.

Amber.

For a split second, the hallway tilted. Amber had been more than Jenna's best friend—she'd been one of the golden girls, one quarter of the flawless cheer squad everyone admired and envied in equal measure. And then, one day, she was gone. No goodbye. No body. Just absence that swallowed the space she'd once occupied.

"Yeah," Lexi chimed in, her tone slick with satisfaction. "How cold do you have to be to tarnish the memory of one of our own?"

Megan didn't turn around. She couldn't. Her chest tightened until her breaths came shallow and uneven, fury and grief tangling together in a way that left her lightheaded. They talked about Amber like she was a shrine no one was allowed to touch—as if searching for answers was some kind of betrayal.

If they only knew.

She fixed her gaze on the tall wooden doors ahead, each step forward an act of stubborn defiance. Her ankle burned with every movement, pain flaring hot and insistent, but she refused to slow down. Stopping meant giving them what they wanted. It meant letting their words sink in and root.

Their laughter chased her anyway, echoing down the concrete steps and worming into her skull. By the time she shoved the doors open and stepped inside, her hands were trembling, her leg screaming in protest.

The hallway closed around her.

Lockers slammed shut. Voices collided and overlapped. Shoes squeaked against polished floors. Life surged forward without pause, loud and careless, utterly indifferent to her spiraling thoughts. Megan stopped just long enough to steady herself, pressing her fingers into her palm until sensation grounded her.

Then she saw him.

Aiden stood at his locker, rifling through his bag, shoulders hunched in concentration. The sight of him—solid, familiar—eased something tight in her chest that she hadn't realized was clamped shut.

"Megan!" He turned, breaking into a smile that felt genuine, unguarded. "Hey. How was your morning?"

She hesitated, the weight of everything pressing against her ribs. "Um… not great," she admitted quietly. "I ran into Jenna, Lexi, and Amy."

Aiden's smile vanished as if someone had flipped a switch. "Let me guess."

"They brought up Amber again," Megan said as they fell into step beside each other, heading toward biology. "Called me heartless. Like I'm trying to ruin her memory." Her voice wavered despite her effort to keep it even. "It's like they don't understand that I'm trying to find out what happened to her."

Aiden's jaw tightened, muscles jumping beneath his skin. "They don't deserve you," he said firmly.

Megan wasn't sure she believed that—but she held onto the words anyway, clutching them like something fragile in a storm.

"They're bullies," Aiden continued after a moment. "That's all this is. They're trying to get a reaction. And they act like Amber disappearing was your fault, which makes zero sense. You weren't even here when it happened."

"I know," Megan said, though the words rang hollow. The hurt sat heavy in her chest, dense and bruising. "It just feels like they're trying to erase me. Like if they say it enough times, I'll disappear too." She forced a weak smile. "Besides, I'm leaving soon anyway. Joke's on them."

The joke tasted bitter. It didn't land the way she wanted it to.

The biology classroom swallowed them in harsh fluorescent light and restless chatter. As they slid into their seats, the noise dulled to a distant drone. The teacher launched into the lecture, voice flat and relentless, diagrams flickering across the board.

Megan tried to focus.

She really did.

But her thoughts kept drifting—back to the forest, to the cabin crouched like a wound among the trees. To the brittle parchment. The symbols carved and inked again and again with obsessive care. They hadn't felt random. They'd felt purposeful. Demanding.

And the dead end they'd hit gnawed at her relentlessly.

Then it clicked.

Mrs. Archer.

Megan's pulse quickened, excitement sparking through the haze. She leaned toward Aiden, barely moving her lips. "I just thought of something. Mrs. Archer."

He glanced at her, confusion creasing his brow. "What about her?"

"The symbols," Megan whispered, energy sharpening her words. "She might recognize them. She's always talking about local folklore, old beliefs, stuff no one else remembers. If anyone knows what they mean, it's her."

Aiden leaned closer, interest lighting his eyes. "You really think she'd have answers?"

"She gave me a book over the winter," Megan said, voice low but urgent. "I noticed some similar markings in it back then. I didn't think much of it at the time, but now…" She swallowed. "Those symbols weren't careless. They were written over and over, like someone was terrified they'd be forgotten."

"We don't have any other leads," Aiden said quietly.

The bell rang before she could respond, loud and jarring, snapping her back into her body. Chairs scraped. Students surged toward the door. Megan gathered her things, nerves buzzing as she headed for lunch, every step feeling charged—like she was drifting closer to something dangerous.

At the cafeteria table, she pulled out a scrap of paper and began sketching furiously, recreating every symbol she could remember. Her hand shook as she worked, lines coming out uneven, forcing her to erase and redraw again and again. The fear of getting it wrong tightened her chest.

When she finished, she pulled out her phone. Her fingers hovered over the screen longer than necessary.

Then she typed.

She reread the email twice. Then again. Her heart hammered as she hit send.

Relief washed through her—thin and fragile, but undeniable. It felt like a small step forward… and like knocking on a door she might regret opening.

The rest of the day blurred together. Megan avoided her self-appointed tormentors with careful precision, slipping into classrooms early and taking longer routes between periods. Jenna, Lexi, and Amy seemed to be everywhere, their laughter carrying too far, too sharp.

But in Literature class, seated beside Aiden, the tension loosened just enough for her to breathe.

"Did you send the email?" Aiden murmured.

"Yeah," Megan whispered back. "I just hope she responds."

"She will," he said, though his expression stayed serious. "Those symbols mean something. They didn't end up in that cabin by accident."

Megan nodded. "I can't shake the feeling that something knows we're looking," she admitted. "Like it's aware of us."

Aiden glanced around the room, eyes flicking toward corners and spaces people never quite looked at. "You think she'll help?"

"I don't know," Megan said softly. "But ever since the forest, it feels like the air itself has changed. Like it's waiting."

The teacher began discussing The Great Gatsby, enthusiasm filling the room. Aiden leaned closer once more.

"Hey," he whispered. "Are you going to the festival? I heard some seniors talking about a party at the barn by the lake. Bonfire. Music."

Megan considered it.

The festival had been impossible to ignore all day, its presence humming beneath every conversation like background noise no one could turn off. Even the quiet kids—normally content to drift through the halls unnoticed—had been whispering about it, voices threaded with anticipation. Lights. Music. Something to look forward to.

"I don't know," she said slowly, the words careful. "I think the forest was enough excitement for a lifetime." Her gaze dropped to the scarred surface of her desk, fingers tracing a shallow groove carved there long before her time. "And I really don't want to deal with those girls."

Aiden didn't back down. His eyes brightened instead, animated with a hopeful intensity that made her pause. "Come on," he said. "It'll be like a farewell party. Food, games, music. Just one night where none of this matters."

The image crept in despite her resistance—the lake catching firelight in fractured reflections, the steady crackle of flames, laughter drifting through the dark. A place where fear didn't get a seat at the table. For a moment, she let herself want it.

Then Jenna's voice cut through the illusion. Lexi's laughter. Amy's eyes.

"What if they're there?" Megan asked quietly.

"Then they're there," Aiden said without hesitation. "I'll be with you. We'll make our own fun."

Something inside her shifted—not gone, not healed, but loosened just enough to breathe. "Okay," she said at last. "I'll think about it."

Aiden grinned. "Good. Think s'mores."

The word lingered long after he leaned back in his chair. Fire. Sugar. Warmth. Comfort. Yet even as the thought settled, it tangled with images she couldn't shake—trees closing in, unseen eyes, the way fire had never meant safety in her dreams.

When the final bell rang, relief surged through her body. The tension she'd been holding all day released in a rush, leaving her lightheaded. Instead of taking the bus, she walked home with Aiden, favoring her ankle but grateful for the fresh air and his steady presence beside her. The late afternoon sun washed the school grounds in gold, voices and footsteps fading behind them until the world felt smaller, quieter.

"I know you missed it last year," Aiden said, hands moving as he talked. "They went all out this time. Ferris wheel and everything."

Megan smiled faintly. "I didn't know they went that big."

"Oh yeah," he said. "And the funnel cake? It's unreal. Vanilla ice cream, caramel, hot cinnamon apples." He laughed. "You have to try it."

She let herself imagine it—the sweetness melting on her tongue, the noise blurring into something harmless—while darker thoughts waited beneath the surface. Finals. Chicago. Mrs. Archer's unanswered email. "I'll think about it," she said again, softer this time.

The walk home felt longer than usual, but she didn't mind. The breeze cooled her skin, the sun warmed her face, and for the first time all day, the weight pressing on her chest eased just enough to make the dread feel distant. Not gone. Just farther away.

When they reached her house, conflicting emotions tugged at her—gratitude for the normalcy Aiden offered, but reluctance to be alone again with her thoughts. "Thanks for walking with me," she said quietly. "It really helped."

He smiled, easy and sincere. "Anytime. Just think about the festival, okay? We'll have a blast."

"Promise," she said, though the word felt thin, almost fragile. She watched him disappear down the sidewalk before turning back toward the house. The door clicked shut behind her, the sound final enough to make the air inside feel heavier.

She settled at her desk, surrounded by familiar clutter—textbooks stacked unevenly and notebooks with dog-eared corners. Homework demanded attention, and she forced herself into equations and reading passages, but her focus slipped again and again. Symbols crept between numbers. Firelight flickered at the edge of sentences. The festival hovered in her mind like a distant echo—bright, tempting, unreal.

As evening deepened and dusk pressed against her windows, hunger finally pulled her downstairs. She moved carefully, favoring her ankle, and heated the dinner her mother had left. The scent of bubbling cheese and seasoned meat filled the kitchen—basil, oregano and garlic—rich and comforting. Intentional. An apology without words.

This was her favorite.

The realization tightened her chest. Guilt settled heavy in her stomach as she ate. When she finished, she picked up her phone and typed, *Thank you for dinner. I love you.*

Upstairs again, she opened her window, letting cool night air spill into the room. Leaves whispered outside, brushing together softly, almost like distant voices carrying secrets she wasn't meant to hear. She checked her phone once more, hope flickering despite herself.

Nothing.

The dark screen reflected her face back at her—pale, tired, older than it should have been.

She reached for her journal. The pen moved fast at first, scratching across the paper in sharp, uneven strokes, as if it couldn't get the day out of her head quickly enough. *Today had been a rollercoaster. It started with the dream—one where she was suddenly one of the popular kids in Glory, standing at the center of everything, seen and admired. But beneath the smiles, everyone carried something rotten inside them, a private darkness they tried to hide.* She lingered on that part, remembering how good it felt to matter, to be wanted. The feeling had been intoxicating. Still, she wrote, *it wasn't worth losing herself for. Nothing was.*

The memory soured as the day unfolded on the page. Lexi. Jenna. Amy. Three names, written harder than the rest. They had dragged her back into reality without mercy, making it their shared mission to strip her down piece by piece until there was nothing left but embarrassment and anger. She stopped writing, the pen hovering as her hand trembled.

After a long moment, she added one final line beneath the rest, the ink darker, heavier: *If they understood why I'm doing this —why I have to—maybe they wouldn't be so cruel.*

When she finally closed the journal and tucked it beneath her pillow, a thin calm settled over her. She switched off the lamp. Moonlight slid across the floor, pale and watchful.

"Tomorrow is a new day," she whispered, the words more plea than promise.

Sleep came slowly, drawing her under one careful breath at a time.

Chapter 12:

A Stolen Heart

The buzzing of her phone tore her awake. Megan jerked upright, breath ripping from her lungs as her heart slammed against her ribs, the sound too loud in the suffocating quiet of her bedroom. For a disoriented second, she didn't know where she was—only that something was wrong. Her phone vibrated again in her hand, insistent, urgent, and she fumbled it open with shaking fingers.

Aiden's name glowed on the screen.

I don't know how I got here, but something isn't right. Please meet at the old cemetery on the edge of town.

The message was short. Jagged. Wrong.

Cold prickled across her skin as she reread it, her mind snagging on the phrasing. Got here. As if he hadn't chosen to go. As if he'd woken up somewhere he didn't recognize.

Curiosity flared—dangerous and immediate—but dread surged faster and heavier, swallowing it whole.

She didn't think about shoes. Or her ankle. Or how she'd explain leaving if her mother found out.

One moment she was standing in her bedroom, the next—

It felt like blinking.

Megan stood rigid at the edge of town, breath shallow, muscles locked as if her body had arrived before her mind caught up. The cemetery sprawled ahead of her, washed in thin moonlight that flattened everything it touched. The sky hung low and oppressive, swollen with intent, as if it were pressing down on the land instead of arching above it.

Gravestones thrust from the soil at crooked angles, some tilting so sharply they looked mid-collapse. Their outlines stretched unnaturally across the ground, long distortions that crept and overlapped like grasping hands. The air buzzed faintly, charged enough to prickle her skin, and every instinct she had screamed that something unseen lingered just beyond her reach.

She wasn't alone.

Aiden stood several yards ahead among the markers, his posture stiff, shoulders hunched as if bracing for a blow. His face was drained of color, eyes wide and unfocused, darting toward the darker pockets where moonlight thinned.

"What are we doing here?" Megan whispered as she approached, her voice trembling despite her effort to control it.

"I don't know," he replied, barely pushing the words past his lips. He didn't look at her right away. His attention kept sliding behind her, toward the far edges of the cemetery. The stillness pressed in around them, stretched tight, like the night itself was listening.

After a long moment, he finally turned back to her. "Earlier tonight… I saw people in the woods." His hands shook as he spoke, fingers flexing uselessly at his sides. "Just standing there. Watching me."

Megan's stomach knotted. "Who?"

"A small group," he said. "They were wearing old clothes. Not costumes. Real old." His voice cracked. "And their faces…" He swallowed hard. "Empty. Like they weren't looking at me. Like they were looking through me."

Her palms grew slick with sweat. "And then?"

"They vanished," Aiden whispered. "Not ran. Not faded. Just—gone." His breath hitched. "It felt like the ground shifted. Like something swallowed them."

"Did you recognize them?" Megan asked, forcing herself to keep her voice steady.

"No," he said. "But it felt like they recognized me." His gaze flicked away again. "When I woke up, I was here."

The silence thickened, congealing around them.

Then the whispers began.

They didn't come from one direction. They seeped upward from the earth itself, soft at first, overlapping murmurs that slithered across Megan's skin and burrowed beneath it. Her muscles locked.

"Do you hear that?" she asked, dread blooming fast.

Aiden nodded, already moving. He passed through the rusted cemetery gate as if drawn by something he couldn't see. The whispers tugged at Megan's attention, pulling her after him toward an overgrown section where cracked stones leaned together, their names worn down to nothing.

Each step felt heavier than the last. The air thickened, cold pressing against her like resistance, as though she were wading through unseen depth.

Something brushed her arm.

Ice shot through her veins.

Megan spun, gasping, pulse roaring in her ears—but there was nothing there. Only subtle shifts in the moonlight, the land rearranging itself when she wasn't looking.

"What?" Aiden hissed.

"Someone touched me," she said, breathless. The whispers swelled, urgent now, pleading. Help me… over here…

"We're almost there," Aiden said, already moving again.

"Wait—Aiden." Panic snapped sharp and bright. "Where are we going?"

He didn't slow.

"Aiden!" she called, but he kept walking, his movements stiff, unnatural, as if invisible cords were pulling him forward.

The gravestones grew older. Smaller. Time had nearly flattened them. Moss swallowed what little remained of their names. The whispers fused into a low chant that crawled into Megan's skull, words forming just beyond comprehension.

"I don't like this," she said, her voice shaking. "You're not acting like yourself."

They stopped before a single grave, its inscription cracked and nearly erased, the stone stained dark as if something had soaked into it long ago.

The whispers surged, frantic, clawing at her thoughts.

Something was waiting.

The ground shifted violently beneath them.

Megan cried out as a deep tremor rippled up through her legs and into her chest, rattling her bones. Dirt skittered across the stones as both she and Aiden staggered backward, barely keeping their footing.

"Did you feel that?" Aiden shouted, panic shredding his voice.

"What is that?" Megan gasped. Her heart slammed so hard it hurt, each beat stealing air from her lungs. The atmosphere grew heavy and damp, pressing in until breathing felt like theft.

The whispers twisted into something louder—overlapping cries that scraped raw against her nerves.

"Megan!" Aiden seized her arm, fingers biting hard as he pointed.

Movement stirred between the headstones.

A figure stepped forward.

It was a woman.

Her body was half-consumed by darkness, her posture twisted with agony. Moonlight spilled across a tattered gown that clung to her frame like decayed skin. Her eyes were hollow pits, vast and searching, filled with grief so deep it felt bottomless. When her mouth opened, no sound came—only a stretched, silent scream, as if she were trying to warn them of something too terrible to voice.

Understanding hit Megan like a blow.

This wasn't just a cemetery.

They had crossed into something broken. A place where time had split open, where the past bled endlessly into the present. The air vibrated with unseen force, and the cries rose higher, drilling into her skull.

They were surrounded.

"Follow me!" Aiden shouted.

They ran.

Gravel tore into Megan's palms when she stumbled, pain detonating through her ankle as she forced herself upright. The land around them pulsed, the ground flexing unnaturally as they sprinted toward a solitary mausoleum in a clearing—its stone door gaping wide, waiting.

Then Megan saw her again.

The woman stood between two headstones, blocking their path.

Her eyes locked onto Megan's.

They froze.

The woman began to chant.

The language scraped through the air, harsh and wrong, each syllable striking like a physical blow. The earth bucked beneath them as the chant escalated, Megan's teeth chattering violently. Pale shapes flickered into view, circling Aiden—faces half-formed, mouths contorted in endless agony.

"Aiden—" Megan tried to scream.

The sound that followed swallowed her whole.

A sickening crack split the clearing as Aiden's body convulsed.

Bone snapped.

Then snapped again.

His scream tore free—raw, animal, climbing into something higher, unrecognizable—as his body twisted violently, reshaping itself in ways that defied reason.

Megan could only watch.

Helpless.

Aiden's body collapsed inward—and then rebuilt itself wrong.

Bone surged beneath his skin, forcing its way out in violent bursts, splitting flesh with wet cracks that echoed across the cemetery. White protrusions tore through muscle and sinew at jagged angles, glistening in the moonlight, slick with blood that seeped thick and dark, too slow to drip like something already decaying. His arms lengthened unevenly, joints bending backward with sharp, grinding pops. What remained of his skin stretched thin and translucent, clinging desperately to a frame it could no longer contain.

Megan staggered back, sobbing openly now, horror hollowing her chest. "What... what happened to you?" she whispered, the words breaking apart as they left her mouth.

The thing that had been Aiden did not answer.

Its head snapped violently to one side, then the other, vertebrae cracking like brittle twigs. When it moved toward her, it did so in spasmodic jerks, each step accompanied by a hollow creak, as though its body were being hauled forward by unseen hands that didn't care if it survived the motion. Skin rippled unnaturally across exposed bone, sliding and twitching as if it were alive—and panicking.

Jagged spines burst from its shoulders and forearms, tearing free in splintered shards that caught the light as it advanced. Megan's legs gave out beneath her. She hit the ground hard, palms scraping across gravel as the creature clawed at itself, fingers digging into its own chest.

Skin ripped free in long, wet strips, exposing raw muscle that quivered helplessly beneath. Thick, blackened fluid oozed from the wounds, sluggish and foul, dripping onto the earth where it spread and soaked into the soil like poison.

The thing loomed over her.

Human enough to recognize. Wrong enough to shatter reason.

Its mouth twisted into a fixed snarl, lips split and peeling back to reveal teeth broken and jagged, stained dark as if they had been gnawing on rot. Its eyes were vast and hollow, empty sockets that reflected nothing—not moonlight, not fear, not mercy. The air around it compressed, heavy and suffocating, pressing dread straight into Megan's lungs until hope felt like something she'd imagined once, long ago.

Without warning, it charged.

Megan barely had time to inhale before her back slammed into a tombstone. The impact drove the breath from her body in a sharp, soundless gasp. Cold stone bit into her spine as skeletal fingers wrapped around her throat, crushing, relentless.

"You are mine now," it snarled.

Its breath washed over her—icy, thick with the stench of soil and decay. Megan clawed at its arm, her fingers slipping uselessly against exposed bone. Terror flooded her veins, freezing her from the inside out, that familiar paralysis locking her voice away. Black spots crowded her vision.

"Leave her."

The command split the air.

Light erupted in a blinding arc from the woman's outstretched hand, slicing through the night and striking the creature square in the chest. It shrieked—a sound so sharp it felt like glass tearing through Megan's skull—and reeled backward, its grip breaking as it staggered.

"Your evil is not welcomed here!" it screamed—not in Aiden's voice, but something older, warped beyond recognition —before unraveling into nothing, dissolving into the night as if it had never existed.

The silence that followed rang painfully loud.

The woman approached Megan slowly now, her expression stripped of sorrow, hardened into something resolute and dangerous in its calm.

"You're dreaming," she said gently, her voice steady, almost comforting. "Your friend is not hurt. He's safe. Nothing you've seen tonight has touched him." She stepped closer, moonlight catching in her dark eyes. "Fear makes lies feel real."

Megan swallowed hard, her pulse hammering violently in her ears. The air still hummed. The ground still felt wrong beneath her hands. "This doesn't feel like a dream," she whispered. "It feels... solid."

"That's how he works," the woman replied. "The reverend." The word was sharpened and poisoned. "He turns belief into a weapon and calls it devotion. He wears God's name like a disguise, but his bloodline is ancient—spoiled from the root." Her gaze pinned Megan in place. "Men like him ruin lives and name it salvation."

Megan's chest tightened as images flared behind her eyes— firelight, chanting mouths, accusing hands. "He says he protects this town."

"They always do." The woman's voice softened, intimate, warm as a hand against Megan's back. "I know what it is to be hunted by men of faith. To be blamed. Silenced. Destroyed." She lifted her hand, stopping just short of touching Megan's skin, close enough that a faint prickle raced through her nerves. "Women like us survive by protecting each other. No one else will."

The cemetery leaned inward.

Stones groaned faintly beneath the soil, as though straining to listen. Her words settled deep inside Megan, curling around doubts already planted, taking root.

"You feel it, don't you?" the woman murmured. "The way this town tightens around you. The way the reverend watches. He will ruin you if you let him."

The whisper slid through the air—not from one place, but everywhere.

Let me in; I will protect you!

Megan's breath hitched. "Who are you?" she asked, though dread had already begun assembling the answer.

The woman smiled—not cruelly, but with patient certainty. "Someone who understands you," she said. "Someone who can help you survive what's coming."

The voice behind her ear returned, closer now. *Let me in.*

"I must show you one last thing," the woman whispered.

Her fingers pressed against Megan's forehead.

Light detonated.

The world tore itself apart.

When Megan could see again, a towering man from her nightmares stood before her, his presence crushing, familiar in the worst possible way. The woman stood beside him now—her gown soiled, her dark hair hanging loose—and both of them were smiling.

Laughing.

Their joy curdled Megan's stomach.

The scene fractured.

She sat inside the abandoned cabin. Warmth filled the space. The smell of beef stew hung thick in the air. They sat together at a rickety table, eating, talking, their voices low and indistinct. Laughter looped endlessly, repeating, broken, false.

Their smiles never touched their eyes.

The image replayed again.

And again.

Until something inside it split.

A shriek ripped through Megan's thoughts, violent and piercing. When her vision cleared, she stood in an older version of Glory—raw and unfinished. Mud-churned roads replaced pavement. Wooden buildings hunched together under a low sky choked with smoke. The church dominated everything, its steeple clawing upward, flanked by a meeting house and a gallows left in full view.

Townsfolk moved with rigid purpose, their eyes tracking her without warmth or mercy. Fear clung to the air, embedded in wood and soil alike—a place ruled by obedience, where cruelty wasn't hidden, only accepted.

Then they began to close in.

Men in rough tunics and wide-brimmed hats, faces carved from judgment. Women in bonnets, mouths drawn tight with fury.

And Megan understood—

This was where it began.

"A demon has touched him!" they screamed.

"Demon! Demon!"

The word slammed into Megan from every direction, hurled again and again like stones. The crowd surged forward in a violent tide, bodies pressing close, hands grabbing, tearing, dragging. Fingers clawed at her sleeves, her hair, her throat. Their touch was slick and cold, crawling over her skin as if they were less alive than she was. Panic detonated inside her chest, sharp and blinding, as she fought for breath through the stench of sweat, soil, and fear.

She lashed out instinctively, striking whatever she could reach, but the mass swallowed her whole. She was yanked downward, pulled beneath the weight of their rage, boots trampling close, elbows digging into her ribs as accusations poured down like filth.

"Help me!" she screamed.

The sound vanished into the roar.

No one came.

At the edge of the chaos, the towering man and the woman stood together, watching. Smiling. Not intervening—enjoying it.

"Why?" Megan sobbed, the word tearing free from her chest.

Something hard struck her head.

Pain burst white-hot across her vision as a stone slammed into her forehead. She cried out, staggering, warmth spilling down her face. Instinctively, she wiped at it—and froze.

The hands staring back at her were not hers.

They were larger. Thicker. Scarred and roughened with labor.

A man's hands.

Her breath stuttered as the world lurched. She lifted her gaze just in time to see the woman standing alone now, no smile on her face.

For the first time, she looked afraid.

A violent wave of dizziness crashed through Megan, buckling her legs. The ground tilted sharply, the sky spinning as though it had been wrenched loose. She dropped to her knees, retching, her vision tearing apart at the seams. Light and darkness bled together, refusing to separate.

When the spinning slowed, the cemetery was gone.

She stood at the edge of the forest.

The air hung thick with the sour rot of wet leaves and churned earth, heavy enough to taste. Smoke drifted on the breeze—faint at first, then unmistakable. Ahead, a crowd had gathered, their silhouettes restless and hungry.

At the center of it all knelt the towering man.

He was barely recognizable.

His massive frame was bent and broken beneath a storm of blows. Fists and clubs rained down on him with frenzied brutality, striking again and again. Blood soaked the dirt beneath his knees, turning the ground slick and dark. His body rocked with each impact, hoarse sounds tearing from his throat as he struggled to remain upright.

At the front stood the reverend.

He watched with fevered devotion, face flushed, eyes burning with conviction so intense it bordered on ecstasy. His voice cut cleanly through the chaos.

"Keep this demon subdued!" he commanded. "Do not let it escape God's judgment!"

A final blow struck the man's head.

He collapsed forward, his face hitting the dirt with a wet, hollow sound.

Megan's breath caught painfully in her chest.

What remained of his face was ruined—skin split and swollen, one eye crushed shut while the other stared blankly into nothing. His lips were torn, teeth smeared red, his once-proud features reduced to something pitiful and broken. Pain clung to him, soaked into him, etched into every inch of exposed flesh.

"Drag him to the woodpile," the reverend said coolly. "Tie him."

The crowd obeyed without hesitation.

Hands seized the man, hauling his limp body across the ground. Ropes were thrown over him, cinched tight around his wrists and chest, biting deep. Megan flinched as the cords cut into skin, leaving raw channels that immediately welled with blood.

Cries erupted from the onlookers.

"We warned you!" a woman shrieked, her face twisted with fury. "How could you listen to her?"

"She corrupted you!" another screamed. "She bewitched you!"

The man stirred.

One eye fluttered open, dull with pain but still alive. His muscles twitched weakly as he struggled against the ropes, but they held fast, digging deeper with every movement. Something sharp and unwanted bloomed in Megan's chest—not just fear.

Pity.

This was no demon.

This was a man who was destroyed for showing compassion, punished for believing in something beyond their rigid cruelty.

"No—stop!" Megan screamed. "You're wrong! You're wrong!" Her voice shredded itself against the roar, swallowed whole by the mob's righteous fury.

"I watched from here."

The voice drifted out from the trees.

Megan turned.

The woman in the tattered gown stepped into view, her dress soaked and torn, her face streaked with tears. Her hands trembled as she pressed them to her chest. "I watched them take my love from me," she whispered. Together, they stood as torches were lit.

Flame bloomed.

Hungry. Eager.

Megan's pulse thundered. "Help him!" she cried, desperation clawing up her throat. She tried to move but couldn't. Her body refused her. She was locked in place, trapped in a moment already sealed.

The fire caught.

Flames leapt up the stacked wood, snapping and roaring as they wrapped around the man's bound body. Heat blasted outward, forcing the crowd back, bathing their faces in violent orange light. Megan gagged as the smell reached her—burning wood, then something far worse.

Burning flesh.

The man screamed.

The sound was raw and unrestrained, rising and breaking apart in jagged waves that no longer resembled anything human. It echoed through the settlement, carried too far, lingered too long, vibrating through walls and into sleeping hearts. The town itself seemed forced to bear witness.

His skin blistered and split beneath the flames, blackening and peeling away in wet, curling sheets. Fat hissed and popped as if alive. The air thickened with a sickly sweetness that coated Megan's tongue and burned her throat.

Through the smoke, his remaining eye found hers.

Wide. Glassy. Terrified.

It begged without words—for mercy, for recognition, for meaning—and no matter how desperately she tried, Megan could not look away.

The fire consumed him.

His screams weakened, fractured, dissolved into a hoarse rasp—then silence.

The sudden stillness pressed down on the crowd like a held breath.

Then—

Megan jolted upright.

Her phone buzzed violently against the mattress, ripping her from the vision. She sucked in a sharp breath, heart racing, skin drenched in cold sweat. Light filled the room. Familiar shapes surrounded her—bed, bookshelf, posters, the dim glow of the lamp.

Real.

She scanned her bedroom frantically, but nothing felt solid. The memory clung to her, thick and suffocating, replaying behind her eyes.

Am I awake… or not?

The question lingered.

And something, somewhere, listened.

Her hands shook as she reached for the glass of water on the nightstand. The surface rippled from the tremor before she could steady it. She drank greedily, swallowing in desperate gulps, the cold sliding down her throat in sharp relief—but it did nothing to scrub away the residue left behind by the vision. The images clung stubbornly, burned into the back of her eyes, resurfacing the moment she closed them.

"What was that?" she whispered, dragging a damp hand across her forehead.

Her skin was slick with sweat, her pulse still skidding out of control. She sat there for several long minutes, forcing herself to breathe, replaying the sequence again and again, searching for logic—for anything that might anchor it to reason. But the memory resisted analysis. It didn't feel like imagination. It felt imposed.

Eventually, Megan reached for her phone.

A nervous jolt shot through her as the screen lit up. Part of her expected—dreaded—another message from Aiden, proof that what she had seen had followed him beyond her mind. But instead, an unread email waited at the top of her inbox.

Mrs. Archer.

Relief and unease collided in her chest as she opened it.

Mrs. Archer apologized for the late reply, her tone warm and cheerful, maddeningly normal compared to the violence still echoing through Megan's thoughts. She explained that the symbols Megan had described were elemental in nature—air, fire, earth, water, and spirit. Pagan in origin. Old, yes, but not inherently dangerous.

Common, Mrs. Archer wrote. Harmless, when properly aligned.

Megan's stomach tightened.

The pentagram, Mrs. Archer continued, represented life. Connection. Balance between forces. Protection, even.

Then came the warning.

If misaligned…

If drawn repeatedly…

If performed at a gravesite, shrine, or place where death had soaked into the land…

Prayers could reach something else.

Something darker.

Megan's skin prickled as though a draft had slid beneath her clothes. Her gaze drifted to the journal on her desk. The symbols she had sketched stared back at her, no longer academic curiosities or half-forgotten scribbles. They looked intentional now. Aggressive. Hungry.

By the time she reached the end of the email—Mrs. Archer's gentle but firm reminder that black magic was not to be trifled with, that curiosity without understanding could recoil violently, that Megan was too intelligent to endanger herself— the tightness in her chest had become painful.

Use your intellect for something greater, Mrs. Archer had written.

Toodles, she signed off.

Megan leaned back in her chair, the wood creaking softly beneath her weight. Her heart hammered as the implications settled in, rearranging everything she thought she knew.

"I need to talk to Aiden," she murmured.

She checked the time.

Too early.

Frustration prickled through her as she set the phone aside and lay back down. The room felt colder than it had moments before, the air heavier, as though something unseen had shifted closer. Her thoughts spiraled relentlessly—back to the cabin, the forest, the careful repetition of symbols carved and drawn with obsessive devotion. Not random. Never random.

And then, without warning, the images crept back in.

Aiden's body twisting unnaturally. Bone breaking. The woman stood untouched, her voice dismissing the creature with a simple, impossible authority—*Your evil is not welcomed here.*

Megan squeezed her eyes shut, but the thoughts kept multiplying, folding over one another until her mind felt crowded and strained. Each memory drained her further, siphoning strength, dulling resistance. Her eyelids grew heavy despite her efforts to stay alert. Exhaustion crept in like a patient thief, wrapping her limbs, weighing down her chest.

The world blurred.

Despite herself, sleep claimed her.

Yet even as consciousness slipped away, something lingered.

A pressure. A presence.

A voice threaded through her thoughts, intimate and insistent, as though it had been waiting for her to tire.

Trust no one.

The words echoed again, tightening around her mind like a closing fist. Familiar. Poisonous. Each repetition chipped away at something fragile inside her, warping the edges of safety until everything felt suspect.

As weariness pulled her deeper into darkness, the voice faded—not gone, merely retreating.

Waiting.

Chapter 13:
Edge of Recklessness

The school hallway roared with life—lockers slamming, laughter ricocheting off tiled walls, sneakers squealing against polished floors—but none of it reached Megan. The noise dissolved the moment she spotted Aiden leaning against the lockers, one foot braced casually behind him, his attention locked on a glossy science magazine. He looked normal. Too normal. Her chest tightened as she limped toward him, her ankle still protesting every step, the bruises beneath her clothes aching like reminders that the weekend hadn't ended cleanly. Her pulse picked up—not from relief alone, but from the remnants of the dream that still clung to her thoughts, thick and suffocating, like cobwebs she couldn't quite brush away.

"Hey, Aiden," she said when she reached him. Her voice came out smaller than she intended, thin and frayed at the edges. "I had another nightmare last night."

His head snapped up immediately. He folded the magazine shut and slid it into his backpack, his casual posture evaporating as concern took its place. "Another one?" His brows knit together as he studied her face. "What happened? You look like you've seen a ghost."

Megan swallowed, the word "ghost" scraping something raw inside her. She hesitated, that familiar warning whispering through her thoughts—trust no one. Her fingers curled reflexively at her sides. "It felt… real," she said finally. "You texted me. Told me to meet you at the cemetery." A chill rippled through her as the memory surfaced. "When I got there, everything was wrong. The trees were dead—twisted, like they'd been rotting for years—and this fog rolled in, thick and choking. It felt like the ground itself was watching me."

Aiden leaned closer, lowering his voice as students streamed past them. "Okay," he said gently. "What happened after that?"

"You weren't yourself," Megan continued, her throat tightening. "You sounded frantic. Unhinged. Like Charlie did before…" She stopped, the memory cutting too close, then forced herself onward. "You kept saying someone was following you. Watching you. You said there were people in old clothes hiding in the trees—calling out." She cleared her throat, but the image refused to loosen its grip, clawing at her thoughts.

"There's more," she said quietly. "The dream shifted. You disappeared." Her hands trembled as she clasped them together. "Then I heard screaming. Not just noise—screams that scraped inside my skull, sharp and relentless, like they were trying to tear something out of me." Her breath stuttered. "When I opened my eyes, the townsfolk were there again. Dressed like pilgrims. They were shouting, clawing at me, hitting me, throwing rocks." Her voice cracked as the memory surged. "Their faces… they didn't look human. Their eyes were wild—hungry. Full of hate. I couldn't move. I couldn't breathe."

Her heart began to race as she relived it, panic curling tight in her chest. "I tried to fight back, but someone threw a rock. It hit my head, and everything blurred." She shifted her weight, wincing as pain flared through her ankle. "When I came to, I was at the edge of the forest."

She lowered her voice instinctively. "That woman was there —the one from my other dreams. Her skin looked almost translucent. She said, This is when he took my love." Megan's stomach twisted. "Then I saw him. The man who always comes for me." Her skin prickled violently. "He was being burned alive."

The words hung heavy between them. Megan could still smell it—charred flesh, smoke thick enough to choke on. She could still feel the heat pressing against her skin, and hear the crackle of flames devouring him as he screamed. "It didn't feel symbolic," she whispered. "It felt like a memory. Like I was watching something that already happened. He was in so much pain."

Aiden leaned back against the locker, dragging a hand through his hair, his face pale. "Okay. First of all—I would never text you to meet me at a cemetery." He forced out a weak laugh that didn't quite land. "And… yeah. That's a lot." His voice softened. "How are you holding up?"

"I'm okay," Megan said, though the word felt flimsy. "Just shaken." She hugged her arms around herself. "I can still smell it. That's what scares me." She exhaled slowly. "My phone vibrating woke me up. I was almost afraid to look—like I'd still be dreaming." She glanced around before continuing. "It was an email from Mrs. Archer. About pagan symbols. Dark magic." Her voice dropped even lower. "I forwarded it to you."

Aiden frowned. "Dark magic?" he said, half-joking, half-serious. "What did she say?"

"She talked about ancient rituals," Megan replied. "Sacred ground. Shrines." Her heart thudded harder with each word. "It was a lot. But I can't stop thinking the dream wasn't just a dream. It felt like a warning, and it pointed to the reverend."

As the bell rang and they began walking, the hallway noise faded again, retreating into a distant hum. Aiden straightened, resolve settling into his expression. "I'll read the email. Let's meet after school and go through it together."

Megan nodded, nudging him lightly. "Thank you." Warmth flickered through her chest, followed immediately by a sharp twist of guilt. She had never kept anything from Aiden before, and the omission sat heavy in her gut. She hadn't told him everything. She hadn't told him about his face in the dream, the way it warped and split, or how he had turned on her, attacking her and slamming her to the ground. The secret pressed against her ribs, cold and uncomfortable, a lie by silence. But the warning lingered, coiled and insistent. Trust no one. And beneath it all, an unfamiliar pull tightened deep in her gut, instinctive and unyielding, telling her those words weren't paranoia—they were truth.

The rest of the day crawled. Finals hovered at the edges of her mind, but she couldn't focus. The email. The dream. The fire. Clock ticks sounded too loud, too deliberate, as if time itself were taunting her. Her notes dissolved into illegible scrawls, words blurring into nonsense.

When the final bell rang, she hurried home, dumped her bag, and left again, the walls of her house feeling close and oppressive. The library greeted her with hushed stillness, the scent of old paper and dust wrapping around her like a fragile shield.

Aiden was already there. "I read it," he said quietly. "There's more here than I like."

"Did you notice anything at the cabin?" Megan asked, leaning in. "Symbols? A shrine?"

He shook his head. "Nothing. And that's what bothers me."

Megan leaned back, then tapped the table. "The woman said, This is where I lost my love. Maybe the legend—the woodsman and the witch—means more than we think."

Aiden's eyes lit slightly. "It's worth checking."

They approached the librarian, who looked up from her desk as they approached. "Can I help you two?" she asked with a welcoming smile.

Megan took a deep breath, trying to convey the urgency of their request. "We're searching for verifiable proof, or any account, pertaining to the legend of the woodsman and the witch. Do you have anything on that?"

The librarian's expression shifted, a flicker of recognition crossing her face. "Ah, yes. We have old material linked to tales of the woodsman and the witch. One moment, please." She rose from her seat and shuffled through a nearby filing cabinet. After a moment, she returned with a large yellow envelope. "Here is the poem donated to our archive. Unfortunately, it is not empirical evidence or a record of the actual events like you requested, but it touches on the story."

Megan's fingers trembled as she took it. The paper inside was brittle, yellowed, and creased with age. Her breath caught as she unfolded it and began to read.

In the forest's heart, where shadows entwine,
A man of nature walks, his spirit divine.
With whispers of leaves and the song of the breeze,
The axe is his freedom, not swayed by the trees.

But the moonlight reveals a woman of magic.
Her laughter is calm; her presence is dramatic.

With spells woven softly but yet full of might,
She defies the old murmurs that darken the night.

Their gazes collide in a world filled with strife.
Two souls intertwined, defying one's life.
Yet the wind carries whispers, warnings unspoken.
Of a love that blooms fiercely but can lead to the broken.

Stay away from the wild, for danger is near.
The forest holds secrets; its shadows bring fear.
But love cannot wither under chains of despair.
So they dance in the twilight, without one care.

Yet fate can be cruel, the night sharp as knives.
For jealousy brews where the darkness thrives.
In a clash of the elements, the forest will weep.
As nature and magic in violence will meet.

In the silence that follows, the echoes of a curse.
Begging for blood to quench the witch's thirst.
Beneath the great oak where their love began,
The earth drinks their sorrow, as blood stains the land.

Now, legends are told of their tragic embrace.
Where love turned to violence, leaving only a trace.
In the forest's heart, they forever remain.
A haunting reminder of love wrapped in pain.

By the time Megan reached the final lines, her vision had blurred. A single tear slipped free and traced a slow path down her cheek, catching the fluorescent light like a fragile shard of glass. Her chest ached as she lowered the page. "This poem is beautiful," she breathed, awe and grief tangled together so tightly she couldn't separate them.

Across from her, Aiden nodded, though his expression had darkened. He glanced toward the librarian, who was methodically shelving books nearby. "Do you know who wrote it?" he asked.

The librarian paused and turned, her face calm but carefully neutral. "I'm afraid the author is unknown," she said. "It was given anonymously to the church many years ago. Decades later, it was donated here and placed in our archives."

Aiden leaned back with a sharp exhale, frustration bleeding into his voice. "So that's it. Another dead end." He folded his arms across his chest, as if bracing himself. "And from what we've learned, this poem is what started the Woodsman and the Witch story in the first place."

Before the weight of his words could settle, the librarian spoke again, her tone shifting—gentler, but firmer. "That love story," she said, "was told to me by my grandmother when I was a child." She stepped closer, lowering her voice. "This particular poem circulated briefly, yes. But the saga itself is far older. It's been passed down for generations—long before anyone bothered to write it down."

Megan leaned forward, her pulse quickening. "Do you think it could be based on real events?" she asked softly, instinctively lowering her voice, as though the question itself might disturb something dormant.

The librarian didn't answer right away. Her gaze drifted toward the tall windows, where the fading afternoon light cast long, distorted shadows across the floor. "Stories like these often are," she said at last. "Truth tends to be the seed. But time reshapes it. Love, loss, magic—those themes endure because they carry emotional weight. Sometimes heavier than facts."

Aiden exchanged a glance with Megan, then leaned in. "Are you saying this could've been real people?" he asked. "Not just a myth?"

The librarian nodded slowly. "Yes. Many legends begin with real lives. Real heartbreak. Real longing." Her eyes sharpened. "But with every retelling, the truth bends. And with it come shadows."

Megan's stomach tightened. "What kind of shadows?"

For a moment, the air around them felt colder. "Regret or grief," the librarian said quietly. "You have to know the story in order to understand." She straightened, her voice firm once more. "Many years ago, this town was said to be shrouded in superstition—afraid of what it didn't understand."

The librarian glanced up, her cheeks faintly flushed. "The story was told to me when I was a child," she continued. "They said the woodsman and the witch fell in love deep in the forest. They met in secret for months, but when discovered, their love was forbidden—condemned by the town's higher authorities. The woodsman's heart was promised to another."

She paused, her expression tightening. "The witch was exiled to the forest, accused of bewitching him and forbidden to ever return. Not long after, the woodsman fell ill." Her voice softened. "Some say he died of a broken heart," the librarian said quietly. "Others insist he was cursed."

She rose slowly from her chair, the legs scraping softly against the floor. "Whatever the truth was, it's been buried for years now—and there are some things this town has made sure no one will ever truly know."

The warning settled over them like a fog. Aiden glanced at Megan, unease flickering across his face. "What if we open something we can't shut again?"

Fear rippled through Megan—but beneath it, resolve took hold. "This town has survived worse," she said, though her voice wavered slightly. "And if people are being hurt… if someone—or something—is taking them… then we can't ignore it. Protecting people matters."

They thanked the librarian, both of them earnest, and she smiled politely—though there was something knowing in her eyes as she returned to her desk.

Back in the shadowed corner of the library, surrounded by towering shelves that seemed to lean inward, frustration simmered beneath their silence. Old books pressed close, heavy with secrets. The Summer Solstice loomed just over two months away, a deadline neither of them wanted to acknowledge out loud.

Aiden dragged a hand through his hair. "I don't know, Megan. It feels like we're chasing ghosts." He scoffed bitterly. "Every answer comes with another warning. Sometimes I think whatever this is was meant to stay buried."

Megan nodded slowly, unease twisting in her gut. "It does feel that way," she admitted. "But that's exactly what bothers me." Her gaze drifted toward the stacks. "Why so many warnings? Why all the fear around asking questions?" The sense of something vast and malignant lurking just beyond their understanding pressed in on her.

Aiden hesitated, then said carefully, "What if the forest is haunted? What if the townsfolk aren't involved at all—and the dreams are just... your imagination?" His eyes flicked to their notes, pages dense with unsettling patterns and disappearances.

Megan snorted softly. "Ghosts sneaking into town and kidnapping kids?" She gestured dismissively. "Ghosts don't do that." Then her expression sobered. "But the forest— something's wrong with it. Tormented spirits, maybe. Or trapped ones." Her stomach churned as the memory resurfaced. "Whatever we encountered out there... it wasn't natural."

Aiden nodded slowly. "It didn't want us there." His voice dropped. "That vine—whatever it was—it grabbed you. Tried to pull you in." The image still made his skin crawl. "It felt alive. Like the forest itself was aware."

Megan shuddered, her hand instinctively brushing her ankle. "And when we got out," she said quietly, "it didn't follow us." Her breath caught. "Almost like it knew we were leaving. Like it was watching… and waiting."

Aiden straightened suddenly, a grim focus settling into his posture. "I watched a documentary once," he said slowly, choosing his words with care. "It was about a priest—respected, untouchable—who turned out to be a serial killer." He hesitated, the thought visibly weighing on him. "What if the Goodwin family is the same? What if they've been hiding behind religion all along?" His jaw tightened. "If the forest is their graveyard, it would explain the cries you hear. Even the graveyard in your dream."

A cold rush of conflicting emotions surged through Megan. *It doesn't explain your transformation*, she thought, unease tightening her chest. Still, the idea lodged itself deep inside her, twisting her stomach. She wasn't just confronting old legends anymore—she was staring down the possibility of a family steeped in calculated cruelty.

Her mind drifted back to the nightmare. Reverend Goodwin's face—no longer human. His mouth stretched impossibly wide, teeth blackened and crumbling. His eyes were hollow pits, leaking thick black ooze that spilled down his cheeks and pooled at his feet like oil, like rot, like a promise. Even now, the image made her skin prickle.

The fear he commanded in Glory wasn't subtle. It seeped into everything—the quiet glances, the lowered voices, the way people avoided the forest like it might reach out and grab them. Every missing child seemed to pull another thread tighter around the church, weaving a pattern of control and silence. As the pieces aligned, Megan felt something inside her harden. Faith as leverage. Fear as obedience. The forest as a dumping ground for what no one dared question. And beneath it all—restless spirits, trapped and furious.

She crossed her arms, resolve sharpening like a blade. "You might be right," she said. "It does explain the warnings from the woman in my dreams." She moved to the window, staring down at the town square. Everything looked peaceful from above. Too peaceful. "But how much power does Reverend Goodwin really have?" Her reflection stared back at her—eyes bright, jaw set. "If I can't prove what happened back then, I'll make damn sure it doesn't happen again." Her voice dropped, fierce and certain. "This ends with us."

Aiden sighed heavily. "Megan," he said gently, "your dream warned you. The one with the oozing windows. You said to stay away from him." His eyes searched her face. "Even if we're wrong… we're talking about missing kids. People our age."

She turned toward him, her expression softening—but only slightly. "I know," she said. "And if the dreams are telling the truth, then the church is connected." She paced, restless. "We need to question him—but safely. Somewhere public. Somewhere he can't touch us."

Aiden joined her at the window, dread prickling along his spine. "That would only delay things," he said quietly.

"Eventually, he—or his followers—would catch us alone." Despite the fear, admiration flickered through him. "But you're right. If we're doing this, we do it properly. Proof first. Then we protect the town."

They packed up in silence, paper rustling softly in the dim library. "We'll watch him," Megan said. "From a distance." One last glance at the shelves, then they stepped outside into the cool evening air, daylight bleeding away.

As they walked, Aiden cleared his throat. "Hey… the fair's coming up," he said lightly. "Games. Rides. Sugar. Distraction."

Megan laughed despite herself. "You've mentioned it." Her smile faltered. "Finals come first."

"You're going to crush them," Aiden said. "Then we celebrate." His voice dipped. "I just… wanted some fun before you go back to Chicago."

She stopped. "I'm not disappearing without saying goodbye," she said firmly. "Fine. We'll go. Maybe we even get a chance to talk to the reverend." She smirked. "But first—finals."

"Deal!" Aiden grinned. "I'll help with biology if you save me from literature."

They laughed, tension loosening just enough to breathe. Streetlights cast long shadows as they reached her house. Safe. Familiar. Almost comforting.

Before leaving, Aiden paused. "Text me if you dream again."

"I will," Megan said softly. As he walked away, doubt crept in. How could I not trust him? Maybe the warnings were wrong. Maybe dreams lied.

Inside, normalcy wrapped around her—dinner, dishes, homework. Routine. Reassuring. She showered, journaled, and finally slipped into bed.

But in the dark, the poem echoed in her thoughts. The woodsman. The witch. Love lost to fire.

As sleep crept closer, the shadows felt heavier—waiting.

Weeks slipped by, and with them the sharp edge of final examinations dulled until they became little more than distant impressions in Megan's memory. Spring bled fully into early summer, and Glory transformed beneath the sun's steady gaze. The air warmed. Flowers burst open in wild, unapologetic color. Wildflowers swayed along roadsides and fences, nodding lazily in the breeze, while the scent of freshly cut grass drifted through open windows like a promise of renewal. Laughter came easier now. The days stretched longer, swollen with light and the illusion of endless time.

For the first time in weeks, Megan felt unburdened. The tight knot that had lived beneath her ribs during finals loosened, replaced by something lighter—hope, maybe, or relief. She allowed herself to imagine what came next: lazy afternoons by the lake, bonfires that crackled beneath star-thick skies, the ache of Chicago drifting farther away with each passing day. For a moment, the darkness receded.

The morning breeze slipped through her open window, cool and clean, carrying the scent of dew and blossoms. Megan reached for her phone and blinked as the screen lit up.

Just got my grades back! Passed all my finals!

She smiled instantly, thumbs flying.

That's amazing! I aced mine too!

The excitement crackled between them, each message feeding the next.

We should celebrate at the fair later! Aiden wrote.

Ferris wheel first, Megan replied without hesitation. Then funnel cake.

She laughed softly, heart fluttering. The fair—lights, noise, tradition. A temporary escape. Something normal.

She sprang from bed, weaving around half-packed boxes stacked along the walls. Her ankle no longer throbbed; the bruise had faded to a faint shadow. Downstairs, the kitchen glowed with sunlight as her mother wrapped dishes in newspaper, movements brisk but careful.

"I'm sorry I didn't make breakfast," her mom said, brushing hair from her face.

"It's okay," Megan replied, already reaching for a bowl. "Cereal's perfect."

She poured Cinnamon Crunch, the sugary clatter loud in the quiet kitchen, milk pooling around the edges. As she ate, her thoughts drifted to the fair—the music, the rides, the way the night would glow with colored lights. For a few hours, she could pretend nothing was wrong.

Her mother watched her carefully. "You excited about today?"

"Definitely," Megan said. "Aiden and I are going all out."

"Just be safe," her mom said gently. "Keep your phone charged."

"I will," Megan promised, though the words felt automatic.

Later, dressed in a sundress and boots, hair twisted into a messy bun, she caught her reflection and smiled. She looked like herself again—or close enough.

By afternoon, the fairgrounds pulsed with life. Megan arrived early, purchasing a glittering wristband that caught the sun as she stepped inside. The air was thick with sweetness—cotton candy, caramel popcorn, and fried dough. Music thumped from somewhere unseen. Laughter spilled in every direction.

Then the reverend's voice rose above it all.

"Welcome, everyone!"

Megan slowed near the edge of the crowd. Reverend Goodwin stood on the platform, hands raised, smile wide. His words flowed smoothly—blessings, gratitude, prayers for the children of Glory. People listened, rapt. Trusting.

Something tightened in Megan's chest, an instinctive clench she couldn't explain. The fair's lights blurred for a moment, the laughter around her dimming to a dull roar.

Her phone buzzed.

Aiden: *Meet me at the fountain.*

She turned away from the stage and wove through the crowd, shoulders brushing strangers, until she spotted Aiden near the stone fountain. He lifted a hand, his grin easy, familiar—an anchor in the noise and color.

"You missed the prayers," she said when she reached him, forcing lightness into her voice.

Aiden glanced back toward the stage, then returned his gaze to her, the grin fading. His posture straightened, resolve settling in. "Let's talk to him," he said quietly. "Before he disappears into the crowd."

They moved together, threading through clusters of townsfolk as Reverend Goodwin shook hands and exchanged pleasantries. Up close, his smile was flawless—rehearsed. When his eyes landed on them, something flickered there. Recognition. Calculation. Then warmth slid back into place.

"Reverend Goodwin," Aiden began, his tone polite but edged with steel. "We were hoping to ask about the upcoming summer solstice. Are there any special ceremonies planned? Gatherings? Anything involving the church?"

Goodwin's smile thinned, but it did not vanish. "Nothing beyond our usual services," he replied smoothly. "The solstice tends to inspire rumors. We prefer to keep our focus on faith, not spectacle."

Megan stepped closer, close enough to see the faint tension at his jaw. "Funny," she said. "Rumors seem to follow the church a lot lately." She held his gaze. "Did you hear about the teenager who went missing last year?"

Aiden didn't give him time to respond. "And Amber Langley," he added. "She vanished too. Why didn't the church organize a search? Or even speak about it publicly?"

For a brief moment, the fair seemed to exhale. Music dulled. Laughter thinned. Reverend Goodwin's eyes hardened—just a fraction—before the mask settled back into place.

"I expressed my deepest sympathy to Mrs. Langley when Amber and her father left town," he said smoothly. "As for the other teenager, I cannot speculate on why anyone would wander into the forest. Adolescence is a fragile time. Depression can drive young people toward... unfortunate decisions." His voice remained calm, measured. "Tragic stories," he said gently. "And painful ones. But stories nonetheless. No matter, the church prays for all lost souls. We offer comfort, not speculation."

Megan's stomach tightened. She stepped closer, her voice sharp enough to cut through the carnival din. "Forest?" she repeated. "Who said anything about the forest?" Her pulse hammered, as she glanced at Aiden, then back at the reverend. "And you said Amber left with her father—but witnesses saw her enter the forest too, alone."

Aiden didn't hesitate. "You mentioned speculation?" he echoed, his voice cutting cleanly through the noise. "People don't just vanish. And it's hard not to notice how often these disappearances trace the same pattern—same places, same families, same beliefs." He leaned in slightly, eyes locked. "So when do we stop calling it rumor and start calling it what it is?

What about the other missing kids? This isn't just about Amber."

A murmur rippled behind them. Goodwin's gaze flicked briefly toward the onlookers, then returned to Megan—sharp now, assessing. "Careful," he said softly. "Grief can distort perception. And imagination has a way of turning sorrow into accusation."

Aiden stepped forward. "So you're saying the church has no knowledge at all? No involvement? No responsibility?" His voice dropped. "Because it's starting to look like silence."

Goodwin folded his hands together, unbothered. Untouchable. "I am saying," he replied evenly, "that the church and my family have served this town for generations. We do not abduct children, and we do not hide crimes." His eyes lingered on each of them in turn. "You are young. Passionate. But passion without proof is dangerous."

Aiden's mouth curved into a thin, humorless grin. He glanced at Megan first—just long enough to acknowledge what they both knew—then turned back to the reverend. "Proof?" he said lightly, the word sharp beneath the calm. "We did mention witnesses, right?" He tilted his head, studying Goodwin like a puzzle he'd already started to solve. "Funny thing is, those same witnesses didn't just see the kids. They said you were there too. You and other church officials. Same nights. Same places." His grin widened, but his eyes stayed cold. "So maybe the danger isn't passion without proof. Maybe it's pretending certain people are above suspicion."

The warmth drained from Reverend Goodwin's face. The change in him was subtle—but unmistakable. "I'm afraid I can't discuss matters I know nothing about," he said calmly. Too calmly. "Teenagers have vivid imaginations." His eyes narrowed just slightly.

Megan felt it then—a pressure behind his words. Not fear. Control. "We're just asking questions," she said, though her tone betrayed her. "Questions people are too afraid to ask themselves."

"And some questions," Goodwin said, smiling faintly, "are asked by those who don't yet understand the weight of answers."

He inclined his head politely, already stepping back. "Enjoy the fair. Let joy be your focus tonight." A pause. "It's healthier that way."

As he turned away, he stopped and reached into his pocket, producing two food tickets. "Here," he said, pressing them into Aiden's hand. "Enjoy a treat from any booth—with my blessing. I've never had much of a sweet tooth." Then he melted back into the crowd, the noise rushed in again—music, laughter, lights—but it no longer felt harmless.

Megan exhaled slowly as she watched him disappear into the crowd, her pulse still racing. "Did you see that?" she whispered, the words tight with urgency. "He slipped—just for a second." She shook her head, unease curling in her stomach. "He knows more than he's admitting. Whatever secret

Reverend Goodwin is carrying, he's guarding it with absolute certainty."

Aiden snorted softly. "Well, add low-key threatened by a reverend to today's list of achievements." He held up the tickets. "You think this works for a funnel cake."

Megan shook her head. "Always thinking with your stomach." She stared down at the paper in her hand, appetite gone. "I expected more from a man of faith." She exhaled slowly. "You're right. We just painted targets on our backs." She forced herself to straighten. "Let's move. We're not getting anything else from him."

They drifted deeper into the fair, stopping beneath the Ferris wheel as it creaked and turned overhead, its colorful gondolas swinging gracefully against the backdrop of the clear blue sky. "Let's do that first!" Megan exclaimed, her excitement breaking through. "No backing out."

Aiden groaned, a terrified look spreading across his face. "Alright, but you know I'm terrified of heights, right?"

"That's the point," she teased, nudging him forward. "Don't worry, I am here with you." They joined the line, the sounds of laughter and carnival music surrounding them, a stark contrast to the weight of their thoughts.

As they climbed into a gondola and settled in, Megan's eyes sparkled with joy. "Look at the view! This is amazing," she said, her voice filled with wonder as they ascended. The fairground spread out below them, a patchwork of vibrant colors and bustling energy.

Aiden forced a smile, trying to focus on the scenery rather than the dizzying height. "Yeah, it's great from up here," he replied, though his heart pounded with a mix of exhilaration and anxiety.

When they reached the top, they paused for a moment, taking in the sprawling fairgrounds below. Megan pointed at the teacups. "We have to ride the teacups, but first, let's play some games!" Her voice was playful again as they began their descent back to the fair.

They stopped at a ring toss game, where Aiden attempted to throw the rings with determination but missed each time. "Come on, Aiden! You can do better than that!" Megan teased, her laughter ringing like music in the air. Aiden rolled his eyes, trying to redeem himself at a balloon dart game, but his aim was just as poor. "Okay, I admit it. I suck at this!" he chuckled, scratching his head in mock defeat.

Megan couldn't help but tease him further, her playful spirit shining bright. "Maybe you should stick to the rides!" she joked, her eyes twinkling with mischief. "I'll handle the games, and you can just enjoy the spinning. Speaking of spinning, race you to the teacups!"

Megan and Aiden burst into laughter as they raced towards the teacup ride. The air was filled with the sweet melody of carnival music. In the distance she could see the colorful teacups spinning, each a variety of pastel hues, beckoning them with their lighthearted charm. With her bun falling loose and her long hair flowing behind her like a banner of excitement, Megan dashed ahead, her competitive spirit ignited by the challenge.

As they reached the entrance, Megan's laughter rang out, bright and infectious, as she hopped into a teal teacup adorned with cheerful daisies. She turned to Aiden, her eyes sparkling with playful victory. "Looks like I beat you!" she teased, her voice bubbling with joy. The sunlight caught her features, illuminating her playful smirk, and Aiden couldn't help but chuckle at her enthusiasm.

Aiden, slightly out of breath but wearing a grin of his own, pulled himself into the teacup. "Oh, come on! I let you win," he retorted, attempting to maintain a facade of nonchalance, though the twinkle in his eye betrayed his amusement. The ride operator gave a nod, and the teacups spun, slowly at first, then gaining momentum, each rotation sending their laughter soaring into the blue sky.

As the cups spun, Megan squealed with delight, the world around them becoming a blur of color and sound. The sensation of the ride was exhilarating, a delightful mixture of giddy anticipation and dizzying joy. With every turn, she felt the rush of wind against her face, the thrill of motion igniting her senses. The sweet scent of popcorn mingled with the vibrant atmosphere, and the laughter of other riders added to the symphony of joy surrounding them.

"Look at us go!" she shouted, her voice rising above the joyous chaos as she tilted the cup to gain more speed, her playful challenge igniting a competitive fire within Aiden. He grabbed the wheel, twisting it with determination. "Want to see how fast it can spin?" he declared, the challenge adding an extra layer of excitement to the ride.

Megan's laughter echoed as she spun faster, her competitive spirit shining through. "You can go faster than that. Let's go!" she joked, her eyes dancing with mischief as the cups swirled around them, the vibrant colors blurring into a vibrant tapestry of laughter and joy.

As the ride slowed and the cups gently halted, Megan's cheeks flushed with exhilaration. Both breathless with laughter, they stepped out and continued to explore the fair, stopping at the food booth where they decided to share a fluffy funnel cake covered with baked cinnamon apples and two scoops of vanilla ice cream. As they took turns indulging in their blissful dessert, Megan laughed at the way Aiden's face lit up with delight. After finishing the funnel cake, they plunged into the remaining rides and games.

As the sun set, casting warm hues of orange and pink across the sky, Megan and Aiden wrapped up their exploration of the fair. "See? I knew you would have fun!" Aiden said, glancing at her with a smile. Megan nodded, her heart swelling with happiness at the memories they had made together.

"Yes, I had a blast. Today has been perfect," Megan replied, the warmth of the moment wrapping around them like a cozy blanket. "But I'm not sure I'm ready for that party, though!" She glanced at Aiden, who offered her a reassuring smile, but the shadows of doubt still danced in her mind.

"I figured we could just chill by the bonfire!" Aiden suggested, a hint of concern in his voice.

"You're right, let's go!" Megan said, pushing those thoughts aside. She took a deep breath, determined to enjoy the evening despite the looming tension. The flickering light from the bonfire in the distance illuminated the faces of familiar friends and foes alike, each one adding to the electric atmosphere surrounding them.

Chapter 14:

Betrayed by the Night

As Megan and Aiden approached the barn, the soft glow of string lights hanging from the rafters flickered like fireflies against the dusky sky. The barn, a sprawling structure made of aged timber, loomed large before them, its silhouette dark against the fading light. The faint sound of laughter and music spilled out through the open doors, mingling with the sounds of nature—the distant croaking of frogs, the rustling leaves, and the scent of the nearby forest.

"Can't believe I am here?" Megan exclaimed, with a spark of anxiety in her eyes that reflected the twinkling lights.

"Yeah, just hope it's not too crazy," Aiden replied, trying to mask his own apprehension. He knew Megan felt uncomfortable about being there, but with the forest bordering the barn, he had his own concerns, especially with their experience almost two months ago.

They made their way toward the campfire, where a small group had gathered, roasting marshmallows over the crackling flames. The flickering light cast playful shadows on their faces, highlighting the laughter and camaraderie that filled the air.

"Hey, you two! Get over here!" Jenna shouted, waving them over with a marshmallow on a stick. "What took you so long? We're already making s'mores! You can't have a party without s'mores—and a drink, of course!" As she spoke, Jenna waved her red cup around, sloshing some of the liquid onto her arm and spilling it into the dirt beneath her feet.

Megan, perplexed, glanced upward at Aiden, wandering about the current events unfolding in front of them. Just then, Thomas and Lexi forced their way past them, with Thomas taking a moment to ruffle Aiden's hair. "Hey, lil guy!" he exclaimed. Megan's heart dropped; for a brief second, a rush of anxiety slammed into her as she felt her dream coming back to her in waves—only to have reality tear through it like broken glass.

She stopped in her tracks as Jenna locked eyes with her. Jenna rolled her eyes and let out an exaggerated sigh. "They're here? Forget it! Let's just meet up with everyone inside; I need a refill!" With that, Jenna dropped the sticks into the fire and walked off with Lexi.

"Are you coming or what?" Lexi called back, snapping Thomas from his thoughts. With a resigned smile, he joined the group heading into the barn.

Megan and Aiden took a deep breath, settling down beside the bonfire, inhaling the sweet smell of melting chocolate and toasted marshmallows. The warmth of the fire felt inviting, but the darkened woods behind them loomed ominously.

"Well, that went better than I expected," Aiden said, shattering the uncomfortable silence.

"Yeah but I don't want it to ruin my fun." Megan reached over, grabbing two sticks and handing one to Aiden. "Graham cracker, chocolate, marshmallow, and another graham cracker!" she declared, her face lit with enthusiasm.

"That's way too much chocolate. You need balance!" Aiden retorted, smirking as he crafted his own s'more. They laughed, and for a moment, the warm glow of the campfire made it easy to forget the darkness surrounding them.

As the night wore on, the party sounds inside the barn grew louder, the music's beat pulsing through the air. Aiden glanced toward the barn, illuminated by colorful lights that danced along the walls, but he couldn't shake the nagging feeling that something was off.

Megan and Aiden sat by the crackling fire when an eerie rustling emerged from the edge of the woods. Aiden stiffened, his heart racing as he turned to look. The trees swayed, but no wind stirred.

"Do you hear that?" Aiden mumbled, his voice barely audible over the sounds of the bonfire. He paused for a moment, glancing back toward the barn entrance, where everyone seemed to be dancing.

Megan's laughter faded as the sound from the woods reached her ears. She nodded slowly, a chill threading through her chest. "Yeah," she said, forcing the words out. "It sounded like… someone yelling."

Before anyone could respond, the barn doors flew open.

Lexi burst through, the moon hanging low behind her, washing the yard in a pale, sickly glow. Firelight flickered uselessly against the darkness beyond the barn, barely touching it. Tears streaked Lexi's face, catching the light as she stopped at the edge of the wooden platform. She stood there trembling, caught between fury and something that looked dangerously close to breaking apart.

"Babe, I was going to tell you!" Thomas blurted, his voice loud and raw. He stepped toward her, hands lifted as if he could physically pull the moment back together.

Lexi recoiled. Even from where Megan stood, she could see the betrayal burning in Lexi's eyes. "Tell me what, Thomas?" Lexi shot back. Her voice shook, but it carried across the yard. "That you've been lying to me this entire time?"

The fire crackled beside them, the sound sharp and intrusive, each pop seeming to underline her words.

Randy hovered a few steps behind Thomas, shifting his weight like he wasn't sure where to stand. "Guys, maybe we should just—"

"No!" Lexi cut in.

Jenna swayed slightly where she stood, grabbing Randy's arm to steady herself. Megan watched her eyes dart between Lexi and Thomas, wide and unfocused. "This has to come out," Jenna said. "We can't keep pretending everything's fine when it isn't."

Thomas dragged a hand through his hair, his jaw tight. "I didn't want to hurt you, Lexi. I—" He stopped, the words failing him.

The silence that followed pressed down hard, thick and uncomfortable.

"You didn't want to hurt me?" Lexi said quietly. Too quietly. "What about the truth? The truth is already hurting, Thomas. You've kept me in the dark about everything."

Megan felt the argument closing in on itself, sharp and spiraling, when Jake's attention snapped toward the trees.

"Guys," he said, voice low. "Can we talk about this later? There's something out there—"

"No," Lexi said again, louder now. "Tell me the truth. Why would you tell your friends about Miami and not tell your girlfriend?"

Thomas looked like he'd been struck. "I was waiting for the right moment!"

"You thought this was the right time?" Lexi demanded.

Before he could answer, something rustled in the trees.

The sound was close enough that Megan's stomach dropped. Every head turned toward the dark edge of the woods. The firelight didn't reach far—just enough to reveal movement. Then she saw them.

Red eyes.

Low to the ground. Unblinking.

Tyler cursed under his breath and grabbed Zack's arm. "We should get inside. Now."

Thomas hesitated, glancing between Lexi and the woods. "We can't let a little miscommunication ruin tonight. Ruin us. We need to stick together."

Megan watched Lexi's breathing turn shallow, watched anger and fear war across her face. "Together?" Lexi said. "How can I trust you after everything? After—"

The rustling grew louder.

The red eyes didn't move. They just watched.

Megan took an instinctive step back as the group shifted as one, fear replacing the argument in an instant. Whatever had been hiding out there felt closer now—more real than the secrets they'd been shouting about moments before.

Then the bushes parted.

A raccoon stepped into the light.

Then two smaller shapes, clumsy and wide-eyed, trailing behind her. The red eyes softened into something almost harmless as the little family waddled toward the warmth of the fire, noses twitching.

For a heartbeat, no one spoke.

Randy laughed—an abrupt bark that didn't match the mood. "You should've seen your faces."

Relief broke through the tension in scattered bursts of laughter. Even Thomas cracked a smile. "Guess we were just scared of a bunch of furballs."

"Those baby raccoons are adorable!" Jenna exclaimed, dropping to her knees near the fire. Her smile was wide and unguarded as she watched the little ones wobble forward, their dark fur catching the firelight. She reached out toward them before anyone could stop her.

Megan didn't laugh.

She watched Lexi instead.

The anger hadn't left her—it had only gone quiet. And when Lexi turned back to Thomas, her voice cut clean through the remaining humor.

"You think this is funny?" she snapped. "You think it's okay to joke around after lying to me?"

The laughter died instantly.

Thomas opened his mouth. "I wasn't trying to—"

"Save it," Lexi said. "You're not taking this seriously. You think messing with my feelings is a joke?"

As the raccoon family approached the fire, Lexi shouted, "I can't believe you! You're such an idiot for thinking everything is just fine!" The sound sent the little creatures scattering back into the bushes.

Her fists clenched at her sides, she spun on her heel and stormed into the field, her footsteps echoing across the yard. The group exchanged uneasy glances; laughter had vanished, replaced by tight, silent tension.

"Lexi, wait!" Thomas called after her, his voice rising with urgency. She didn't stop. Megan watched her disappear into the shadows, and Thomas froze in place, staring after her.

Something had heard them.

And it hadn't left.

Lexi ran until her lungs burned and her vision blurred, the laughter and music from the party dissolving behind her like something unreal—something that had never belonged to her in the first place. The night swallowed the noise whole, replacing it with a damp, watchful quiet that pressed in on her ears. She didn't slow until she reached the small park down the road, the place where the streetlights thinned and the shadows stretched long and crooked across the sand.

The swings creaked softly in the breeze, an old, lonely sound.

Her legs finally gave out. Lexi collapsed onto one of the swings, the cold plastic seat biting through her thin dress as the metal chains rattled violently under her grip. Tears spilled unchecked, hot and relentless, dripping from her chin into the sand below. She clutched the chains like anchors, her knuckles whitening as if holding on was the only thing keeping her from shattering apart completely.

Her chest heaved as she struggled for air, every breath jagged, shallow. The swing rocked beneath her—back and forth, back and forth—too gentle, too calm, mocking the storm ripping through her chest. The rhythmic creak of the chains grated on her nerves, each sound stretching the silence thinner, sharper.

Footsteps crunched behind her. She stiffened before she even looked up.

"Lexi—wait!" Thomas called, jogging toward her, his voice strained, breathless. "Please. Can we just talk?"

She squeezed her eyes shut, then sprang off the swing, her shoes sinking into the cool, damp sand. She wiped at her face angrily, smearing tears instead of stopping them. "Talk about what, Thomas?" she snapped, turning on him. "Leaving me behind while you run off to college in Miami?" Her laugh broke, brittle and sharp. "Apparently that decision didn't include me."

He stopped a few feet away, hands hovering uselessly at his sides, guilt and frustration warping his expression. "I was going to tell you," he said quickly. "I tried. We kept getting interrupted, and I thought we had more time to figure this out together."

"Together?" The word tasted bitter. Lexi scoffed, disbelief rising into anger. "That's funny, considering you made the whole damn decision alone." She stepped toward him, finger stabbing the air between them. "We agreed on Virginia Tech. Together. We planned our future—together."

Her voice cracked as she turned away from him, wrapping her arms around herself like she could hold herself together through sheer force. "But Miami?" she whispered, then spun back around, fury blazing. "You chose that alone. You chose to throw us away—alone."

"I'm not throwing anything away!" Thomas protested, desperation leaking into his voice. "Miami is a huge opportunity. I thought you'd be happy for me."

"Happy?" Lexi whirled on him, her scream tearing into the night. "Why would I be happy about you lying to me?" Tears streamed down her face again, unstoppable now. She pointed at him, her hand shaking. "When I mentioned California, you said long-distance never works. You said you wanted us close." Her voice dropped, trembling. "So I turned down UCLA. I gave it up—for you."

The words hung there, heavy and damning. Her anger surged hotter, sharper. "But now suddenly long-distance is something we can 'figure out'?" she demanded. "So when it comes to dreams and goals, only yours matter?"

Thomas stepped closer, reaching for her hand. "Lexi, please —"

She jerked away from him as if burned. "Don't." Her voice broke completely. "Don't touch me."

"I didn't mean to hurt you," he said softly. "I'm sorry. Can we just—can we try to figure this out?"

"Figure out what?" she cried. "How long distance doesn't work? How you lied to me? Or how you convinced me to abandon my dreams so you could chase yours?" Her breath hitched violently. "I need space. Just—just tell Jenna and Amy to come meet me. Okay?"

"Lexi—"

"Please," she cut in, her voice suddenly flat, final. "Just go. I want you to leave." She sat down hard, eyes fixed anywhere but on him, the chains creaking again as the swing began its lonely sway.

Lexi remained on the swing, alone beneath the dim lights. The park was quiet, the slow, endless creak of metal rocking her back and forth like the echo of a future unraveling.

Thomas stopped a few feet away, saying nothing, just watching. She felt his presence press against the edges of her thoughts, heavy and unspoken. Slowly, she turned her face away, letting the swing carry her instead, and watched him fade into the darkness, swallowed by the night. He walked away from the park, shoulders hunched under the invisible weight of their argument, each step slow and deliberate. Every instinct told him to move faster, to shake off the tension, but his feet wouldn't obey, and the quiet of the night pressed against him like a physical force.

As he turned away from the park, the weight of his argument with Lexi still heavy on his shoulders. Each step reminded him of the tension that had just unfolded. He made his way back to the party, the lively music and laughter beckoning him like a moth drawn to a flame, promising a temporary escape from his worries. As he stepped inside, the bright lights and cheerful chatter enveloped him, and he scanned the crowd, searching for familiar faces in the sea of people.

Spotting Randy sitting with Zack, Jake, and Tyler, he approached them, hoping to drown out the turmoil swirling in his mind. Their laughter was infectious, a welcome distraction from the emotional storm he had just left behind.

"Hey, man! What happened with Lexi?" Randy asked, leaning back in his chair, a smirk playing on his lips, eager for the latest gossip.

"She's blowing things out of proportion," Thomas replied with a sigh, taking a seat beside him. He felt the pressure in his chest lessen, finding comfort in his companions, even briefly.

"Yeah, I told you, bro. Long-distance relationships are difficult, but they're not catastrophic," Tyler chimed in, letting out a chuckle. "She must consider the potential future that you two share and how this decision will benefit you both."

"I know she does not see the bigger picture." Thomas said, feeling a flicker of relief at the friendship surrounding him. It was nice to have his guys rallying behind him. "She's being selfish. It's a wonderful opportunity for me; she ought to be supportive."

Jake nodded, raising his cup in a small toast. "You've got to focus on what's best for you. Miami is going to be amazing. Imagine the adventures awaiting you there!"

As the guys continued to talk, sharing jokes and stories to lighten the mood, Jenna stumbled over, her cheeks flushed from the effects of the drinks she had consumed. Her eyes narrowed as she took in their conversation. "What are you talking about?" she asked, suspicion lacing her tone as curiosity sparked about their animated conversation.

Thomas exchanged a glance with his friends, knowing they would not share the details to keep the mood light.

"Just some guy talk," Randy said, but Jenna wasn't having any of it.

"You're talking about Lexi, aren't you?" she said, her voice rising, filled with concern and frustration. "That is your girlfriend, you shouldn't be talking behind her back!"

"Come on, Jenna. It's just the truth," Thomas replied, trying to keep his tone calm and even. "She needs to stop being so negative about everything. It's my opportunity, which she ought to grasp.

Jenna's expression hardened. "Just like California was an opportunity for her—oh wait, you know what happened to that." She crossed her arms across her chest, her disappointment clear. "If you cared about her, you would have told her about Miami long ago! She deserves better!" Her firm voice and the disappointment in her eyes cut deeper than any criticism.

With that, she turned on her heel and stormed off, leaving the guys in stunned silence, the lively atmosphere of the party feeling heavy and tense. The laughter and banter faded, replaced by an uncomfortable realization of the impact of their words.

"Wow, I didn't see that coming," Randy said, shaking his head in disbelief.

"Ignore Lexi and Jenna; they will understand," Thomas said, attempting to brush off the tension Jenna had left behind. "Let's focus on the good times ahead. Miami is going to be epic!"

Subsequently, talk reverted to college experiences, with spirits lifting as the fellows cheered, sharing football stories. "To Thomas and breaking records at Miami!" Randy shouted, raising his drink high above his head, his enthusiasm infectious.

"Let's go, Canes! Let's go, Canes!" they roared, their cheers echoing through the barn as they celebrated the future. Laughter and excitement filled the air, drowning out any lingering worries they had, making them feel invincible.

Anthony and Amy pushed through the barn doors, the roar of laughter and shouts pressing against them like a living thing. The warm, musty air hit first, thick with the smell of sweat and spilled drinks, then the lights—strings of flickering bulbs casting uneven, jittering shadows across the floor. Amy's eyes landed on Jenna almost immediately, her voice slicing above the crowd, high-pitched and harsh. She was yelling at a group of guys, her body wobbling, her balance uncertain. One second she was there, the next, she stumbled backward and vanished into the darker recesses of the barn, swallowed by shadow.

"Yo, fellas! Did I miss anything?" Anthony's voice cracked through the noise.

The guys spun toward him, grinning wide, arms outstretched. Hugs, pats on the shoulder, laughter that bounced off the rafters like loose gravel. Amy lingered at the edge, sensing a flicker of something wrong beneath the cheer, a tremor in the energy she couldn't name. Anthony caught it too—his brow flicked, lips twisting into a question he didn't voice.

"Well, you missed a little drama," Thomas said, exhaling like he wanted to wipe it off the floor. He shoved a cold can into Anthony's hand; condensation slicked his fingers. "But it's fine. You're behind, Ant—time to catch up."

"We aren't drinking," Amy said, cutting through the false cheer.

Randy let out a playful boo, and the others laughed along, but Amy felt the bubble of levity crack. The tension she'd sensed tightened, a thread stretched to breaking.

"What just happened with Jenna?" she asked, her voice lower now, sharp as broken glass. "And where's Lexi?"

"Jenna's drunk and Lexi," Thomas said, jerking his head toward the door. The guys snickered, a ripple of mockery that made Amy's stomach turn.

"Yea Lexi?" Amy pressed.

Thomas's shrug came slow, measured. "We got into it. She stormed out. She's at the park. Told me to leave her alone—but asked for you. And Jenna."

The laughter drained. Silence fell like a weight, heavy and watching.

"What do you mean you got into it?" Amy said, eyes scanning the group. Faces avoided her gaze, expressions closed off. "What happened?"

Anthony stepped in, tone sharper than usual. "Did you tell her about Miami?"

Amy's head snapped to Thomas. Her heart thudded, sudden and hard.

"Miami?" she demanded. "What about Miami, Thomas?"

Thomas shrugged, uneasy. "Opportunity came up. I took it. Lexi didn't take it well."

"You think?" Amy's voice sliced through the space. "She sacrificed for you. Everyone else knew before she did. That's—" Her words choked off as the weight of silence pressed in, the guys' discomfort visible even through their feigned casualness.

"You guys are such assholes," Amy muttered under her breath, frustration and hurt sparking sharp. She turned and left before anyone could answer.

The night air hit her like a wall—cool, damp, carrying the distant flicker of the bonfire. Megan and Aiden sat near the glow, leaning toward each other, soft smiles cutting through the dark. But movement shifted at the edge of Amy's vision. Jenna stumbled toward them, face tight with anger, eyes wild.

"Hey—" Amy called, breaking into a jog.

Jenna didn't slow. "What the hell are you looking at, Megan?" Her words ripped through the night, jagged and bitter. "Haven't you gotten the clue nobody wants you here? Why don't you and your wannabe boyfriend crawl back under whatever rock you came from?"

Megan and Aiden exchanged a glance but stayed silent, the fire popping between them like nervous breaths.

Amy moved faster, stepping between them. "We're going to find Lexi," she said, gripping Jenna's arm. "We're done here."

Jenna scoffed, swaying slightly as Amy steered her away. "Yeah. Don't want to waste time with losers anyway."

They threaded through the thinning party crowd, the barn's yellow lights shrinking behind them until they barely touched the edge of the field. Amy felt the air change as they neared the trees—cooler, heavier. Crickets rasped from the grass, loud and relentless, while frogs croaked from somewhere deeper in the woods, their calls uneven, overlapping, then stopping without warning. The sudden silence made Amy's shoulders tense.

Jenna slowed. Amy watched her expression shift—curiosity pulling her forward while fear crept in beneath it, tightening her mouth, widening her eyes. She stared into the narrow break between the trunks like she was trying to convince herself something was there.

"Hey," Jenna said softly, lifting a finger. "Do you see that?"

Amy followed her gaze. Nothing solid, just darkness folding in on itself, a faint movement sliding behind bark and leaves. Her stomach clenched. "See what?" she asked, even though her pulse had already started to race. "Come on, Jenna. Lexi won't wait for us."

Jenna didn't answer. The forest smelled damp and old, like rot hidden under soil. Amy stepped closer and grabbed Jenna's wrist. "You know I don't like this forest," she said, her voice lower now. "It never feels empty." The words sounded wrong the moment she said them, like an invitation.

Jenna took a step, hesitated, and her foot caught. She went down hard, the thud of her body against the grass muted by the night. She laughed as she rolled onto her back—too loud, too sharp, the sound cracking through the quiet like something breaking. The crickets started again, slower this time, and Amy couldn't shake the feeling that whatever Jenna had seen hadn't moved on. It was still there, hidden just beyond the treeline, listening.

Amy tugged Jenna forward. A step too late: Jenna tripped, rolling onto the grass with a soft thud. Her laughter erupted, wild and unsteady, breaking the eerie quiet of the night.

Amy exhaled, frustration and worry coiling tight. The barn behind them had gone quiet—too quiet. "Come on," she urged, helping Jenna up. "We need to keep moving."

Jenna rolled onto her back, gazing at the star-strewn sky. "The stars are so pretty tonight, Amy!" she said, eyes bright, oblivious to the tension still pressing in the shadows.

"Are you serious?" Amy groaned, irritation creeping in, but it vanished the moment she spotted Lexi, sitting alone on a swing, her silhouette fragile against the shimmer of moonlight. "Come on, Jenna, let's go. Lexi's over there!"

"I'm fine! Go ahead. I'll catch up," Jenna insisted, rolling onto her stomach, propping herself on her elbows.

Amy stood over her, watching Jenna laugh, a sound bubbling up from somewhere light and unrestrained. It made Amy's chest tighten, a strange mix of relief and lingering concern. "Are you sure you're okay?" she asked, trying to read the state of her friend beneath the surface of that carefree grin.

"I'm fine!" Jenna repeated, eyes sparkling with mischief, waving her off as if worry itself were ridiculous.

Amy let out a sigh, shaking her head. She turned and sprinted toward Lexi, leaving Jenna in the soft grass. "Lexi!" she called, breaking into a run. Relief washed over her when they collided, arms locking in a tight embrace. For a moment, the chaos of the party fell away, leaving nothing but the warmth of friendship.

Amy and Lexi stepped back from their hug, concern etched across their faces. "What happened?" Amy asked, scanning Jenna's expression.

Lexi's voice shook. "Thomas accepted a scholarship at Miami… and didn't tell me until tonight. I can't believe he would make a decision like that without even talking to me first."

"What a jerk!" Amy's anger flared. "He should have told you earlier! It's not okay to just drop that on you."

"I thought we agreed," Lexi said, wiping her eyes with the back of her hand. "It feels like he doesn't care about the plans we made—about the future."

"Because he's being selfish," Amy said firmly. "You deserved better. You both talked about Virginia Tech, and now he's leaving you hanging, especially after you passed up UCLA."

Lexi's worry shifted instantly. "Where's Jenna? Is she okay?"

Amy's eyes darted toward the patch of grass where Jenna had lain. "I think she's still over there." But as they approached, the expanse was empty. An uneasy silence had settled, heavy and unnatural.

"Jenna?" Lexi's voice trembled, anxiety threading through every word. Shadows swayed and stretched across the dim landscape, darkness curling between the trees, twisting familiar shapes into something foreign and sinister.

Then, a figure emerged at the treeline, drifting toward the forest's mouth. "There she is!" Lexi's voice brightened briefly with hope—but it faltered as Jenna disappeared into the opening between the trees.

"Jenna, wait!" Amy shouted, panic lacing her tone, but the darkness swallowed her friend. She vanished, consumed by the towering, silent guardians of the woods. The air seemed to tighten, compressing around Amy and Lexi, as if the forest itself had drawn a deep breath and was waiting, patient, aware.

"Come on!" Lexi grabbed Amy's hand, pulling her forward, urgency propelling them toward the treeline. Cold air wrapped around them, carrying the scent of earth and decay.

"No, no, no! This isn't good! We have to find her!" Lexi's words trembled with fear.

"Jenna!" Their voices merged, calling into the shadows, but only the rustling of leaves answered. The forest pressed in closer, alive with movement, whispering secrets just beyond reach.

"Where could she have gone?" Lexi's voice barely rose above a whisper, though terror coated every syllable.

No one answered. The trees waited, their gnarled limbs twisting, the windless branches shifting like eyes. Then a crack —a branch breaking somewhere deeper, closer than comfort allowed.

Footsteps followed.

Slow and deliberate, heavier than any animal should be. No form emerged. No sound accompanied it, only the suffocating sense of being watched, measured, judged.

Lexi's gaze drifted back to the black mouth of the forest where Jenna had disappeared. The woods gave nothing in return. It waited. And when they went looking, it would be ready.

Chapter 15:
The Long Way In

Left alone, Jenna's stomach clenched as the shadow at the forest's edge pushed back into her thoughts. She told herself it was nothing, shook her head hard enough to make her vision blur—but the sound came again. A low murmur slid through the branches, threading between the chirring insects, wrapping around her ears like something whispered too close. Her pulse spiked. A cold pressure bloomed behind her ribs, stealing the depth from her breaths.

The darkness along the treeline shifted. Not with wind. With intent. It swelled and stilled, rising and falling as if it were drawing air, inviting her nearer while daring her to refuse. Fear locked her legs, rooted her to the damp grass.

The party's laughter dulled, thinned, then disappeared entirely. The world narrowed to the trees and the hush between them.

Then she saw her.

Amber stepped forward from the shadows, outlined in a pale, wrong light that didn't reach the ground beneath her feet. Relief punched tears into Jenna's eyes. She scrambled upright, heart hammering so violently it hurt

"Amber!" Her voice broke.

"It's me," the voice drifted back, soft and achingly familiar, yet off—too smooth, too steady. The fine hairs along Jenna's arms lifted. "I've missed you."

"I miss you too!" Jenna ran toward her, instinct screaming too late. Amber retreated, slipping backward into the trees.

"Wait!" Jenna shouted, feet pounding the earth. "Please—don't go!"

She lunged for the glow—and it vanished. The forest closed around her, swallowing the light, leaving only the echo of Amber's shape and the certainty that Jenna had gone too far to turn back, and the world behind her vanished. Her pulse hammered against her ribs, her breath catching as if she'd crossed a line that could never be uncrossed.

The laughter and music from the fair didn't fade—they snapped off, sharp and absolute, as if the sound itself had been shredded. The silence that followed rang in her ears, heavy and alien.

Blackness pooled between the trees, thick and spreading, swallowing the narrow path behind her until it no longer existed. The forest closed in layer by layer—towering trunks jammed together, roots heaving from the soil like bones, branches bent into twisted angles that clawed at the sky. Above it all, the pale moon hung motionless, its light ruptured into cruel shards, illuminating only the patches of ground where her friends had disappeared.

With each step, the world tilted out of alignment. Trees leaned inward, massive trunks warped and swollen, bark puckered like diseased skin. Faces emerged in the wood: mouths frozen mid-scream, hollow eye sockets, expressions warped with agony. She blinked, forcing her eyes away, but the sensation of being watched didn't fade. Shadows flickered at the edges of her vision, darting like living things. Each turn of her head made them vanish instantly, leaving behind the suffocating certainty that she was being measured and evaluated.

Leaves rustled above her, though no wind stirred. The sound layered, forming low murmurs that slithered into her ears like secrets pressed against her skull. Her throat tightened, saliva thick and bitter, dread crawling steadily upward from her gut. Then the voice came again.

"Jenna…" It was everywhere at once, vibrating through the ground beneath her feet and the bark against her skin. Achingly familiar, soft, and coaxing, yet threaded with something rotten, something wrong. Her stomach dropped. More voices joined, overlapping and harmonizing into a chorus that pressed in on her, urging her forward. Hope flared despite terror, tangled with it until she could no longer separate one from the other. Her legs moved before her mind could stop them.

Then she saw her. Amber stood a few feet away, her silhouette framed by splintered moonlight. Relief detonated inside Jenna, almost making her sob. "Amber!" she cried, arms outstretched, stumbling forward. But the pressure twisting her gut intensified. Amber's form shimmered unnaturally, edges blurring and rippling like heat over asphalt. When Jenna reached out, her hands passed through her friend's body, encountering only a freezing void that burned against her skin.

Jenna staggered, breath hitching, confusion flooding her mind. Amber was still there, but her face had changed. The familiar features stretched hideously, her mouth widening far beyond human limits, skin splitting at the corners as jagged, bone-white teeth emerged, polished and sharp. Her eyes sank inward, glowing faintly with a sick, yellow light. The air dropped several degrees, biting into Jenna's lungs as shadows thickened, crawling across the forest floor, swallowing the moonlight entirely.

An unholy shriek tore from Amber's throat as her flesh began to rot, peeling away in wet, tearing strips to reveal something ancient and inhuman beneath. Limbs elongated, joints cracking as long, claw-like fingers unfurled, talons darkened with old blood and decay. The thing wearing Amber's face leaned forward, its grin splitting wider.

"You shouldn't have come here, Jenna," it hissed, layered with whispers, growls, and something far older that vibrated with hunger.

Before Jenna could react, Amber lunged, claws slicing through the air with impossible speed. The sharp tips tore through her shirt, shredding the fragile fabric. Pain shot through her side, and she fell backward, gasping. Scrambling away, adrenaline surged like fire through her veins.

"Get away from me!" she screamed. Her voice echoed as she sprinted, the forest alive with the crunch of leaves and twigs beneath her feet, a stark contrast to the oppressive silence that had fallen moments before. Behind her, Amber's ghastly figure moved with fluid, unnatural grace, sending waves of terror crashing over her.

"Run, Jenna! Run!" the voices cackled. She obeyed, primal instinct taking over, darting deeper into the forest. Branches clawed at her as if trying to hold her back, but she pressed on, driven by fear and the desperate hope of escape.

Shapes emerged from the shadows. Not just Amber, but deformed, slithering creatures, bodies twisted beyond comprehension. Skin glistened with slick rot, bone exposed in grotesque patterns, moving with a sickening elegance that churned her stomach. With every glance over her shoulder, Jenna saw their hollow eyes fixed on her, a soulless hunger lurking within. The forest was alive, a breathing nightmare, each step dragging her deeper into a realm where reality bent and twisted like the warped trunks around her. The air pressed down on her, thick and suffocating, as though the trees themselves weighed on her chest.

"Jenna…" Amber's voice hissed from the shadows, smooth, seductive, and sinister. "You can't escape. We are everywhere."

Jenna stumbled, foot catching on a root that jutted from the soil. She fell hard, the impact knocking the breath from her lungs. Cold, clammy fingers brushed against her ankle, slick and rotting, sending a wave of revulsion crawling up her spine. Instinctively, she kicked out, feeling the putrid flesh yield beneath her foot, and scrambled back onto shaking legs.

Amber loomed larger than life, the moonlight igniting an unholy glow around her. "You can't hide from me!" she shrieked, a voice equal parts rage and delight. Jenna gasped, chest tightening, turning to run as the forest closed in—branches whipping at her face like the jagged claws of some ancient predator.

She burst into a clearing, heart hammering, only to freeze at the sight. A circle of gnarled, decomposing trees surrounded her, roots writhing across the ground like bony fingers. The air reeked of death, heavy and suffocating, as though the forest had claimed this as a sacrificial ground. The earth trembled beneath her feet, and the voices swelled until they pressed against her skull like a physical weight.

Amber and the creatures emerged from the shadows, eyes glinting with unnatural hunger. Jenna's screams tore from her throat, echoing into the void as she curled into a tight fetal position, trembling uncontrollably. The forest exhaled, a slow, oppressive breath that pressed down on her like a suffocating blanket. When she dared to lift her head, the clearing was empty—only darkness swirled around her, alive, sentient, watching.

A crackling sound broke the silence—a deliberate, crunching step that echoed across the ground. Jenna's palms grew slick with sweat as she turned toward the noise, terror pooling in her stomach.

In the clearing, bathed in the fragmented moonlight, a massive figure loomed. Its presence was oppressive, a living nightmare pulled from the soil itself. Muscles bulged beneath mottled, earthen skin; thick red moss clung to its face, dripping like the remnants of forgotten blood; thorny vines twisted around its limbs, writhing as if with a mind of their own.

Jenna's gaze locked on its yellow, bloodshot eyes, molten with hunger, glinting like pools of fire in the darkness. Its mouth, wide and grotesque, revealed jagged, rock-like teeth jutting at unnatural angles, a grin that promised annihilation. Every step it took reverberated through the forest floor, vibrations hammering into her bones, an unrelenting reminder of her fragility.

A guttural roar erupted, tearing through the night like a chorus of agony. The putrid stench rolled off it in waves, acrid and rancid, filling Jenna's nostrils and choking her with the weight of its presence. Jagged teeth glistened in the silvery light, and every instinct screamed at her to flee, yet her legs burned with exhaustion, barely carrying her forward.

She ran, branches lashing at her like living weapons, the shadows shifting, shapes writhing in the periphery. The forest became a labyrinth of terror, walls closing in, every twisted tree a sentinel of the nightmare. Behind her, the woodsman moved with horrifying purpose, a predator born of earth, moss, and vine, each step closer making her chest constrict, each breath a razor against her lungs.

Jenna understood, in a bone-deep shiver, that this creature was not just a monster—it was the forest's vengeance, the embodiment of all the fear and darkness festering in the shadows. There was no escape. Every path led deeper into its grip, every tree a trap, every whisper a promise of something worse waiting ahead. She raced toward the abandoned cabin she glimpsed through the gloom, heart hammering, yet the true horror pressed in around her: this nightmare had no exit, and the woodsman would ensure she never found one.

The forest seemed to breathe around her, inhaling her fear and exhaling it back as a tangible weight. Every snap of a twig made her stomach lurch, every rustle of leaves felt like a hundred eyes watching from just beyond the shadows. Her skin prickled, tiny hairs standing on end, as if the darkness itself had teeth. She could feel the damp earth shift beneath her sneakers, roots writhing like snakes trying to trip her, claws of bark snagging at her sleeves.

The stench of decay intensified, thick and cloying, clinging to her hair and clothes, burning her nostrils. Somewhere close, a wet, slapping sound echoed—flesh meeting flesh?—and she shuddered violently, forcing her legs to move even as her mind screamed to stop. Heart hammering against her ribs like a trapped animal, she could taste copper and bile, the tang of panic thick on her tongue.

The shadows intermingled around her, moving just beyond the range of her vision. Shapes twisted in impossible ways: limbs too long, torsos bent at cruel angles, faces with eyes sunken too deep, mouths gaping unnaturally wide, teeth sharp and glinting like obsidian knives. They whispered, low and urgent, their voices crawling over her skin like crawling insects. She couldn't look directly at them, and yet she could feel their gaze boring into her chest, into her mind, reading every fear she had ever tried to bury.

Then came the crunching step again, slow, deliberate, each one pressing through the forest floor and into her bones. She could hear it behind her, then to her left, then ahead—as if it were everywhere at once, circling, stalking, laughing in a language older than the trees themselves. Her lungs burned as she gasped for air, and her legs screamed with exhaustion, but she could not stop. Stopping meant death.

The woodsman emerged from the shadows, larger now, impossibly so, the red moss dripping from his face like blood from a wound that had never healed. His vines writhed with a life of their own, curling and snapping like whips. The air around him shimmered, almost liquid, a distortion that made the trees bend toward him. His yellow eyes locked on hers, unblinking, unrelenting, and she felt herself shrivel under the heat of his stare.

A low growl rumbled from his chest, resonating in her ears, vibrating through the soles of her feet. It was not a sound meant for hearing—it was a force meant to shake her bones, twist her insides, unravel her sanity one vibration at a time. She stumbled over a protruding root, mouth dry, chest heaving, and felt the first brush of something sticky along her arm. It wasn't moss, not exactly—something cold, wet, and breathing, wrapping itself around her skin like a living curse.

The forest itself joined him. Branches reached down, snapping at her, trying to claw, to hold, to drag her into the earth. Roots thrashed at her ankles, tangling, constricting, threatening to pull her to the soil that was now pulsing like a heart beneath her feet. Every step she took seemed slower, more resistant, as if the world itself was conspiring to keep her there, to hand her over to the monster that had claimed this place.

The shadows of the forest stretched and twisted, twisting her sense of distance, making the path ahead both impossibly far and maddeningly close. She could hear Amber laughing, or was it screaming?—the sound fractured and warped, coming from everywhere, nowhere, as if the forest had stolen her friend and was now echoing her torment back at her.

The woodsman took another step. The earth groaned under his weight. Jenna felt it through the soles of her feet, through her knees, through her teeth. She tried to run, but her legs buckled, and the ground seemed to pulse in rhythm with the predator behind her. A vine lashed out, wrapping around her ankle, yanking her forward, scraping her palms raw as she clawed at dirt and roots. Panic was a living thing inside her, clawing at her throat, choking her, spurring her into desperate, erratic motion.

She stumbled, rolling, scraping, twisting. The moonlight glinted off jagged rocks, and she could swear the shadows themselves had faces, grinning at her, whispering, "Not fast enough. Not fast enough." She forced herself upright, running blind, every nerve screaming, every sense drowning in terror. The woodsman's presence was a hurricane, a tidal wave of malice and hunger pressing down on her, leaving her mind raw, screaming, trembling under its weight.

Ahead, the rotting and warped cabin, barely visible through the darkness, offered a promise—a fragile, desperate hope of sanctuary. Every step toward it was a battle against roots, against branches, against the suffocating grasp of the forest itself. She could hear the woodsman behind her now, his roar shaking the very air, his vines snapping like whips, his eyes burning like coals through the dark. She ran. She had no choice but to run, praying the cabin would offer protection from the forest, and its monstrous guardian attempting to claim her.

From where Megan and Aiden sat near the bonfire at the barn, the fairground looked almost harmless, a pocket of warmth carved out of the encroaching night. The bonfire snapped and hissed, flames licking upward in jagged bursts, sending sparks spiraling into the air like tiny dying stars. The heat pressed against Megan's face, but it did nothing to settle the cold coiled deep in her gut.

She stared into the fire, watching the flames twist and collapse in on themselves, shadows stretching unnaturally across the dirt and the barn wall. The shapes lingered a second too long, twitching at the edges before snapping back into nothing. Her mind refused to stay present. It dragged her backward, replaying Jenna's earlier behavior frame by frame, twisting it darker with every repetition.

Aiden grabbed another log and tossed it onto the fire. The wood cracked sharply, sparks scattering into the dark, momentarily breaking the oppressive quiet Megan had sunk into. "You've been quiet for a while," he said, glancing at her, concern flickering across his face. "Are you okay?"

His voice should have grounded her. Instead, it felt distant, as if it had traveled too far to reach her intact. Megan forced her lips into a smile, brittle and rehearsed. "Yeah," she said softly. "I'm just… thinking about what happened with Jenna."

Aiden frowned, shifting his weight. "I mean, I thought it was kind of funny at first," he admitted. "But yeah—she was completely out of it."

Megan folded her arms across her chest, suddenly aware of how thin the night air felt against her skin despite the fire's warmth. "I can't believe she just walked up like that and embarrassed us," she said, irritation sharpening her tone, though it failed to mask the worry underneath. "We were literally minding our own business. What was she even thinking?"

The fire snapped again, embers scattering. Somewhere beyond the circle of light, the carnival laughter dulled and thinned, as though distance—or something else—was swallowing it. Megan's gaze drifted past the fire toward the edges of the field, where darkness pooled thickly, pressing close, waiting just beyond the flames' reach. Her pulse quickened as that familiar sensation crept over her: the unmistakable feeling of being watched.

"It just feels… off," she murmured, eyes flicking toward where she had last seen Jenna and Amy. "I know Jenna's never exactly been nice to me, but she was clearly drunk." Megan hesitated. "And people don't just disappear from parties like this."

Before Aiden could respond, a faint sound cut through the night—not laughter, not fire, not music. A whisper, thin and desperate, carried on no discernible wind. Her breath caught. The word was indistinct, but the intent was unmistakable: *help*.

Megan straightened abruptly, heart hammering against her ribs. "Did you hear that?" she asked, scanning the darkness.

"Hear what?" Aiden replied, already moving as a blur of motion caught his attention.

Lexi and Amy came running from the direction of the forest, stumbling over uneven ground, their faces pale and streaked with sweat. Panic radiated off them in waves. The sight alone sent a jolt of dread through Megan's chest.

Aiden was on his feet instantly. "What's wrong?" he asked, his voice sharp now, alert.

Lexi didn't slow as she shouted, her voice breaking. "Help! We need help!" Her eyes darted wildly, as if expecting something to leap from the darkness behind her. "Jenna—she walked into the forest. She just... kept walking, and we can't find her!"

The words struck like a hammer.

Nearby, people paused, conversations stalling as confusion rippled outward. From the barn, the guys—Thomas, Anthony, Zack, Randy, Jake, and Tyler—emerged, drawn by the commotion. Thomas's casual expression vanished the moment he saw Lexi's face. "What's going on?" he demanded, eyes snapping between them.

Amy bent over, hands braced against her knees, struggling to breathe. "She fell in the grass and started laughing," she said, voice shaking violently. "I thought she just needed a minute. Lexi and I went back to help her, and she was already walking toward the trees." Tears streaked her cheeks. "We called for her. She didn't turn around. I was only gone for a minute. One minute."

Randy's temper flared instantly. "What the hell, Amy?" he snapped, stepping forward. "You don't leave someone like that alone!"

Anthony moved between them before it could escalate, his tone firm. "Enough. Blaming her isn't going to fix this." He glanced toward the tree line, jaw tightening. "Jenna drinks when she's upset. You all know that. If she went into the woods like that, we don't have time to argue."

An uneasy silence followed, thick and heavy, broken only by the distant carnival music, now strangely thin and out of place.

Thomas swore under his breath. "Great," he muttered. Then louder, "Okay. Someone needs to call the sheriff. Now."

Phones were pulled from pockets, faces turned toward the forest, and Megan felt it again—that tightening in her chest, that crawling certainty beneath her skin. The bonfire crackled behind them, bright and warm, but the darkness beyond the field felt closer than before.

Randy stepped forward, jaw clenched, firelight casting harsh lines across his face, highlighting the anger and fear burning behind his eyes. "We're not leaving her out there alone," he said, voice cutting through the murmurs around the bonfire. "We go after her. Now."

No one answered.

The silence that followed was heavy, suffocating, almost physical. The fire popped behind them, embers lifting into the dark, but no one moved. Randy's gaze swept across the group, daring someone to challenge him, daring someone to care enough to act.

"Screw this," he snapped when no one spoke. "I'm going." He took a step toward the tree line, into the wall of darkness swallowing the edge of the field.

Thomas lunged forward, grabbing his arm, fingers biting down hard. "Hold up," he said, sharp and urgent. "It's pitch black out there, Randy. You know what people say about that forest." He released him but didn't back away, pacing as his thoughts raced. The bonfire cast his shadow long and distorted across the ground, stretching and bending in unnatural ways. "Running in blind is how people get lost—or worse."

Randy yanked free, breathing hard. "So what, we just stand here?"

"No," Thomas said, control threading his voice. "We think. We plan. We don't make this worse." He stopped pacing and faced them all. "We stick together. Grab lights. Bring something to defend ourselves with. And if something is out there—" He paused, letting the unsaid hang heavy in the air. "—we don't face it unprepared."

Uneasy glances passed between them. The carnival's laughter felt miles away now, thin, artificial, like a memory of safety that no longer applied. The darkness beyond the field pressed closer, encroaching on the weak ring of firelight.

Megan's pulse hammered as she looked at Aiden. She didn't need to speak; the same thought lived behind his eyes. They could not stay behind. They could not pretend this wasn't happening.

"We should help," Aiden said quietly, leaning toward her. "She shouldn't be out there alone."

"Of course we should," Megan replied immediately, voice tight but steady. "Whatever Jenna's done, she doesn't deserve this."

Randy turned on them, crossing his arms. "Stay out of it," he snapped. "This isn't one of your attention-seeking stunts. We don't need you involved."

The words hit harder than Megan expected. Her stomach sank, but she swallowed the response burning on her tongue. Arguing would waste time Jenna didn't have. She stayed quiet, watching as Thomas took control, his tone shifting from frustration to command.

"Flashlights," Thomas said sharply. "Check the barn. We need as many as we can find."

Aiden didn't hesitate. He sprinted toward the barn, ignoring Randy's glare. Moments later, he returned with two heavy-duty flashlights, clicking one on. The beams cut through the darkness, slicing a narrow path ahead, illuminating dust motes and drifting smoke. But it felt inadequate against the vast black waiting beyond the field.

"Zack, Anthony," Thomas continued, already moving. "Pull your trucks around. Aim the high beams toward the tree line. I want as much light as we can get."

Engines roared to life, headlights swinging across the field. The beams washed over the forest's edge, revealing nothing but tightly packed trunks and tangled undergrowth, shadows layered so thick they seemed almost solid.

Randy grabbed a baseball bat leaning against the barn wall, his grip white-knuckled. "Let's go," he said, voice low and hard. "We're not losing anyone tonight."

Jake glanced toward the shed. "We should grab tools. Just in case."

"Wild animals," Tyler added quickly, already heading for the shed. "Or anything else."

They returned with a grim assortment of implements—a pitchfork, a rusted machete, garden tools meant for dirt, not flesh. Anthony eyed them carefully. "Careful with those," he warned. "It's dark. Don't swing unless you're sure. We're here to find Jenna, not hurt each other."

The night pressed in closer, every sound amplified. Leaves rustled without wind. An owl cried out and fell silent too abruptly. Megan's skin prickled as if something unseen had turned its attention toward them.

"Did Jenna say anything before she left?" Thomas asked, turning to Lexi and Amy.

Amy's face crumpled. "She said she saw something in the forest," she admitted, voice shaking. "She laughed right after. I thought she was just drunk. I didn't think—" Her voice broke.

Megan felt the words sink into her chest like ice.

Thomas nodded once, grim. "Alright. We move together. No one wanders off. If you hear something, you say it. If you see something—anything—you stop and tell us."

The group gathered at the edge of the field, flashlights raised, tools clutched tightly. The forest waited—vast and unmoving, its darkness dense and expectant.

Megan felt it with chilling certainty: they were no longer choosing to enter the woods.

A grim resolve settled over the group. Whatever secrets the forest held, they were no longer distant rumors or drunken stories passed around bonfires. Those secrets had reached out and taken someone. Now they were going after her.

"We can't waste another minute," Thomas said sharply. "Lexi, Amy—show us exactly where she went in."

Flashlights flicked on, beams cutting jagged paths through the darkness as they approached the tree line. The carnival behind them dissolved into hollow echoes, laughter and music feeling unreal, distant, like something remembered from another life. Lexi and Amy led the way, pace uneven, panic riding every breath.

"This is it," Lexi said, stopping abruptly at the edge of the woods. She pointed to a snarl of underbrush, branches bent inward as if something had pushed through. "This is where we last saw her."

The forest opened before them, dense and oppressive. Tall trunks blackened with age and dampness, their branches interwoven overhead like a cage. The temperature dropped the moment they crossed the invisible threshold. The air smelled wrong—wet earth, decay, and a faint metallic tang that made Megan's stomach twist.

"Stay close," Aiden murmured, voice low as if the forest could overhear. He pressed a flashlight into her palm. "I grabbed an extra. Don't let go."

Megan tightened her grip. The beam trembled as she swept it across bark and shadow. Everywhere the light touched, darkness recoiled reluctantly, thickening just beyond its reach.

Lexi stepped forward, voice cracking as she called, "Jenna!" The sound vanished almost instantly, swallowed by the trees.

Thomas exhaled slowly, forcing calm into his tone. "We split up to cover more ground," he said. "Two teams."

Megan's stomach knotted.

"Team One," Thomas continued, pointing. "Randy, Amy, Tyler, Anthony. You take this flashlight." The beam sputtered once before steadying. "Team Two is me, Jake, Zack, and Lexi."

"No," Lexi cut in sharply, eyes blazing. "I'm not going with you right now. This isn't about you being in charge. This is about Jenna."

The tension snapped tight. Even the forest seemed to lean closer.

"I'm going with Randy, Tyler, and Zack," she said. "You take Amy, Anthony, Jake, or whoever else you want."

Thomas scoffed, folding his arms. "Fine. Do whatever you want." The irritation in his voice was unmistakable, but Lexi had already turned away.

Anthony stepped in quickly. "Listen," he said firmly. "We stay within sight. No running. No wandering. If you hear or see something, you stop and call it out."

Megan stood beside Aiden, pulse hammering. "Looks like it's us," he whispered, forcing calm into his voice.

She nodded. "Outer edge. She couldn't have gone far."

The cold intensified as they moved deeper into the forest, seeping through Megan's jacket and into her bones. Leaves crunched unnaturally loudly beneath their feet, echoing between the trunks. Somewhere deeper, a branch snapped with deliberate slowness.

Megan's skin prickled. The sensation of being watched grew stronger with every step, as if unseen eyes tracked them from behind the trees, studying them with patient interest. She glanced at Aiden, jaw set, flashlight sweeping steadily.

"We have to find her," Megan said, more to herself than him. Speaking it aloud felt like holding onto something solid.

"We will," Aiden replied, though uncertainty laced his words. "Stay alert. Stay close."

Behind them, the carnival lights dwindled into nothing, erased by shadow and distance. Ahead, the forest closed around them, branches knitting tighter overhead, darkness thickening with intent. Megan understood with chilling clarity: the forest was no longer just a place to search.

Chapter 16:

The Decent into Shadows

Lexi pushed forward into a cavernous maw, the forest opening around them like the throat of some living beast. Jagged branches locked overhead, crooked teeth in a mouth of shadows, pooling between the trunks in thick, black swells that seemed to pulse with anticipation. She forced herself onward, ignoring Thomas's strained breathing somewhere behind her, fingers gripping the flashlight so hard her knuckles ached. The beam quivered violently, carving a narrow, fragile path through the darkness. Damp air pressed against her face, heavy with the stench of wet soil, decomposing leaves, and something far older—something metallic and sour that clung to her tongue, and burned the back of her throat. A chill slithered down her spine, crawling vertebra by vertebra, slow, deliberate, and unrelenting.

Her gaze flicked to the others, heart hammering. "Are we really doing this?" The whisper barely escaped her lips, swallowed immediately by the forest.

"We have to find Jenna," Randy said, shifting the bat on his shoulder. His jaw was tight, eyes flicking into the shadows, expecting them to move. "Standing here won't bring her back. If she's hurt—if she's out here alone—" He cut himself off, but the thought lingered between them, raw and poisonous.

Tyler and Zack nodded, gripping their tools so tight their knuckles whitened. Zack tried to smile; it fell apart as quickly as it formed, his gaze flicking to the darkness pressing in from every side. "We go in, we find her," he said quickly, as if speaking it could make it true. "Then we leave. No wandering. No splitting up."

The moment they crossed the tree line, Lexi felt it—the chest-tightening noose of the forest closing. The air thickened, cold biting at her skin, as if she had plunged underwater. Her flashlight flickered, the beam warping the bark into faces stretched and twisted, eyes bulging, mouths frozen in silent screams. Shadows snapped back and recoiled, testing her reactions.

"Stay together," Lexi forced out, panic grating her words. Silence pressed down with a weight that could crush. Every step against the carpet of dead leaves echoed far longer than it should, every rustle a scream in her mind. The forest was listening.

"Jenna!" Randy's voice tore through the trees. "Where are you?" The words vanished—devoured, erased. Lexi's gaze darted to Tyler and Zack, the fear settling in her chest like cold cement.

A low growl rolled through the undergrowth, resonant, deliberate, vibrating in the ground beneath their feet. Lexi froze, breath catching. "Did you hear that?"

"Probably a deer," Tyler said, but the edge in his voice betrayed him. Knuckles tightened on the shovel until they hurt.

A pale mist snaked between the trees, sliding across the forest floor with unnatural speed. It wrapped around their legs, climbing higher until Lexi could barely see her boots. The flashlight's beam waned, illuminating only a trembling circle around her. "Stay close," she urged, panic bleeding into the words.

When she turned, stomach dropping, the others were drifting apart.

"Just a little farther," Randy called, moving into the fog. Lexi hesitated, glancing back at Tyler and Zack, who seemed hypnotized by the shadows. "Guys, wait!" Her words were swallowed by the mist.

Branches groaned softly as the forest shifted, alive, aware. Lexi pushed forward, flashlight shaking violently. "Randy! Tyler! Zack!" she screamed. Her voice returned, warped, hollow, mocking.

From the corner of her vision, it appeared—a face bulging from the bark, twisted with rage, eyes faintly glowing beneath the wood's surface, straining to break free. Lexi gasped, spinning toward it, pulse roaring in her ears.

"Lexi!" Randy's voice, sharp with fear, echoed somewhere deeper in the mist. "We need to regroup!"

She stumbled forward. Shadows writhed and recoiled as if the light itself were an intruder. "Randy!" Her scream died in the fog.

Another growl thundered through the trees, heavier now, vibrating through her bones. "We need to get out!" Her words were swallowed again, smothered by the unnatural silence.

The ground shuddered beneath her.

Lexi felt it—a presence immense, crushing, and radiating malice. Slowly, she turned.

A massive figure emerged from darkness, half-concealed in shadow and mist. Sickly yellow eyes, bloodshot and unblinking, burned into her. Red moss clung to a face that could not be human, tangled in a beard of pulsing vines and thorns. Its grin was wrong, too wide, jagged, teeth like fractured stone.

Lexi staggered back, terror jolting through her. When her eyes snapped to the spot again, there was nothing there.

"Lexi, where are you?" Tyler's voice rang somewhere nearby, fragile but alive.

"I'm right here!" she screamed, voice trembling, hope igniting with fear.

Then the ground beneath her convulsed, erupting with a rumble from the earth itself. Vibration shot up her legs, rattled her teeth, and the trees shuddered, leaning inward, bark splitting as if strained by invisible hands. Branches swayed, and snapped, alive with fury. And the voices came—dozens of them, layered, distorted, circling her head in a storm of malice. They mocked her, whispered intimate, poisonous truths: *You shouldn't have come here…* Slithering straight into her skull, bypassing sound, sinking into her bones.

Panic detonated inside Lexi's chest. She ran blindly into the fog, lungs burning, flashlight beam jerking with every frantic stride. "Randy! Tyler! Zack!" Her voice shredded itself raw, yet the mist devoured it instantly. The forest drank her fear without echo, without mercy. Shadows slithered just beyond the edges of her light, pacing her movements with patient, predatory precision. She felt it now—something vast stalking—not chasing, not rushing, but herding.

Branches whipped at her face and arms, drawing thin, stinging lines across her skin. Each breath scraped her throat raw, each heartbeat pounding dread into her bones. Hope fluttered weakly—her friends were out there, somewhere. But it was crushed as quickly as it surfaced. The forest did not allow hope. It fed on certainty. Jenna had been taken.

The mist thickened, clinging like wet fabric to her skin, coating hair, clothes and lashes; muffling sound and distorting distance. The forest felt endless and claustrophobic all at once. Then she stopped short.

A massive shape loomed ahead.

It stood between two ancient trees, impossibly still, a hulking silhouette pulsing faintly as though breathing. As the fog shifted, it revealed itself—an abomination sculpted from the forest itself. Compact earth and jagged stone formed its muscles, soil cracking and shifting as it moved. Thick vines wrapped its limbs like veins, pulsing slowly with something dark and alive. Red moss hung in heavy mats over its head and shoulders, draping its face like a rotting beard.

Its eyes found her.

Sickly, bloodshot yellow, wet, and intelligent. The mouth stretched into a hideous grin, jagged teeth smeared with something dark and slick. This was no spirit, no hallucination—it was a guardian, a predator, ancient and elemental, bound to the forest, feeding on trespassers.

Lexi's scream caught in her throat.

The creature stepped back, dissolving into fog, shadow, nothing, as though the forest had swallowed it whole. She stood frozen, shaking violently, lungs tearing with each shallow breath.

Then—scream. High, desperate, human. Followed by a wet, choking gurgle that cut off in sickening finality. It echoed just long enough to carve itself into her memory, then vanished.

"Randy!" Lexi screamed, spinning blindly toward the sound. She collided hard with something solid, the impact stealing her breath. Recognition brought a ragged cry.

"Lexi," Randy gasped, face ashen, eyes wide with raw terror. "Did you see it?"

"It was—" Her voice trembled violently. "Monstrous. Not human. Part of the forest."

The air went unnervingly still. No wind. No insects. The forest held its breath. Wordless, they moved together, cautious, every step a knife-edge of fear.

The creature reappeared at the edge of sight, eyes flickering between trees. They dove behind a massive trunk, pressing against the bark as vines brushed their legs. Lexi's pulse thundered, every nerve straining to detect movement through the fog.

"Do you think it saw us?" Randy whispered.

"I don't know," Lexi said, tears streaking her cheeks. "But we can't stay here."

Something warm splashed across her face.

Instinctively, she wiped at it—fingers slick and dark. Slowly, dread dragging her gaze upward, she saw him.

Zack.

Impaled through the chest by a jagged branch, his torso sagging unnaturally, ribs splayed, blood pooling through his soaked shirt. Eyes glassy, open, frozen in pure agony.

"Zack!" Lexi screamed, knees buckling as nausea surged.

Randy grabbed her arm, yanking her back—but the forest shifted. Leaves rustled. Branches groaned.

And then Randy was gone.

No sound. No struggle. Erased as if he had never existed.

"Randy!" she shrieked, spinning. Mist swirled tighter, suffocating. Her own ragged breathing layered over the whispering forest, inescapable.

The trees twisted unnaturally, branches stretching like hands, faces bulging from bark, hollow eyes watching, mouths frozen in silent delight.

"No," she sobbed, backing away. "Please. Please come back."

Nothing answered. Only the wind threading through branches and the soft, hungry shifting of something immense deeper within the fog.

Lexi took a trembling step forward, tears blinding her, dread pooling thick in her gut.

She was alone.

And the forest had only just begun.

Thomas stepped toward the forest, unease coiling tight in his chest. He cast one last glance at Lexi. She stood several yards away, rigid, withdrawn, already moving toward Randy, Tyler, and Zack. Pale, jaw clenched, bracing. He opened his mouth to call out, some instinct screaming to stop her—but she vanished into the treeline before he could speak, leaving a sour, crawling foreboding deep in his gut.

The darkness swallowed Thomas, Amy, Anthony, and Jake the instant they crossed beneath the trees. Damp, cold, thick air pressed against their skin, carrying the stench of rot and stagnant earth. Thomas swung the flashlight beam ahead—a fragile tunnel through blackness. Tangled roots writhed across the ground like coiled snakes, trees pressed too close together, trunks swollen and warped as though born under immense pressure.

"Stay close," Thomas said, forcing control into his voice. "We find Jenna and we get out. No wandering."

Amy gripped Anthony's arm with white-knuckled desperation. "I hate this," she whispered. "It feels wrong. What if something happens?"

"Nothing's going to happen," Anthony said automatically, eyes flicking toward every shifting shadow. Behind them, Jake trailed, pitchfork clutched like a lifeline, palms slick with sweat despite the cold.

The mist rolled in abruptly, unnatural, deliberate, crawling between the trees. It crept up their legs, soaked clothes, blurred the ground until depth and distance became meaningless. The flashlight flickered, bending bark into grotesque shapes—faces mid-scream, mouths stretched, eyes bulging.

Gooseflesh rippled along Thomas's arms. The forest no longer felt empty. It was watching.

"Guys," Jake whispered, voice trembling, pitchfork raised. "Something just moved over there. That wasn't mist."

Thomas followed his gaze. The shadows recoiled slightly, then settled. "It's just fog," he lied, pulse quickening. The eyes, the forest… something tracked them.

Then the growl came. Low. Wet. Powerful. Vibrating through the ground and up his legs. Not an animal. A warning.

"You heard that too, right?" Thomas asked, throat tight.

Jake nodded violently. "Not a wolf."

Anthony swallowed hard. "Stay calm. Wolves don't hunt people like this. Keep moving."

Voices sliced through the fog, soft, layered, distorted. Whispering his name.

"Thomas…"

"Over here…"

"Please… help me…"

Familiar. Female.

"Did you hear that?" Thomas asked sharply, spinning. "Someone's calling us."

Amy shook her head, terror flashing across her pale face. "I don't hear anything. Stop it. You're scaring me."

The flashlight died. Darkness fell like a weight, crushing, immediate. Amy screamed, clutching Anthony. Thomas fumbled blindly, hands shaking.

"There's someone there," he said, panic rising. "I saw someone."

Before anyone could stop him, Thomas stepped forward, drawn by the voices threading through the mist. "Jenna?" he called, dread and hope tangled in his chest. "Is that you?"

"Thomas, don't!" Anthony shouted—but the fog surged, swallowing him whole.

The flashlight flickered weakly back to life. Whispers pressed in, circling, overlapping, fingering his thoughts like cold glass.

"I'm here…"

"Come closer…"

"I'm waiting…"

He spun, breath ragged, straining to locate the source. "Jenna!" His voice returned warped and distant, mocked by echoes.

Then the growl again—closer. Trees shook. Bark split. Leaves rained down. Thomas froze as something massive shifted just beyond the fog.

Amy clung to Anthony, tears streaking her face. "We have to find him," she sobbed. "He can't be out there alone."

Jake staggered backward, pitchfork rattling. "Something's behind me. I can feel it."

The mist thickened, forest creaked and groaned, and whatever hunted them began closing in.

"Jake, stay calm!" Amy screamed, her voice fracturing inside the choking fog.

Shadows peeled back. A shape forced itself into definition. A massive silhouette emerged, fused partially with the trees. Bark split as a face bulged free, wet and tearing. Sunken cheeks plated with dirt and moss, a beard of tangled red vines crawling with insects. The grin split too wide, jagged, stone-like teeth clacking as it inhaled. Yellow, bloodshot, unblinking eyes locked on Jake.

The forest fell silent, holding its breath.

"We can't stay here," Jake choked. "Run!"

He bolted blindly into the fog, branches tearing at arms and face. The creature did not rush. It did not need to. Its form dissolved, reappearing ahead, herding him deeper.

Thomas heard Jake's scream tear through the forest and surged forward, lungs burning, feet pounding against the wet, uneven ground. He caught a glimpse of Jake sprinting ahead, wild-eyed, arms flailing, but the fog swallowed him before Thomas could reach him. The relief lasted a heartbeat—then Jake vanished completely, dissolved into the mist as if the forest itself had swallowed him.

A narrow stream appeared through the fog, moonlight shimmering weakly on its shattered surface. In its center, a small figure stood, trembling, half-hidden in curling mist.

"Jenna?" Jake gasped, hope stabbing through him.

The figure lifted her head. Fragile. Desperate. Perfectly pitched to lure him closer. "You found me," she whispered. "Please. Help me."

Relief crashed through him like a wave. Jake waded into the water, arms wrapping around her body—but his hands met wrongness immediately.

Her skin was slick and cold. Vines writhed beneath his touch, thick cords of living plants tightening around his wrists. Bones cracked and shifted, expanding into bark and stone beneath the surface.

"No—no!" he screamed, thrashing.

The creature rose. Towering now, its disguise gone, revealing its true, ancient form. Eyes yellow, unblinking, burning with awareness. Its mouth stretched into a grin, jagged stone teeth gleaming wetly. Insects poured from its beard and mouth, skittering across his skin.

The world narrowed to water and grip and impossible weight. Jake's ribs protested as the creature lifted him with effortless strength, slamming him into the stream. Cold water surged over him, filling lungs, splashing eyes, as he clawed at stone-hard, moss-slicked limbs.

His lungs burned, vision dimming. Above him, the creature's presence was patient, unhurried, omnipotent. It allowed him to fight just enough to taste terror.

Thomas burst through the trees, his flashlight beam slicing a path through the fog. "Jake!"

He saw the nightmare.

Jake flailed beneath the surface, eyes bulging, mouth open in a silent scream. The creature's massive form was anchored to the riverbed, vines rooting deep into the soil. One hand forced Jake under; the other pressed his head down, over and over, patient, precise.

And then—slack.

The body floated up, face-first, eyes open, glassy, streams of water spilling from his mouth. Thomas froze, vision swimming, chest heaving. The creature turned its head toward him, grin widening, awareness radiating like crushing pressure.

Something inside Thomas snapped. He ran.

Branches lashed at him, roots snagged boots, mud sucked at his feet. The fog rippled around him, alive, bending, watching, allowing flight because fear was its delight.

He tripped on a root, sprawling down a short embankment, landing inches from a jagged branch, heart hammering. Sweat stung his eyes. He scrambled upright, breath ragged, muscles screaming.

A scream tore through the mist.

A figure burst forward, stumbling, erratic, human but broken by panic.

"Lexi!" Recognition slammed into him.

She collided with him, arms locking around his torso, shaking violently, sobbing into his chest. "Thank God," she gasped. "I thought—I thought I was alone."

Thomas held her, breathless, heart hammering. Relief crashed through him, only to be buried under the memory of the stream, the lifeless body. "Jake's dead," he choked out. "It killed him. I watched it."

Lexi stiffened.

The ground trembled beneath their feet. A low, subterranean growl rolled through the forest, rattling bones and mud alike. The fog moved in deliberate swells, the stink of rot and wet soil thickening the air.

"It's coming," Thomas said, panic clawing up his throat. "We have to move. Now."

Lexi tightened her grip. "We don't split up," she said fiercely.

The roar came again, closer, bending trunks inward, lifting roots like grasping fingers. The forest itself began to close in around them.

Thomas grabbed her hand. They ran.

Blindly, desperately, into darkness. Fog clawing at them, branches tearing at their skin. Somewhere behind, the creature followed, pacing with confidence. It didn't need to chase. Fear alone was enough.

The mist clung to Megan like wet gauze, pressing against her throat and lungs as she and Aiden sank deeper into the forest. Every step sucked at the mud beneath their boots, a sick, sucking sound that felt deliberate, almost hungry. The trees leaned inward, their gnarled branches clawing at the fog, twisting into shapes that weren't entirely natural. Megan's pulse thundered in her ears, echoing the certainty that they were not alone.

"I didn't think I'd ever come back here," Aiden said quietly, his voice tight. His eyes scanned the haze, searching for movement that never fully revealed itself. "It's like the place remembers you. Pulls you in whether you want it to or not."

Megan let out a dry, brittle laugh. "You've always had terrible instincts." The words cracked under the weight of the fog, shattered when whispers teased at the edges of her mind—voices just shy of language, brushing against her thoughts. Real. Unmistakably real.

The cabin emerged slowly, crouched among the trees like a waiting predator. One window glowed faintly, the light inside flickering as if something moved just behind it. Megan's stomach knotted. "Of course she's here," she muttered. "This place never lets anything go."

They reached the door. It creaked open with a long, aching groan that vibrated through Megan's bones. The air inside was stagnant and sour, thick with mildew and the sharp tang of iron. Her throat constricted as her eyes adjusted to the dim light.

Jenna was crumpled against the far wall, knees drawn to her chest, hair matted, eyes wide and glassy with terror. She rocked back and forth, whispering under her breath, her voice shredded and raw. "Please... don't hurt me... don't take me back..."

"Megan and Aiden. It's us," Megan said, stepping forward cautiously. "You're safe."

Jenna snapped her head up.

"No!" she screamed, scrabbling backward until her shoulder slammed into the wall. "You're not real. He sends you first. He always does!" Hysterical sobs tore through her as she clawed at the floor, desperate to escape something only she could see. "You're here to deliver me!"

"Megan, stop," Aiden warned sharply. Her fear was tangible, clawing through the room, wrapping around his chest.

"We're trying to help you," Megan said again, louder, forcing steadiness into her voice. The shadows along the walls shifted deliberately, curling and stretching like smoke drawn toward a flame.

A low growl rolled through the forest outside, vibrating the cabin walls and sinking into Megan's bones. Somewhere in the distance, a scream cut abruptly short.

Jenna seized a jagged shard of broken glass, gripping it until blood ran freely down her palm and splattered across the wood. "He's coming!" she sobbed. "You're going to give me to him!"

Aiden froze, dread etched across his face. "Megan… who is she talking about?"

Before an answer could form, the cabin shuddered violently. Dust rained from the ceiling as the floorboards bowed beneath a massive, unseen weight. The door rattled and hit once—hard—splintering wood along its frame.

"Get away from her!" Aiden shouted, planting himself between Jenna and the entrance. His voice was raw with urgency.

The door burst inward. Randy staggered inside, slamming it behind him as if something were mere inches from tearing through. His face was gray with terror, eyes wide, breath ragged. "We're not alone," he choked. "It's out there. It killed…"

"Randy," Megan said, rushing toward him, relief and horror colliding. "Jenna thinks someone is hunting her."

Randy's gaze locked onto Jenna. His grip tightened on the baseball bat until his knuckles turned white. "Back away from her," he said, his voice sharp. "Right now."

The growl outside rose again—closer, heavier—followed by the slow, deliberate scrape of something massive moving along the cabin walls.

"Everyone shut up," Aiden whispered. "It's listening."

The shadows thickened, crawling up the walls and pooling along the ceiling like living veins. The air grew dense, pressing down until every breath was laborious, as if the cabin itself were squeezing them.

Jenna's breathing became frantic, sharp gasps ripping from her throat. She clutched the shard of glass to her chest, blood dripping onto the floor. "He's here," she cried. "I can feel him. Under the floor. In the walls. Listening."

A deep, grinding vibration shook the cabin, rattling boards beneath their feet and sinking into their bones, cold and undeniable.

"He got Zack," Randy blurted, hoarse and uneven. "We can't stay here. He tore him apart like he was nothing."

Megan's heart slammed violently. "What do you mean he got Zack?" she demanded. "Randy, what is out there?"

"Don't play dumb," he snapped, backing toward the door, bat raised. "You brought this thing back. I won't let it take us."

The growl shifted. Slowed. Deepened. Twisted into a low, deliberate laugh that pulsed through the trees and seeped into the cabin walls. Intelligence. Malice. Enjoyment.

Jenna screamed—raw, piercing, and full of the certainty that they were prey.

The cabin shook as something massive dragged itself along the exterior walls. Dust fell. Floorboards bowed. Megan felt it in her feet, traveling up into her spine: the forest, the cabin, and whatever hunted them—all one, alive, patient, waiting.

"We cannot leave her," Megan said, her voice hard, forcing herself forward despite the claws of fear scraping at her chest. "Running will get us killed. Whatever this thing is, it wants us scattered and terrified."

Randy's eyes snapped to hers.

The bat swung.

Aiden reacted instantly, throwing himself between Megan and the blow. The bat struck his raised arm with a sickening, splintering crack that echoed through the cabin like a hammer on bone. Aiden cried out as the force sent him slamming backward into Megan. They hit the bookshelf together, the old wood shattering with a cascade of splinters and books tumbling in every direction. Pain ripped through Aiden as he hit the floor, the bat clattering to the boards beside him.

"You stay back!" Randy shouted, voice raw and shaking, snatching the bat again. He yanked the door open. A fetid gust of air surged in, damp and rotten, carrying with it the unmistakable stench of death. "On three—we run."

Jenna scrambled for the fallen flashlight, her hand slick with blood.

"One," Randy whispered.

A growl pressed against the cabin walls, close enough to make their teeth rattle.

"Two."

The trees outside shifted, shadows bending unnaturally toward the doorway, leaning like predators poised to strike.

"Three."

They vanished into the night, the door slamming shut behind them with a hollow, final report.

Silence descended, thick and terrible. Megan dropped beside Aiden, her pulse roaring as distant screams pierced the forest, each cut short before it could reach resolution. She fumbled for her phone, activating the flashlight, the beam jittering violently across Aiden's pale, sweat-slick face.

"Aiden," she cried.

He clenched his jaw, struggling to sit upright while gripping his injured arm. "Randy... he wasn't thinking. He—he was gone. Completely gone."

"We have to move," Megan said urgently, helping him upright. "Right now."

Another scream tore through the fog outside—brief, abruptly silenced. Megan froze, the hair on her arms rising. Her light drifted across the wreckage of the bookshelf and landed on a carved symbol, deep into the back panel: an inverted pentagram, circled with burned runes that pulsed faintly, alive. She recognized it instantly. This was no decoration. This was ritual.

"This explains everything," she whispered, the weight of dread compressing her chest. "This cabin... it was used for summoning."

Visions flooded her mind: the reverend standing where she now was, voice raised beneath the rafters, scripture twisted beneath the words, each line a transaction, each blessing an invitation. The congregation unaware, their faith redirected—reshaped—into something far older, far hungrier.

"The reverend kept the balance," she breathed. "He chanted the prayers that told the demon it was remembered, that it was honored, that it was still welcome."

The symbols weren't commands. They were cycles. Repetitions. Rituals of offering and renewal. The inverted seal at the center was an anchor, rooting the demon here, giving it a permanent place to return to, to grow, to feed. Megan's phone trembled as her eyes traced the grooves in the wood.

"Megan, do not touch it!" Aiden shouted, panic threading his words.

Her fingers brushed the carved symbols anyway.

Pain detonated. Ice surged up her arm and into her chest, locking muscles and ripping her breath from her lungs. Her back arched violently as something invisible seized her from within.

"Megan!" Aiden screamed, crawling toward her.

The cabin dissolved around her. Darkness pressed in, thick and alive, whispers now clear, insistent and hungry.

Her phone slipped from her grasp, clattering to the floor. Its beam danced across the ceiling, illuminating Megan's rigid, contorted body.

Aiden froze beside her, terror coiling in his throat. "What… what did you do?"

The cabin pulsed once, a violent heartbeat. Outside, something massive shifted, and a towering shadow crawled across the doorway. The growl returned—slow, deliberate, satisfied.

Whatever had been awakened was fully aware.

And it was coming for them.

Chapter 17:

Hearts in the Twilight

Amy and Anthony stood locked in the center of the clearing, afraid to move, afraid not to. The silence was total—so absolute it amplified everything else until it felt unbearable. Amy could hear her own heartbeat hammering in her ears, each thud loud and wet, as if it were echoing through the trees instead of her chest. The forest surrounded them in a perfect ring, trunks rising straight and unyielding like blackened pillars beneath the last scraps of dying light. Above, the branches had knitted together so tightly that the sky felt smothered, as though the woods had sealed them inside on purpose.

This was supposed to be harmless. A stupid night. Flashlights and laughter and pretending they weren't scared of a place everyone whispered about. Somewhere along the way, the woods had changed the rules. What had begun as a joke had curdled into something hostile, something watchful. The air itself felt crowded, pressing against their skin, waiting.

"Where is everyone?" Amy whispered. The sound of her voice startled her—it felt loud and fragile. She turned slowly, pivoting in place, her gaze skimming the tree line again and again, searching for a familiar shape, a face, anything human. "Thomas?" she called, then quieter, "Tyler?" Each name seemed to drop dead the moment it left her mouth, swallowed whole by the dark.

Anthony scrubbed a shaking hand down his face. Sweat slicked his skin despite the cold seeping through his clothes, despite the way his teeth threatened to chatter. "This isn't funny anymore," he said, raising his voice, pushing it outward like a challenge. "Seriously. Knock it off." The forest didn't answer. No echo. No movement. Just the same oppressive quiet, thick as packed earth.

Something shifted.

Amy's breath hitched as motion flickered at the edge of her vision—too fast to track or dismiss. "Did you see that?" she asked, pointing, her arm trembling so badly she had to clutch her wrist with her other hand.

Anthony snapped the flashlight toward the spot, the beam wobbling violently. Pale light scraped across bark and dead leaves and nothing else. "Probably an animal," he said, but the words sounded brittle, already cracking apart. His pupils were blown wide, swallowing the whites of his eyes. "Just… just stay close to me."

"That wasn't an animal," Amy said. Panic bled into her voice despite her effort to swallow it down. "Something's wrong. We need to find them. Now."

They took a step together, then another, the crunch of leaves beneath their feet sounding obscenely loud. That was when the laughter began.

It rippled through the trees—high-pitched and bright, playful in a way that made Amy's stomach twist. It didn't come from one place. It came from everywhere at once, bouncing unnaturally between trunks, sliding through branches like breath through hollow bones. It sounded like children. Real children. The kind of laughter that should have belonged to daylight and scraped knees and playgrounds.

Amy's blood turned to ice. "Do you hear that?" she whispered. Her throat tightened, the words barely escaping. "That sounds like kids."

Anthony swallowed hard. His Adam's apple bobbed painfully. "There aren't any kids out here," he said. "There can't be." Even as he spoke, mist began to creep across the ground, thin at first, then thickening, curling around their ankles with slow intent. It was cold enough to burn, clinging to their legs as if feeling them out, memorizing their shape.

The laughter drew closer.

Shadows began to separate themselves from the trees.

They were small—child-sized—but wrong in every way that mattered. Their forms looked stitched together from smoke and absence, edges blurring and reforming as they moved. They darted and skipped with jerky enthusiasm, circling just outside the flashlight's reach, limbs bending where joints shouldn't exist. Heads tilted too far to one side, then snapped back upright as giggles spilled from them in wet, choking bursts.

"Anthony," Amy whispered. Terror flooded her veins, hot and electric.

One of the figures sprang into the beam of light.

It had no face—just a hollow void where features should have been, split open by a grin packed with thin, needle-like teeth. Its eyes were pits, empty wells that swallowed the light instead of reflecting it. It shrieked with delight, a sound sharp enough to stab straight into Amy's skull, then burst apart into shadow, scattering back into the mist.

More surged forward. A dozen. Maybe more. They rushed them in waves, darting close enough that Amy felt a brush of cold against her cheek, her arm, her throat—each touch lingering just long enough to promise something worse before vanishing again. Their laughter climbed into a shrill, overlapping chorus that vibrated inside her head, pressing against her thoughts, scraping and clawing at the edges of her sanity.

"Stop!" Amy screamed. The word tore out of her raw and broken. "Please—stop!" She squeezed her eyes shut and covered her face as the shadows closed in, their voices layering over one another, chanting nonsense syllables that felt ancient and cruel, sounds meant to unmake her piece by piece.

Anthony yanked her against his chest, locking his arms around her as if he could fuse them together. His heart slammed wildly beneath her ear. "I've got you," he said, forcing steadiness into his voice even as fear crawled up his spine and lodged in his throat. "Just breathe. Don't look. Don't listen."

Then—nothing.

The laughter cut off mid-note, like a cord being severed. The pressure vanished. The shadows thinned and unraveled, dissolving into the mist until only the trees remained. The silence that followed felt wronger than the noise had—sudden and very heavy, as if the forest itself were holding its breath.

Amy and Anthony stood trembling, gasping, afraid to open their eyes.

Then Amy did—and saw him.

"There," she said hoarsely, her voice scraped raw. "Anthony… look."

A figure stood between the trees ahead, perfectly still. Human-shaped. Familiar.

"Tyler!" Anthony shouted, relief exploding through him as he dragged Amy forward. "Tyler!"

But with every step closer, the air grew colder, denser, sinking into their lungs like water. Tyler didn't turn. He didn't move. He stood facing the trees, shoulders slumped at an unnatural angle, head tilted as if his neck had forgotten how to hold itself upright.

"Tyler?" Anthony called again, slowing now, dread crawling back in, slow and venomous. "Hey, man. You okay?"

No answer.

Amy's heart battered her ribs as they reached him. "Tyler," she whispered, her voice breaking apart.

Anthony stepped around him—and froze.

Tyler's chest was split open from throat to stomach, his ribs forced outward like shattered gates. Thick, pulsing vines had grown through his torso, erupting through flesh and bone, slick with blood and something darker. They throbbed wetly, as if still feeding. His eyes were wide and glassy, staring at nothing, his mouth stretched into a silent, eternal scream. Blood had dried in dark, flaky streaks down his chin.

The vines twitched.

Then they withdrew, sliding back into the earth with obscene patience, tearing free chunks of meat and sinew as they went.

Amy screamed as Tyler collapsed to the ground.

The trees answered with a deep, grinding groan as roots shifted beneath their feet. Somewhere deep within the forest, something massive exhaled—slow, heavy, and satisfied.

Anthony grabbed Amy by the wrist and twisted, instinct screaming louder than reason. They took two stumbling steps—

—and the laughter returned.

It was different now. No longer high and bright. No longer pretending to be innocent. It rolled through the trees low and drawn-out, saturated with knowing. A predator's patience had replaced the children's glee. Whatever had been playing with them had decided the game was worth finishing.

The hunt was not over.

Anthony's stomach knotted so tightly he thought he might vomit. His mind screamed at him to run, to drag Amy as far away from this place as his legs could carry him—but his body betrayed him. He kneeled down his hand reached out on its own and clamped down on Tyler's shoulder.

The flesh was cold.

He pulled.

The breath ripped from Anthony's lungs in a broken gasp.

Tyler's face was no longer a face. It was a ruin—something torn apart and rearranged without care or mercy. Deep, ragged slashes carved through his features, splitting skin and muscle from cheekbones down across his throat and chest, as if something had tried to peel him open and grown impatient. The wounds gleamed wetly in the moonlight, edges swollen and dark.

Then Tyler's mouth twitched.

Thorny vines forced their way out through his lips and eye sockets, pushing and tearing as they emerged, splitting flesh with slow, obscene persistence. One vine flexed, barbs scraping bone as it withdrew with a soft, sucking sound, dragging blood and shredded tissue with it before slipping back into his throat.

"No—no, no, no!" Amy screamed.

She staggered backward, hands flying to her mouth as the sound ripped out of her raw and uncontrolled. It wasn't fear alone—it was recognition. This was wrong in a way her mind could not correct or escape.

Anthony moved without thinking, stepping in front of her, his body a shield he knew was useless. The image seared itself into his brain anyway, permanent and vivid, burned into the back of his eyelids.

"It's okay," he whispered, even as his voice fractured and his heart slammed so hard it hurt. "Don't look. Don't—"

He stopped.

Behind Amy, the mist thickened.

It didn't drift this time. It parted.

Something enormous pushed through it, slow and deliberate, displacing the air with its mass. The creature revealed itself inch by inch, as if savoring their understanding. Moonlight caught on a towering body formed from compacted mud, splintered bark, and layered rot, its shape vaguely human but bloated and warped, as though the forest itself had tried to imitate a man and failed.

Vines crawled across its frame like veins beneath translucent skin, pulsing with stolen warmth. From its torso spilled long, slick tendrils that dragged along the ground, carving deep grooves into the soil as they moved.

Its mouth stretched wider than anatomy should allow, splitting its face into a rictus grin. Inside, rows of jagged, glass-like shards clicked softly together as it breathed. The sound was intimate. Anticipatory.

Its eyes locked onto them.

Yellow. Bloodshot. Intelligent.

They did not flicker or wander. They fixed.

Thick vines burst from its fingers, twisting into clawed shapes, each thorn sharp enough to strip flesh clean from bone.

The forest fell silent—not in peace, but in submission.

Then it stepped forward.

The sound was wet and heavy, each movement accompanied by a deep squelch, as though the ground were being peeled open beneath its weight.

"Run!" Anthony screamed.

He grabbed Amy and dragged her forward just as the creature's attention narrowed fully onto them. They tore through the trees, branches lashing their faces, splitting skin, roots snagging their feet as panic fueled their flight. Their lungs burned. Their muscles screamed. Behind them, the earth trembled with every step of pursuit.

They slammed behind a massive tree trunk, pressing themselves flat against the bark, chests heaving as they fought to keep silent. The wood vibrated against their backs as heavy footsteps circled, slow and unhurried. The thing was not rushing.

It didn't need to.

"Where did it go?" Amy whispered, peeking around the trunk, hands shaking so badly she could barely hold herself upright. The clearing stood empty. No movement. No sound. "What if it left?"

Anthony opened his mouth to answer—

—and something tightened around his ankle.

He looked down just as a thick vine snapped fully closed around his leg. It coiled instantly, hard as iron, constricting with brutal force. Bone ground against bone with a sharp, sickening crack as pressure crushed his calf.

"Amy!" he screamed.

Pain detonated through him, blinding and absolute. He clawed at the vine, nails tearing, but it only tightened in response, thorns punching deep into his flesh, drawing hot streams of blood.

She rushed to him, grabbing the vine with both hands and pulling with everything she had. It pulsed beneath her grip—alive, responsive, almost curious. With a violent jerk, Anthony tore free.

The sudden release sent him crashing backward.

His skull struck a rock with a dull, brutal thud.

Light exploded behind his eyes. The world pitched sideways.

"Amy…" he whispered, barely conscious.

"I'm here!" she cried, dropping beside him, hands slick with his blood. "Get up—please—we have to go!"

The creature stepped into view again.

It moved calmly now, confidence radiating from every heavy step. Its gaze swept the clearing, then settled on them with quiet certainty. Anthony tried to stand, but his leg folded uselessly beneath him, agony flaring white-hot.

"Go!" he shouted. "Just go!"

"I won't leave you!" Amy sobbed.

The creature lunged.

Amy threw herself over Anthony without hesitation, wrapping her arms around him, her body trembling as she screamed, "No!"

It loomed above them, blotting out the moonlight entirely. One vine-wrapped arm lifted a massive fallen log from the ground as easily as lifting a twig.

"Amy, move!" Anthony screamed, shoving weakly against her.

The log came down.

The impact was catastrophic.

Bone shattered. Flesh collapsed. The sound tore through the forest like a tree splitting under lightning. Pain erased everything—thought, breath, identity—until there was only blinding white and then nothing at all.

In their final moments, they clung to one another, foreheads pressed together, breaths mingling, terror and love tangled so tightly they became indistinguishable.

The forest accepted them without ceremony.

Their bodies sank into the soil, feeding the roots beneath the ground.

Another offering taken.

Another life consumed.

Deep within the trees, the thing that ruled this place settled back into the earth, stronger than before.

As Thomas held Lexi against him, her warmth felt like the last fragile proof that he was still alive. The fog closed in from every direction, thick and wet, clinging to their skin and clothing as if it were trying to pull them back into the nightmare they had barely escaped. His heart slammed against his ribs, not only from the sprint through the trees, but from the certainty that whatever hunted them was still close. Still listening.

"Where is everyone else?" Thomas asked, his voice tight as he scanned the shifting mist. Shapes moved at the edges of his vision, trees warping into hulking silhouettes that seemed to lean toward them.

"Randy… he left me," Lexi whispered. Her voice broke, barely carrying through the fog. "He said he'd come back. He promised he'd help me find you." Tears spilled over, streaking down her dirt-smeared face, and for a moment Thomas's fear was eclipsed by a hot surge of anger.

"Forget him," Thomas said sharply, pulling her closer. "I've got you now. We stick together. Just you and me." He meant it, but the tremor in his voice betrayed how thin his resolve felt beneath the weight of the forest.

Lexi swallowed hard, her eyes darting toward the shadows threading between the trees. "Did you see it?" she asked. "Did you see what ripped Zack apart?"

The memory slammed into him without mercy. Jake's body was thrashing in the water. The impossible strength dragging him under. Those yellow, bloodshot eyes staring up through the murk with cold intelligence. Thomas's stomach twisted violently. "I—I don't want to talk about it," he said, the words scraping his throat raw. He saw it again—Jake frozen in place, terror locking his body while Jake drowned—and shame coiled around his lungs.

"You have to," Lexi insisted, panic sharpening her voice. "We can't survive if we don't understand it. We need to know what we're dealing with." She hugged herself, shaking as cold sank into her bones. The fog thickened, rolling around their legs like something alive and searching.

Thomas forced a breath into his chest. "It wasn't an animal," he said quietly. "It knew what it was doing. It grabbed Jake like he weighed nothing, dragged him under, and didn't even struggle. Its eyes were glowing. Its teeth... they weren't right. That thing wasn't hunting to eat. It was hunting because it enjoyed it."

Lexi's face drained of color. "It got Jake too?" Her voice dropped to a whisper. "Then we're already next."

The forest seemed to lean in, listening.

"We can't stop," Thomas said, forcing strength into his words. "We have to get out of the low ground. Somewhere open. Somewhere we can see it coming."

"Safe?" Lexi whispered, glancing around wildly. "There's nothing safe out here. We'll get lost."

Thomas clenched his fists until his knuckles burned, grounding himself in the pain. He pointed into the fog, arm rigid, as if certainty alone could carve a path through the woods. "We came from that direction," he said. "I'm sure of it. If we keep moving, we'll find something—anything." The words sounded thin the moment they left him, but stopping felt worse. Stopping felt final.

He stepped away from the water's edge and pulled Lexi with him. The mist tightened instantly, coiling around their legs and waists, cold and invasive, crawling beneath their clothes like damp fingers. It clung to their skin as if the forest were memorizing them.

They moved deeper between the trees. Branches scraped along their arms and faces, leaving stinging lines in their wake. Every snapped twig detonated in the silence, sharp and accusatory, as though the woods were cataloging their mistakes. The air grew heavier with each step, thick with rot and wet soil, pressing down on Thomas's chest until every breath felt borrowed, temporary.

"Thomas," Lexi whispered suddenly.

He felt it before he heard it—the way her grip tightened, the way her body went rigid beside him. "Do you hear that?"

He stopped.

At first there was only the whisper of wind threading through the branches. Then something underneath it stirred. A low, guttural sound rolled through the trees, deep and deliberate, vibrating through the ground itself. It wasn't loud. It didn't need to be. It carried weight. Intent.

Thomas's blood went cold. The growl traveled up through the soles of his boots, into his legs, settling in his chest like a second heartbeat—slower, heavier, not his own. He tightened his grip on Lexi's hand.

"We need to move," he said, already walking faster. "Right now."

"Wait!" Lexi hissed, yanking his arm hard enough to hurt. Her nails bit through his sleeve, into skin. "What if we're walking straight toward it?"

Thomas didn't slow. He couldn't. The idea of standing still made his skin crawl. "Then we don't panic," he said, forcing his voice steady while his pulse thundered in his ears. "We stay low, stay quiet, and stick to the trees. If it hears us…" He swallowed. "We're done."

A sharp crack split the air behind them.

Both of them froze.

Thomas spun, swinging the flashlight in a wide arc. The beam cut through tangled brush and slick leaves, illuminating nothing but trunks and shadow. The forest stared back, unmoving. Waiting.

Then the sound came again—closer this time. The growl deepened, fractured, layered with something else beneath it, something wet and hungry. It rolled through the earth, climbed Thomas's legs, and lodged in his ribcage, rattling his bones.

It wasn't searching anymore.

It had found them.

"Run!" Thomas shouted.

He yanked Lexi forward, and they bolted. They crashed through the trees, branches lashing their faces, tearing at hair and skin. Roots reached up from the mud, slick and treacherous, snagging their feet as the fog thickened until the world collapsed into breath, burn, and blind panic. Behind them, the growl split into snarls—too many throats, overlapping and wrong—each step of pursuit heavy enough to shake the ground.

"Where do we go?" Lexi gasped, her words shredding apart as her lungs fought for air. "I can't—Thomas—I can't keep up!"

"Just a little farther!" he yelled, dragging her uphill as the ground pitched steeply beneath them. His chest burned, each breath tasting metallic, sharp. "Look for—"

The sentence died in his throat.

Something exploded out of the darkness.

The impact was violent enough to erase sound. Thomas was lifted clean off his feet and hurled backward, slammed into the ground with crushing force. The flashlight tore from his hand, spinning once in the air before vanishing into the brush. Darkness swallowed everything.

"Thomas!" Lexi screamed.

Pain detonated through him as immense weight crushed him into the earth. The creature's breath washed over his face— hot, foul, reeking of churned soil and decay. Claws tore into his side, sharp points driving between his ribs. He screamed and thrashed, hands sliding uselessly against bark-slick flesh and writhing vines that pulsed beneath his fingers.

The thing pressed down harder.

Lexi grabbed the first thing she could reach—a thick, broken branch—and swung with everything she had. Wood cracked against something solid and alive. The creature snarled, the sound so deep and furious it rattled Thomas's skull, reverberating inside his teeth. For half a heartbeat, the pressure eased.

Then it shifted.

The weight came down again—heavier, merciless. Thomas felt his chest compress inward. He heard it before he felt it: a wet, catastrophic crack as his rib cage folded under the force. Agony tore through him, blinding and absolute. His lungs seized. No air came. No sound.

"Get away from him!" Lexi shrieked. Her voice broke apart on the words.

The pressure lifted.

Thomas sucked in a broken gasp, choking on air and pain as the creature rose. His vision pulsed dark at the edges. He lay twisted in the dirt, every breath a knife grinding deeper into his chest.

Then the creature turned.

Its attention slid away from him and locked onto Lexi. Yellow eyes burned with focused hunger as it stalked toward her, unhurried. Vines dragged behind it like living chains, carving grooves through the mud.

Lexi stumbled backward, terror freezing her limbs. "Thomas!" she cried, looking at him helplessly.

He could barely see her. The world throbbed. His lungs screamed. But he saw the way the thing loomed over her, the way its shadow swallowed her whole.

Something inside him snapped.

With a raw, animal sound torn from somewhere deeper than thought, Thomas forced himself up. His body rebelled, pain ripping through his torso, but he ignored it. He staggered once and then ran.

"Lexi, run!" he roared.

He slammed into the creature shoulder-first. The impact shuddered through both of them, bone and rot colliding. They crashed together, tumbling down the slope in a violent tangle of limbs, vines, and snarling fury. Thomas rolled hard, the world spinning, pain screaming as the creature slid past him, tearing through brush, snapping branches, before disappearing into the darkness below.

The forest fell silent again.

Thomas lay in the dirt, gasping, chest crushed, knowing with sick certainty that silence didn't mean safety—it meant the woods were listening, deciding what to take next.

Thomas collapsed onto his side, the world tilting violently as his body finally gave in. Every breath was a war—short, shallow gasps that scraped through his chest and caught on shattered ribs like broken glass. The pain wasn't sharp anymore. It was crushing, suffocating, as if something heavy still sat on him, even after the creature was gone.

Somewhere nearby, Lexi sobbed his name.

And farther still—far enough to pretend it wasn't real, close enough to feel in his bones—something moved. Retreating. Withdrawing. Not fleeing.

Waiting.

"Thomas!" Lexi screamed. Terror split her voice open as she scrambled to him near the edge of the ridge. She grabbed his arm and hauled him upright despite his weight, despite the sound he made when she did it—a low, involuntary cry torn from his throat. "Are you okay?" Her eyes flicked wildly to the slope below, swallowed by fog and darkness. "I don't see it. Where did it go?"

"I—I don't know," Thomas gasped. Speaking felt like swallowing razors. Each breath scraped, caught, burned. His lungs refused to fill properly, panic blooming alongside the pain. He barely had time to steady himself before the mist ahead of them began to stir.

The forest exhaled, fog rolling apart as something stepped through it.

The creature emerged slowly, deliberately, as if it wanted to be seen. Its massive form resolved piece by piece—bark grinding against bark, mud sliding and reforming, vines dragging along the ground like living restraints. Its body looked unfinished, constantly shifting, as though the forest were still deciding what shape it should take. Those sickly yellow eyes burned through the mist, fixed on them with patient, unmistakable hunger.

Thomas felt something cold uncurl in his gut.

"Run!" he shouted.

He shoved Lexi forward, and they bolted, plunging back into the trees as the creature's growl rolled out behind them—

deep, layered, vibrating through the earth and into their bones. It wasn't a sound of rage.

It was the sound of anticipation.

They crashed through dense undergrowth, branches slashing at their faces and arms, tearing skin, drawing blood. Thomas stumbled again and again, pain flaring white-hot in his chest, his legs buckling as the damage caught up with him. Each breath came with a wet hitch. Lexi refused to let go. She dragged him forward when his body faltered, her grip iron-tight, desperate.

He risked a glance over his shoulder.

The thing was gaining on them.

Its silhouette warped through the fog, stretching and compressing unnaturally as it moved, vines snapping back and forth like whips. The ground shook beneath its steps, the rhythm of pursuit steady and inevitable.

"Where do we go?" Lexi cried as they burst onto a narrow, barely-there path. Her voice broke completely. "Thomas, please—"

"Just keep running!" he yelled. Ahead, something flickered through the fog. A faint, steady glow. Unmoving. Human. "I see light!"

Hope sparked—sharp and dangerous.

They ran harder. Lungs burned. Legs screamed. Behind them, the growl swelled into a thunderous bellow that echoed through the forest like a warning bell, shaking leaves loose from branches. The darkness pressed in from all sides. Trees leaned closer, branches twisting inward, closing ranks, as if the woods itself were trying to seal them inside.

The roar came again—closer.

Lexi sobbed as she ran. "Thomas," she whispered, barely audible over the pounding of their feet. "It's right there."

"Don't stop," he forced out, teeth clenched as agony ripped through his ribs. Every step felt like punishment. "Don't look back."

The light sharpened, resolving into something solid. Familiar.

"It's—" Thomas sucked in a ragged breath. "It's Tyler's truck!"

They burst through the thinning mist and out of the trees. The forest released them all at once, fog peeling back like a disappointed thing denied its prize. Tyler's truck sat at the edge of the clearing, dull metal catching the faint glow of the night sky.

Relief hit Thomas so hard his knees nearly buckled.

Before he could collapse, hurried footsteps broke through the clearing. Two figures rushed toward them from the road—the sheriff first, face pale and drawn, flashlight sweeping wildly, and then Reverend Goodwin, coat flapping open, all composure stripped away.

"Thomas!" the reverend shouted.

Then he was there, arms crushing his son against his chest, holding him with a fierceness that stole what little breath Thomas had left. The smell of cold night air and worn cloth grounded him—real, solid—cutting through the nightmare still clinging to his skin.

Lexi stood frozen beside them, shaking.

The sheriff swept his beam toward the treeline, jaw clenched tight. The fog lingered there, thick and watchful.

"You were never supposed to be in there," Reverend Goodwin said quietly. He pulled back just enough to grip Thomas's shoulders, searching his face for injuries, grief and relief warring in his eyes. "The forest is forbidden to the people of Glory. Always has been."

Thomas stared up at him, shuddering. "Then why—" His voice cracked. "Why does it keep happening?"

The reverend's gaze slid back to the trees.

"Because the evil in that forest cannot be destroyed," he said. There was no sermon left in his voice now—only truth, heavy and exhausted. "It can only be contained."

He hesitated, fingers tightening as though the words themselves hurt to hold. "There are rites older than this town," he continued. "Older than the church. Older than the names carved into our graves."

Thomas felt something settle, cold and sick, in his stomach.

The reverend swallowed, his eyes shining with restrained grief. "For generations, the burden of containment has been passed down," he said quietly. "Each shepherd before me made the same choice. Each summer solstice, one soul is sent beyond that treeline."

Lexi sucked in a sharp breath.

"They are not forced," Goodwin said, voice trembling, as he looked around for understanding. "They are prepared. Guided. Taught to believe their offering is holy. An honor. A necessary devotion to God, to Glory, to the children who must never know what truly lives in that forest."

His hand tightened on Thomas's shoulder, pain etched into every line of his face. "It is the price we pay to keep the curse contained. To ensure this town survives. Thrives."

Silence stretched between them, thick and unbearable.

"Now," the reverend said at last, his gaze drifting back to the woods, "all we can do is pray your friends are strong enough to survive what they have already endured." Beyond the clearing, beneath tangled roots and shifting fog, the forest waited— holding its breath around the souls still lost within its depths, patient as it closed in on the others who hadn't made it out.

Chapter 18:

Blood and Ash

Megan felt suspended in time, as if the world had stopped spinning, her body a vessel she could barely recognize. She looked down at herself—or rather, at what remained of it—limp and lifeless on the cabin floor. Panic surged in her chest—raw and unfamiliar, yet sickeningly recognizable—like the aftershock of every nightmare she had ever survived. "What happened? Did I die?" she whispered, her words unraveling into the mist that coiled around her fingertips. The fog slid around her ankles, soft but unrelenting, tugging her forward into an abyss where the line between life and death felt thin, brittle, and easily torn. She remembered touching the symbol carved into the cabinet, the sudden jolt that raced up her arm, the way the room had collapsed into absolute blackness—and then this.

"Megan!" Aiden's voice cut through her daze, sharp and urgent. "Stay with me! We need to get out of here." His words were tethered to the edge of reality, grounding her, yet the shadows at the corners of her vision seemed to pulse and twitch, as if listening.

"Where… where am I?" Megan's voice trembled. The mist beneath her swirled with a cold, tangible intent, spinning into a miniature tornado that clawed at her senses. Panic sought to take hold, but she remembered Sister Abigail's advice—breathe. Visualize your protected place. Hold onto it.

She focused, inhaling slowly. In her mind, she drew a circle of light, a small sanctuary carved from memory and will. Within it, she could move, observe, and act. The fog responded, hesitating, curling around the edge of her sanctuary but not inside it. Her pulse slowed as the world sharpened, colors deepening, the acrid scent of burnt wood rising from the charred remnants ahead. A grotesque monument loomed in her mind's eye—a memory, yes, but more visceral than mere recollection could account for. Something terrible had happened here. She could feel its weight, the air vibrating with hatred.

A voice brushed against her awareness, faint and almost imperceptible—a chant woven into the wind, threading through the trees like a dark melody. "What is that?" Megan whispered, heart hammering. The sound drew her forward, curiosity pulling her feet even as her instincts screamed retreat.

She advanced slowly, feeling the underbrush scratch at her skin, shadows stretching and twisting like they were alive. Then she saw her: the woman from her dreams, kneeling at the edge of the forest, tears streaming down her face, her expression torn between grief and fury. Her lips moved, forming words Megan could feel more than hear:

"I curse you! I curse you all. You will answer to me… just you wait."

Megan's chest tightened. The words throbbed like a physical blow, vibrating with an unnatural resonance that seeped into her bones. Time shivered, the air folding in on itself, revealing fleeting glimpses of the town swallowed by creeping darkness —streets empty, buildings bending under the shadows that stretched like living things.

The woman's movements were ghostlike as she approached the charred remains, half-buried in ash that still breathed heat from the funeral pyre, a crude tower of blackened logs where her lover's body had burned down to ruin. She knelt and began to gather what was left, digging through scorched flesh and fused muscle with trembling, reverent hands. She lifted the skull first, its surface split and blistered, the jaw warped open as if locked in a final scream. Then came the long bones, cracked and ivory-bright beneath soot, splintered femurs and warped ribs that flaked apart when she touched them. Smaller fragments followed, shards of spine and knuckles, pieces of a life ended too soon and refused rest.

The air grew heavy, pressing inward with a suffocating fury, an ancient, consuming wrath that vibrated through the ground itself. What clung to the woman was no longer devotion but a ravenous obsession, something feral and unholy that clawed at the edges of Megan's sanctuary, testing it, probing for weakness. A chant began to echo, low at first, carried on no clear voice, then rising and multiplying until it surrounded Megan from every direction. The words pulsed and called, dragging at her thoughts, beckoning her back to the cabin.

Megan squeezed her eyes shut and forced herself to focus, pulling inward, imagining the walls, the floorboards, the smell of damp wood and rot. She concentrated on the sensation of being there, of leaving this place behind, pushing against the pressure until it burned behind her eyes. When she opened them, the ash and fire were gone.

Megan was back in the cabin.

The woman rose with the bones clutched tight against her chest, then crouched in the corner and spread them across the cabin floor one by one, her face stretched into a grin of wild, unrestrained triumph.

She leaned closer, daring to look over the woman's shoulder as her hands moved feverishly, carving a symbol into the wooden slab, the blade chewing into the grain with splintering force. Megan could see the purpose etched into every motion, the frantic insistence driving her magic forward, right up to the moment the pentagram was completed.

"Arise, my love," the woman whispered, a tremor of despair and rage intertwining. "Let the spirit of earth empower you and vengeance consume you."

A vibration thrummed through the cabin, low and insistent, like the heartbeat of the forest itself. Megan could feel the dark power coiling, dense and suffocating. She focused, centering herself within her circle of light, and for the first time, she saw the truth behind the woman's eyes—the madness, a fracture of grief amplified into obsession. After Hank's death, the woman had broken completely, and now her sorrow and rage vibrated through the shadows, clawing at reality itself.

The shrine she built for him seemed to breathe. Candles flickered violently, throwing monstrous shadows that danced across the walls. The skull and bleached bones of the altar pulsated with a life of their own, casting a hellish glow. Megan felt the air thicken, each inhalation a struggle as the oppressive energy gnawed at the edges of her mind. Yet, through it all, her protected place remained a bubble of clarity, her focus a shield against the onslaught of visions.

She stepped forward, curiosity and courage intertwining, drawing closer to the woman's voice. The chanting became louder, each word a strike, each syllable a vibration that seemed to warp the very walls of the cabin. Megan could see it—the destruction of the woman's mind, the slow dissolution into obsession, the raw, aching desire to reclaim what had been lost. Every movement, every spell, every whispered incantation was a spiral deeper into madness, yet it was also a precise, intentional act of summoning.

And then she noticed the movement in the shadows just outside the cabin, the stirring of something immense. Megan's pulse raced, but her focus did not waver. She realized the woman was calling forth more than just grief or rage—she was summoning Hank. Not the man he had been, not the familiar woodsman of the town, but something else. Something monstrous, fused with the forest itself.

Megan's vision contracted and expanded as she observed the process. Vines slithered from the mud and across the forest floor, and bright red moss clung to form shapes, twisting and rising, forming the outline of a massive figure. The eyes, yellow and intelligent, opened and burned with a hunger that seemed endless. Teeth, jagged and uneven like broken rocks, clicked as the mouth flexed. Megan's stomach churned, yet her protected space held firm, letting her watch without being consumed.

The woman lifted her voice higher, channeling rage and grief into Hank's body, animating it with the forest's dark essence. Megan could feel the surge, the pull, the sense of life returning not through compassion but through vengeance. Hank moved, slow at first, as if testing his newfound strength, then faster, the monstrous form fully realized: mud crusted like armor, bark splintering over muscles, thorny vines crawling across limbs, hair and beard of bright red moss twisting and writhing. Every step he took left a ripple in the air, a whisper of destruction.

The horror was both intimate and vast, pressing close while stretching far beyond Megan's grasp. She understood then that the woman's evil was not confined to flesh or blood; it seeped outward, fouling the air itself, warping the world into a waking nightmare capable of devouring anyone who wandered in unguarded. At times, the woman's consciousness shattered and faltered, jerking in and out as she clawed at her own skull, her mouth open in a soundless scream while black smoke bled from her skin, crawling over her like a sentient shroud.

Megan felt the edges of the vision press in, but she breathed and held onto her protected place, letting the scene unfold, taking in every detail: the oscillating rage in the woman, the monstrous perfection of Hank's new form, the subtle destruction that threatened to consume the town completely.

And still, she stayed.

Her mind, sharpened by fear and will, observed the careful choreography of grief, vengeance, and dark magic. Every scream, every flaring of fire, every twitch of Hank's pointed fingers was accounted for. Megan marked the threads of magic, the origin of the woman's power, and the moments where madness collided with creation. This was the truth, unflinching and raw, and for the first time, she felt the weight of knowledge as a weapon as much as a burden.

The cabin's walls seemed to vibrate with the pulse of the ritual, a low, resonant thrum that Megan could feel beneath her feet, in her chest, in the marrow of her bones. The woman's grief had become her power; Hank, the monstrous incarnation of that grief, was her instrument of devastation. Megan's heart raced, yet the clarity in her mind allowed her to see beyond the immediate chaos.

She whispered to herself, low and deliberate, "Show me more." At once, the vision twisted again, the mist thickening and coiling around her like smoke from a dying fire, drawing her forward toward the next horror, the next revelation, and the confrontation waiting to claim her.

The night air slammed against Megan as she stepped from the cabin's threshold, the chill biting at her skin, mingling with the residual heat of the vision. She staggered forward, drawn by a dark rhythm she couldn't name—footsteps, heavy and purposeful, thundering through the town ahead. Her chest heaved as she ran, the forest behind her swallowing her in shadow, while the faint glow of fires flickered at the edges of her vision. The scent of smoke and charred wood rolled over her in waves, thick and suffocating, coating her lungs with every breath.

And then she saw him.

Hank. Or what had once been Hank. The monstrous form moved with terrifying precision through the burning streets, his frame enormous and twisted by the forest's dark will. Mud and bark fused across his body like grotesque armor, thorny vines crawling over limbs, snaking across his chest and arms. Bright red moss formed hair and a beard that bristled with unnatural life. His eyes burned yellow, luminous in the infernal glow of the flames. Each breath drew steam from the heat, carrying with it a raw, animalistic hunger. His teeth, jagged and sharp like broken rocks, caught the firelight, glinting with the promise of violence.

Megan froze, heart hammering, as Hank's gaze swept the square. He lifted a massive hand, crushing a wooden post with ease, the wood cracking and snapping under his strength. Megan's stomach twisted as she realized what the woman had done: she had given life to pure vengeance, and now it walked the earth, unstoppable and monstrous.

The woman's voice—a thread in Megan's mind—wove through the chaos, guiding Hank with a dark rhythm. Megan's stomach turned at the intimacy of it, the realization that Hank was no longer himself. He was an extension of her grief and madness, a living weapon forged from loss, rage, and the deepest corners of the forest's hunger.

Flames spread across the buildings, licking the sky in angry tongues, and from the center of the square came the first screams. Megan could see the town unraveling: doors splintered, roofs collapsing, smoke devouring the streets. And in the middle of it all, Hank moved like a predator, calculated and terrifying, the debris of destruction scattering at his feet.

As Megan's energy slowly diminished, her consciousness wavered, slipping in and out as the world dissolved into white-hot clarity before snapping back into the vision she had fought to keep moving forward.

She saw a man hurled against the splintered ruins of a building, but before she could grasp more, her vision snapped away. Later, a woman's scream pierced the air as thick, writhing vines erupted from the earth, and Megan knew instinctively that Hank was behind it, though the exact details were shrouded in shadow and distance. It was as if the forest itself, fueled by the woman's wrath, was instructing Hank in the art of ruthless destruction, letting the imagination of terror fill every unseen gap.

Megan could see the woman now, moving slowly through the edge of the chaos. Her form wavered, appearing as if it were part spirit, part physical, ghostly threads peeling in and out of her body as she extended her will over Hank. At one moment she walked; the next, she was suspended above the ground, hands clawing at her skull, emitting a soundless scream that vibrated through the ether. Smoke and blackness wrapped around her, coiling like serpents, and Megan felt the pure, unfiltered malevolence radiating outward. The woman exuded a presence so absolute that even Hank's monstrous form seemed subservient, a tool to enact her rage.

Megan swallowed hard, feeling the pulse of her heartbeat sync with the vibration of the woman's madness. This was power intertwined with insanity, grief weaponized, and the echoes of countless deaths rolled through the air like a tide. She realized with a cold, sinking dread that the woman's pleasure was absolute; she was watching the chaos unfold, her spirit floating in ecstasy as the town burned, as lives were torn apart.

She saw Hank lift a man with his massive hands, crushing him and tossing the body as easily as a toy, yet she also saw the infernal precision in his movement, the subtle pauses, the way he seemed almost to stalk, testing barriers, savoring the effect of fear. She felt a terrible kinship with the woman's vision, as if she could feel the edges of the magic that animated Hank.

Megan forced herself to breathe, to pull in the sharp night air, to focus on the details that anchored her to the moment. She could see the people fleeing the square, their movements frantic, and hear their cries as Hank advanced. She could see the flames reflect off his jagged teeth and yellow eyes, but her mind filled in the gaps of the violence, leaving the exact acts to the imagination, as if the forest respected some unspoken boundary. She could feel the weight of every action, the consequence of every motion, without being directly consumed.

Then a flicker of recognition struck her—the woman, hovering at the edge of the firelight, had paused. Megan could see her hands twitch as though she were feeling Hank's actions across the distance, and the spiritual connection intensified. The woman's scream, silent yet deafening, tore through the vision, and Megan felt it reverberate inside her skull. The black smoke swirled thicker, feeding on her fear, pushing against the edges of her focus.

But Megan pushed back. She recentered, drawing on her protected place, slowing the vision, sharpening the clarity. She watched as Hank paused near the center of the square, looming over the terrified reverend and townsfolk. He tilted his head, the moss in his hair catching the flickering flames, vines twitching at his sides. Megan saw the interaction with eerie precision: the reverend raised a trembling hand, calling out words she could almost hear, and Hank responded with a subtle motion, almost imperceptible, that sent the townsfolk scattering.

A sound tore through the night—human, terrified, pleading —and Megan felt it strike her chest like a hammer. She could not see the specifics, only the impact: chaos, fear, destruction. Hank moved again, faster now, each step sending tremors through the ground. Megan's stomach clenched as she realized the woman was feeding off every moment, extending her consciousness into the night, relishing the terror as if it were sustenance.

Megan's vision flickered again. For a heartbeat, she was outside herself, floating above the square. She could feel her body moving mechanically through the town, limbs propelling her forward while her spirit clawed at her mind, fighting to remain anchored. The fire and smoke swirled around her, yet her mind remained a lens, observing the unfolding horror.

"Halt!" she whispered into herself, forcing focus. Her sanctuary of thought held. She could witness without succumbing, could catalog the evil without surrendering. Hank's monstrous form now stalked back and forth through the square, pausing at intervals, lifting bodies, bending the scene into a tableau of terror. The woman's fragmented consciousness pulsed behind every movement, a living tether of grief, rage, and insanity.

Megan noticed a moment of pause in Hank's rampage. He lifted a body—a young woman, pale and trembling—clutching her as the firelight reflected off the jagged teeth and the yellow glow of his eyes. Megan's stomach rolled, but the image was incomplete, left for her imagination, yet enough to convey the horror. Then Hank vanished into the smoke and shadow, the woman's influence drawing him away with invisible threads of magic. Megan's heart pounded as she realized the full scope: the woman could manipulate, extend, and displace her will across the distance, her madness a conduit for devastation.

The woman stepped forward slowly and deliberately, into the town's edge. Megan could see her body falter in flickers, a spirit partially unanchored, moving mechanically while her consciousness trembled, clawing inside her skull. Black smoke coiled from her form, eyes gleaming with a horror so pure that it seemed almost physical, wrapping around her like a cloak of darkness. Megan felt a pull in her gut, a cold awareness that the woman was absolute evil, unrestrained, and utterly untethered from mortality.

Yet Megan did not retreat. Her protected place remained firm, her mind a fixed lens in the chaos. She stepped closer, heart hammering, observing the woman and the monstrous Hank as they interacted, noting the precision, the cruelty, the surreal nature of what was happening. The fire, the screams, the shadows—they all moved in response to the woman's will, yet Megan's focus allowed her clarity.

"I will not be consumed," she whispered to herself, steadying her breathing. The black smoke seemed to hiss, as if reacting, yet Megan's mind refused to yield. She saw the terror, the devastation, the manipulation, and she cataloged it all—the essence of the woman's power, the monstrous reshaping of Hank, and the subtle threads of chaos that could be traced back to grief turned absolute.

The town burned. Hank's massive form stalked through it like a predator guided by the woman's fragmented spirit. The screams echoed, overlapping, yet Megan remained anchored, her focus sharpening. She realized she could see it all, hold it all, and survive. Her mind, sharpened by fear and will, began to map a path forward: observe, understand, confront.

And in the flicker of flame and shadow, the woman paused, sensing Megan's presence, the first crack in her control.

The town square trembled under the echoes of destruction. Flames licked the edges of broken buildings, casting long, dancing shadows across the twisted cobblestones. Hank's massive form had vanished into the smoke, leaving only the faint crackle of fire and the echoing terror of those still scattered through the streets. Megan's chest heaved, every inhalation sharp and jagged, but she forced herself forward, the protective circle in her mind holding her steady even as the world around her seemed to collapse into chaos.

From the corner of the square, a voice rose—a sharp, accusatory sound that cut through the smoke and fire. "You did this to him!"

The reverend stepped forward, his face pale beneath the flickering firelight, hands trembling. "What does she mean? What has happened?" he shouted, the desperation of a man who had lost control dripping from every syllable.

Megan's eyes scanned the burning town, searching through the haze for the source. The woman's form hovered at the edge of the square, partially wreathed in shadow and smoke, her body flickering as if caught between the material and the ethereal. Each movement was deliberate, mechanical, and terrifyingly graceful. Her arms extended at odd angles as if pulled by threads only she could see, fingers clawing the air, grasping at some invisible connection that tethered Hank to her will.

"Forgiveness isn't an option," the woman's voice echoed, deep and tremulous yet clear as a bell. "You took something from me. Now we take something from you."

Megan's stomach clenched, panic pooling low and hot. Every instinct screamed to flee, but her protective circle anchored her, giving her the clarity to observe, to understand, to act. Her eyes burned as she forced herself closer, keeping her mind tethered to her sanctuary, resisting the pull of the darkness surrounding the woman.

The reverend's face twisted in confusion, anger, and fear, and he barked into the chaos, "What do you want from this witch?"

"Sacrifice," the voice hissed, filling the town with a resonant certainty. "Every year, before the sun rises on the day of the summer solstice, you will offer one pure of heart, or my love will destroy your precious town and all within it."

Megan's stomach dropped. The weight of the words pressed against her ribs, threatening to crush the breath from her lungs.

She saw the reverend lunge forward, desperate and resolute, in a heartbeat, he gripped a young woman from the crowd, raising a dagger with a trembling hand. Megan's blood ran cold as she understood the ritual would be enacted, and yet she could only watch, rooted in her protective space.

The knife came down. Megan's mind recoiled as metal tore through flesh, slashing her throat with a wet, ripping force. Blood spattered across the reverend's face, streaking his eyes and chin, while a crimson torrent poured from the woman's body. Her gurgling cries fought to escape, jagged and choked, as her frame sagged and collapsed under its own weight. Around them, the townsfolk gasped, the twisted mixture of complicity, fear, and inevitability radiating through the square like a living, suffocating presence. With a grim finality, the reverend grabbed the lifeless body and tossed it toward Hank, where it landed with a wet thud in the mud at his feet.

The reverend raised his bloodied hands, his eyes sweeping over the frozen townsfolk. "We... we have no choice," he stammered, his voice shaking with both fear and authority. "I must protect my sheep from the wolf... in God's name... her sacrifice... it will be for the good of the many..." His words trailed off, heavy with a grim, unspoken finality. One by one, the townsfolk lowered their heads, murmuring in unison, "In God's name... for the good of the many..."

Hank shifted at the edge of the scene, the monstrous mass of mud, bark, and thorny vines observing, pacing, and waiting. His massive hands twitching as though savoring the anticipation of the ritual's completion. Then, with a sudden, fluid motion, he seized the body and vanished into the smoke, leaving the townsfolk paralyzed with terror.

The woman's voice rang out again, triumphant, chilling. "The woods are mine now. All who enter will die. Never forget!"

A heat unlike anything Megan had ever felt swept over her, as if the inferno itself had wrapped around her, flames licking the edges of her skin, searing her soul. Her vision flickered between the fiery square and the cabin where the woman's rituals had begun.

The whispers grew louder, rising to an almost unbearable pitch. Megan could feel the threads of the woman's madness brushing against her mind, trying to ensnare her, trying to pull her consciousness into the black smoke that wreathed the witch's body. The air around the woman seemed alive, vibrating with power and rage, the shattering of a spirit unhinged.

And then, almost instinctively, Megan shouted.

"Sarah!" The name broke free, carried on a trembling, urgent whisper that seemed to hang in the fire-lit air. "You lied to me! You are the reason for all of this!"

The woman paused, her form flickering violently, and for a moment, Megan glimpsed the true horror beneath the surface: not just power, but a complete surrender to grief, rage, and unrestrained evil.

"You speak as if you understand," the woman replied, her voice curling around the edges of Megan's mind, a sibilant, intoxicating whisper. "Witches must stick together. I showed you that those without power… they will turn on you. They will consume you. The world has no mercy for weakness."

Megan's hands balled into fists, heart hammering. "I will use whatever power I have for the weak and never be consumed by darkness!" she yelled, her voice shattering the smoke around them.

The woman's scream tore through the air, a banshee's wail that rattled Megan's skull and made the ground tremble. "If you cannot stand by women who share a similar connection of blood then you are nothing to me!" The words slashed at Megan's ears like blades, black smoke surging forward as if to envelop her.

Megan's protective space tightened, a bright, lucid core amid the black tendrils. She focused on her anchor, the clarity of her vision, the knowledge that she could resist, that she could see through the manipulation. She watched the woman, her madness unraveling in waves, her consciousness shattering and reforming like brittle glass. Every flicker of the woman's form radiated pure, untempered evil, yet Megan remained.

The heat intensified, flames licking her senses, pressing against her body with a terrifying intimacy. She gasped, choking on the suffocating mix of fire, smoke, and psychic energy. The square, the town, Hank's monstrous form—all of it blended into an unbearable crescendo of horror. She felt herself slipping, consciousness wavering between life and vision, but she anchored herself, forcing her mind into clarity, forcing it to remain separate from the darkness.

Megan stepped forward, voice steady now, cutting through the banshee's scream. "This ends. I see your lies. I see the manipulation. I will not follow, I will not yield, and I will not let you consume me!"

The witch shrieked again, a sound that seemed to tear the night itself. Smoke coiled violently, blackness surging, and for a heartbeat Megan feared her sanctuary would fail. Yet she held, every nerve taut, every thought focused on resistance, clarity, and truth.

The flames peaked, roaring around her, and then she felt the sudden shift. The heat receded, the smoke dissolved like mist, and Megan's body jolted violently. Her eyes snapped open, chest heaving, the world solid and cold around her.

"Megan!" Aiden's voice cut through the residue of fire and vision. "What happened?"

She trembled, fighting to steady herself as the lingering heat and pressure of the vision vibrated through her veins. She had survived; her mind remained her own, yet the weight of what she had witnessed—the destruction, the manipulation, the raw, consuming evil—pressed against her soul like a shadow that refused to lift.

Hank's monstrous form, the woman's fractured fury, the town's screams—they all lingered at the edges of her vision, ghosts clawing at her awareness. Megan drew a shuddering breath, anchoring herself in the solidity of her own body, her senses sharp and alive.

She had seen the truth. She had stared into darkness and pulled herself back. Deep down, she knew the woman's wrath, the forest's corruption, and Hank's monstrous rage were far from finished.

Slowly, she rose to her knees, hands pressed to the floor, trembling but unbroken. "I… I'm not hers," she whispered, voice raw but unyielding. "I am mine. I will see this through."

A gust of cold night air swept the room, brushing against her like affirmation. The shadows shifted, but her heart did not falter. The visions, the fire, the monstrous forms—they were memories now, sharpened lessons she would carry forward.

Her gaze lingered on the remnants of the horror, the echo of the woman's madness. She would remember. She would resist. She would fight—not just for herself, but for all who remained trapped in the darkness.

Chapter 19:

The Sacrifice we Make

The forest closed in on them; moist air clung to Jenna's skin, the fog sliding up her ankles and calves with slow intent, seeping into her shoes and soaking her socks until every step felt invasive, intimate. Wet leaves crushed beneath her boots, each step hammering against her chest as if the forest were counting her breaths.

Randy's grip locked around her wrist, tugging her forward, anchoring her to something human. Even so, his touch felt distant, dulled—as if the woods were already thinning the space between them, stretching him into something less solid.

"I knew I didn't like them," Jenna whispered, her voice shaking apart the moment it left her mouth, swallowed by the fog and the towering dark. "But how could they do this?"

Randy stopped long enough to look at her, moonlight flashing in his eyes, fear stripping him bare. "Megan and Aiden?" he asked, the question brittle. "Are they messing with us?"

The answer arrived before she could speak.

A sound moved through the trees—not loud, not fast, but heavy. It slid through the soil and into their bones, a low vibration that settled in Jenna's chest and stayed there, humming with promise. It wasn't a growl so much as a signal, something ancient announcing awareness.

Her throat tightened. "This isn't a game," she said. "The whispers are back. Amber's whispers."

Randy shook his head hard, hands coming up to frame her face, grounding her with pressure. "Amber's gone," he said. "She's dead. The voices aren't real. None of this is real."

Jenna barely heard him.

She could feel it now—certainty curling inside her gut, cold and unrelenting. Whatever wore Amber's face was wrong. It wasn't grief. It wasn't memory. It was something hollow pretending to ache.

The fog thickened, wrapping tighter around her legs, tugging at her knees like it wanted to pull her down. Movement flickered just beyond her vision—shapes that never fully formed, outlines that collapsed the moment she tried to focus. Then the face surfaced.

Not Amber.

The skull stretched unnaturally wide, skin pulled tight over angles that should not have existed. Its eyes were nothing but deep pits, lightless and endless, and its mouth split open far past human limits. The air around it throbbed, rhythmic and wrong, like a heartbeat dragged out of the ground itself.

The smell hit her next—sweet rot, wet earth, old blood. Jenna gagged, bile flooding her throat as the scent soaked into her lungs.

"No," she screamed, clawing at her head. "You're not real!"

The form shrieked, the sound tearing through her head and caving in her chest all at once. It wasn't a voice—it was the land itself howling through stolen flesh, the trees grinding their roots together, the soil splitting open, the wind exhaling a scream that had been buried, starving and feral, for centuries.

Rational thought evaporated in a single breath. Jenna's legs buckled, useless beneath her, as she staggered backward. The dark pressed closer, not rushing—advancing with patience— while the whispers swelled until they clawed at her skull, each voice dragging the nightmare out of memory and into the dirt at her feet.

"Jenna, get back!" Randy shouted.

He moved without thinking, instincts overriding fear. The bat arced through the air, his muscles screaming as he brought it down. Wood collided with something that should not have had a face. For a heartbeat, Jenna caught the thing's expression— before it unraveled into vapor that scattered with a hiss, leaving behind a brutal cold that stung her lungs.

The silence barely had time to settle when a low growl rolled through the fog. The air thickened, sour and wet, carrying the stink of rot and old graves. Something vast began to take shape, dragging itself out of the haze. Its body gleamed like slick hide stretched over swollen muscle, veins pulsing beneath the surface. Its eyes burned with intent—not rage, but appetite. It advanced slowly, the earth shuddering in submission.

"Come on, Jenna!" Randy called. "We can't let it trap us!"

Randy seized Jenna's wrist and yanked her forward. They tore through brush and roots until the trees thinned, moonlight spilling into a clearing where a pile of stones resembling an altar squatted at the center, blackened with age and stained by remnants of things never meant to be named. Jenna broke away and ducked behind it, her back slamming against the stone. It was icy and uneven, scraping her skin as her breath came apart in ragged pulls.

Something wet dragged across the ground behind them. Branches bent inward, creaking under unseen pressure, the forest leaning closer, watching. And then it stepped forward.

Yellow eyes locked onto its prey, unblinking and merciless. Thick black ooze spilled from its mouth, stretching in viscous strands before dropping to the ground like the drool of something long starved. The creature's bulk followed, massive and roughly human in outline—but assembled wrong, proportions twisted, weight distributed in ways that made the air feel heavier around it. Its body glistened with slick, living flesh smeared in mud and fragments of bark, the surface rising and falling as if something beneath were breathing out of sync.

Randy charged.

Hope flared—brief, stupid, desperate.

The bat struck the creature's side with a crack that echoed through the clearing. The impact drove it to one knee—but it laughed. A wet, rasping sound peeled from its throat as it caught the bat mid-swing. Its mouth split wider, teeth jagged and crowded, savoring the moment.

Randy swung again

The bat struck the woodsman once more, solid and loud—but the creature didn't stagger. It smiled. In one violent motion, it ripped the bat from Randy's hands and flung him backwards. His body slammed into the altar with a hollow, bone-jarring thud before crumpling to the ground. He gasped, air torn from his lungs, fingers clawing uselessly at the dirt as pain seized him whole.

"Randy!" Jenna screamed.

The creature loomed over him, its grin stretching impossibly wide. The whispers returned, threading through her thoughts, urging surrender, urging stillness. The darkness felt heavier now—closer.

"Get up, Randy!" she shouted, forcing the words past her terror. "Don't let it win!"

Mist churned violently as the creature advanced. Thick, vine-like tendrils unfurled from its arms, slick and pulsing, flexing with every step as though eager to taste flesh. Jenna watched from her crouched shelter, heart hammering so hard it hurt. Then fear snapped into fury.

She grabbed a stone and ran towards the creature but never reached it.

The creature moved with sudden, impossible speed. Its thorn-wrapped fist backhanded her mid-stride. The impact crushed the air from her chest and sent her tumbling across the ground. She hit hard, vision flashing white as breath refused to return.

"Randy," she rasped.

The monster bent low, its repulsive expression twisted with glee, and smashed its fist into Randy's face. The thorns tore through flesh with a sickening crack, blood spraying like a morbid fountain as Randy lay defenseless beneath the weight of despair. In that moment, the creature snatched up the bat, its grip tightening around the wood as vines slithered around it, morphing it into a deformed axe, dripping with a thick slimy ooze and barbed with thorns.

With a sickening thud, the axe sunk into Randy's skull, a gruesome explosion of bone and brain matter scattering like grotesque confetti. His wide eyes stared blankly into oblivion, body twitching in a final, futile gasp as the world around him faded to darkness. Jenna's screams echoed in her ears, but all she could see was the horror before her—the end of hope, the finality of despair.

All that remained was the body, broken beyond recognition, and the creature standing over it—patient, satisfied—while the last fragile thread of hope snapped in her chest.

Jenna's stomach churned violently.

But beneath the terror, something hardened. Heart hammering, lungs screaming, she seized a jagged stone from the clearing floor. Her legs moved almost independently, powered by desperation and fear, each step a defiance of her instinct to collapse in terror.

The creature's head tilted, yellow eyes locking on her as she moved forward. Its grin widened, exposing jagged, rock-like teeth, and the air vibrated with anticipation. Jenna hurled the stone. The impact echoed like a gunshot in the silent, suffocating night. The creature recoiled slightly, mist curling where it had been, but it advanced relentlessly.

Another stone burned in her clenched fist as Jenna wound up again, her body rotating on pure instinct. Her arm surged forward—then the motion fractured, stretched impossibly thin, as if time had been yanked apart and left quivering.

The stone tore through the fog and struck the woodsman square in the face. Red moss exploded on impact, ripping free in wet clumps as the blow snapped its head sideways, the creature's hunger stuttering for a single, brutal heartbeat.

As Jenna forced air into her lungs. One breath. Then another. Her heartbeat thundered so hard it blurred her sight, but she kept moving, teeth clenched, nails digging into the soil until pain anchored her. The whispers flooded in, no longer separate voices but a single rhythm, relentless, pounding in time with her pulse.

You must survive.

Jenna staggered back, chest heaving, the taste of blood sharp on her tongue. Her body shook uncontrollably, nerves flayed and drowning in adrenaline, every sense firing at once with nowhere to go. The forest continued its slow, patient breathing around her, branches creaking, mist shifting, the night holding its ground.

Across the clearing, the creature's head rolled slowly back toward her. Red moss crept over the place where the stone had struck, knitting itself together in wet, twitching strands, reforming its ruined face with deliberate patience. Its yellow eyes found her again and locked on, unblinking.

She forced herself to stay upright.

She would not break here.

Not yet.

Megan stirred awake with a violent jolt, her heart hammering so fiercely she feared it would burst through her ribcage. The cabin was suffocating, the air thick with the scent of dust, rotting wood, and something else—something faintly acrid that set her stomach roiling. Moonlight filtered in through the grimy windows, striking across the floorboards like cold fingers, casting long, spindly shadows that writhed as if alive. The shadows seemed to shift in her peripheral vision, crawling closer with every blink.

Aiden knelt beside her, his hands brushing her shoulders with a trembling steadiness, trying to tether her to the world. "Megan… are you okay?" His voice was soft, but there was an edge of alarm threading through it, a tether to sanity in the fog of her terror. "You looked like you were having a seizure."

Her gaze fixed on him for a heartbeat, wide-eyed, unblinking. "I… I saw her again," she whispered, her voice quivering so violently that it sounded almost like a scream smothered by fog. "The woman from my visions… all of it… everything we were wrong about, it was not the Reverend!" Panic pressed at her chest, constricting like iron bands. "She cursed the town. Every year. A sacrifice. Or else." Her voice caught on the last word, as if saying it aloud could summon it into being.

Aiden's brow furrowed. "What do you mean? What did you see?"

"She… she took the bones of the woodsman, and she—" Megan's words stalled. Her eyes darted instinctively toward the dark corner where a shadow-cloaked shelf leaned against the wall. Impulsively, she sprang forward, yanking it from its hinges. Wood splintered and shattered on the floor, sending up a spray of dust and darkness. Behind the wreckage, cloaked in shadow, lay a shrine: a shrine of bones and candle wax, of dark intention and quiet malevolence.

"Megan, wait!" Aiden shouted, horror lacing his voice. "What are you doing? Don't—"

But she didn't hear him. Her hands shook as she pried loose the human remains, fingers curling around the smooth, cold surfaces of a skull and two femur bones. They felt alive in her grip, humming with a faint vibration she could feel even in her teeth. Her heartbeat escalated, a frantic drum keeping pace with the terror that pulsed in the shadows. She slammed the bones against the jagged window frame, cracking and splintering them further. The shards gleamed ominously in the dim moonlight, sharp and glinting like tiny shards of promise.

"You can't just—" Aiden's voice cracked, rising to an urgent pitch. "What if these belong to someone?"

"They belong to Hank! He was the woodsman—the monster from my nightmares!" she shouted, eyes wide and blazing with a mixture of fear and revelation. "She turned him into something else… she used him to curse this town!"

Aiden stumbled back, his face pale, confusion wrestling with terror. "Wait… what? You're saying… the woman in your visions—the witch—she's behind everything? She's responsible for the disappearances, the… the destruction?"

"Yes!" Megan's voice was sharp, slicing through the stagnant air. "She resurrected Hank as… as something else. A force of death. And the reverend—he was forced into a deal with her to save the town. Every year, he has to offer someone pure of heart before the Summer Solstice, or she destroys the town!"

Aiden staggered, running a hand through his hair, the dawning horror twisting his expression. "This… this can't be real," he muttered, voice trembling. "Curses, sacrifices, monsters… Megan, this sounds insane!"

She pressed the bones tighter to her chest, the energy vibrating faintly under her fingers. "I don't know how else to explain it. I can feel it. They're tied to the woman, to Hank, to the curse. We can't stay here. We have to move."

A tense silence hung between them, punctuated only by the creaking of the cabin settling. Aiden's shoulders tensed, then slowly, reluctantly, he nodded. "Okay," he whispered, his voice low, heavy with dread. "We leave. Let's… let's go before it finds us here."

They stepped into the night, the forest swallowing them in an instant. The moonlight struggled to pierce the mist, which now thickened into a wall of gray-white, curling and writhing around their feet. Every movement felt laborious, as if the mist itself were tugging at their legs, resisting their escape. The air was damp, suffocating, pressing into their lungs with the weight of unseen eyes.

Shadows moved just outside of her vision, flickering and twisting unnaturally. She squinted into the fog. "Aiden… do you see that?" she whispered, her fingers tightening on the fragments of bones, her pulse a jackhammer in her ears.

He shook his head, his gaze scanning the opaque gray that pressed in from every direction. "I… I don't see anything. Just… shadows."

The whispers returned then, soft at first, curling into her ears like smoke. Names, words, voices she knew but didn't, seeping in through the cracks of her mind: Amber… spirits… the woman… they're all watching… waiting… She stumbled, knees weak, and pressed a trembling hand to a tree, the bark rough and wet under her fingers.

"Don't let it see you panic," she muttered to herself, trying to anchor her mind. Her breath came in ragged gasps, fog of it condensing and swirling around her head, forming ghostly shapes that flickered and vanished. Every sense screamed at her, telling her to run, to hide, to collapse—but she forced herself forward.

A low, wet rasp rolled through the fog, vibrating in her teeth. She didn't look up. She didn't need to. She could feel it— slithering, patient, stalking. The darkness pressed closer, almost tangible, like a living cloak that weighed down her shoulders and slid its icy fingers around her spine.

A shadow moved. Too big to be a deer or some other animal. The forest seemed to breathe around it, sucking the warmth from her body. Her pulse spiked. She could hear the snap of twigs, too methodical, too heavy to belong to any ordinary creature.

Her grip on the bone fragments tightened. She could feel the subtle vibration emanating from them, a resonance that hummed faintly with life—or something like life. Her chest heaved as the whispers became voices, calling, coaxing, accusing. *Run. Run. Run. You can't escape. You will be next.*

Jenna's memory of the night in the forest—the screams, the chaos, the monstrous visage—flickered in her mind like a film strip set ablaze. She imagined Hank's hulking, grotesque form: skin slick like oiled leather, muscle and mud intertwining; vines coiling around his limbs, thorns jutting outward like weapons; moss-red hair and beard bristling and tangled; and those sickly yellow eyes, burning with a malevolent awareness. Every flash of memory set her stomach churning, every imagined step of his monster's advance pressed into her like a warning.

The mist thickened further, and for a heartbeat, it felt as if the forest itself had condensed, folding in around them. The ground squelched beneath her boots. Shapes lurked in the fog, fleeting glimpses of pale faces, twisted mouths, and eyes too bright in the dark. She pressed forward, forcing her legs to move despite the nausea clawing at her gut.

Aiden whispered something, words lost in the mist, but she couldn't hear him clearly. Every sense was heightened, every nerve ending alight with terror and adrenaline. Shadows flickered and stretched as the laughter of children echoed around them; the faint, wet stench of decay crawled into her nose. The bones hummed faintly in her hands, a pulse that resonated in tandem with her heartbeat, grounding her just enough to keep moving.

The mist swirled, alive. Shadows danced. Laughter clawed her insides. And somewhere, just beyond sight, the forest waited.

The fog twisted and writhed before Megan's eyes, curling around her ankles like living smoke. From its depths emerged a figure—petite, almost fragile in stature, her features impossibly beautiful, pale as moonlight, her hair cascading like a river of midnight. Megan's chest constricted, a wave of icy dread pressing into her lungs, as though the forest itself had leaned in closer to listen.

You will not take him from me! The woman's voice slithered into Megan's mind, a melody that dripped with venom and sweetness all at once, curling around her skull and rattling her thoughts. It wasn't just sound—it was a presence, pressing against her temples, threading into her nerves, a living thing of malice and command. *Leave him with me… he belongs to me.*

Megan's knees hit the damp earth, and her fingers trembled as they clenched the skull and femurs, her knuckles bleaching white under the strain. Every heartbeat pounded like a drum of warning in her chest, each pulse echoing the terror clawing at her ribs. Her breath came in ragged bursts, sharp and uneven, as if the night itself had wrapped around her throat.

"No!" Megan's voice cracked, sharp and desperate, yet defiant. She hoisted the skull high above her head, trembling, as if sheer will could turn the fragile bone into a weapon against the dark force before her. "I will free everyone from your torment! Every life you've stolen, every scream you've caused— I will undo it!"

The moonlight caught the skull and reflected off its surface, igniting it with an almost supernatural glow, as though it held a fire that defied the woman's command. Shadows twisted and writhed around Megan, flickering like tortured spirits, responding to the clash of wills. The woman's presence surged, a black tide pressing in on all sides, and Megan could feel it, heavy and suffocating, gnawing at her resolve.

You think you can defy me? The woman's voice tore into her mind, silky yet cruel, filling every corner of Megan's consciousness. *You are nothing but a flicker of flesh and fear.*

Megan's teeth gritted against the panic bubbling inside her. She rocked slightly, the weight of the bones grounding her in a small, defiant heartbeat of reality. "I am not nothing!" she shouted into the night, though the fog swallowed her voice like it had swallowed so many others. "I will not let your darkness consume me. I will fight. I will fight until there's nothing left of your curse!"

The wind shifted around them, carrying the echo of the woman's laughter—a high, chilling sound that cut through the mist and threaded itself into Megan's chest. The shadows seemed to lean closer, whispering threats, caressing her with imagined hands that burned and clawed.

The woman's expression twisted instantly, morphing into pure rage. Her scream tore through the fog like shattered glass, shrill and penetrating, vibrating in Megan's teeth, in her bones, deep within her chest. It was not just a sound but a force that shoved the air from her lungs.

Fury radiated from her, tangible and cutting. *I thought you were one of us! I showed you the evil that has killed so many, and you turn your back! You are a traitor!* The words were sharp, clawing at Megan's mind, sinking into the edges of her sanity.

The woman's form warped before Megan's eyes. Once human, now demonic, her body stretched and contorted: long, needle-sharp nails glinting in the moonlight; teeth like tiny knives flashing in a grin that promised nothing but pain; eyes that were voids of pure black, sucking in the surrounding light, devouring hope.

You will pay for your betrayal! Her voice echoed unnaturally, stretching, vibrating through Megan's skull. The air grew thick and heavy, pressing into her chest, each breath a struggle. And then, in a sudden gust of wind, the figure erupted into a dense, choking cloud of darkness, spiraling before dissipating, leaving only the echo of her fury lingering in the mist.

Aiden knelt beside Megan, eyes wide and trembling. "Megan… are you okay? What… what is happening to you?" His voice was shaky, barely a tether to reality.

Megan gasped, clutching the bones as though they were the only thing holding her from falling into the void of the forest. "I can hear her… the woman from my dreams… inside my head. She's here."

The fog shifted around them, retreating only slightly, yet the forest felt alive with menace. Every step forward pressed down on Megan's chest, an invisible hand tightening with every heartbeat. The whispers threaded through her ears again, jagged shards of warning and accusation: *You have betrayed us… you will fail… you are not one of us…I will take everything from you.*

The clearing opened slowly, moonlight spilling across the ground like silver blood. And then Megan's stomach dropped.

Randy's body lay twisted before the altar, mutilated beyond recognition. But it was the figure beyond him that stole her breath: Hank. The woodsman. Her nightmare made flesh.

He moved with an unnatural grace, colossal and terrifying. His form was a grotesque fusion of earth and monster. Skin like mud and bark stretched across a muscular frame, layered in thorny vines that writhed as he moved. Bright red moss tangled in his hair and beard, and his jagged, rocklike teeth glinted as he growled low in his throat. The sickly yellow of his eyes burned in the dim moonlight, each glance a promise of devastation.

Hank's enormous hands gripped Jenna with ease, hoisting her like she weighed nothing. Megan's scream tore from her throat. "HAAAANK!"

The woodsman paused, confusion flickering across his massive, monstrous features. Then, almost casually, he dropped her, letting her body hit the earth with a dull, sickening thud. Megan's stomach churned as Aiden dove forward, dragging Jenna behind the jagged altar stones. Her skin was bruised, her forehead split, but she was alive.

The forest held its breath. Shadows stretched unnaturally, and the woman's voice—low, reverberating—rolled through the clearing: "Join them… in hell." It was not Hank speaking, yet it carried from him, seeping from his very presence, infecting the air around him.

Megan's legs trembled, but she seized her courage, clutching the remaining femur bone. "Aiden, we have to stop him!" she yelled. Her voice bounced off the trees, a desperate echo, mingling with the mist and shadows.

Aiden charged, gripping one of the bones tightly, stabbing it into Hank's shoulder with all the strength his small frame could muster. The woodsman's roar—a sound like grinding stone and broken trees—shattered the silence. He jerked violently, muscles rippling beneath mud and bark, then flung Aiden clear across the clearing. Aiden hit the earth with a brutal thud, gasping for air, pain and terror mingling in a bitter cocktail.

Hank turned, slow and deliberate, a predator assessing prey. Megan saw the power in his movement, the alien intelligence behind each step. Every inch he closed was a promise of annihilation. She lunged, her bone raised like a dagger, but a vine—thick, spiked, and pulsating—lashed out, colliding into her stomach with a force that sent her sprawling.

Her skull hit the ground with a sickening crack. Bones slipped from her hands, rolling across the mossy, cold floor. Panic erupted, claws tearing at her throat and chest. "Megan!" Aiden shouted, crawling to her, fear etched into every line of his face.

Jenna, bruised and shaken, lunged for a bone, trembling with fury. "You killed Randy, you bastard!" she screamed, but Hank's attention shifted instantly. With a fluid, horrifying movement, he whipped the bone from her grasp.

Her scream faltered as the woodsman's massive hands closed around her leg, lifting her into the air effortlessly. The sensation was a living nightmare, a weightless terror as she dangled, body flailing. "No! Let me go!" Panic tore through her, her lungs burning, chest tight as iron bands.

Megan felt bile rise, a metallic taste in her mouth. She pressed forward, willing herself not to collapse, bones clutched like fragile talismans, whispering to herself that there was still a chance, a thread of control. But the air was thick with death, the mist curling and thrashing, whispering around her like hands trying to drag her mind into the shadows.

Hank's growl rumbled through the clearing, deep and resonant, vibrating in Megan's teeth. The forest seemed to pulse in sync with his rage, leaves trembling, shadows quivering. And then, just for a heartbeat, their eyes met—her terror, his incomprehensible, unnatural intelligence. In that moment, the world seemed to tilt, and Megan realized the truth of what she faced: this was no ordinary monster. This was Hank, yes, but transformed beyond recognition—fused with the forest, the curse, the witch's will.

And the woman—her voice whispered in her head, sharp as knives: *You have betrayed us. You will fail.*

Megan pressed her eyes shut, inhaled, and steadied her trembling hands, readying herself for the impossible.

Without hesitation, the woodsman's mouth opened wide, a cavern of jagged, rock-like teeth glinting in the faint moonlight. Megan's stomach lurched as he lunged with inhuman speed, sinking those grotesque fangs into Jenna's face. The scream that tore from her lips was a raw, guttural sound, a mixture of shock, agony, and the primal terror of someone caught in the jaws of something not meant to exist. Blood sprayed into the air, mingling with the metallic tang of the earth, filling Megan's nose with the coppery scent of pain. She couldn't move. She couldn't breathe. All she could do was watch.

The woodsman flung Jenna across the altar with brutal force, her body hitting the stone with a sickening thud that seemed to echo in the very marrow of Megan's bones. Her upper body crumpled beneath the impact, arms flailing uselessly, blood flowing from Jenna's ripped open face. Each heartbeat reverberated painfully, a drum of helplessness as her mind grasped for some thread of hope in the suffocating night.

"Noooo!" Aiden's voice tore through the fog, raw with rage and fear, as he scrambled toward her. Megan's eyes followed him, heart hammering, as he leapt toward the towering form of the monster. But Hank's massive frame, hulking and fused with mud, bark, vines, and thorny red moss, blocked him like a living mountain. The sickly yellow of his eyes caught the moonlight, burning with an intelligence and hatred that froze Megan's blood.

"Hey! You ugly pile of garbage!" Megan's voice rang out, more desperate than brave. She flung a jagged stone with all her strength. The rock bounced harmlessly off Hank's chest, but it drew his attention, and he let out a roar that split the night and rattled Megan's very bones.

Aiden's eyes locked onto the second femur bone lying where Jenna had dropped it. Gripping it tightly, he surged forward, a raw, trembling determination carrying him across the clearing. "Get away from her!" he screamed, a desperate plea mingled with the violence of impending combat.

The bone drove deep into Hank's chest. A crunch of flesh and snapping vines echoed like thunder, and for a heartbeat, the creature froze. Its glowing yellow eyes widened in shock, then in fury. It collapsed to the ground with a deafening roar, writhing as its massive, grotesque body shuddered. The forest groaned as Hank finally gave way. His enormous body sagged, vines withering and snapping as mud peeled from him in wet slabs. The red moss in his beard blackened and bled into the ground while roots unraveled from his ribs and slid back into the soil.

His legs vanished first, then his torso, the ground turning soft and ravenous as it hauled him under. Stone-jagged teeth clacked once before mud jammed his mouth and his head disappeared beneath the surface. When it was finished, only a dark, churning stain remained—gore, pulp, and soil slowly flattening as the forest closed over him in defeat.

The earth did not stop there. It shifted and writhed, thick vines forcing their way up to reclaim what he left behind. Pale bones were dragged under one by one, the skull rolling once before sinking into the moss as if the forest itself were feeding.

It was finally over. A rush of relief surged through Megan as Aiden sprinted toward her, his face breaking through the chaos.

"Aiden!" she screamed, stumbling forward, heart leaping as the distance between them closed.

The forest answered with cruelty. Hank's head snapped back up through the soil. Vine-wrapped limbs lashed out in a sudden blur.

Time fractured. Megan watched, helpless, as a thick, gnarled vine punched through Aiden's back with a wet, brutal sound. His body jerked mid-stride, breath ripping from his lungs as blood slicked the vine pinning him to the ground. His eyes found hers—wide, shocked, already dimming.

Hank would not leave alone. With one final, desperate act of vengeance, he dragged Aiden into the dark with him.

"Noooo, Aiden!" Megan screamed, her knees slamming against the cold, wet forest floor as she crawled to him. Her hands shook violently as she pressed against his chest, feeling the warmth of life ebbing through her fingers. Panic gripped her throat, choking the sound from her own voice.

Hank's head began to slowly melt back into the earth, grotesque and loathsome, a slow, deliberate mockery on his features. Every line of his monstrous face carried a cruel amusement, as if savoring her despair as he vanished. Megan's mind screamed, but words were inadequate against the presence of pure, physicalized rage. *You cannot save him; he is mine now*, a voice whispered in her head, low and venomous, crawling along her nerves and coiling around her skull.

Tears streamed down Megan's cheeks as she pressed her ear to Aiden's chest, searching desperately for the thrum of life.

"Please… stay with me… don't leave me," she whispered, her voice cracking, almost drowned by the roar of the forest and the pounding of her own pulse.

Aiden's eyes fluttered, struggling to stay open, and a faint, broken smile trembled across his pale, sweat-slicked face. Blood bubbled at his lips as he drew a shallow, rattling breath. "I… I'll watch over you… always," he whispered, each word tearing its way out of him like it might be his last gift to her.

Megan gathered him against her, sobs wracking her body as she clutched him tighter, desperate to keep him here. She felt the heat leave him inch by inch, his weight growing heavier in her arms, the rise and fall of his chest slowing—then faltering. His fingers twitched once in hers, then went still, and the soft, living presence she loved slipped away, leaving only cold flesh and the unbearable silence of his death.

She pressed her face into her hands, trembling, crying not just for Aiden, but for every life lost to the darkness that had crawled from her nightmares into her reality. The shadows of the trees seemed to leer, bending toward her as if to whisper in twisted sympathy, echoing the hollow ache of her soul.

And then, through the mist, shapes began to take form— human shapes. The silhouettes of the Sheriff, Thomas, and Lexi emerged, their movements urgent and protective. Megan felt the warmth of human touch again, a balm to the cold terror that had suffocated her. Lexi's arms wrapped around her, steady and strong, while Thomas whispered in her ear, grounding her frayed nerves. The Sheriff stood vigilant, scanning the forest edges, a silent promise that some measure of protection remained.

The three guided her from the clearing, each step leaving the carnage behind: twisted bodies, scorched earth, the lingering cries and echoes of terror that clung to the fog like cobwebs. Sunlight bled over the horizon, a pale, fragile light that seemed almost cruel in its serenity, casting the ruined forest into stark, unforgiving relief. Blood-soaked ground, broken trees, and the hollowed remnants of terror were laid bare in the cold clarity of dawn.

Megan's stomach churned, nausea rising as her gaze swept over the scene. Every fallen friend, every monstrous transformation, every howl of the woodsman replayed in her mind, searing the images into memory. Dawn's light offered no salvation, only exposure, only truth. She had survived—but at a cost that weighed more than life itself.

She stumbled forward, shoulders shaking, tears still streaming, heart heavy with grief that pressed like stone. The forest receded behind her, but its shadow lingered in her chest, in her pulse, in the hollow echo of Aiden's last words. Megan knew this loss would not fade, that she would carry the memory of fire, blood, and the monstrous fusion of nature and curse for the rest of her life.

For the first time in hours, she dared to breathe, though the ache remained, gnawing, relentless. Survival had a bitter taste, and the dawn only reminded her how thoroughly darkness had claimed what she loved.

Epilogue:

Five years had passed since the night the Forbidden Forest devoured the town of Glory and left its survivors permanently altered. In the years that followed, the headlines faded, the memorials weathered, and life—at least on the surface—returned to something resembling normal. No bodies were found in the woods again. No hikers vanished. No one reported sightings of the Woodsman lingering between the trees or watching from the forest's edge. Yet no one dared enter the forest either—not for shortcuts, not for dares, not for curiosity or nostalgia. The trails remained untouched, overgrown and choked with rot, as if the land itself had been quietly marked off-limits. The town endured in silence, as though whatever had been awakened that night had finally gone dormant—and everyone understood, without ever saying it aloud, that tempting the forest again would mean inviting it to wake.

For Megan, Lexi, and Thomas, time did not erase what the forest had taken from them. It only taught them how to live around the absence.

Megan stood outside a crowded coffee shop in downtown Los Angeles, the afternoon sun spilling across the sidewalk, warm and ordinary. Cars rolled past. People laughed. Life moved forward with careless ease. Yet a familiar tension coiled low in her stomach, the same quiet warning she had learned never to ignore. It had been years since the three of them stood together like this, unguarded and exposed beneath an open sky.

The years following the massacre had reshaped her entirely. After returning to Chicago with her mother, Megan buried herself in words, turning terror into structure, memory into narrative. Her first novel, Mysteries of Glory, found an audience she never expected—readers drawn to its raw honesty, its insistence that survival did not mean forgetting. But success came at a cost. Every page reopened doors she had tried to seal shut, and some nights the forest still crept into her dreams, dragging its cold breath across her skin.

Megan glanced at her watch, her thoughts swirling with both pride and fear. She had poured herself into her writing, yet the fear of revisiting the past was ever-present. Unbidden, vivid nightmares persisted; chaos, helplessness, lost individuals: these replayed, drawing her back toward the forest's darkness. But with each passing day, she learned to wield her pen like a sword, using her trauma as a tool for healing.

Just then, she spotted Lexi and Thomas weaving through the crowd. Lexi's blonde hair shimmered in the sunlight, and her infectious smile was a beacon of warmth. Thomas stood beside her, looking sturdy yet burdened, the weight of his own struggles clear in the shadows under his eyes. As they approached, a wave of nostalgia washed over Megan, a reminder of their unbreakable bond forged in the fires of shared trauma.

"Megan!" Lexi called out, her voice bursting with excitement as they embraced. "I can't believe you are finally in Los Angeles!"

"Yeah I am finally here!" Megan replied, her heart swelling with a mix of joy and anxiety. Yet, as she pulled back, she caught the flicker of worry in Thomas's eyes. "It's so good to see you. How have you both been?"

Lexi's smile dimmed. "Busy, but amazing! I'm working on a project to restore parts of the redwoods here in California," she said, her voice brightening with passion. "It feels good to give back, but sometimes it's overwhelming."

Thomas nodded, his expression serious. "I'm studying psychology now, trying to help others with their trauma. But I still have those nightmares," he admitted, glancing down as if ashamed. "The memories refuse to fade."

Megan felt a pang in her heart, the familiar ache of understanding. "I get it. The past is a heavy burden," she whispered. "But I believe we can face it together."

As they settled around a small table on the patio, the afternoon sun dipped lower in the sky, casting a warm golden hue over their reunion. Megan looked at her friends, feeling a mixture of pride and fear. They had survived the worst, yet the trauma still clung to them like a second

skin. She could sense the tension in the air, the unspoken words that hovered between them, and the memories that still haunted their hearts.

"Your book is incredible, Megan," Lexi said, her voice filled with admiration. "It's like you've captured everything we felt during that time."

"Thanks," Megan replied, her voice wavering. "But it was hard to write. Each page offered a repeat experience of that horror.

"But you did it," Thomas said, his eyes meeting hers with a fierce intensity. "You turned that pain into something beautiful. That's powerful."

The weight of his words settled over her like a warm blanket, yet the shadows of doubt crept in. "I just hope it helps someone. I hope it gives a voice to those who can't speak about what they went through," she said, her throat tightening. "But sometimes I wonder if I'm just dragging us all back into the darkness."

Lexi reached across the table and squeezed Megan's hand. "You're not. You're healing, and you're helping us heal too. It's okay to remember, Megan. It's okay to feel," she said, her voice steady. "We can face it together."

As they continued to talk, Megan could feel a sense of friendship building, the laughter and shared stories pushing aside the weight of their past. But just as she relaxed, a sudden chill coursed through her, a sense of dread creeping back in. She glanced down the street, and her heart plummeted as a horrifying vision invaded her mind.

Aiden stood there, bloodied and bruised, his eyes wide with terror. *They won't let me go!* he screamed, his voice filled with anguish and desperation as it echoed in her mind. The image appeared so lifelike, so authentic; she experienced the sensation of being present, immobilized by terror.

"Megan?" Lexi's voice cut through the haze, but it felt distant, muffled, as if she were underwater. The vision tightened its grip on her, terror clawing at her insides.

The blaring of a car horn jolted her back to reality, and she instinctively dropped her coffee cup. It shattered against the cement, the sound of breaking porcelain echoing like a gunshot in the afternoon air.

"Megan! Are you okay?" Thomas rushed to her side, concern etched across his face as he knelt to help her gather the pieces of the cup.

Her heart raced, and she struggled to catch her breath. "I—I'm fine," she stammered, forcing a smile that felt brittle. She couldn't share the vision, the unease that swirled within her. Suppose this originated solely within her imagination? What if it meant nothing? "Just a little clumsy," she added, brushing off the moment.

As they gathered the remains of the broken cup, the weight of their past loomed over them like a dark cloud. The shadows of the Forbidden Forest still clung to their lives, and now Megan could feel something unsettling wash over her. But for now, she tucked the vision deep inside, unwilling to share the burden with her friends. Instead, she focused on the warmth of their laughter and the friendship they had built. She would confront her fears alone if she had to.

With newfound resolve, Megan looked at her friends, determination igniting in her chest. "Let's talk about something fun," she suggested, pushing back the shadows. "I want to hear all about your adventures!"

And so, under the fading light of the afternoon sun, the three friends stood together, their laughter filling the air as they pushed aside the remnants of their past, ready to face whatever challenges lay ahead. The echoes of the forest may have haunted them, but they would no longer run from the shadows; they would confront them together—though Megan would carry a hidden weight, one that might one day demand to be unveiled.

As the sun dipped below the horizon, casting long shadows on the pavement, Megan felt a mix of hope and apprehension. She was a survivor, a writer, and a friend. She would continue to face her fears, knowing that in doing so, she would help herself and those she loved heal from the wounds that still ached beneath the surface. The image of Aiden resided within, an ominous reminder, a troubling whisper yet unrevealed.